HER WARTIME SECRET

www.penguin.co.uk

HER WARTIME SECRET

Emma Hornby

BANTAM PRESS

TRANSWORLD PUBLISHERS
Penguin Random House, One Embassy Gardens,
8 Viaduct Gardens, London SW11 7BW
www.penguin.co.uk

Transworld is part of the Penguin Random House group of companies
whose addresses can be found at global.penguinrandomhouse.com

First published in Great Britain in 2021 by Bantam Press
an imprint of Transworld Publishers

A CIP catalogue record for this book
is available from the British Library.

ISBN 9781787634688

Typeset in 12.60/15.25pt ITC New Baskerville by Jouve (UK), Milton Keynes.
Printed and bound in Great Britain by Clays Ltd, Elcograf S.p.A.

The authorized representative in the EEA is Penguin Random House Ireland,
Morrison Chambers, 32 Nassau Street, Dublin D02 YH68.

Penguin Random House is committed to a sustainable
future for our business, our readers and our planet. This book
is made from Forest Stewardship Council® certified paper.

For Sonny and Mary Ellen – the perfect 'match'.
And my ABC, always x

This precious stone set in the silver sea . . .
the envy of less happier lands.
This blessed plot, this earth, this realm, this
England.

William Shakespeare

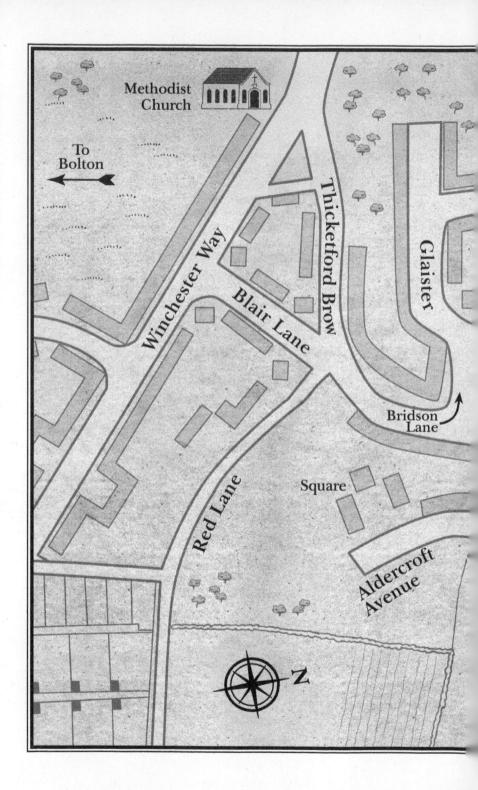

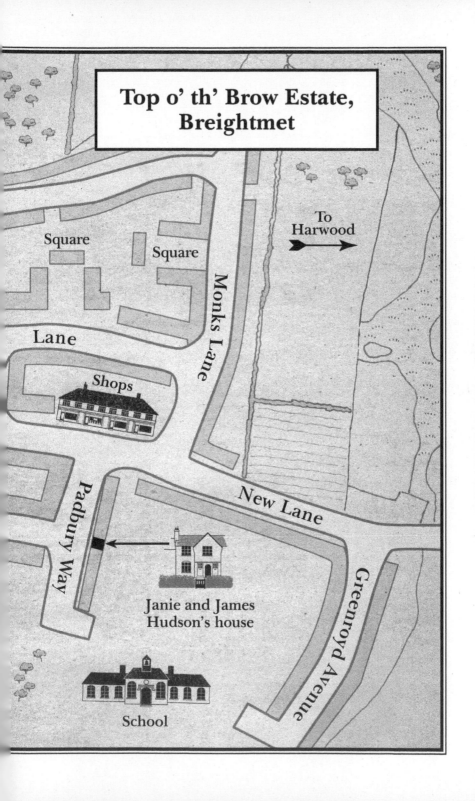

Top o' th' Brow Estate,
Breightmet

To
Harwood

Square

Square

Monks Lane

Lane

Shops

New Lane

Padbury Way

Greenroyd Avenue

Janie and James
Hudson's house

School

Chapter 1

Bolton, Lancashire
January 1940

'TELL ME YOU'RE having me on, James.'

'Love . . .'

'Please. *Please* say you haven't really gone and done it.'

A torturous silence hung between them. Then:

'I can't do that, for I have. I leave for training in t' morning. I'm sorry.'

Janie Hudson dropped, trembling, into a chair. The air felt as though it was caving in on her; she could barely snatch a breath. 'I knew summat was wrong the minute you arrived home from work,' she murmured, dazed. 'And you barely uttered two words throughout the evening meal and beyond. I knew.'

'I thought it best to wait 'til the kiddies were abed so's we could talk proper, like.'

Raising her eyes from her clasped hands on the tabletop, she stared at him through a haze of hurt and angry tears. 'Why did you do it?'

'I had to. The urge . . . it's like a hunger inside of

1

me. It's my duty, love. The duty of every right-thinking Britisher—'

'No. No! I'll never accept it. You've let me down, James. You *promised.*'

'Aye, you're right. Thing is, I made a pact with myself as well, one you knew nowt about.'

'What pact?' she asked, removing her shoe in an automatic action as she spotted through the corner of her eye a cockroach scurrying along the mantel beside her. She brought the footwear down with a resounding whack, rendering the intruder senseless on its back on the hearth. One dark antenna twitched then was still. Janie reached for the small shovel hanging by the fire, scooped the bug up and tossed it into the flames. 'Well?' she continued, straightening around to face her husband again. 'What pact, James?'

'I told myself that, for your sake, I'd hold off doing owt rash forra couple of months, see how things went.' He lowered his stare. 'And that if Christmas came and went and the war weren't yet won, as we'd been assured it would, then I'd join up.'

'You were plotting all this behind my back?'

'I couldn't tell you, love, could I? You'd have tried to talk me out of it and . . . well, I didn't want to risk that.' James reached for her hands and held them between his own. His voice was low with passion. 'I have to do this, Janie. I must. Have you any idea how it feels, seeing lads nearly half my age parading round the streets in uniform? Every which way I turn, they're there: ready, proud, *brave.* Willing without a

2

second's thought to give their lives to King and country, they are, every last one. Nobbut boys, most of them. And all the while, here's me, bumbling about the bloody fields . . .'

'But your job on t' farm is just as important—'

'No, it ain't. It can never be.' His words had an angry urgency to them now, his gaze likewise. 'Don't you see what I'm saying? I want to feel useful. *Really* useful. It's my country too, damn it. I need to feel I've done my bit. I must, Janie, for as God is my witness, I'll regret it always. When our future grandkiddies ask me in years to come what I did in t' war, I want to be able to say I helped boot Jerry's arse to kingdom come – not that I shied away nice and safe at home, planting tatties and milking bloody cows! Tell me you understand. Please, lass.'

She didn't – *couldn't.* The stakes were far too high to ever attempt it. That she could very well lose her husband, the children their father, and for the sake of what? Male ruddy pride? The notion was utterly incomprehensible – and completely avoidable. He needn't risk it. He couldn't!

'It's too late, now,' he went on, as though reading her mind. 'What's done is done. There's no backing out of it for me, even if I wanted to.'

'Which you don't, at any rate.'

'No.'

Shaking her head, she rose and, wrapping her arms around herself tightly, paced the room.

When Britain had entered the war four months earlier and conscription came into force, requiring

3

all men between the ages of eighteen and forty-one to register for service, James had been adamant he must do his bit in helping to defeat 'that crazed bunch of buggers'. They would have the Nazis licked in no time. Germany hadn't stood a chance against their powerful little island and her allies last time around, had it? Those namby-pamby Jerries just didn't have it in them, he'd told her confidently.

The speeches had only increased in zealousness. Adolf Hitler had swiftly become his main topic of conversation, and she'd listened on with a growing mix of incredulousness and dread. It had felt like her father all over again. He too had caught 'battle fever' during the Great War, had marched from their lives to the trenches of France and, ultimately, his death, with his chin held high and a great daft smile on his face. Janie had been but a girl at the time but the memory was clear as crystal. Only now could she appreciate fully what her poor mother had suffered.

Now, here they were again. New generation, new fight. Another eternity of destruction and heartache to follow, millions more heads destined for the chopping block. And James Hudson was one of them. *Dear God.*

Plunged into a second world war in their lifetime. How, after the horror of the last one, the unfathomable loss, had they found themselves in the grip of another? It beggared belief, it did. Just as everything was going all right, too.

To her mind, the solution was simple: let these cossetted world leaders battle it out between themselves.

Chuck them in a boxing ring, aye, have them duff it out one on one – why must the rest of them be hauled into the madness? The average man, woman and child living their day-to-day lives, not bothering anyone, suddenly thrust – nay, *forced* – into these conflicts between fellows of power they had never even met? Conflicts to the death. *Conflicts* they had had no hand in creating. The ruddy cheek, the soul-corroding injustice of it. It made not a jot of sense and never could.

'No need.' The dull words fell from her lips on a whisper. 'There wasn't any *need* for you to hand yourself over to this bloody stupidity. Industries vital in keeping the country going are classed as reserved occupations – farming amongst them. You were safe. But that didn't stop you, oh no.'

'Like I said—'

'Aye, I know.' Her interjection was harsh. 'Milking and tattie planting, keeping your countryfolk fed, ain't glamorous enough for you, is it? Holding a hoe in your hands don't cut it, no – it's the feel of the rifle you hanker for. Does your dad know?' she asked, the thought occurring to her suddenly. Then, when James glanced away: 'Aye, 'course he does. I should have guessed. He probably encouraged it, didn't he? Never grows tired of harking on about how the fearless Hudson men have fought in every British battle since day dot, does he? So you're the next in line, eh? And who's to work the farm, like, in your absence? Have the pair of youse thought of that?'

'I'll not be leaving Dad in t' lurch. We thought . . . well, happen our Joey could take my place.'

5

'You really have planned this out all nice and bonny, ain't you?' The sear of betrayal was indescribable. 'Hand on heart, I didn't see any of this coming at all.'

'I worried mebbe . . . you've had no night sight?'

She shook her head. A 'night sight': that's what her granny, who had passed away when Janie was still a babe in arms, used to call it according to her mam. Truth in a dream. A blessing they were bestowed with and one they must use when they could to help others, bring comfort. Janie, however, was of the same mind as her mam had been: the sporadic visions of the future that the females of her family experienced were more a curse than a gift. But, by God, she wished she'd had one with this. At least then she'd have been prepared.

For a full minute, rain tapping at the thin panes filled the silence whilst she struggled to rein in her emotions.

'All them weeks of me pleading . . . it worked. I persuaded you not to get involved, made you see sense.' She gave a hollow laugh. 'Or at least I thought I had. I feel such a fool. You went and did it anyway, lied about your occupation, secured yourself a nice warm welcome into the army – and shattered my heart to dust in the process. It's all been for nothing. Even were I to beg on my knees, it'd make not the slightest difference, now.'

Her husband made his way across to her. He tried to take her into his arms, but she shook him off. He sighed. 'I know you're disappointed—'

'No, James. Devastated is what I am. Nineteen

forty were meant to be our year, remember? A clean start. We were set to leave Velvet Walks and this stinking hovel behind us. We've a fresh new house waiting for us. A better *life*, don't you see?'

'And nowt's changed there, not really. You and the kiddies will be starting that new life a bit earlier than me, that's all. I'll be back and joining youse in it soon enough.'

'Will you?' Turning now to face him, she bit down on her bottom lip, but a small cry escaped anyway. She reached out and smoothed his dark hair from his forehead then caressed his cheek tenderly. 'We're thirty-four years old, lad, and all our lives ahead of us ... I want to grow old with you, have you by my side for ever. I love you, James Hudson, with every single piece of me, have done since the day I clapped eyes on you and always will. Should you ... I don't know what, what I'd do, I ...'

'Eeh, love, love ...'

Now, when he drew her towards him, Janie didn't resist. All vestige of anger dissipated, leaving only terror in its wake. Her body heaving with sobs, she clung to him desperately with a feeling of drowning. 'Don't leave me.' Pointless, but she uttered it anyway. 'Please don't leave me.'

'I must. But, Janie ...' Holding her wet face in his hands, he gazed into her eyes with such sincerity, such conviction, it stole her breath and she allowed herself to hope that his next words could be the truth: 'I'll come back to you. I will. I promise.'

That night, their lovemaking had a different urgency

to it. Their hungry hands explored every inch of each other, desperate to imprint there the feel for when the time came that memory was all they had. Limbs entwined as though of one body, their hearts beat in perfect tandem. They tasted the salty tang of their tears in their kiss, and long after they had climaxed Janie held James deep inside her, her legs tight around him, loath to let him go.

When later he slept, his head cushioned on her bare breasts, she stroked his hair in the weak candlelight and stared unseeing at the damp-patched ceiling, thoughts galloping, mind snared in misery.

This was the beginning of the end for them all.

She needed no night sight to predict that.

A pale sun was struggling to claw through the yellow-tinged clouds the following day when James rose to don his coat.

The children, sombre-faced and quiet, put down their spoons, their porridge forgotten, and watched as their father did up the buttons and straightened the collar. His brown stare came to rest on them in turn and his brows met in the middle in an expression of guilt tinged with regret.

'Right, then. I'd best be off.'

Janie couldn't respond, refused to attempt it for fear of breaking down completely. She reached behind her for her cigarettes atop the mantel and lit one with shaking hands.

'Come here, you two.' James held out his hands and his young daughters bolted from their seats and ran to him to throw themselves into his arms. Holding them near, he closed his eyes. 'You'll be good lasses for your mam?'

Hilda and Elsie nodded in unison. 'Aye, Dad.'

James kissed them both on the forehead then turned to look at his son. He cleared his throat once, twice; still, when he spoke, a quaver sounded in the tone. 'Lad.'

Eyes downcast, Joey scraped back his chair and made his way across. Biting his lip, he halted a few steps away from his father.

'I'm leaving my three girls in your capable hands. All right?'

Glancing to his sisters and mother, Joey nodded solemnly. 'Aye.'

'Remember, you're the man of the house whilst I'm away.'

At this, the fifteen-year-old seemed to grow several inches in height. His shoulders went back and his chin lifted with clear pride at the responsibility with which his father was entrusting him. 'Aye, Dad.'

James shook his hand then on impulse clasped him to his chest in a swift hug before turning and heading for the door. In a world of pain, Janie rose from the table and followed her husband out.

Alone together in the minuscule hall, they gazed at each other in thick silence.

'James . . .'

'Janie. My own sweet love.'

They wrapped their arms around each other. Rocking slightly, they breathed in one another's scent, eyes closed, making the precious moments last as long as they were able.

'How could you do it, James?' Janie's voice was a choked whisper. 'I can't bear this, I can't!'

'Aye, you can, for you're strong, love. More than anyone else I know.'

'Oh, lad.'

'I'm sorry ...' With evident reluctance, he extracted himself from her hold. 'I need to be making tracks else I'll miss my train.'

Janie received a last lingering kiss from the man she loved, then he was gone.

Locked in shock and despair, she remained rooted to the spot, gazing at the closed front door for an age. When movement sounded from the room behind her, she shook herself – the children needed her. She was all they had for now. She nodded, though her heart felt as though it was genuinely breaking, and took some deep breaths. Then she lifted her head bravely, determinedly, and returned to the kitchen.

'Come on, then, youse three,' she said in her usual fashion, smiling, passing the girls their coats and tossing her son his flat cap. Normality was what was needed here – now more than ever. 'Time you were away to school and work else you'll be late.'

Joey, employed as a little piecer in a nearby cotton spinning works since leaving school last summer, normally walked ten-year-old Hilda and five-year-old Elsie to their classes on his way each morning – now, he shepherded them out into the freezing street. 'You're all right, Mam?' he asked quietly before leaving.

Janie swallowed several times before plastering back in place a smile. 'Aye, lad,' she reassured him. 'Go on, now. I'll see you later.'

They disappeared around the corner and she let her shoulders slump, the pretence leaving her in a rapid rush. Mouth drooping, eyes gritty, she turned back inside.

'Morning, lass!'

Lord, not now. Glancing around towards the source of the greeting, she threw her neighbour a brief wave. 'Morning, Mrs Reilly.'

'Janie love? Eeh, what's to do?'

'Nowt, I . . .' She broke off with a small sigh – the elderly woman was hurrying across to her. Knowing escape was an impossibility, Janie folded her arms and waited for her to reach her.

'Ay, you've been crying. What's occurred?'

Janie attempted to make light of the woman's concern, but tears were welling again; to her dismay, she burst into silent weeping. 'Oh, Mrs Reilly. It's my James. He's only gone and friggin' joined!'

'Nay, he never has! Eeh, lass.' She put a twig-thin arm about Janie's shoulders. 'The daft ha'porth, why's he done that?'

Five narrow steps led up to Janie's front door – she lowered herself on to the middle one, tucking her dove grey skirt around her calves, and Mrs Reilly plonked herself down beside her. 'He feels it's his duty. You know how men are.'

Her neighbour plucked a clay pipe from a pocket of her long skirts. Matches followed next and she struck one and held the flame to the dark tobacco in the bowl, sucking in her cheeks as she puffed it to life. 'That I do. Left for training, has he?'

Janie nodded. 'Weeks he'll be gone for. What will I do, Mrs Reilly? We ain't never spent even a single night apart since the day we said our vows. I'll miss him summat awful.'

'Aye well, it'll be sound practice for thee, lass, for once he's away fighting overseas . . .' The old woman paused to sigh. 'I mean not to be harsh, you know, only it's best you're prepared.'

Though it pained Janie to hear it, she knew Mrs Reilly spoke the truth – she bobbed her head again. 'It'll be hit and miss if and when he gets leave, won't it? It could be months at a time that we don't see him for. Mebbe even years . . .'

'Ay, don't say that! Surely to God, this war won't drag on as long as the last.'

'Who knows with that swine Hitler? He got his grubby mitts on Austria and Czechoslovakia but weren't happy with that, oh no. Nor will he be content now he has Poland as well, you just watch. Wants to conquer the world, he does, I reckon. And aye, I get that he must be stopped, I do really. But still . . .'

'Not at the expense of someone you love.'

Janie had the grace to blush. 'By, it sounds selfish, don't it?'

'Not at all, lass. You're frickened of losing your man – no shame in that, none at all. There's folk aplenty of the same mindset, I'll be bound.'

'It's the kiddies I'm most sorry for, Mrs Reilly.

D'you know, they were that brave earlier when we sat them down and told them what was what. Upset they were, I could see it in their little faces, but they didn't let it show to their father. Our Joey's to take his place on the family farm, will give his notice at work today.'

'The lad shan't mind that, leaving his pals at the mill?'

'He didn't say owt. He's took it in his stride, like; you know how he is. Lord, *why* did James *do* it?' Janie lambasted in a whisper after some moments, couldn't help it. 'I'll never understand, you know.'

The old woman shook her head gravely. 'And you just about ready to up sticks to your new dwelling. When is it, the big move?'

'Saturday.'

'Will youse still go?'

'I'd rather we didn't, not now. Not without James. Mind, he insists we must, and I suppose he's right: look how long it took us to secure one of them lovely new houses. If we let it go to someone else, who knows whether we'll be lucky enough to snag another?'

They lapsed into silence, their gazes straying about their cramped and tumbledown lane. A black rat, scratching about in the refuse that clogged the gutter running down the centre of the street, caught their attention, and they eyed it warily. It scurried off to squeeze its furry body through a gap in the boundary wall to their right, and they breathed in relief.

'Buggers,' muttered Mrs Reilly, her gnarled fingers going beneath her ancient shawl to rub at her arm.

'Is that nip what you copped for still giving you bother?'

'A bit, aye.'

Janie shook her head. 'You ought to get the doctor to look at it, really you should. God alone knows what you might have picked up – riddled with disease, them dirty things are.'

She brushed aside her concerns. 'Nay, lass. I'll be reet soon enough. It'll take more than an overgrown mousey to finish me off!'

Though Janie let the matter drop – Mrs Reilly was a stubborn piece, all right – she couldn't contain a shudder of revulsion. The woman had awoken one night last week to find a huge rat sitting on her chest in bed. She'd raised an arm instinctively to shield her face and, whether from hungry desperation, fear of attack or just plain wickedness, the intruder had lunged and delivered a nasty bite. Though the four-legged beasts were a common sight in this street and others of its ilk, the incident had nonetheless horrified its residents. Now more than ever Janie couldn't wait to get her family far from this dung pit they called home.

Until relatively recently, Bolton's inner-town poor had had no alternative but to make their homes in the clusters of slums that teemed throughout the area. The late-Georgian and early-Victorian cottages and terraced housing, thrown up quickly and cheaply by private landlords during the cotton industry's boom and subsequent flood of people who arrived in search of work, had been built solely with profit in mind – certainly with no thought for the multitude forced to inhabit them – and were unfit for purpose even then. A hundred years later, long-departed generations would have found nothing unrecognisable in the appalling conditions in which their descendants were living. There had been virtually no improvement; if anything, matters had only worsened.

Crumbling with age and neglect, stained black with a century's worth of soot from the surrounding factories' spewing chimneys, overcrowded, insanitary and overrun with vermin, the decaying dwellings' true horror had to be seen to be believed. Dark ginnels and entryways choked with rubbish, and pail closets – hit and miss as to when they were emptied – overflowing with human waste and heaving with disease added to the misery.

Then several years ago, seemingly out of nowhere, something unbelievable had occurred: the government awakened from their apathetic slumber and took notice.

At last, the desperate need for improvement was acknowledged and local authorities had taken over the long-overdue task. During the interwar years, the housing shortage was addressed and slum clearance slowly but surely took root.

The programme gained momentum following the 1930 Housing Act, when a widespread survey had finally shone a spotlight on the shameful situation, and the worst of the inadequate abodes were wiped away. In their place, brand-new houses erected by the council had mushroomed throughout the town. Low cost, but of a much superior quality to anything the working class had ever experienced, the modern accommodation couldn't have come soon enough.

Flicking her gaze once more around *their* narrow 'pocket of poverty', as Janie was wont to refer to Velvet Walks, another ripple of disgust ran through her – only this time, it was tinged with anger. Situated close by the River Croal and snaking off the main thoroughfare of Deansgate, it was allegedly named so owing to its historic production of the costly, smooth tufted fabric, which had involved tenants walking up and down the long attics between the benches working the material. The street and its three-storey dwellings should have been amongst the first to be ripped down, long ago, in her opinion. It was no way for human beings to live.

Albie Hudson, James's father, had been the one to inform his son about the new estate that was set to be developed no great distance from where his farm was situated. He'd offered to keep his ear to the ground for news on how they might secure one of the brand-spanking-new properties to rent, and James and Janie had readily agreed.

That had been some ten years ago.

To their dismay, upon completion, the houses had been snapped up in two blinks, and the family had been awaiting a vacancy ever since.

Now, finally, it had happened. They had been approved, and in two days' time number thirteen Padbury Way would become their new home. Though Janie and the children were yet to see it and the area, James's journey to and from work took him through

16

the heart of the estate each day, and he'd assured her with a wink that it would more than meet with her approval. Further details he'd laughingly refused to divulge, wanting her first viewing to be a nice surprise – Janie had barely been able to contain her anticipation. Yet that excitement had dulled somewhat in light of recent events. Embarking on this fresh beginning just wouldn't be the same without her husband by her side. How could it?

'I'll be away in, lass,' Mrs Reilly announced now, ambling to her feet and scattering Janie's brooding thoughts. She shot the moody sky a weary glance. 'White stuff's on its way, God help us.'

'You reckon?'

'Oh aye, I can smell it in t' air.'

Lifting her gaze, Janie bit her lip. 'Let's hope it holds off a while longer. My father-in-law's lending us a hand with the move; everything's arranged.'

'I'll keep my fingers crossed for thee, lass. You'll be all reet, aye?'

'I will. And thanks,' she added earnestly, giving the woman's bony shoulder a gentle squeeze. She felt a little better now she'd got some of her worries off her chest.

'Any time, you know that. Ta-ra for now.'

Watching her go, Janie felt a pang of impending loss. A yearning for betterment she might well harbour, but by, she'd miss the old girl and the other neighbours when she was gone from here.

As Janie entered the house, shutting the door behind her, the first wispy snowflakes began to fall.

Chapter 2

THE NIGHTS WERE by far the worst.

Janie had worried that the long days stretching ahead of her once the children had gone to work and school would be the crux, but no. She found her time taken up with the usual household duties, alongside packing up the remainder of their possessions for the move. Moreover, there were always the neighbours to talk to. The twilight hours, however, were another matter entirely.

The marital bed had felt huge and so very empty last night – the first of James's absence. Janie had quietly cried herself to sleep.

Tonight was proving no different. She tossed and turned for hours, her yearning for her husband intermingled now with both anticipation and dread of tomorrow's relocation, before finally drifting into a fitful slumber as dawn approached.

By eleven o'clock that morning, everything was set. Their belongings were packed neatly beneath the living-room window and Janie had swept and scrubbed their home for the last time to within an inch of its life. Decrepit the place might be, but she wouldn't dream of leaving it in a less than satisfactory state – her pride would never have allowed it.

'When's Grandad going to be here?' asked Hilda. Perched on a wooden chair by the front door, swinging her spindly legs, her eyes remained rooted to the street corner.

'Soon.'

'Well, he'd best get a shimmy on. It's snowing again.'

'Frig, that's all we need,' Janie muttered, craning her neck to catch a glimpse of the sky. Sure enough, fat flakes were floating down like confetti to add themselves to the previous dusting they had received on and off over the past few days. If Albie left it much longer, they would be in danger of having to postpone the move altogether.

'Not that he'll even notice me and Elsie when he does arrive. He never does,' Hilda went on in a wry mutter. 'Never wants nowt to do with us, he don't, oh no, us being only lasses. Now, our golden boy Joey on t' other hand . . . Well. Grandad will be all over him, you watch and see.'

She's got a point, Janie thought to herself. However, she couldn't let an impertinence towards one of her elders go unchecked. Give their eldest daughter an inch and she'd take a mile. Almost as tall as her mother and possessing the same light blonde hair and large violet eyes she might be, but physical traits were where the similarities ended. Sharp as a tack and hot-headed with it, Hilda had her father's temperament, all right.

19

'We'll have none of your lip today,' Janie told her. Then, in a softer tone: 'Don't take it to heart, lovey, it's just his way.' To her relief, the girl let the matter drop with a shrug.

'Mam?' Little Elsie tugged at Janie's skirt. 'It's going to snow for ever! Can I play in it? Can I?'

'You cannot! You'll catch your death of cold, lass.'

'He's here,' Joey announced suddenly, killing possible protests from his youngest sister. 'Ready, Mam?'

But Janie couldn't respond. A panic had overtaken her and she struggled to regain her composure. It was really happening. After all these years, they were leaving this place and its people for good.

'Mam?'

'Aye, lad,' she managed. She nodded with a shaky breath. 'Aye, I'm ready.'

The horse trotted to a standstill at the bottom of their steps. Albie climbed down from the cart and doffed his flat cap to them. 'Morning.'

Though she did her level best, Janie couldn't keep the slight edge from her tone as she returned the greeting. He was one of the reasons her husband wasn't here to share this experience with them today, she was certain of it. She could just hear him in her mind now, his disapproving sniffs and barbed remarks as to why his son hadn't been born with the backbone of his Hudson ancestors – Albie himself included. He'd harangued her husband into this fresh war – he had, just as surely as if he'd shoved him headlong through the recruiting office door with his two hands. May God help him should harm – or worse – come to James.

20

Albie and Son: it had been but the two of them for more years than they could count. James had lost his mother to a stroke during his tender years, and his father became the central focus in his life – and vice versa. Janie only had to glance at her father-in-law to see how her husband would look in later life; the resemblance was striking. Albie was more whiskered and weathered than his son, it was true, but the similarities were there nonetheless, even down to the same untameable hair and cleft chin. The sight of him today brought her loss home to her ever more.

'You're all reet?' Albie asked Janie now, his eyes meaningful, his tone uncharacteristically amiable.

'I have to be, don't I?'

'He's done the right thing, you know. He'd have regretted it else. Every fella needs a good war; it's their due, part of growing up. James'll come back from this a new man, you'll see.'

Not trusting herself to speak for fear of creating a row, she clasped together her hands, which were trembling with suppressed anger, and turned back inside the house, saying over her shoulder, 'Best we make a start lest this weather worsens.'

Albie followed her inside and his large frame filled the doorway behind her. He rummaged inside his trouser pocket and brought out a handful of coins. These he sorted through, selecting several and holding them out to her.

'What's that for?'

'Fare for t' tram. You and the lasses here go on in front, get the new place opened up, like. Me and

21

Joey shall see to your stuff.' He turned to his grandson with a hard nod. 'Man's work, lad, am I right?'

'Pompous, patronising prat,' Janie muttered beneath
her breath, taking the money from him with much
reluctance. Arguing the toss with him, however, was
pointless – he'd shout a body down into submission
every time. Janie had discovered this, and that to
have it appear he was getting his own way led for a
more peaceful life, very early on in her marriage.

'Right then, we'll be on our way,' she announced,
reaching for her gas mask then lifting the large
wicker basket she'd packed especially earlier, and
which contained the most essential items, so far as
she was concerned: the kettle, cups and teapot, tin
caddy, milk and sugar. The last thing she'd wanted
was to arrive at the new house gasping for a brew
and have the palaver of rifling through boxes in
search of the tea stuff. She checked her coat pocket
for the new front-door key and, satisfied, nodded.
'Ta-ra for now.'

'Oh, I meant to tell you,' Albie said as she turned
to leave.

'Aye?'

'I had a hundredweight of coal delivered to Padbury Way – it should be there all ready for you and
should see youse through the week.'

Janie blinked at him in shock. 'You didn't have to
do that, but I thank you for it all the same.'

He shot her a brief smile. 'I figured it'd be one less
thing for you to have the bother of when you get there.'

It would, he was right, and Janie knew a prickle of

guilt for her standoffishness with him since he'd arrived. He really hadn't needed to do that, had he, after all? Not to mention the fact he'd taken the time out of his busy day to help them with the move. By, but she could be a bit of a bitch at times. 'Ta, Albie,' she told him with feeling. Then, glancing outside: 'It *is* a good thing you did, all right – just look at this now.'

'Aye,' he agreed, a frown appearing at his brow at the sight of the worsening snow. 'I don't like the look of that. Come on, lad, let's get cracking,' he added to Joey, and the two of them headed for the stairs to make a start.

Janie shepherded the girls towards the door. 'I'll just say a quick goodbye to everyone,' she told them, 'then we'll be on our way— Oh!' Her words died, the exclamation of surprise with them, to spot the crowd gathered out to see them off in the street. Others stood smiling from doorways and some leaned from the attic windows waving. 'Eeh, what's all this?' she asked tearfully, smiling at each of her neighbours in turn.

Mrs Reilly shuffled to the front of the group. In her hands she held a large spider plant in a bright lilac pot. 'A little summat, lass, for the new house. We all chipped in, like.'

'I don't know what to say, I . . .' Janie was quite overcome. 'Thank you – all of you.'

'We'll miss thee.'

'And I youse,' she responded earnestly. 'I'll visit, I will, honest.'

'You'd better!' Mrs Reilly warned, pulling her into a firm embrace. In Janie's ear, she murmured, 'Now you be strong, d'you hear? This war will be done with and James will be back with you afore you know it, I'm sure. Be happy, lass.'

Tears ran freely down Janie's cheeks. Letting her gaze travel around her, she knew a sense of gut-wrenching sadness. Then her daughters were tugging at her hands, impatient to be off on the new adventure, and she nodded. It was time.

'Ta-ra, Janie love, lasses. Ta-ra!'

The farewells wrapped around them like a blanket, shielding them from the cold and filling their hearts with warmth as they walked away.

Unbroken uniform grey gave way to a jade-coloured horizon as the tram turned off Crompton Way and clanked northwards along the centre of Thicketford Road. Heads close together, the potted plant balanced on the bench between them, Hilda and Elsie gazed through the window at scenery they were encountering for the first time. This route was also unfamiliar to Janie and she too took in their surroundings with growing interest.

Though her father-in-law paid them regular – albeit short – visits at Velvet Walks, he himself wasn't overly keen on receiving guests at his small farm. Children in particular quickly proved a strain on his misanthropic disposition, and the family had made the journey to his home only a handful of times over the years. When they had, they had always taken the main Bury Road – thus, this part of the town was altogether new to them.

On towards Winchester Way, they passed the plain block building of a recently established Independent Methodist Church before turning left on to Blair Lane. Finally, the tram came to a stop on New Lane and the Hudsons alighted and looked about.

'Well, would you look at that,' Janie murmured to her daughters, motioning ahead with her chin to the snow-smudged fields dominating the skyline in the distance. 'Bonny, eh?'

It was indeed an apt description of here, on the breezy rise that was Breightmet.

The Old English place name translated simply as 'Bright Meadow' – Janie could well appreciate why. Only two miles from their former home in the centre of town it might be, but the difference was staggering. Made up of hilly land dotted with farms and woods, the area was a thing of beauty – a word severely lacking in their previous surroundings. Space – green at that – and proportionally fewer smoking chimneys meant cleaner air: far healthier for the body as well as the mind and eye, she was sure.

Their home belonged to Breightmet's new estate of Top o' th' Brow, literally so-called due to its position on the brow of a hill. Cushioned between Harwood and Tonge Moor, the estate itself was comprised of less than a dozen neatly laid streets. These revolved around a central row of small shops: a grocer's, butcher's and a confectioner's, which stood directly facing the slight incline of Padbury Way.

'Which one is ours, Mam?' asked Elsie, hopping from foot to foot, desperate to explore.

'Aye, come on, let's have a look-see!' chipped in Hilda, grabbing her sister's hand and dragging her off on a skip in front.

Janie hitched up the spider plant that was resting on her hip and repositioned the wicker basket swinging from her other arm. Then, smiling, she joined her children in the search for number thirteen.

The short, tidy street of eighteen houses fronted by clipped privet hedges and picket fences was like nothing they had known before – mother and daughters stopped dead in their tracks in wonderment. That they would have the privilege of calling such a wholesome spot home seemed like a stolen dream belonging to someone else. Suddenly diffident now, they continued on tentatively, as intruders might.

'Eeh, Mam . . .' the girls breathed in unison when they reached their destination.

'A garden,' Janie whispered back, marvelling along with them entirely at the sight of the small patch of grass. After swinging her head and squinting down the road at the street sign attached to the corner dwelling, just to be sure they were indeed at the right place, she double-checked the door number then pushed open the wooden gate.

Still not quite believing this was right, when she put the key in the hole and the lock sprang back with a welcoming clink she gasped in surprised delight. Taking a deep breath, she led the way inside.

Hilda and Elsie dashed straight upstairs to inspect

the three bedrooms whilst their mother made a bee-line for her chief domain and the hub of every house.

'Oh my . . .' Janie gazed around open-mouthed. The room boasted a serviceable yet attractive fitted kitchen in brown and beige units, and – wonder of wonders – hot running water! Kettles and pans heated on the fire were what she'd always known; now all she had to do was turn a tap? It was a far cry from the ancient slop stone and single cold-water tap she was accustomed to. She could scarcely compre-hend the incredible changes. Never in her life had she known such luxury.

She'd just wandered back to the living room and was peering about in a daze when her daughters yelled down to her to come and see. Excited as a child herself, she deposited the plant and basket on the windowsill and hurried upstairs to find out what fresh discoveries awaited her.

'We've gorra bathroom, Mam! A proper 'un, look!'

'There never is . . .' Janie began, but the girls were right – God in heaven above!

'An inside toilet!' Hilda squealed, clapping her hands.

'A bath, an' all – and oh, it's massive!' added Elsie, beaming. 'Can I have one now, Mam?' she begged. 'Pleeease?'

Janie laughed through her tears. 'Later, love. We've a lot of work to do just now, getting everything sorted. Speaking of which, your grandad and our Joey will be here soon with the first load, so I'd best get the kettle on. They'll be parched, I'll bet.'

However, despite her words, when the children had skittered off she didn't follow right away. She remained where she was for a minute, shaking her head and smiling. No more having to share dank and stinking communal toilets with the rest of the street – now they had one all of their own. No more dragging the tin tub in front of the fire or a weekly trip to the slipper baths on Bridgeman Street in town – they would wash and bathe here in the comfort of their home. All that had gone before was a thing of the past. And her James had been the one to help make it possible.

'I wish you were here to share this day with us, lad,' she mouthed to the ceiling, closing her eyes. 'I love you and miss you. And I thank you, aye. By, I do.'

After crossing the landing and shooting a quick look around the spacious bedrooms – larger than anything they had ever known, at any rate – she sighed happily and headed back downstairs.

She found the children in the kitchen, struggling with the lock on the back door, and held her hand out for the key. 'Let me try; it's probably a bit stiff is all.'

If their eyes had been out on stalks when they spied the front garden, now they almost fell clean from their skulls upon discovering an even larger patch of green at the rear of the property, too. An Anderson shelter, erected by the last tenants, squatted in one corner.

'Eeh, it truly is magic here!' Janie cried, and her daughters were swift to agree.

An open playing field backed on to this side of

Padbury Way's gardens and on closer inspection they saw it belonged to a modest school stretching across a concrete yard to their right.

'Is that where me and Elsie will go?' Hilda asked, her nose pressed against their fence.

'It is. A bonny little building, in t' it? I'll call in first thing Monday morning and put your names down.'

'I'm going to make lots of new friends,' Elsie announced. 'Our Hilda will, an' all. I like it here, Mam.'

Janie held her little body close. 'A fresh start, this is, aye – and a better one at that, God willing,' she added quietly, with her husband in mind once more. Then, shaking herself before her emotions got the better of her, she turned back indoors, saying brightly, 'Come on in, lasses, out of the cold, and we'll have a nice hot brew.'

A small door set into the far corner of the kitchen revealed, when Janie went to investigate, a well-stocked coal shed, just as Albie had promised there would be. Smiling, she reached for the shovel hanging on the wall inside. In no time at all, she had a fire blazing merrily in the living-room grate, which took the winter bite from the air and instantly made the place feel more homely. Whilst she emptied the basket of its tea things and put the kettle on the heat, the girls sat on the windowsill and kept a look-out for the horse and cart. Janie had just poured hot water into the pot, scalding the dark leaves within, when Hilda spoke:

'There's someone 'ere, Mam.'

'Who, lass?'

'I don't know, a woman. She's coming up our path.'

'And she's got two babbies with her, Mam, and aw, they are bonny!' Elsie added.

Frowning, Janie abandoned the tea to investigate. She'd just reached the living room when a knock came at the door. Pulling a 'who the heck can this be?' face to her daughters, she crossed to the tiny hallway and hesitantly opened the door.

'Morning! Or is it afternoon by now . . . ? Anyroad, I'm Lynn Ball and I live next door,' chirped the woman on the step. Tall and plump with a wide mouth, rich raven hair styled in a neat shingle bob and bright eyes framed by thick lashes, she was as dark-featured as Janie was light and cut a striking figure. 'You've taken the place on, then?'

'That's right,' Janie replied, her hand involuntarily moving upwards to touch her own hair, the long, soft waves rolled and tucked at her neck in a faux bob. She would never have had the courage, she didn't reckon, to have it cut so short as Lynn's – and doubted that James would have been pleased about the look if she did. Her eyes travelled next to her plain cream blouse – glaringly drab and in stark contrast with the pretty patterned lemon garment Lynn wore. Nevertheless, she couldn't help returning the infectious smile. She'd have placed Lynn in her mid-to late twenties, a little younger than herself, and was drawn to the sunny woman instantly. 'I'm Janie Hudson and these are my girls, Hilda and Elsie,' she told her, motioning inside. 'I've a son, an' all: our Joey. He's away helping his grandad with the move.'

'These two terrors of mine are Bobby and Brian,' said Lynn, jiggling the chubby youngsters in her arms up and down and making them laugh. 'Twins, I ask you! By, they're tiring!'

'I'll bet,' Janie chuckled. Then, remembering her manners, she shook her head: 'Sorry – will you come in?'

'You sure? You must be up to your eyes in it; we'll not be in t' way?'

'No, no,' Janie assured her, holding the door wide. 'We're still waiting on t' cart.'

Nodding, Lynn followed her inside. 'Hello, girls.'

'Hello,' the sisters said in unison, scrambling from the windowsill and hurrying over to chuck the babies under their chins.

'Here, sit and play with them if you like,' Lynn said, lowering the boys to the floor, and the delighted girls readily agreed.

Janie's smile returned as she watched on, then she turned and headed back for the kitchen, asking over her shoulder, 'Can I offer you a sup, Lynn? I've just brewed a fresh pot.'

'Ta, thanks.'

She poured out four cups, adding extra milk to those of her daughters to help cool the piping drink, and handed them around. 'Have you lived here long?' she asked the woman before taking a sip of her own tea.

'Nearly three years now. Me and Duncan – that's my husband – moved here shortly after we were wed.'

'In t' army, is he?'

'That's right.'

'My James has gone the same road. He left for training two days ago.'

'Duncan joined up in September, right at the start of things. Miss him summat awful, I do,' Lynn added softly. 'The twins had only come along a few months before in the May, and he's only managed to get home and see them the once since, is missing out on so much . . . But well, we mustn't grumble, eh?' she continued with determined conviction. 'That rabble-rouser Hitler needs putting in his place, all right, and our men are the ones to do it. Every one of us, in fact – this is all of ours fight, the fight for the good. We all must make the sacrifice if we're to live in peace; that's the price, aye, and we must accept it. Ain't that right, love?'

Though Janie knew she spoke sense and truth, she was unable to be so readily accepting of the situation as Lynn, and no doubt many others along with her. In time, perhaps she might, but not now. Not just yet. The anger and pain of loss and separation was just too raw.

What made matters more difficult, she reckoned, was the fact it didn't really *feel* like their country was at war. True, men were consistently leaving the cities and towns, but there was no great change here on the home front, not really.

It had become evident that war was inevitable when blackout and evacuation were introduced on the first day of September last year – though, thankfully, owing to theirs being a neutral town, Bolton mothers were spared the heartache of sending their offspring to live with strangers; a necessary evil, maybe, but Janie could imagine nothing worse – and therefore, when the terrible news was officially announced two days later, it came as little surprise. National Registration Day, when details of every householder were collected for the issuance of identity cards, swiftly followed, as did the distribution of gas masks. And then . . . nothing.

It had been widely predicted that this time around would prove a far more personal affair and that suffering would be shared more equally between soldier and civilian. Aerial bombardment posed a very real threat. Enemy planes would darken their vulnerable skies, and gas bombs and high explosives would devastate Britain. Except they hadn't – at least not yet.

Janie well remembered the tense atmosphere shared by all, that quiet yet palpable panic that had gripped the nation during those early days. Indeed, they had awaited with bated breath and gritted teeth the expected attacks from the air and bombs to begin raining on their heads within moments of the Prime Minister delivering his speech. But no. Nothing had occurred and the people drifted day to day in a queer kind of limbo; still did.

Understandably, it was quickly dubbed the 'phoney war'. The skies remained quiet and, by Christmas, many homesick evacuees had returned to the bosom of their families. Life was simply continuing as it always had – and that was what Janie found impossible to fathom: the sheer normality of it. If it wasn't for the absence of their menfolk, it would be difficult to imagine they were even at war at all.

With a shrug and a sigh, she returned her attention to her cup.

'Mind you,' Lynn went on, unperturbed, 'I'd not have managed without the help and kindness of the residents hereabouts. We're a close-knit lot here, us Top o' th' Brow folk. You'll learn that for yourself soon enough.'

Janie was certainly relieved to hear this. 'They're a sound bunch on this here estate then, aye?'

'Oh, champion.'

'I must say, I have been worrying summat awful about leaving my friends and neighbours behind. They're a grand bunch back there.'

'You've come from the centre of town, aye?'

'That's right. By, but the state of the place ... You'd never believe it, Lynn.'

'Rough, was it?'

'Oh, rougher than a tramp's chin!' Again, Janie trained her gaze around the space, and her heart gave a flutter in response. As with the rooms upstairs, a subtle floral-patterned paper hung at the walls and, though faded, there were no tears that she could see. It was in good condition still and would serve them well until they ever managed to save enough money to redecorate. The skirting boards and doorframes could have done with a lick of paint but would have to make do with a thorough rub-down for now. The previous tenants had looked after the place well, for which she was more than grateful. 'Top o' th' Brow is a paradise in comparison.'

Lynn nodded understandingly. 'Me and my Duncan

were making do with renting a single poky room in cramped lodgings before we got the house here. We thought we'd died and gone to heaven when we first clapped eyes on it, still do, and that's the truth.'

The women lapsed into companionable silence and, as they drank their tea, Janie listened to her daughters, who by now had wandered off again to explore. Clattering up and down the stairs, they filled the rooms with the sweet sound of free and exuberant laughter, bringing tears to their mother's eyes.

Never in their short lives – hers and James's also, for that matter – had they experienced such a level of luxury, and it showed. In that moment, buried amidst the rush of pure happiness, she knew a shiver of rage for how life had been up to now. How it would remain, until who knew when, for countless of her townsfolk born on the wrong side of the class barrier.

Not that everyone had been encouraging of the changes, however. Janie gave a small shake of her head in remembrance. Those belonging to higher sections of society and of the opinion that the toiling masses were a savage, uncivilised lot who enjoyed living in their own squalor had regarded the lifesaving venture as a waste of time and money. Dwellings would be uncared for and fall into ruinous disrepair in no time at all, of this they were convinced. The wholly unjust misconception had rankled and, so far as she'd witnessed up to now of this development at least, served only to prove the narrow-minded wrong.

Boltonians were by and large a decent and dignified lot. They were brave and proud and generous to a fault – she felt lucky to call herself one of their number. Just as she'd known they would, it appeared folk free from the stink and rottenness were flourishing in their fresh surroundings. They had simply been without the means before – a silk purse from a sow's lug thou canst make, after all – and the majority looked to keep their homes sparkling like new pins.

Mind you, it had to be said there were some amongst the working class, too, who were averse to the idea of the new estates – though for widely differing reasons to those of their more privileged counterparts. It wasn't that they enjoyed being slum dwellers – who in their right mind *would* choose such a thing? No, it was fear of change which held some prisoner.

Older residents in particular – stubborn and stuck in their ways, and claiming they were content with their lot for it was all they had ever known – were reluctant to even consider the bold new phase. Friends and neighbours would be separated and close-knit communities that had been nurtured for generations torn apart and lost for ever, many insisted. One day, of course, the choice might be made for them, but for the present, 'they were stopping where they were, thank you very much'.

Mrs Reilly was amongst them. She and several others had voiced their shock and concern when Janie had shared the news of their plan to up sticks. Though Janie herself had harboured similar worries to begin with, the overwhelming urge for betterment had won through; now, she once more thanked God that her family at least had striven to wave Velvet Walks goodbye for good.

Steadfast in their belief her old friends might be, but Janie's confidence in proving them wrong was steadily growing. They had their opinion, they insisted, and nothing would persuade them otherwise – however, if what Lynn Ball had told her was true, then the move hadn't been a bad decision after all. Hopefully, she'd discover that change didn't have to be for the worse, that fresh friendships could be forged and new communities born. And she'd do what she could to make the others see this too, she told herself, vowing that, if all turned out well, she'd pay the elderly woman a visit soon.

No one could deny the tide was turning. The country was heading in the right direction and a better quality of life was at long last emerging – she only wished it could have come sooner. It *should* have come sooner. Unhealthy warrens and back-to-back housing – ideal for cramming as many folk as was possible into the smallest of spaces – had for many, the Hudsons now amongst their number, come to an end and descriptions of 'fetid' and 'comfortless' ceased to apply. For many, yes, but not all. There remained still much to be done. The onset of this latest war had stalled the housing progress but was set to resume when peacetime was restored. *Peacetime* . . .

'Did you hear me, love?'

Pulled back to the present before thoughts of James had a chance to gather, Janie shook her head with some relief. 'Sorry, no,' she admitted. 'I were in a world of my own.'

'I were just saying: I'll introduce you to the street when you're settled in,' Lynn repeated.

'Oh ta, I'd appreciate that.'

'Aye, I think you're going to like it here.'

'Aye, I think we are,' she agreed, smiling.

'It's Grandad, Mam,' Hilda called out just then, and the women made across to look through the window. Sure enough, Albie's horse had stopped by the roadside and Joey was already swinging down from the laden cart. Janie let the front door off the latch then hurried to pour man and boy a much-needed hot drink.

'By, it's cold enough to freeze the devil!' her son announced, rushing across the room to warm his hands at the fire. 'We're not done yet neither – it's going to take another trip.'

'Here, lad, get that down you,' Janie told him, handing him a steaming cup then passing over another to her father-in-law as he entered. 'That'll see you right before you have to set out again. Oh, Albie, Joey, this is Lynn Ball,' she added, introducing them to her new neighbour. 'She lives next door.'

The woman flashed them a smile. 'Pleased to meet you both. Now then, where do you want me?'

'Where do we . . . ?' Albie was flummoxed.

'Aye, what do you need my help with?' Lynn pressed on. She glanced back to the waiting cart outside and rolled up her sleeves. 'I'll just make a start with what's on top, shall I, whilst you finish your brews?'

Janie felt laughter bubble up in her throat at the old man's expression. He was gazing at the woman as though she'd spoken in a foreign tongue and he was finding her announcement impossible to process. 'But . . . that's man's work,' he stuttered.

'And that's daft talk! Do I look like a jelly-muscled damsel to you?' Lynn asked, stretching to her full height and puffing out her chest, whilst Albie simply stared back open-mouthed. 'Girls, you'll keep an eye to the twins, won't you?' she continued to Hilda and Elsie, and at their nods: 'That's settled then.' Then, turning to Janie, she said, 'Come on, love, let's get cracking,' before leading the way.

Outside, Janie doubled over with mirth. 'Eeh, what are you like! Albie's face!'

Lynn's own face stretched in a grin. 'Serves him right – man's work indeed. We'll show him!'

Within ten minutes, the cart was unloaded. Puffing and red in the face but proud of their efforts, the women waved Joey and a silent Albie off on their final journey from the gate, with Janie promising them she'd have a hot meal waiting for them upon their return.

'I don't think your father-in-law likes me very much,' whispered Lynn out of the side of her mouth as the cart rattled away, her shoulders shaking with amusement.

'Well, I wouldn't lose much sleep over that, love. Albie Hudson's been put in his place for the first time in his life today, I reckon. He's met his match in you and boy does he know it!'

Dissolving into laughter, they linked arms and made their way back to the house.

The snow, which had fallen steadily all day, still showed no sign of abating. In fact, it had only increased in intensity following the cart's departure, and Janie was beginning to grow worried.

'They should have been back by now. I hope nowt's occurred; it's turned treacherous out there. They could have got into difficulty, had a mishap . . .'

'They'll be here, love, soon enough. You'll see,' Lynn reassured her. 'They'll be taking their time is all, lest the horse loses its footing. I'll make a fresh pot of tea, shall I, to calm your nerves?'

'Ta, Lynn,' Janie told her with feeling, relieved to have the woman's soothing presence. Her steady-naturedness right now was a comfort. It was queer, really – it was as though they had been friends all their lives. Janie knew she was fortunate to have found her. Nicer still, it seemed the sentiment was mutual. 'You're right; I'm just being daft.'

'Anyroad, Albie won't be able to resist me for too long,' her neighbour purred in her best imitation of the famous entertainer Mae West. Hands on her round hips, she tilted her head and pursed her lips in a pout before bursting out laughing. Janie couldn't resist joining in.

'Eeh, Lynn, you're a tonic. Mad as a basketful of wasps, mind, but a tonic all the same!'

'I try my best,' she said with a sultry wink.

Still chuckling, Janie crossed once more to the

window – and, to her great relief, she saw the horse and cart drawing to a halt outside. 'Oh, thank the Lord, they're here!' she cried, rushing into the hall to let them in.

On instruction from her mother, Hilda had called to the nearby shops earlier and purchased eggs and a small loaf to go with the bacon Janie already had. Their neighbour came through for them with the lend of her frying pan and some plates, and Joey and Albie's meals had been kept warming in the small kitchen oven. These, the girl now went to fetch in for the shivering and ravenous males, whilst Lynn busied herself with cutting the bread and pouring each of them a piping cup of tea.

As her son and father-in-law tucked into the food gratefully, Janie went to collect another shovelful of coal for the fire. Then, without a word, she and Lynn moved towards the door. To her surprise – and not a little amusement – this time, despite his bushy brows drawing together in a disapproving frown, Albie made no attempt at protest. Hiding their smiles, the women donned their coats and, braving the thick-falling snow, went to empty the cart of the last items.

'Ta for today, Albie,' Janie told him earnestly a little later as he was leaving. 'I appreciate it.' And despite his habit of getting under her skin at times, she meant it. 'You'll be all reet getting home?'

Evening shadows were rapidly drawing in and the weather had worsened yet further. Nevertheless, he nodded. 'Aye, it ain't far.'

'Well, if you're sure . . . Thanks again.'

41

'Ta-ra for now.'

'Ta-ra, take care.'

He said his goodbyes to the children then threw a reluctant nod to Lynn, who returned the farewell with a film star smile, before heading off back to his farm.

'Aw, I'm a swine, ain't I?' Lynn giggled as the front door banged shut.

'Aye, you are!'

'Sorry, I couldn't resist.'

Janie rummaged in a box and brought out a length of material. Smiling, she shook her head. 'It's all reet, I'll forgive you. *If* you lend me a hand to get the blackout blind up, that is,' she added wickedly, arching an eyebrow.

'That's bribery, that is!'

'Aye, I know. Come on, then, shake a leg,' she ordered in mock sternness, and, grinning, they got to work.

That night, with the blizzard shut out and the orange flames licking over the coals in the grate and bathing the room in a cosy glow, Janie sighed in contentment. Lynn had left with the twins with the promise of calling back in in the morning, which Janie was already looking forward to, and the children were washed and fed and tucked up in bed. She'd had a long soak in the bath herself and felt all the better for it. Now, dressed in an oversized shirt of her husband's upon which lingered his comforting scent, she tucked her bare feet and legs beneath herself and snuggled deeper into the fireside chair.

Hands wrapped around a cup of Ovaltine, she took a sip of the milky malt drink.

Pure and simple bliss.

She hadn't dreamed she could be this settled, this happy. The upheaval was done with and things had gone better than she'd ever dared hope.

If only James . . .

'Oh, lad,' she whispered out loud, and a solitary tear escaped to roll down her cheek.

Chapter 3

BULLETS, LIKE THICK swarms of angered bees, whizzed through the grey dawn from all sides. Deafening thumps of bombs rocked the very world, snaring the mind and senses. Beyond and above, the thunderous drone of tanks and aircraft hacked air that was choked with the stink of smoke and destruction. Everywhere, the screams and shouts of man added to the carnage chorus.

Thousands upon thousands of flesh and bone fighting machines – khaki-clad soldiers, too many barely on the cusp of adulthood – yelling and cursing, weeping and praying, bellowing orders and silent in grim focus, battled on and died on the blood-drenched sands. Still the assault raged, relentless.

Looking on in numb horror, Janie Hudson doubted it would ever come to an end.

Then she saw him.

Her James, her husband. His handsome face, its every contour as familiar to her as her own, was almost lost beneath week-old stubble, general grime and other men's blood. Almost, but not quite – besides,

44

she would have recognised him anywhere. With broad back and shoulders iron taut in quiet trepidation, and hooded eyes locked on the enemy in the distance, he was crouched by the water's edge, weapon poised in readiness.

Janie knew he would be shot.

As always, she could but watch the scene unfold. There would be nothing she could do; there never was.

Then it came: ear-splitting cracks as a German machine-gun vomited forth rounds of ammunition, one of its lethal missiles making a beeline for James's head. She saw her husband raise his arm instinctively, then all was still. Sound and smell died and the vision went black.

Bolting up in bed, Janie groped for her cigarettes on the night table and lit one with trembling hands.

'Friggin' 'ell. Oh, friggin' *hell.*'

She took several long drags and blew the plumes of smoke into the shadows, but this went little in the way of soothing her shattered nerves.

She hated having this part of her that she could do nothing about, hated catching glimpses of the future, both the good and the bad, for it wasn't the natural way of things, was it? An oddity, that's how she'd always felt. Folk *shouldn't* know what fate might deliver, they shouldn't. So why did God deem it right to burden a select few with the ability?

Admittedly, she did feel fractionally better now, having 'seen' him – in no matter the capacity – she was forced to concede after some minutes. Over

45

eight weeks had passed since James had left, and she'd heard not a whisper, knew not whether he was still at training, had been assigned to defend vulnerable points in England or some such, or had been shipped overseas into battle without first obtaining leave. Moreover, at least she knew now that wherever he may be, he wasn't dead. She'd feared it constantly of late, that uncertainty. He'd be shot, but he wouldn't succumb to the injury – this time at least. She knew this without a single shred of doubt. Yet it did nothing to ease her anxiety in the long run, not really. Next time . . .

She'd rather not see, *not* know. It would be bad enough if . . . but to witness it like that, watch his suffering, his demise, for herself . . . It would finish *her*, that would. *Damn it, why me?* But no answer was forthcoming; there never was.

When her husband's face trickled back to her mind and refused to leave it, her eyes grew gritty with tears. 'God, how I miss you . . .' she whispered. Then, in the next breath, firmer now: 'No.'

She shook her head and rose from the bed swiftly, determinedly. Yielding to her emotions was something she wouldn't do. She'd had no choice but to learn to harden herself to her pain as time went on, had toughened, felt it with the days. Aye, she could have done with a good bawl – who couldn't with the way their world was these days? – but what good would it do? None, that's what, so where was the point?

'Keep calm and carry on.'

She repeated the strengthening mantra to herself as she dressed.

'You must, Janie Hudson, for the kiddies' sakes, if nowt else. Chin up and chest out, girl. James would expect nowt less.'

The worn linoleum was cold on her bare feet and she hurried her step down to the kitchen. Before making for the gas lamp bracketed to the far wall, she groped her way through the thick darkness to check the window.

It came automatically, this, now, for them all. Woe betide anyone careless enough to be showing a chink of light when the ARP warden passed by on his obligatory patrol of the streets.

She'd soon come to discover that Ralph Robertson wore his blue overalls and black steel hat stamped with its large white W with pride and took his role very seriously. He was a stickler for the rules. His cutting cry from outside of 'You there, number thirteen!' – or three, or seven or ten, depending on the culprit – 'Turn that bleedin' light out! D'you want to guide the Luftwaffe to our doorsteps, is that it? Happen you've a mind to invite Jerry in for a sup of tea and slice of cake whilst you're about it, eh!' had become a familiar one. A lecture right now Janie could well do without.

Feeling along the blackout blinds and satisfied they were in place, she turned once more and made for the box of matches on the far shelf. She struck one and brought the lamp hissing and popping to life. After securing its milk-white, frosted glass globe

carefully – the delicate mantles it protected, responsible for producing the light, were the devils themselves; even after being soaked in vinegar to lend
them strength they were prone to disintegrating
at the least knock, which resulted in regularly fork-
ing out for a replacement at the oil shop – she took
out another match and headed for the gas stove to
make tea.

As she waited for the kettle to come to the boil, she
pulled out a chair and sat at the table. The low glow
had scattered with its halo of flickering gold the
early-morning darkness, and she let her gaze travel
around the room of the neat little house of which
she was so proud.

Eeh, but they had been over the moon, the stars –
heaven itself – when they had secured this place,
hadn't they? Every day since, not a single one went
by that she didn't remind herself how lucky they
were, and luckier than most. And the people? Well.
They made this bright and airy estate what it was, oh
they did. Lynn Ball had been correct about that, all
right.

Pouring hot water into a large cream teapot,
Janie's mind remained on the past and a wistful smile
touched her lips. She well recalled the old place and
always would, could never erase from her memory
the smell, the bugs and rats. Like others, she'd spent
every spare penny on disinfectants to combat the
filth and damp and infestations, but it had made little difference. How could it, really? It had been an
impossible battle they could never win – and one

which seemed like a lifetime ago now. However, she also remembered the folk there: the best friends she could ever have wished for, never dreaming there could be anyone else to match them. Yet now look at her – she *had* found that here, after all.

She'd been so very, very fortunate. Secluded on their peaceful development, the people of Top o' th' Brow rubbed along in their own little world almost. Everyone quickly grew to know everybody else, she'd found, and a deep and meaningful group spirit was adopted. Children went to school and played in the streets together. Housewives popped into one another's kitchens for a pot of tea when they had completed their morning chores, and men conversed over their fences whilst tending to their gardens at weekends. The shops and tram stop were also perfect meeting places to chat and exchange local news; residents were even on first-name terms with the store owners and conductor.

In such a tight-knit setting, company and support were never in short supply. The co-op builds that offered such privileges were worth every copper farthing and breadwinners were happy to work overtime to cover the few extra shillings on the weekly rent. Nonetheless, she was determined not to lose contact with the Velvet Walks lot, would make the effort to visit them – and hopefully that would be soon, given that more clement weather had finally arrived.

With a nod, Janie now rose and made for the fire, where she dropped to her knees and raked out the dead ashes. Minutes later, flames were tickling the coals. The radiating warmth was quick to take the chill from the room, but as she went to fetch the bread for toasting for the children's breakfasts she shivered nonetheless with remembrance of the winter just gone that they had struggled to endure.

No one could remember weather like it. Everybody said so. What had started out as a mild autumn, followed by fogs and frosts, had given way to a ferocious season of freak blizzards.

The arrival of the snow at the outset of the Hudsons' house move failed to cease – it had fallen relentlessly for weeks. Its timing had been a sure gift from God. Life had rapidly ground to a halt as the first winter of war wreaked havoc across Britain and much of Europe.

Canals and harbours were paralysed, and London's River Thames was lost under a sheet of ice for the first time in over a century. There were reports that even the sea froze over in some parts of the country.

The north of England was hit especially badly and a blanket of white several feet in places had smothered their world. A simultaneous coal shortage hadn't helped matters. Those unable to lay in fuel stocks suffered more than most, as did the weak and infirm. Even industry was afflicted, and agriculture particularly. Farmers had found it a near-impossible task to work through the drifts and stranded livestock had starved to death in the fields. No one, it seemed, was spared the effects.

It had felt as though the sky was falling in on them

and that the sub-zero temperatures would never abate. Yet, in the midst of their own misery, no one could fail to empathise with the plight of the poor boys fighting abroad. As if the German army wasn't enough on its own for them to contend with!

As March approached, the fierce conditions had finally juddered to an end. The results were dreadful flooding – though, mercifully, they had been spared this added trouble owing to Breightmet's elevated position.

Janie had consoled herself that the weather was behind James's lack of correspondence and return. It had to be, surely? Travel would have been out of the question, after all. If so, what had that night sight meant? Was he really in some foreign land right now, at the mercy of enemy fire? Or had the vision been a hint of things to come? The uncertainty of it all made her chest ache. *Lord, just where was he? Why, why had he ever joined?*

Why? The word whispered at her on repeat as she reached for the long fork hanging on its hook by the hearth, and she swallowed down another sigh. Familiar melancholy was creeping in – restlessly, she turned and crossed to the window.

Dawn light was staining the sky. Peeping through the side of the blinds, Janie followed the silver-blue tracks of the new day with a sorrowful smile. She'd found herself doing this often since James went; for her, it brought a modicum of comfort to know they shared this expanse, that he too might be looking up at the same moment and thinking of her and home. *He'd be shot.* The memory hit her again and she sucked in a breath. *But he'd survive.*

'He will,' she told the empty street, desperate to reaffirm the fact. Then, in a trembling murmur: '*Bloody* war.'

When footsteps overhead pulled Janie from her ruminations she let the blackout material fall back into position. By the time the door opened and her son entered the room, she was crouched once more by the fire, an easy and much-practised smile firmly in place.

'Morning, Mam.'

'Sit down, lad. Toast is on t' go.'

Smothering a yawn with one hand and dragging the other through his tousled dark hair, Joey went to fetch himself a cup from the dresser. Taking a seat at the table, he reached for the teapot, asking, 'D'you want another sup pouring, Mam?'

'Aye, go on.'

'Ta,' he said as she put a slice of browned bread and the butter before him. 'Here, think on and go easy with that, only a thin scrape,' he added before his mother had chance to issue the warning, shooting the small golden block in the dish a rueful look. 'Don't you know there's a war on?'

Although she clicked her tongue at his mimicry, Janie couldn't suppress a smile.

Though widespread rationing had come into effect in the enemy's fatherland at the very start of hostilities, in Britain petrol had been the only commodity to be controlled. All that changed, however, just days after the Hudsons' relocation.

The introduction hadn't come as much of a shock to the adults. After all, those old enough remembered well the food shortages during the Great War. Naturally, these had affected the poor most, and many were going hungry by the time rationing came into force towards the end of the conflict. This time around, the government had been prepared. Suspecting for several years beforehand that another war in Europe was imminent, they had put plans in place for the equal distribution of food early on.

Now, six months in, butter, sugar and meat were all 'on t' ration', and the younger generation, in particular, were finding it difficult adjusting to the restrictions. Not that they had a choice in the matter. It was said that even the royal family had ration cards – no one was exempt.

Aye, folk would soon get used to it, Janie knew – and the sooner the better, for it was inevitable that other staples would shortly follow suit. Rumour had it that eggs would be next; thank God for kindly old Reuben Trent across the road at number six, that's all she could say. He'd kept hens in his back garden for years, would see that Padbury Way's residents didn't go without if shop supplies did grow short.

Lifting her refilled cup, a sudden thought occurred and she sent up a silent plea to the Almighty that tea wouldn't find its way on to the list – Lord, it didn't bear thinking about! A good strong brew was all that saw her through her trials some days!

'What's tickled you, Mam?' Joey asked, noticing her grinning.

'Nowt much, lad, only I've just come to realise I'm a bit of a hypocrite underneath, you know,' she admitted, chuckling. 'Here's me, forever harking on at youse all for grousing over shortages, when truth be told I reckon I'll hit the roof should tea finish up the same road.'

Joey joined in her laughter. 'Eeh, imagine it.'

'Perish the thought!'

'Aye,' he agreed, and his eyes creased impishly. 'Besides, what would you find to do all day without your endless pots of tea?'

'Cheeky young devil, you!' She cuffed him around the head playfully. 'I'll remember that remark well, my lad, when you next need your belly filling or your clothes washing or the million and one other things I see to in this house—'

'I were only joking with you, Mam,' he cut in, throwing her a wink, and reminding Janie just how much he resembled his father the older he got.

Her voice was soft. 'Aye, I know. Now, come on, you'd best be making tracks, else you'll be late.'

Nodding, her son swallowed the last of his toast and, as he crossed the room to collect his jacket and cap, Janie watched him go with a small smile. He was a good boy, her Joey. He'd never given her any trouble, not like other young lads with their mams, and had proved a comfort to her whilst James was away. By, but she was proud of him – proud of all her children. She and her husband had done a grand job with them, that they had.

'I'll see you later, then, Mam.'

'All right. Here, lad, don't forget your box,' she instructed in time before he ducked out of the kitchen.

'But, Mam, no one bothers with them any more.'

'Well, they should, for none of us knows what's round the corner, do we? D'you want a chestful of mustard gas, is that it? Aye, good at that, them Germans are. I remember well enough the last war and the state some of our boys lucky enough to make it home arrived in. Lungs eaten away from the poison, poor souls . . . Go on,' she added, sterner now, when he rolled his eyes. 'Anyroad, you know what Ralph Robertson's like should he spy you in t' street. Your grandfather an' all, for that matter; it'll be an ear-bashing you'll receive if you turn up at the farm without it.'

Sighing in defeat, Joey did as she bid, slinging the string of the small, oblong-shaped cardboard box containing his gas mask over his shoulder. 'Ta-ra.'

She walked with him whilst he collected his bicycle from the narrow, arched ginnel they shared with next door. Cut into the adjoining wall between their front doors, the entryway gave access to their coal sheds, into which the coalman deposited fuel directly on delivery day – a boon to housewives to not have to suffer him hauling his filthy sacks through the home proper.

'See you this evening, lad,' she told her son, waving him off from the front step as he pedalled down the path and through the gate then turned right towards Harwood.

Returning indoors, she sent up a quick thanks for her father-in-law. Who knew where her family would have been just lately without Albie, despite his faults? He was proving particularly helpful now with regards to rationing. That he provided his grandson with his dinner each day eased the burden on her stretched resources tremendously.

Nonetheless, Janie couldn't suppress the niggle of anger that was wont to creep up on her in these moments as she saw her son off to work. It should be James still that was cycling away to the fields each morning, not their Joey.

'What else could I have done?' she asked of the kitchen as she refilled the kettle to make a fresh pot of tea. 'James had made up his mind and, stubborn swine that he is, he'd never have budged.'

Their son had stepped into his shoes at the farm gladly. Strong and energetic and with a love of the outdoors like his father, he'd taken to it right away. Be it helping with the lambing or tending to the horse, delivering milk or toiling in the fields alongside his grandfather, he revelled in every aspect. He'd proven himself especially so during the recent bad weather, had worked like a Trojan around the clock, sometimes not arriving home until almost midnight, and always without a word of complaint.

His sense of accomplishment and gratification

56

when he handed over his wage to her each week was evident. That he'd had the role of man of the house thrust upon him he was acutely aware, and he took the new position extremely seriously. Janie couldn't be more proud of him if she tried.

She just hoped and prayed all this was over and done with before he reached age . . .

Unequivocal terror seized her at the prospect. Never. No *way* would the army get her lad. James was bad enough, but not her Joey. Not the both of them. *Oh God, when would this end and life return to normal?*

'Morning, Mam.'

Hauled from her fretful thoughts, Janie spun around to find her elder daughter standing in the doorway, rubbing a tired eye with her bunched fist. 'Morning, my lass.' She returned the greeting as brightly as she could muster, however there was no fooling Hilda.

'Mam, what's wrong, you're crying.'

'No, no.' Janie swiped at her cheeks with the corner of her pinny. 'Steam from the kettle is all it is,' she said, thinking on her toes. 'I leaned over the spout reaching for summat and . . . the steam caught me. It's made my eyes water, that's all. Daft ha'porth that I am.'

'Aye,' Hilda responded, clearly in full agreement that her mam was indeed daft – Janie couldn't help but chuckle.

'Bold article, you. 'Ere, has our Elsie roused yet?'

'Huh, that one.' Hilda's brows knotted in deep indignation. 'I'm *sick* of her, I am, the big bloody babby!'

'Hey you! Less of the language, missy. What's Elsie done?'

'What's she done? What d'you think! Look, Mam, look at that!' Twisting her body on the spot, Hilda revealed a wet patch on the side of her nightdress. Her features puckered in disgust. 'She's gone and peed the bed again, ain't she? Why do I have to share with her, Mam, why!'

'All right, all right. The poor mite can't help it, can she?' said Janie soothingly, struggling not to laugh – Hilda's anger had a habit of forcing her face into one resembling a wizened old woman's. 'Go on and get yourself washed and changed, there's a good lass.'

Shooting a black look to her sister, who had appeared in the doorway and stood wearing a look of contrition, her thumb planted firmly in her mouth, Hilda stomped upstairs to dress.

'Morning.' Janie held out a hand and the youngster hurried across to her. 'You wet again, Elsie lass?' she asked gently.

The girl answered in a whisper. 'Aye, Mam. I did try the toilet before I went to bed last night, honest I did!'

'I know, don't fret now.'

'Sorry.'

'It's all right.'

A smile lifted Elsie's face momentarily before her mouth drooped at the corners once more. 'Hilda's hopping mad.'

'Aye well, when is she not?' Janie said lightly, winking. 'That lass could put the willies up Hitler hisself when she starts, I'm sure.'

58

Elsie giggled. Then suddenly her face contorted and she winced. 'Aw, Mam!'

'What, lass? What's to do?'

'My arm's sore.'

'Our Hilda's not thumped you one, has she? She better not have—'

'No, Mam. It's just sore.'

Frowning, Janie inspected the little limb, but could see no obvious reason for her pain. 'Never mind, lass, you've likely just slept on it funny, that's all. Come on, eh. Let's get you out of them wet things and then you can have some breakfast.' She shepherded her towards the open fire. 'You wait there whilst I fetch your clothes.'

Along with her daughter's blue cotton frock, Janie returned with a warm flannel rubbed with carbolic soap, which, after stripping the girl of her soiled nightdress and underwear, she used to wash her with all over. She then reached for a dry pair of drawers from the clothes rack suspended above the fire and, after helping her to dress, led her towards the table.

Having returned to the room, Hilda joined her sister, selecting the chair furthest away from her, her mood clearly not improved; busy now filling the teapot, Janie rolled her eyes.

'Here,' she instructed, 'pour you and Elsie a cup of tea whilst I make youse some toast.'

'That one can pour her own.'

'For pity's sake, lass. Give over, will you?' Janie's patience was wearing thin and, to her chagrin, she

59

felt tears prick once more. 'Don't you think I've enough to deal with without you griping on—?'

'That's the door,' Hilda cut in mildly as a knock sounded.

Janie's anger rose further at her daughter's obstinacy. 'Go and see who's calling, then, eh.'

'You know who it'll be: Lynn, same as it is every morning.'

'Well, let her in then. Go on!'

Sighing theatrically, the girl scraped back her chair and dragged herself to the front door.

'Ooh, what's up with you, then? You've a phizog on yer that could sour milk,' Janie heard her neighbour exclaim to Hilda – and her daughter's retort: 'Leaky arse Elsie as usual, what d'you think!'

Janie's mouth dropped open in mortification. 'Oi! What have I told you about that gutter tongue of yours? Right, you, you young devil, in here now and get this breakfast down you, then get on out of it to school! Sorry about her, love,' she added to Lynn, who had followed Hilda into the room and was struggling to keep a straight face. 'She'll be the death of me, I swear it.'

A baby perched as usual on each hip, the woman shook her head, eyes dancing with suppressed amusement. 'And I thought these two were a handful now.'

'Oh, you've got it all to come!' Janie told her, adding, 'Have you time forra quick sup afore you leave for work?'

'Aye, go on.'

'You'll not be late?'

Lynn shrugged. 'Owd Seymour Briggs can like it or lump it.'

Chuckling, Janie went to fetch her a cup, saying over her shoulder, 'Come on, now, girls, else youse'll be the ones who are late. Get your cardigans on. You, Elsie, bring me the hairbrush from the sideboard drawer, there's a good girl.'

Within minutes, she'd unravelled the youngster's untidy dark plaits and redone them neatly, tying the ends with lengths of faded red imitation silk. She repeated the action on Hilda, who, despite her mother's best efforts at gentleness, huffed and yelled and stomped her feet as the knots were teased from her locks.

'Hang about,' Janie told her, securing her plaits in place with similar ribbon in pale yellow as she made to dash for the door. 'Right, go on, you're done. And 'ere, don't forget your gas masks.'

In contrast with Joey's reaction shortly before, Hilda's scowl vanished instantly at the instruction and was replaced with a dazzling smile that lit up her face. 'Oh aye!' she exclaimed in delighted remembrance, hurrying to fetch hers from where it hung from a peg in the tiny hall. 'Lynn, look! In t' it bonny? My friends'll be green with envy when they see this.'

'Oh aye, that's nice.' She surveyed the box, the drab cardboard exterior of which had been covered with pretty fabric. 'Yours has had a makeover as well, has it, Elsie love? Eeh, ain't you lucky lasses, eh?'

61

'It's from an old frock,' Hilda informed her, stroking the white material patterned with pink flowers. 'Mam did it.'

'That's 'cause you've gorra good 'un who goes out of her way to make you all happy.' Lynn's tone was soft. 'In't that right?'

'Aye,' Elsie readily agreed, rushing across the room to plant a kiss on Janie's cheek.

Watching on, Hilda lowered her eyes with a nod. Then she too was running to her mother. She stroked Janie's hand and smiled. 'Ta again. And, Mam? Sorry for being a bi—witch,' she amended in time, a grin spreading across her face.

Overcome at this rare show of affection from her elder daughter, Janie could only nod.

Spotting their mother struggling to hold back her emotion, Lynn was swift to step in. 'Off to school, now,' she told the children, guiding them out. 'See youse later.'

The moment the front door closed behind them, Janie's resolve crumbled; gasping on a sob, she dropped her head in her hands.

'Hey now.' Lynn deposited her sons on to the rug and hurried to put an arm around her friend's heaving shoulders. 'Love, whatever's the matter?'

'Oh, Lynn. It's nowt really, I'm just . . . being daft . . .'

Lowering her plump body, Lynn crouched by Janie's feet. 'I'll be the judge of that. Come on, girl, out with it.'

'It's James.'

'He's not . . . Oh, Mother of God, you've not had a telegram—?'

'No, love, no. He . . . I saw him get shot.'

'Shot?'

'I saw it, and there were nowt I could do and I . . . I didn't want to worry the kiddies, but it's been playing on my mind all morning. I just . . . I just . . .'

'Eeh, Janie.'

'He'll live, mind. That, I know, is a blessing. I just can't stop thinking about him, Lynn. God, I miss him so friggin' *much.*'

That she could discuss this openly went some way towards easing her pain – she'd be lost without this woman, Janie knew. She'd been terrorised at school because of her 'gift', had made the mistake of telling one or two other children, hadn't realised that not everyone saw things in their dreams, as she did. Consequently, as had her mother before her, she'd suffered every cruel name under the sun right throughout her childhood, learned very quickly to keep that part of her to herself. Only her husband knew – and, just recently, Lynn.

The women had formed a close bond over the passing months and each viewed the other rather more as a sister now than a mere friend. Like James, Lynn hadn't made her feel queer for having this thing she couldn't shake or control, and she loved her all the more for it. She'd have trusted the pair of them with her life.

'I understand how you feel there well enough,' her

neighbour murmured now, her normally twinkling gaze clouded with the pain of longing. 'I'd do owt to feel my Duncan's arms around me, Janie. Owt.'

She was instantly sorry. Here was she, prattling on about missing her man . . . As if she was the only woman in the land enduring such loss. 'Eeh, 'course you would, love. Take no notice of me; I'm having a moany morning is all.'

'You're sure you're all right? I can always find someone else if you're not up to minding these two terrors today—'

'No, no need for all that. Honest, love,' she insisted, horrified at the prospect – she needed all the distraction right now that she could get.

'Right, then, well . . . I'd best be off.' Lynn pulled an apologetic face. 'Sorry, Janie, only you know what Seymour's like . . .'

'I know. Don't fret! You go.'

'You're *sure* you'll be all right?'

'Aye.'

'We'll talk later, eh?' Lynn promised, and at her friend's nod slipped reluctantly from the house.

Alone with her doomy thoughts once more, Janie was quick to turn her attention to the two small boys in her care. She'd been looking after Bobby and Brian whilst their mother went to work at the local grocer's for a number of weeks now. Their previous minder, Renee Rushmore, a girl from nearby Monks Lane, had suddenly upped sticks without notice to join the Women's Land Army, leaving Lynn without childcare, and Janie had happily stepped in to help

64

her friend out. She was only rattling around the house all day once her own kiddies had gone to work and school, after all – and besides, the few extra shillings a week that Lynn paid her came in handy.

'Come on then, little loves,' she told them, lifting them from the rug. 'Let's find you some of our Joey's old toys, shall we, whilst I get my jobs done?'

An hour later, Janie had stripped her daughters' wet bedsheets and put them in to soak, scoured with Lanry bleach then donkey-stoned the front step, cleaned the kitchen and swept the floor and dusted the front-room furniture. With nothing more pressing to do just yet and the boys growing restless, she went to fetch her coat and basket.

Their daily drop-in on Sadie Hodgkiss several doors down had become a pleasant routine which they all enjoyed. Janie had first caught the woman's attention a few days into her new role as the twins' minder. Sadie had been watching the world go by from her gate one morning as the trio passed on their way to the shops and had struck up conversation – Janie was thankful she had. She'd learned that Sadie was in her middle sixties and widowed, had never been blessed with children of her own and had little in the way of even distant family; in short, she was desperately lonely. Her eyes had lit up at the sight of the boys, and when she'd invited them all in for tea and biscuits Janie had been happy to oblige her.

The twins lapped up the attention that Sadie showered upon them and, as well as being grateful for some adult conversation during the long day, Janie was pleased she was able to make a poor soul's otherwise empty world a little more meaningful. Sadie lived for their visits, she knew. Her life was richer for their acquaintance – Janie would never take that away from her now.

After double-checking she had her ration books and purse, Janie carried the boys outside to the shared ginnel, where was stored their pram, and bundled them inside. Cooing and smiling at the children, she manoeuvred the cumbersome item down the narrow path and out into the street.

'Janie love!' Sadie welcomed them with an empty-gummed grin.

'Morning, Mrs Hodgkiss.'

'Eeh, come on in.'

Parking the pram outside beneath the woman's front window, Janie carried the boys into the warm and homely kitchen. A pot of tea and plate of custard creams stood waiting in the centre of the table atop the snowy lace tablecloth – she smiled in their direction. 'Just what the doctor ordered!'

'Well, sit thee down and take the weight off, lass. 'Ere, pass them little cherubs across to me for a cuddle.'

Janie watched on with a laugh as the twins wrapped their podgy arms around Sadie's neck and hugged her back. 'They really enjoy coming to see you, Mrs Hodgkiss,' she told her as she poured out tea.

'And I enjoy seeing the three of youse, an' all. Now then.' Sitting a child on each knee, she pulled the biscuit plate across. 'Tuck in, my little loves!'

The children readily obeyed. By the time Janie rose to resume her journey to the shops, their hands and faces had been wiped clean and they were seated on large cushions on the floor playing with Sadie's cat. Smiling, she went to stand over them, hands on hips. 'Right, laddies, time to go.'

At the prospect of being separated from their furry friend, the boys' bottom lips wobbled and they shook their heads.

'You could allus leave them here whilst you make your purchases, lass,' Sadie was quick to offer.

Janie was reluctant. They were a boisterous pair at the best of times, could be a handful for someone half Sadie's age – could the woman cope? 'Oh, I don't know . . .'

'They're in capable hands, lass, I promise thee.'

'You're sure you'll manage?' It would make her trip easier all round, she had to admit. Bobby and Brian grew fractious whenever they spotted their mother at work in the grocer's, and tears were inevitable when the shopping was done and it was time for Janie to take them back home. 'They do get clingy with Lynn, grow upset when they realise they can't stay with her . . .'

'There you have it, then. They'll stop here with me – problem solved.'

Nodding, she thanked her and lifted the basket. 'I shan't be long, Mrs Hodgkiss. You two be good, now, d'you hear?' she added to the boys.

'We'll be fine, lass; go on!' Sadie shooed her out with a chuckle. 'And don't hurry back.'

The walk to the small row of stores took half a minute and by the time she pushed open the grocer's door Janie's thoughts had switched from her charges to the ever-present worry of food. Certain items were becoming increasingly unobtainable of late – a daily trial for housewives with the family's evening meal in mind.

Lynn was serving a customer – catching her eye, Janie waved. 'The kiddies are with Mrs Hodgkiss, love,' she explained. 'I hope that's all right, only she insisted . . . ?'

'Aye, course it is.'

Janie headed for the shelves of tinned goods and, after bidding the customer goodbye, Lynn came around the counter and joined her.

'How you feeling? Sorry I had to love and leave you earlier.'

'Now don't be daft. I understand, I told you that. I'm all right, ta. Keeping busy the best I can is all I can do; it takes my mind off it.'

'By, I've been busy myself, but not through choice. I'm fagged.'

'Is Mr Briggs not around to help you?'

With a snort, Lynn shook her head. 'No, he hot-footed it out of here the minute I arrived. He's likely trying to punish me for being five minutes late this morning, owd swine that he is.'

Janie hid a smile. Lynn and her boss had what could only be described as a challenging working relationship. Her friend's temperament, teasing by nature with a quick tongue to boot, coupled with Seymour's over-serious demeanour and pedanticism for the rules, saw them locking horns on an almost daily basis. However, both knew which side their bread was buttered, ensuring things never got too out of hand. Lynn needed this job and the money that came with it, and Seymour was well aware he'd be hard-pressed to find another such hard-working assistant to replace her. In fact, for all their grumbles, Janie suspected they were fond of one another and found their harmless squabbles entertaining deep down.

'Oh, here we go, speak of the devil . . .' muttered Lynn out of the side of her mouth and rolled her eyes as the door opened and in walked her employer. Then, raising her voice, she addressed him, saying in mock surprise, 'Seymour Briggs, is it really you? By, it is! I hardly recognised you, it's been that long since last we met . . .'

'Now don't you start, missy,' he was quick to shoot back. 'I've had just about enough of your cheek for one day— Oh.' Spotting Janie, his reprimand died. He removed his dark bowler and smoothed down his thinning hair, a smile surfacing. 'Good morning, Mrs Hudson.'

'Morning, Mr Briggs,' she responded, doing her best to ignore Lynn's discreet elbow jab to her ribs. 'You're well, I hope?'

'Fair to middling, lass, fair to middling. And yourself?'

'Oh, you know. Can't complain.'

'Good, good.'

There followed an awkward silence, then several fresh customers entered at once and Seymour took himself off to see to their needs. Left alone with Lynn, Janie held up a warning finger before her grinning friend had the chance to crow. 'Just don't you say it!'

'Say what?'

'Oh, you know, missis. The same thing you're always for saying lately.'

Swallowing back a guffaw, Lynn shook her head. 'I'm right, though, ain't I? He's after you, he is. Fancies you summat rotten, aye – dirty sod.'

Janie bit her lip. Though she didn't like to admit it, it would appear that her friend's opinion might hold some truth in it. Since she had moved to this estate, Seymour Briggs seemed to have taken an instant shine to her. Janie hadn't heard him speak as kindly to any other customer as he did with her, nor show anywhere near as much attentiveness to her wants in the shop or her daily life in general. And yet . . . Surely not, her mind insisted once more. He was well aware that she was married, after all. Not that that would have been the only obstacle in his path – he was old enough to be her father, for goodness' sake.

'You can't blame the randy owd swine, mind,' Lynn was saying now. 'After all, you're the bonniest woman around these parts for miles, and that's the truth.'

'For God's sake, will you give it a rest,' Janie hissed,

glancing around for eavesdroppers, her colour mounting. The very last thing she wanted was for rumours to start – and travel at speed they would here, in such a tight-knit community. She'd die from the shame, she would. 'Mr Briggs doesn't fancy me and that's an end to it. And well, even if he did, it's of no consequence. Anyroad,' she added, remembering her friend's last remark, 'what d'you mean with all that daft talk – bonniest woman around indeed! You're pulling my leg.'

'You really don't see it, do you, love?' Lynn indicated Janie's shapely calves, trim waist and full bust. 'You're a bloody stunner, girl. And that hair . . . all natural, too, I might add. That blonde ain't from a bottle, is it?'

'Certainly not,' Janie confirmed.

'Well, there you are then.'

'Can we just drop it now?' Janie asked. 'Please?'

Chuckling, Lynn nodded, and the women turned their attention back to the shelves.

'Corned-beef hash this evening, I reckon,' Janie said, moving to the pyramid of tins to her right and plucking one from the stack. 'Simple but filling, aye.' *And James's favourite.* The thought came to her from nowhere, making her pause.

It happened often, that did. Her husband was never far from her mind and, sometimes, she was wont to forget. Something she'd seen or heard or read about in the paper which she knew he'd find interesting or funny would have her opening her mouth to call his name. Then reality would slam in,

71

the crushing pain of remembrance with it, and it was like losing him all over again. *Lord, where was he?*

'You all right?'

Pulled from her ruminations, Janie swiped at eyes she hadn't realised had grown wet and nodded to her friend. 'Aye, ignore me. I were just . . .' The words died in her throat.

'Love?'

Janie heard her friend speaking but not for anything could she have responded. Tongue frozen, her feet rooted to the spot, she watched in a daze the soldier in full khaki garb who had just entered the shop make towards the counter. Snatches of his speech as he addressed Mr Briggs rapped at her ears: *Janie Hudson, aye, that's right . . . tried at home, but she's not in . . . wondered if you knew her and where I might find her . . .'*

'James?' The name fell from her lips on a feathered whisper.

He turned as though on instinct.

'Oh, James!'

'Lass!'

Catching her in his arms as she dropped the tin of corned beef and ran across the floor, James buried his face in her neck. 'God, Janie, I've missed you.'

'Eeh, lad.' Laughing through her tears, she covered his face in kisses whilst the customers present looked on with happy sighs and smiles. 'Where have you *been*? I've been going out of my mind, was imagining all sorts, I . . . Oh, I can't believe it!'

James covered her mouth with his and she returned

72

the kiss hungrily. It was Lynn's cough that brought Janie back down to earth with a bump. Glancing around the shop, she blushed scarlet then giggled. 'Oh dear, you'll have to excuse me. For a moment there . . .'

'You forgot where you were?' asked Lynn, eyes twinkling.

'For a moment I did. Eeh, but I'm that happy . . . !' She turned to her husband. 'This is Lynn Ball, lad, our neighbour. Lynn, this is my husband,' she finished, bursting with love and joy and pride.

'Well, I didn't suspect it was the coalman, lass!' Grinning, Lynn shook James's hand warmly. 'Nice to meet you, I'm sure.'

'Nice to meet you, Lynn.'

'Well . . . we'll be off then . . .' Janie could feel her flush resurfacing at the amused, knowing looks being shot in her and her husband's direction – none more so than from the incorrigible Lynn. 'James has yet to see the new house, you see, and . . . and I'm sure he'd welcome a cup of tea, so . . .'

'Go on, off with the pair of youse.' Lynn shepherded them towards the door. Before seeing them out into the morning sunshine, she leaned in close. Tongue in cheek, shoulders shaking with suppressed laughter, she winked. 'Enjoy that brew, now, won't you?'

'She's a card, that one,' Janie chuckled as, pulling James along, she hurried him across the road and on towards Padbury Way. 'They all guessed what we're rushing home for, you know!'

'And what of it? We're a respectable married

couple, after all.' His arm travelled south to snake around her waist. 'I'm famished for you, Mrs Hudson, and if I choose to ravish your beautiful body in the middle of the day, I'm ruddy well entitled to do so – and will. Now, have you any objection to that?'

Pulling him to a stop, she gazed up into his dancing eyes with such an overwhelming feeling of adoration it stole the breath from her. 'No objection whatsoever, lad,' she whispered.

Grinning, they clasped hands and set off on a run the rest of the way home.

Chapter 4

'I TELL YOU, it were as though I'd conjured you up. There I was one minute, just thinking to myself how much you liked corned beef, and in the next you were there. Strange ain't in it.'

Their lusts spent, Janie and James were lying naked on the living-room floor. The second they had entered the house, their hungry hands had taken on a life of their own; unable to make it upstairs, they had removed each other's clothing feverishly, right there in front of the fire. Now, limbs entwined, cheek against cheek, they stared, drowsy with contentment, at the ceiling.

'Corned beef?' James asked in bemusement after some moments, and Janie laughed.

'Aye. Oh, it don't matter.' Nothing did. Not now he was home.

By, but he looked good. The intensive training had knocked years off him, it seemed – he was more like the youth she'd met all those years ago than the husband she'd waved off just a few months past. His face and eyes shone with vitality and his upper body had

75

definitely broadened; he seemed altogether fitter, stronger, and it suited him. Truth be told, she knew that for as long as she had him here she'd have a struggle on her hands to keep her eager mitts off him.

Sitting up, she wiggled towards the sofa on her bottom and leaned her back against it, pulling her crumpled coat, which was lying in a heap, around herself. James lit them both a cigarette then moved to join her, and they snuggled up beneath its woollen folds.

'When do you go back?'

Clearly reading the pain in her question – the question she'd been loath to put to him since he arrived but was acutely aware had to be voiced sometime – James drew her closer against his warm chest. 'Let's not think about that just now—'

'Tell me,' she cut in thickly. 'How long?'

'A fortnight.'

Janie closed her eyes then nodded bravely. What alternative was there? It was what it was. Not for anything would she mar this precious time. 'And will they ship you abroad?'

'We reckon so, aye.' He spoke quietly, reluctant to meet her stare. 'Rumour has it our battalion will be sent to join the other Loyals with the British Expeditionary Force, aiding our lads defending the Belgian–French border.'

'I think that's where Lynn said her husband Duncan is.'

'We'll know for definite soon enough.'

Again, she bobbed her head. However, she wouldn't

allow her mind to dwell on the gut-churning night sight she'd had – evidently an occurrence to come once he left these shores – and what it would mean for him, for them all. 'Then we'd best make sure we make the most of every millisecond, hadn't we?'

'I love you, lass, so very much.'

'And I love you, lad. More than you could ever know.'

Releasing a simultaneous sigh, they smoked their cigarettes without another word.

A little later, fully dressed once more and seated at the table with a cup of tea, they discussed all that had transpired during their separation. James told of the new friendships he'd made with other men of his unit, and Janie told him of the move to Top o' th' Brow and filled him in on its people.

'It's a cracking little place, lad. As for this house . . .' She smiled. 'It's like nowt I'd imagined. I love it – we all do.'

'The girls have settled in at their new school?'

'Oh aye, they have. They've made loads of friends. 'Ere, that's a thought,' she added, sitting forward in eagerness at the sudden idea, 'why don't we walk up there at home time? Surprise them, like. Eeh, their little faces when they see you will be a picture!'

James smiled agreement. 'Aye, all right.'

'I know our Joey will be just as delighted, an' all, when he gets home.'

'How's the lad coping on t' farm?'

'Oh, gradely. Took to it like a duck to water, he has.'

'And my dad? He's well?'

She nodded. 'Albie's been a sound help to us whilst you've been gone, lad. Aye, he has.'

Taking a sip of his tea, James raised his eyebrows in surprised relief at the clear warmth with which she'd spoken of the senior Mr Hudson. 'You're not angry with him no more, then, for me joining up?'

'Well, I wouldn't go that far,' she told him with a crooked smile. 'But . . . Let's just say I've seen another side to him lately, and I suppose . . . well, I suppose he's not all bad.'

James grinned, Janie followed suit, and they lapsed into companionable silence.

It was whilst clearing away the tea things some time afterwards that she remembered. Spotting the colourful spinning top by the sideboard, which she must have missed earlier when tidying the toys away, she slapped a hand to her mouth in horror. 'Oh, my friggin' God. The twins!'

'Eh? What twins?'

Janie supplied a quick explanation as she shrugged on her coat. 'So you see I must hurry,' she finished, heading to the door. 'Poor Mrs Hodgkiss. She'll be run ragged! And oh, there's still the evening meal to buy yet . . . 'Ere, why don't you take yourself off to Harwood, go and surprise your father and Joey at the farm.'

James nodded. 'You wouldn't mind?'

'No, no. I've things to be getting on with anyroad. Besides, they'll be over t' moon to see you.'

'Wait about,' he said, rising from the table as she made to enter the hall. He closed the space between them in a few strides and wrapped his arms around her, lifting her off her feet. 'You're sure you can spare me for an hour, 'cause I don't think I can be parted from you for that long.' He nuzzled her neck, making her giggle. 'Eeh, lass, it's glad I am to be back.'

'Aye, and me.' She pressed her lips to his in a tender kiss. 'Now go on, get going, before I change my tune. No longer than an hour, mind, or I'll have your guts for garters. It's selfish of me, I know, but I want you to myself today. Deal?'

'Deal,' he vowed.

A last, lingering kiss, and they parted ways.

Janie almost floated the short distance to Sadie's house; so consumed with happiness was she that it felt like she was walking on air. Nor could she keep the soppy smile from her face when delivering her apologies – Sadie noticed the change in her instantly.

'You favour you've lost a pebble and found a diamond, lass. Has summat occurred?'

'It has. My husband's home, glory be to God.'

'Ay, that's music to my ears, that is,' the kindly older woman trilled. 'Right, well, the babbies can stop here with me the day until their mam finishes her shift – and no arguments!' she insisted when Janie made to protest. 'You must make the most of every moment he's here, every moment.'

'Eeh, thank you, Mrs Hodgkiss.'

'Ta-ra, love.'

'Ta-ra – and thanks again!'

Her next port of call was the shops – before entering, Janie paused outside the grocer's to steel herself for the holy ribbing she just knew Lynn would be ready to deliver. Hiding her smile and shaking her head, she pushed open the door.

'All right?'

'Aye,' Janie answered her friend as casually as she could muster – then cursed the blush that instantly sprang to her cheeks. She wagged a finger. 'None of your smut, girl; I'm here to shop and nowt more.'

Lynn wiggled her eyebrows with a grin and, despite her warning, Janie couldn't hold a straight face any longer – the two of them burst out laughing.

'You're terrible, that's what you are,' Janie told her, making for the second time that day towards the shelves of tinned goods. She selected corned beef once more – sighing happily to herself this time around when again it conjured up thoughts of James – and headed for the counter. 'I've some carrots and potatoes at home, so just two large onions as well, please, Mr Briggs, if you have them,' she told him, going inside her coat pocket for her purse. 'Oh, and a quarter of tea.'

The grocer duly fulfilled her requests. 'There you are, Mrs Hudson. And here, take these.' He reached into a glass cabinet displaying cigars and cigarettes and pulled out a packet of Woodbines, which he nestled amongst her other purchases inside her basket. 'For your husband – on me.'

Janie was extremely touched. 'Oh, ta very much. That's very kind of you, Mr Briggs.'

He bobbed his greying head towards her in a nod.

'Don't mention it. I'm very pleased for your sake that he's home.'

'Thank you. Well, ta-ra for now. Ta-ra, Lynn!' she added over her shoulder, beating a hasty retreat before Lynn could waylay her. She was well aware that her friend had just witnessed her exchange with the grocer, and also knew that Lynn would certainly have something fresh to say on the matter. 'Can't stop, love, sorry. Must dash!'

Janie would have loved to have been a fly on the wall in there right now to see Lynn's face! Chuckling to herself, she hurried on for home.

True to his word, her husband was back within the hour – and with Joey in tow. In light of James's return, Albie had given his grandson the rest of the day off, much to the lad's delight.

Peeling and chopping the vegetables in preparation for tea, listening to father and son in the living room chattering nineteen to the dozen about the farm, Janie could have burst with heady fulfilment. It was almost like normal, as though nothing had changed and war wasn't hanging over them and their future like a dirty great cloud. *Almost.* Nevertheless, as Sadie Hodgkiss had advised, she intended making the most of every single moment. By God she did.

When later the two of them walked the short distance to the school to meet their daughters, Janie observed the appreciative looks directed at the uniformed James from the other mothers with quiet satisfaction. Oh, but he did look handsome, she told herself for the dozenth time that day, linking his arm that little more tightly. Obviously, it went without saying that she'd rather have never had to have seen him in khaki. But here they were all the same. It had happened, and there was no going back. What's more, and much to her surprise, she knew now, buried amongst the rest of her feelings, a deep sense of pride.

Boys and girls began pouring through the school doors, and Janie and James peered out over the sea of heads for a glimpse of those of their children. Then there they were. Hilda, striding across the playground in front, whilst Elsie's little legs scurried to keep up with her, spotted her parents first. Slowing, she frowned and squinted ahead. Then her brow cleared, her eyes grew wide and she was running full pelt to greet them.

'Eeh, lass.' James caught her in a bear-like embrace then stooped and extended an arm to include Elsie. 'Me and your mam thought we'd surprise youse both. My big, bonny lasses. Ay, they've grown, you know,' he said thickly to his wife over his shoulder, 'they have, all three of 'em.'

'I missed you every day. Are you back for ever, now, Dad?' Elsie asked, her innocent gaze bright with expectancy.

''Course not, dafty.' Hilda rolled her eyes. 'He needs to beat Hitler and all the other Germans first. He's been away practising how to do it, that's all, and will be off to the real action soon. Ain't that right, Dad?'

Face creasing, James could only nod.

'Will you bash every one of them, Dad? All on your own?' Elsie was suitably impressed.

'Not bash, ki—'

'That's enough, Hilda,' Janie cut in quietly. The child didn't need to hear about such things as destruction and death. This kind of talk wasn't doing her husband – or herself, for that matter – any good either. 'Oh, how's your arm, lass?' she asked, switching her attention to Elsie as the complaint from this morning came back to her. 'All right, is it?'

The girl wiggled the small limb this way and that, then smiled. 'Aye, Mam. It is now Dad's here.'

'Good. Come on, then, let's get home. I've a pan on t' stove, and our Joey will let the food burn dry before he ever thinks to turn the heat down.'

That evening, with their meal eaten, the curtains drawn against the gathering dark and the room cosy and warm, Janie glanced around through the flickering gaslight as she cleared the table and smiled. Sprawled on the sofa, Joey had his nose buried in a comic. Across the room, James had his eyes closed in his fireside chair whilst at his feet his daughters sat cross-legged, heads cocked towards the wireless set, engrossed in *The Children's Hour* story and song show with Uncle Mac on the BBC Home Service channel.

A typical family scene. Ordinary, comfortable. Just as it used to be – and now, after so many weeks, was again. *For one precious fortnight, at least,* her mind was quick to remind her, much to her disgust. Telling it

83

to shut up, she turned her attention back to her chore.

When the time reached six o'clock, it brought with it through the fabric-covered speaker the blare of the news broadcast. As the room filled with the male reporter's familiar refined, austere tones, James was suddenly on his feet. Striding across to the polished wooden box, he turned the knob, extinguishing the service.

Having assumed he was snoozing, Janie shot him a surprised frown. 'You all right, love?'

'Aye, I just . . .'

He broke off, and she nodded in understanding. She too had had enough talk, enough reminders of war for one day.

'Why don't we nip forra drink? I'm sure our Joey won't mind keeping an eye to the lasses.'

'Aye?' Janie's face spread in a smile. Then, realising he probably wasn't aware, him only just becoming acquainted with the place: 'It's a different kettle of fish, here, mind. We'd have to catch some transport into town.'

For many who had relocated, daily travel to places of work in the centre of Bolton was now done by tram, which separated the two worlds – and this was also the case for those with a penchant for alcohol.

Housewives with husbands fond of a tipple found that the moves had thrown up an unexpected advantage: there were no pubs on the new estates. The trek to regular watering holes was now undertaken once a week rather than every day; the added expense of transportation there and back ensured this. Thus, women unfortunate enough to have shackled themselves to men who turned wranglesome when in their cups not only saw an increase in the family purse but a decrease in black eyes.

Mrs Fiennes at number one was a prime example. It was no secret she'd suffered for years her husband's free fists when in drink, but since coming to Top o' th' Brow, her Terry was a new man. For her and others of her ilk, it had made a marked difference in every aspect. A happy husband and wife made for happy children, and you couldn't put a price on that.

'We might as well make a proper night of it, then? How's about I treat you to the pictures afterwards?'

'Eeh. I'd like that, love, aye.'

'Fingers crossed we'll manage to get some seats on the back row, eh?'

'James!' Janie scolded, her cheeks pinkening as the children grinned at his quip. 'What are you like!'

With a wink and a smile, he took himself off to fetch their coats.

Owing to the threat of air attacks, the Home Office had deemed it wise to order the closure of all places of public entertainment – cinemas included – at the outbreak of war. However, within weeks, the decision was revoked and venues had reopened, much to the populace's relief. They were integral in boosting British morale – more so these days than ever before. Who wouldn't want to escape reality, to lose themselves in another world of make-believe and forget their troubles for a few short hours?

Bolton certainly seemed to think it essential. With an impressive twenty-two cinemas, its residents were spoilt for choice. Thousands flocked to the 'flea pits' and the grander 'palaces' every week, drawn to the glamorous stars who inhabited the dazzling world of film on the silver screen like moths to a flame.

Janie and James favoured the Queen's. After a glass of sherry and pint of mild in the Balmoral Hotel, they cut through town, busy with dance halls, cafés and pubs, towards the junction of Bradshawgate and Trinity Street, where the cinema was situated. Mindful of the risks the blackout posed, they kept a sensible step. Not only was this strict regulation a hindrance, but it proved a danger, too. Falls and trips were commonplace – even death resulting from such accidents occurred. Holding tight to her husband's hand, Janie allowed him to lead the way.

When they emerged from the picture house two hours later – relaxed and fuzzy inside with the sheer completion of being together – it was drizzling with rain. Not that they were going to allow that to dampen their spirits. Laughing, they headed out into the star-pricked dark, hastening inside a fish-and-chip shop at the first opportunity. Feeling sixteen again, they ate their supper straight from the salt-and-vinegar-soaked paper, under the shelter of a nearby doorway. Finally, tired but happy with their evening, they set off once more to catch the last bus back.

'All right, love?' Having heard their return, Lynn popped her head outside her front door as they were putting the key in the lock of their own. 'Good night, was it?'

Telling her husband to go on in and warm himself by the fire, that she'd follow in a minute, Janie bestowed a dreamy smile on her friend. 'Oh, champion, Lynn. Just champion.'

'Eeh, I'm that pleased for you that he's home.'

The remark had been completely sincere and without a hint of envy or bitterness – Janie was instantly ashamed. 'Lynn ... Oh, love, I am sorry,' she murmured. 'I wish to Christ your Duncan were home, an' all.'

'I know, don't feel guilty, girl. My turn will come soon, God willing.'

'And one day, which I can only pray is soon, it'll be for good. Life can get back to what it ought to be, for us all.'

Tears had formed on her friend's lashes. 'You really think so, love?'

'I do. I do, Lynn. They'll come back, you know,' she added with feeling, reaching for her hand and squeezing. 'They will, the pair. I know it.'

'You mean ... your visions? You've seen *that*, too?'

Oh, dear God. Why had she said that? Now Lynn thought ... But Janie hadn't received proof of this, had she? There had been no night sight as to whether their husbands would indeed get through the war in its entirety unscathed – and absolutely nothing at all with regards to Duncan Ball. And yet ...

In that moment, loath to wipe the desperate joy

from her friend's face, Janie did something she knew she shouldn't: she lied.

'Aye.'

The whispered word fell from between her lips before she could stop it.

She just hoped beyond hope that she wouldn't live to regret it.

Chapter 5

AS IS OFTEN the case, swiftly flies time most precious –
before they knew it, the days were gone.

Slouched on the bench of the tram bumping them
ever nearer to the station, Janie felt sick to her stomach. Beside her, caught in broody silence, James
stared unseeing through the window.

An April chill breathed down their necks, binding
them closer still as they stood locked in each other's
arms on the platform. The stretch of ugly concrete
teemed with others whose faces mirrored their own:
uniformed men with mothers or sisters, sweethearts
or wives – all preparing for loss. A flurry of activity up
ahead, then the distant puff of an approaching train
snared the air. Women started to weep.

'James . . .' There was little point in begging him
to be careful – wouldn't he be shot after all, regard-
less? – but she did it anyway. 'Oh, lad, please. Come
back to me.'

'I promise, Janie,' he swore fiercely into her hair.

The men were pouring into the carriages – James
followed. He managed to secure a space at the

window, opened it and reached through to grasp his wife's outstretched hand. Eyes closed tight, he pressed his lips to it for an eternity.

A whistle shrilled. The train shifted and picked up speed. Then he was gone.

Some chased after the steam-belching metal monster taking their loved ones off; others stood waving handkerchiefs, calling goodbye. Janie did neither. Tears cascading down her face, she stood as though in a trance. Her blurred gaze remained glued to the train until it was but a smudge in the distance, then she turned and walked away.

Her feet took her in the familiar direction of old; her mind had no say in it. Minutes later, she found she was standing at the entrance to Velvet Walks.

Mrs Reilly answered her knock with a gasp of delight. But one look at her former neighbour's face and her words of welcome swiftly fizzled out. She hooked her arm around Janie's shoulders and led her inside her house.

'Sit thee down, lass, I'll brew a sup of tea.'

'He's gone, Mrs Reilly.'

The woman bobbed her shawl-covered head. 'I figured as much. How you feeling?'

'Heartsore. Numb. Sick.'

'Aye.'

They sat by the paltry fire and waited for the ancient black kettle to come to the boil. Looking around at the walls, their rotten brick exposed in large patches where the plaster had fallen away from the damp, Janie gave a discreet shake of her head.

Being away from here only highlighted the grim conditions further still. It was like she was seeing the place through fresh eyes, and the contrast between this and her neat new house was stark. She just hoped she wouldn't carry any fleas or worse back with her, a problem which was clearly very much still prevalent at Velvet Walks – there was a definite pong of sulphur candles in the air.

'Why don't you leave this crummy hole, Mrs Reilly?'

'Oh, 'tain't so bad.'

Janie let the matter pass. 'Sorry for dropping in on you like this and burdening you with my troubles, only I didn't know where else to go . . .'

'Burdening indeed! That's daft talk forra start; ain't we friends?'

'Aye.'

'Well then.'

'He will come back to me, my James, won't he, Mrs Reilly?'

The old woman responded pragmatically as always, as Janie knew she would: 'That's summat neither I nor anyone else but the good Lord in the clouds above can answer, lass. We can but pray it'll be so. It's all we have.'

'The leave he's just had . . .' Hugging herself, she smiled. 'By, it were magical, honest. Every second.'

Busy with the teapot, Mrs Reilly nodded. 'I bet the kiddies were glad to have their father home.'

'Oh aye. The lasses, in particular, have been like new people since he's been back. Our Hilda – well, you know what a madam she can be, don't you! – she'd

91

grown cheekier still over the weeks. But her mood changed like that when James returned,' she said, clicking her fingers. 'As for Elsie, well, she's a sensitive thing at the best of times. She got herself into the habit of wetting the bed, but lo and behold, she didn't do it once whilst James was here. Not that I let on to him how things had been in his absence, mind. He's got enough on his plate, after all.'

'They've had some big changes to get used to, ain't they, poor loves,' the woman observed, pouring Janie a cup of tea and passing it across. 'Their father going away, the upheaval to Breightmet town, new school and new friends . . . It's a lot for little ones to take in. But they'll be reet. Everything settles itself eventually, lass, fret not.'

'Aye, you're right.'

'No sugar, I'm afraid, bleedin' rationing,' her friend grumbled, easing back into her chair.

'It's all right.' Janie meant it. Sweetened or not, the brew was like nectar in her current state, was just what she'd needed to lull her frayed nerves. 'It has been nice seeing you, Mrs Reilly. I've missed youse all here. Sorry I've not been to visit until now, only I've not had a minute what with one thing and another.'

'I'll bet. Them twins you're minding of a day must keep you busy enough!'

Janie blinked in surprise. 'How d'you know about that?'

'Your Joey were telling me.'

'Joey? When?'

'He's up this way every weekend. Didn't you know?'

'I didn't. He's likely been seeing his chums. Deserves the break, an' all, he does – he don't half toil hard. Mind, he loves it on t' farm.'

Mrs Reilly flashed a smile then changed the subject. 'So you'll be all right, then, aye, whilst James is away?'

'I have to be, don't I? It's just a shame he had to return today of all days . . .' Tears welled, and she cleared her throat. 'You see, it's our wedding anniversary.'

'Ay, lass.'

'Seventeen years.'

'Well, that's more than some folk get, eh?' Mrs Reilly said softly, eyes kind. She patted Janie's hand. 'Come on now, wipe them peepers, chin up. Moping won't do thee no good.'

'I just miss him. And I love him, oh so much.'

'Well, 'course you do. He's barmy over thee an' all, I've seen it. Your pain is summat to be thankful about, really, for it proves what's in your hearts for one another, and that it's true. It proves you've summat special. It wouldn't hurt like it does else.'

'Eeh, Mrs Reilly.'

'You've a strong and solid union,' the woman added, wiping Janie's wet cheeks with a gnarled hand. 'A bit *too* strong in a way – intense is how I'd describe it, if I'm honest. So it's little wonder you're feeling this rotten at being parted. But you'll bear it, you will. Like you say: you have to, don't you?'

Waving goodbye to her friend a short time later, Janie felt better than she'd dared believe she could. The sage advice had done her the power of good;

shoulders back, chin high, she set off for the tram stop with renewed vigour.

'I've got a poorly arm again, Mam.'

'Oh, have you, lass? The same one?'

'Aye.'

Frowning – it was obvious Elsie was in some discomfort – her mother put down her fork and beckoned her over. However, as with before, there was no sign of injury, no mark or redness whatever; Janie was stumped.

'I can see nowt what could be causing it, love. You must have just banged it or summat and forgot, and it's bruised a bit on t' inside. I'm sure it'll right itself soon enough. It did before.'

Satisfied with this, the girl walked back to her chair and resumed her meal, and Janie turned her attention to her son. 'How are your mates doing, lad?'

'My mates?'

'Aye. I went to visit Mrs Reilly today and she said she'd seen you up that end last week. They're all right, I hope?'

'Oh. Aye.'

Watching him, she was filled with confusion; his face had bloomed in a bright blush and he was struggling to meet her stare. 'Lad? What is it?'

'Nowt, Mam.'

'Don't come that – you've gone as red as a ruddy beetroot.'

'I ain't.'

'Oh yes you have! What's up?'

'Nowt, honest.'

Unconvinced, she probed on. 'Will you be calling on them again this weekend?'

'I might.'

'Well, I think you should, anyroad. It'll do you good. You work hard and deserve a bit of enjoyment in your free time.'

Eyes fixed firmly on his food, he responded with but a nod, and Janie let the matter drop. She wouldn't get anything out of him when he got like this; stubborn as a mule, her Joey was, when the mood took him. If and when he wanted to talk to her, he would; it was no good pushing him. He'd likely had some petty row or other with one of the friends and didn't want to discuss it. No doubt it would blow over in a few days. These things usually did.

Later, when the children had gone to bed, Janie ran herself a hot bath and treated her tired body to a nice long soak. Returning downstairs, she stood for a moment in the middle of the living room and looked around. It seemed so dead and empty without James. She'd got used to their nights in front of the fire at the end of the day. The closeness, their cuddles and easy chatter. His presence. All gone again, for goodness knew how long. God, but it was unfair! Swallowing down her emotion, she made towards the kitchen to put the kettle on.

'Janie? It's only me, love.'

The quiet call reached her before she got to the

door – frowning, she turned back and crossed to the hallway. 'Who is it?' she asked.

The voice floated through the letterbox again: 'Lynn. Open up, lass, it's bloody freezing out here!'

Smiling, she unlocked the front door and let her friend inside, saying, 'What you doing here at this time of night?'

'Well, that's nice, in t' it? I think I'll go out again and come back in; I might get a better welcome!'

'Sorry. 'Course you're welcome. Come on through.'

'Ta.'

Janie nodded to a chair and sat in the one opposite. 'So, what can I do you for?'

'I thought you might like some company, what with James gone and it being your anniversary and all.'

'Eeh, that were thoughtful of you.' She could have hugged her. 'What about the twins, though?'

'They're all right; fast akip the pair are. I'll keep nipping in on them, make sure they're all right.'

'That would be nice, then, aye. I don't half feel lonely without him.'

'Maybe this'll help – look what I've got.'

Gazing at the two bottles Lynn had whipped out from inside her coat, Janie's mouth fell open. 'Wine? How've you afforded that!'

'Not me, owd Briggs.'

She was stunned. 'Seymour? What's he giving you wine for?'

'It's for you. Insisted, he did.'

'But why?'

'To cheer you up.' Lynn grinned. 'And 'cause, like

I keep telling you: he's in love with you, yer daft ha'porth!'

Tut-tutting, Janie went to fetch some glasses. 'Don't be starting all that again. He's likely being kind is all.'

'Kind my left foot! All right, all right,' she relented, holding up her hands, when Janie sighed. 'I'll not mention his name again. Will that do you?'

'Aye. Now come on, get it opened and let's have a taste. I've never had wine before.'

'Nor me, but it looks like a good 'un. He must have more money than sense, that fella.'

Several glasses of the strong, tangy beverage and lots of laughter later, Janie felt infinitely better. 'He's a good egg, you know, Mr Briggs. Aw no, he is!' she insisted when Lynn scoffed. 'He didn't have to gift us this, did he?'

'You're squiffy, you are.'

Squinting through one eye, Janie nodded agreement. 'I am a bit, aye, but still . . . Right generous, it was. If he was here now, I'd give him a great big kiss on t' cheek, I would!'

At that moment, a loud rap came at the door. The women gazed towards it in astonishment.

'Eeh, maybe you'll get your chance!' cackled Lynn, hauling herself up and making her way unsteadily to the hall. 'Watch this be him, the owd bugger, trying his luck, hoping to catch you alone!'

Janie was horrified. 'Ay, he wouldn't. It can't be!'

'Well, there's only one way to find out, in t' there?' Puffing out her chest as though getting ready for battle, her friend marched off to open the door.

Slapping a hand to her mouth to smother a bout of nervous giggles, Janie bolted out of sight behind the chair.

'Love?' Having returned, Lynn held on to the table, could barely breathe from laughing. 'Where the devil are you?'

Popping her head out of hiding, which made her friend double up even more, Janie glanced about. 'Was it really him . . . ?'

'It were the soddin' air-raid warden, Ralph Robertson. You've a bit of light showing, you scatty mare, yer!'

'Oh, ruddy hell . . .'

Watching Janie drag herself to her feet, pink with embarrassment, her friend had tears of mirth coursing down her face. 'Lass, this has made my night. You're a bloody riot, you are, and I love you for it.'

'You tell anyone about this, Lynn Ball, and I'll skin you alive,' she warned, her own face breaking into a grin.

'Now, would I do a thing like that?'

Janie couldn't rightly say. However, there was one thing she *was* sure of: being the butt of the jokes or not, she was glad of tonight. It had certainly managed to take her mind off what had started out as one of the most painful days of her life. She smiled.

'See to them blackout blinds, you bugger, whilst I pour us another drink.'

Chapter 6

'GOOD GOD, IT'S like a troupe of Morris dancers have taken root inside my skull. It's friggin' banging.'

Gingerly making her way to the table and sitting down, Lynn nodded agreement. 'I feel rotten an' all, right enough.' Winking, she added, 'Fun, though, weren't it?'

'Aye, but we'll pay for it today. Rough or not, we've both got to work.'

Burying her head in her arms, her friend groaned. 'Be a mate, love, and stick the kettle on.'

Two cups of tea and an aspirin each later, the women were feeling fractionally more human. Janie glanced to the clock.

'Lynn, look at the time! Mr Briggs is going to kill you.'

'Oh, he'd better not give me no grief today, because I won't be responsible for my actions,' she growled, lumbering to her feet. 'This is all his fault anyroad – him and his bloody posh plonk.'

'Come on,' Janie told her, chuckling, 'I'll walk with you. I could do with a bit of fresh air.'

With the twins secured in their pram, Janie led the way through the front gate whilst a reluctant Lynn trailed behind. As they made to turn right in the direction of the shops, a door across the road opened and Reuben Trent – a firm favourite in the street – emerged into the weak sunlight. Tall and lean with neatly combed white hair and impeccable dress, he was, as usual, the epitome of gentlemanliness, and had the manners to boot. Janie called to him a good morning, but today he didn't return it. Instead, he beckoned them across.

'Is everything all right?' she asked when she reached him. Then, noticing on closer inspection his tight expression and the grim set of his mouth: 'Mr Trent? What's wrong, what's happened?'

'Hitler's invaded Denmark and Norway.'

His words robbed the colour from the women's faces. No . . .

'Can you believe it?' the old man went on in a murmur. 'Just what is this world coming to? That mad swine wants every corner of the planet, I'm sure.'

The truth of it rang in their ears. Further talk was useless. For this morning at least, British bravado and the 'no defeatist talk' mantra was forgotten. Would they hear the sound of Jerry's boots pounding their own green and pleasant land one day soon? The prospect wasn't an altogether preposterous one any more. In a daze, the trio turned as one and headed for the shops.

The news was the gossip of the grocer's. Strained-faced customers milled around discussing the bleak report in subdued voices. The enemy, it seemed, was unstoppable. Who would be next? they all wanted to know, at the same time in dread of the answer.

Just four weeks later, they found out.

On 10 May, the announcement screamed from every paper and wireless in the country: German troops had invaded Holland, Luxembourg and Belgium. Fear for neighbouring France in light of this crushing development was a very real one.

The nation was united in dumbfounded devastation. The Phoney War, as they knew it, had come crashing to an end.

Then, later that same day, a beacon of light emerged through the wreckage which lent the people of Britain much-needed hope: Winston Churchill replaced Neville Chamberlain as Prime Minister. Most agreed he'd make a fine leader. Surely this was the man to steer them to victory?

At Padbury Way, the following days passed in a blur for Janie and Lynn as they anxiously waited for word of their husbands. Unsure where precisely they were and in what danger, the what-ifs were agonising. Then, one blessed, blue-skied morning towards the month's end, the postman's arrival finally put them out of their misery.

'Janie! Janie!'

Wrenching open the front door at the excited call, her own precious letter clasped to her chest, Janie ushered her friend inside. 'Oh, Lynn. He's all right.'

'My Duncan, too.' Lynn waved the sheet of paper under Janie's nose. 'Eeh, thank the good Lord.'

101

When they were seated with a cup of tea, they pored over their correspondence yet again. Having been first checked by the censors at the local headquarters – a necessary precaution to ensure soldiers didn't inadvertently reveal military secrets – blocks in black ink blotted out some of the text. What they had been left with, they savoured, every word.

'We'll have the Jerries on the run in quick time,' Janie read out. 'Look after the children and give them my love. Try not to worry, lass. I'll be back just as soon as I can be.'

Lynn joined in, and now it was Duncan's message that whispered around the room from across the miles. 'I long for the day I get to see you at last. The boys, too. How is it nearly their first birthday already? They must be getting so big. Give them both a kiss from me, and here's one for you: X.'

'Take care, my Janie . . .'

'Until we meet again, dear Lynn . . .'

'Your loving husband,' the women finished in unison.

They returned the notes to their envelopes, the flaps of which were emblazoned with the letters SWALK – sealed with a loving kiss. Wiping away a tear, they smiled at one another across the table.

'Soppy buggers,' said Lynn on a watery laugh.

'And we wouldn't have them any other way.'

'D'you think this lot will be enough?'

Running her eye over the spread, Janie nodded. Two days had been and gone since they'd received word from their men and, despite the ever-present worry as to their well-being and the mess of the world in general, today was a special one that couldn't – shouldn't – be left unacknowledged. They were determined to have a good time if it killed them. 'Aye, I reckon so. We can always make up a few more butties later on if we start to run low, and I've half a steamed date pudding and jug of lemon sauce keeping fresh in t' larder. Don't fret, lass. Under the circumstances, you've done the lads proud.'

Owing to the shortage of butter and sugar, a conventional celebration cake had been out of the question. Lynn gave the small plain sponge in the centre of the table a disgusted sniff. 'Friggin' war. I'd wring that Hitler's scraggy neck for him given the chance.'

'You'd have to get to the back of the queue, love. I'd be in there first to give him the thumping of his life, oh, would I.'

Voices began to filter through the open back door; glancing outside and seeing schoolchildren on the yard beyond the garden fence, Janie was shocked. 'Is it home time already? The hours have flown! Right then.' She removed her pinny and crossed to the mirror above the fire to check she was presentable. 'Hilda, Elsie and the other kiddies from the street know to come straight here from school, so that just leaves the twins. I'll go and fetch them from Mrs Hodgkiss, shall I?'

Lynn nodded. 'Aye, please. Eeh, their first party. I can't wait to see their little faces!'

Janie was just drawing level with Sadie's house when

she spotted her son turning the corner of their street. Frowning in surprise, she walked on to meet him. 'All right, lad? What are you doing home at this time?'

He greeted her with a swift kiss to her cheek, making her smile. 'Grandad were happy with my work so let me off early.'

'Well, that were good of him. 'Ere, you're just in time for the jollifications – I'm on my way to collect the babbies now.'

'Oh, well . . .'

'What is it?'

Joey pulled an apologetic face. 'I don't really fancy it, Mam, if I'm honest. Anyroad, I thought I'd get the tram into town.'

Janie nodded, understanding. 'I don't suppose a houseful of screeching kiddies would be many young men's idea of a good evening, would it? Go on then, you take yourself home and get washed and changed and get off to your mates. I'll see you later, love.'

'Mam?'

Having reached Sadie's front door, Janie glanced over her shoulder to see her son had paused a little further up the road. 'Aye?'

'It's just . . . Oh, nowt. It don't matter.' He threw her a smile. 'I'll see you later on.'

'Ta-ra. And oi, make sure you keep out of trouble!' she added to his retreating back, at the same time aware that her warning was more through habit than genuine concern – her Joey was a good lad after all, had never given her cause to worry on that score.

'Are you ready for them, lass?' asked Sadie upon

answering Janie's knock; she seemed as excited as the birthday boys themselves.

'Aye. Thanks for keeping an eye to them whilst we got everything ready.'

'It were my pleasure, as always,' Sadie insisted as she handed the children over, adding, 'hang on, won't be a minute.' She disappeared back inside the house and returned with two brightly wrapped presents, which she held out. ''Tain't much, you know . . .'

'Oh, that's kind of you, Mrs Hodgkiss. But won't you want to see them being opened yourself?'

Her mouth spread in a brilliant smile and it was like the sun had come out behind her eyes. 'You mean I'm invited? To the party, like?'

''Course you are!'

'I'll not be in t' way?'

'No, no. What little kin Lynn had were dead and buried years ago, poor lass. And what with Duncan Ball hailing from Wales . . . his family ain't able to make it. There'll be but us and a bunch of kiddies, that's all. And I just know Bobby and Brian shall want you there.'

'Eeh, well, if you're sure . . . I'll get my coat!'

Poor Sadie, too, Janie thought to herself as she waited for her to lock up. How incredibly sad not to have a soul in the world to call your own. How lonely she must have been all these years. But not any more, she reminded herself with an inward smile, pushing the pram with one hand so she could offer an arm to the woman to link. No, not now she was amongst friends.

Over the following hours, the children had a whale

of a time. They stuffed their faces with mint jellies and cheese sandwiches, danced and sang songs and enjoyed what seemed like a hundred rounds of blind man's buff, bumping into furniture and screaming in glee with every game – eventually, Lynn ushered them all into her front garden with a rubber ball to play catch.

'Gawd, I'm fagged!' she announced as she poured out tea for Janie, Sadie and herself. 'A bit of peace at last.'

Janie puffed out a long breath of agreement. 'It's been worth it, though, to see them all smiling and happy, with no reminders of war forra little while.'

Sadie nodded. 'Well, I for one have delighted in every single second of today, aye. Ta very much for asking me along.'

'Any time, Mrs Hodgkiss, you know that,' Lynn told her, patting her hand. 'You've become like a granny to them boys of mine; love the bones of you, they do.'

'Eeh, lass.'

'That's right, ain't it?' Lynn had turned to Janie for confirmation, but her friend was only half listening. 'Love?'

'Sorry, I . . .' Frowning, Janie cocked her head further towards the open window, where, from outside, the children's chatter had grabbed her attention. 'What *is* the issue there, at all?'

'With what?'

'Our Elsie. Listen.'

The other women leaned forward to hear.

'So you see, I can't play ball with youse all, sorry,' the youngster was saying to another girl.

'Well, your arm don't look bad. You've not got no cuts or owt on it, have you?'

'No, but it's still sore,' Elsie insisted.

'You're just lying 'cause you're rubbish at catch, that's what, Elsie Hudson.'

'I'm not, I'm not!'

Seeing the quarrel was getting out of hand, Janie knocked on the pane and pointed a warning finger. 'That's enough, now, you two. Play nice or it'll be time to go home.'

The children apologised and skittered off to resume their games, and Lynn scratched her head. 'What were all that about, then?'

'The lass and her arm. She's been complaining it hurts forra while, but so far as I can see, there's nowt wrong with it. It got mysteriously better when James were home, but she started up about it again as soon as he'd left. And the same is true with her bed-wetting. I just don't know what to make of it.'

'It's likely nowt more than a cry for attention, love. You know how kiddies can be.'

'Aye, Lynn, mebbe. I'll give it a bit longer, eh, see how she is. If nowt improves, I'll ask the doctor to check her over, put my mind at ease.'

When she put the suggestion to Elsie that night, however, the girl was insistent she didn't need to see a medical man.

'No, Mam, I'm not sick.'

'But your arm—'

'Oh, that'll get better again when Dad's home. Anyroad,' the child added matter-of-factly, 'it's our Hilda what needs medicine, not me.'

'Eh? What you going on about?' her sister scoffed, snuggling down deeper in the bed they shared. 'Why would I need medicine then?'

''Cause you're poorly, our Hilda.'

''Course I ain't, stupid! Mam, will you tell her!'

Rolling her eyes, Janie tucked the blankets around them. She and Lynn had worked hard today and she was bone-tired – the last thing she had energy for tonight was a squabbling match. 'That's enough, now. Get some sleep, good lasses.'

'Mam?'

Blinking in the darkness of her room, Janie frowned to see Hilda's figure hovering at the foot of the bed. 'Lass? It's the middle of the night. What's wrong?'

'Mam, I don't feel so good.'

Scrambling up and fumbling for the matches, Janie lit the lamp and drew her daughter closer to the guttering light. She looked pained and groggy. Feeling her forehead, Janie gasped. 'Oh, you're burning up enough to fry an egg on that! Eeh, lass, come on in here.' She pulled back the bedclothes and helped the girl settle in the bed. 'You don't feel like you need to be sick, love, do you?'

Hilda shook her head.

'Right, well, you lie still now and rest whilst I go and make you a cup of tea.'

By dawn, Hilda's temperature had risen further and she'd developed a headache so severe it was reducing her to tears. Flummoxed and with her concern mounting, Janie went to waken her son.

'Lad, I need you to go and collect the doctor.'

'Eh?' he slurred sleepily. 'What, Mam?'

'The doctor. Our Hilda's not right. Hurry up, now, come on!'

Her words sinking in, he was on his feet in a flash. His deep love for his sisters was no secret; but also, hadn't he promised his father he'd do his utmost in his role of man of the house, that he'd look after their female folk whilst he was away? The responsibility was etched clearly in his face and he was out of the door and pelting down the road without even pausing to put on his jacket or cap.

The doctor's examination was over in less than five minutes. Nodding to himself, he snapped shut his Gladstone bag and ushered Janie on to the landing.

'Well, Doctor?' she asked in a dread-filled whisper. 'Do you know what ails her?'

'Indeed I do. Hilda has rubella.'

'German measles?' Janie was incensed. 'Oh aye, aye, of course it would have to be . . . Those bloody Jerries! Won't they ever just leave us in peace? The evil, black-souled—!'

'Mrs Hudson.' The doctor tugged at his lips as though trying not to smile. 'Rubella is also known as German measles merely due to the fact that German physicians first described and studied it many years ago. I understand we're living in worrying times, but I can assure you this is no secret weapon, no slight upon us by the enemy, just . . . unfortunate timing, shall we say. Large parts of the country are suffering just now from a wave of the disease. Try not to take on so.'

Running a hand over her eyes, Janie sighed. 'Aye. Sorry, 'course you're right. I'm just exhausted, Doctor.'

'Get some rest. The draught I've just given to Hilda will help her to sleep – I suggest you snatch a few hours yourself. Now, the spotty pink rash behind her ears will spread to her head and body – don't be alarmed, it's its natural course. Treat her aches and fever with aspirin and see she gets plenty of fluids. School, of course, is out of the question, given its contagiousness. I would suggest you limit her contact with other family members and neighbours for the next few days as well – particularly pregnant women, for whom the disease can be highly dangerous.'

'Aye, Doctor. I'll have her in my bed with me for the duration. I'll make sure she don't move a muscle from it neither 'til she's well again, however much she might kick up a fuss.'

'Separate cutlery, cup, plate and towel for her use only would also be wise. Rubella is unpleasant, but not so dangerous given the right care,' he went on, and his words had a sympathetic undertone to them now for this mother afraid for her child. 'Your daughter should be recovered in about a week. However,

110

should you need my services again at all, don't hesitate to send for me.'

'Thank you.'

'Good morning, Mrs Hudson.'

'Ta-ra, Doctor.'

Joey saw the man out then came to sit beside his mother on the sofa. Putting an arm around her shoulders, he released a breath of relief. 'She'll be all right then. Thank God.'

'Aye.'

'Shall I make you some tea?'

Smiling, Janie nodded. 'Eeh, please, lad. My nerves are in bits.'

'I, erm, overheard him mention summat about the illness being serious to pregnant women,' her son remarked with his back to her as he mashed the tea in the pot. 'Is it right, then?'

'I expect so, if he says it is. Why?'

'No reason. I just wondered.'

'I'm not in t' family way, lad, if that's what's concerning you,' she assured him with a chuckle. 'Don't fret none over that.'

'Aye. Here you are, Mam.' He handed her the steaming brew then turned and headed for the door. 'I'd best get ready for work.'

Alone, she sipped at her drink with closed eyes. In her mind, she spoke to the Lord. She told Him how grateful she was to Him for sparing their Hilda from something more sinister and asked if He would see to it that she got better quickly.

'I wish you were here, James,' she finished on a

111

whisper. 'I need you – we all do. Don't you understand that?'

'Mam?'

Dragged back to the present, Janie looked across
the room and smiled to see Elsie in the doorway. She
held open her arms and the girl hurried across to
snuggle down beside her.

'See, Mam. I told you.'

'Told me what, lass?' she asked mildly, smothering
a yawn with the back of her hand.

'I told you our Hilda was poorly and not me.'

A shiver of remembrance, icy in its truth, washed
through her. She gasped. 'You did as well, didn't
you . . . Elsie, how . . . How did you know that?'

Her daughter shrugged her shoulders. 'Just did.'

'Elsie. Lass.' Janie's heart was thumping. *She just
knew* . . . 'Do you sometimes see things, things in
your sleep? Things that you just sense are going to
come true?'

Her answer came without hesitation: 'No.'

'But . . . Then how—?'

'Not when I'm asleep, Mam. When I'm awake.'

'When you're awake?' Janie was flummoxed. The
females in her family 'blessed' with this ability only
ever received the visions in their dreams. What could
this mean? 'Are you sure?'

'Aye, Mam. It's like talking in my head, but not all
the time.'

'You hear . . . Not pictures, then?'

'No, just words. They tell me what's going to
happen.'

That one of her daughters had inherited the ability shouldn't have overly surprised her – hadn't she sometimes wondered if it would be the case? And yet, it nonetheless did. More so in fact given Elsie's description of *her* experience. She received the sights whilst awake? But how?

Snippets of memory started to trickle back, and she nodded slowly. She recalled the day they had moved to this house, the day the blizzards began, and how Elsie had innocently remarked that it would 'snow for ever'. *She'd been told.* Of course, it hadn't continued for as long as that, but for a child of her tender years months would indeed seem an eternity. Then there was Hilda's rubella. Again, she'd said her sister would 'need medicine', and she'd been proven right. It was true. There could be no denying it. *God help the lass.*

'Does it mean I'm barmy, Mam?'

Gazing down into her confused little face, Janie bit back a sob, understanding her worry completely. Who, after all, could relate to the child's dilemma more than she? No one, that's who. 'No, my lass. No, it doesn't, not a single bit, and you must never think it either. Promise? You're different, aye, but in a good way, not bad. You're special. Just *special*, that's all. Like me.'

Satisfied, Elsie nodded.

'Now. You go on up and get washed and dressed for school and I'll make you some breakfast. All right?'

Janie kept her smile in place as her daughter skipped to the door. Only when her footfalls sounded on the stairs did she allow herself to close her eyes in despair.

113

Chapter 7

DUNKIRK.

The word meant little or nothing to the inhabitants of a sleepy suburban estate in northern England. Yet it soon would.

Towards the beginning of June, startling reports regarding the state of affairs abroad began to filter through to the public. The British Expeditionary Force had stumbled obliviously into a trap set by the Germans advancing into France. With cunning strategy, the enemy had flanked the defending armies, almost completely surrounding them. Overwhelmed and forced to retreat, the Allies found themselves hemmed in on the beaches of the French port town of Dunkirk.

Their situation seemed doomed, defeat certain. Withdrawal from the Nazi snare their only hope from obliteration and the sea their last route to safety, Operation Dynamo sprang into action. Over the course of nine days, almost 340,000 British and Allied soldiers were rescued from the sands and transported across the Channel to the English coast – a monumental number and a magnificent success. A potential military disaster became a mission of heroism. In the words of the Prime Minister himself, the operation was a miracle of deliverance.

Desperate to keep up to date with events, Janie and Lynn, along with the rest of the nation, pored hungrily over every newspaper they could get their hands on. They devoured the articles, scoured each grainy accompanying image in the remote chance of catching a glimpse of their menfolk. They winced together and wept in private over the details. And they prayed. *Oh, did they.* It was all anyone seemed to do these days.

All was so nearly lost. But, in true tradition, Britain had survived to fight on. The small victory, however, had come at a hefty cost.

Tens of thousands of their boys were captured or dead, gone for ever. Many others were injured. Yet amidst the human wreckage emerged stories of unwavering valour and remarkable teamwork.

Owing to the difficulty of larger naval ships approaching the beaches' shallows, a request for small craft which could navigate these waters was put out. The call was immediately answered and resulted in a plethora of offers from civilian fishermen willing to aid the cause. Despite the dangers, some even sailed their private boats to Dunkirk personally. By the time the evacuation reached its conclusion, close to nine hundred vessels had played their part.

From huge warships and destroyers to littler pleasure steamers and yachts, barges, tugs and paddle steamers, fishing boats, cargo ships and rowing boats – under Allied air and ground cover, the mixed armada worked coolly and methodically to rescue as many rest-deprived, battle-stunned troops as possible. All the while, they were fiercely attacked from all sides. Machine-guns and artillery blazed; the bombardment was incessant. They were far outnumbered in the skies: a storm of German bullets and shrapnel bombs swept their ranks. Yet, strafed by a ceaseless enemy or not, they had clung on for survival doggedly. Their tenacity was staggering.

The accounts horrified and awed those on the home front in equal measure. For Janie, the wait for word on not only James but Duncan was a continual ache in her breast. What she'd told Lynn . . . why, *why*, had she said that both men would survive this hell? Never had she regretted something as much. Just what if Duncan had been one of the many to perish at Dunkirk, what then? Lynn would never forgive her.

As for her own husband – well. He had escaped with his life, the night sight said so. Then again, what if, for the first time, her visions were wrong? And even if it did prove correct, in what state would he return? Just how much of the James they knew and loved was left? And on and on the skittish worries harangued, allowing her no respite.

Despite her turmoil, life had to go on. Whether her troubled mind was only half here in the present most days or not, this she strove to do. She cooked and cleaned and shopped. She minded the twins as usual and got her own children off to work and school. In between it all, with gentle care, she nursed Hilda back to health. All this she performed with as much of a smile on her lips as she could force. Yes, she did it. For she had to, just as every other wife and mother in the country must. Then Lynn received a postcard with news of her husband which shattered the normal routine – and shook Janie's resolve to the core.

Duncan was alive.

Grasping her friend in a tight hug, Janie wept with her. *Thank God.* 'Eeh, I'm that pleased for you.'

'You were right all along, Janie. He got through – and he'll continue to.'

'Aye,' was all she could choke.

'He's arrived in England safely and says I'll be seeing him shortly. Oh, love. I can't tell you how relieved—' Lynn broke off abruptly and glanced to the floor. 'Sorry, Janie, I wasn't thinking . . .'

'Don't apologise! You're over t' moon, and so you deserve to be.'

'Aye, but what about you? *You're* no closer to knowing . . . I'm sure James will get in touch soon,' she insisted, squeezing Janie's hand. 'Then we'll both have cause to celebrate – and ay, when they're both back home, we'll have the best bloody knees-up that Top o' th' Brow's ever seen! Just you wait.'

With a nod and a smile, Janie inclined her head to the table. 'Sit down, love. I'll brew us a pot of tea.'

Whilst Janie waited for the kettle to come to the boil, her mind was locked in turmoil. Lynn was chattering through to the kitchen to her, but she barely registered any of it. Why hadn't she heard from her man? Just where was James? Was he injured so badly that he was unable to send out word to her? Perhaps his postcard had merely become lost in the post? Or maybe he wasn't even back in England at all. Maybe he'd been left behind in France – it was surely possible. Was he lying on some godforsaken battleground? Miles from his loved ones and home, alone and in pain . . . ?

'Stop it,' she growled to herself harshly beneath her breath. 'Just you friggin' stop that before you drive yourself mental. Have patience. You'll know well enough soon.'

The Balls' reunion soon after was a beautiful sight to behold. It was Lynn's day off from the grocer's, and she and Janie had been standing by their front doors, nattering over events in the warm sunshine whilst the twins played amongst the daisies and wild cornflowers in their garden, when the tall figure, kit-bag and rifle slung over his shoulder, turned into their road.

It was Janie who spotted him first. For the briefest moment, she thought it was James – but no. Realisation had slammed, crushing her joy in its tracks. Then, as she recognised him as the man in the framed picture standing proudly on Lynn's mantel-piece, her smile returned with understanding of what this meant to her friend. Nudging her, Janie had motioned down the street.

'Duncan!' Setting off at a sprint to meet him, the woman had fallen, laughing, into his arms.

'Lynn.' He swept her off her feet and twirled her around, his face wreathed in the biggest smile. 'My love. Oh, how I've missed you!'

As her friend returned the sentiment and professed her undying love to him, Janie slipped away into her house. The last thing they wanted right now was an audience. Time alone was what they would have on their minds – didn't she know that more than most?

Lynn and her husband called around later that evening, and Janie greeted him warmly. To say her friend appeared happy was putting it mildly – Lynn positively glowed. It warmed Janie's heart something lovely to witness.

Thanking his neighbour, Duncan took the seat she offered him and lifted his sons into his lap. Light-haired and blue-eyed with a wide mouth seemingly rarely short of a smile, Janie could well see what had attracted her friend to him. They were much alike, she soon learned – Duncan's sparky personality and rich laughter mirrored his wife's completely. They made a perfect match.

'Eeh, guess what?' Lynn squeaked when they were sipping tea, grasping Janie's hand in her excitement. 'I called at the shop forra few bits earlier and Seymour says I can cut my hours – with full pay! – for as long as Duncan's home. I were shocked when the owd bugger gave me the twins' birthday off last month, but this . . . Fancy! From now on, I only have to work the morning shift – we'll have the rest of the days all to ourselves. That's champion, in t' it?'

'It really is, love. See, he ain't all bad, eh?'

'Suppose not.' Lynn nodded in agreement. Then, eyes dancing with mischief, she turned to her husband, saying in amusement, 'Mind you, Janie here would say that. Likes my boss, she does. And aye, he's gorra soft spot for her, too, all right!'

'Lynn!' Janie was mortified. 'For goodness' sake, won't you ever grow bored with that nonsense? It's a good thing the girls are out playing in t' street and our Joey's up in his room, and that they aren't around to hear you; imagine such talk getting back to James! It's not funny,' she added when her friend doubled forward with laughter.

'No? So why are you smiling?'

Holding a hand to her mouth and inwardly cursing Lynn – she could never stay angry with her for long – Janie shook her head. 'Because you're a swine, that's what! Saying such things indeed . . . what must Duncan think of me?'

The man was grinning. 'Fret not, Janie, I believe you. I know my wife and her antics only too well!'

'Oh aye, ganging up on me now, are youse?' Lynn began in mock offence. But before she could go further, she was cut off by a thunderous knocking at the door. Almost jumping from her skin, she held a hand to her thudding heart. 'Who the devil . . . ?'

'James. It has to be!' Janie was out of her chair and dashing for the hallway in a trice. 'Wait, I'm coming!'

'Mrs Hudson?'

Staring in bewilderment at the woman on the step, Janie had to bite back tears. Her sheer disappointment was like no other. 'What?'

'I said, are you Mrs Hudson?'

'Aye, but who—?' The enquiry lodged in her throat as, flicking her head in an angry nod, the unwelcome visitor barged past her into the house. Janie was stunned. ''Ere, now just you hang on—!'

'Where is he?'

'Where's who?'

The fat and none-too-clean-looking newcomer, the front of her hair scraped back in several dinky curlers, scanned the room in search of whoever it was she sought. Clearly failing to find them, her nostrils flared. She swung around to face Janie, hands on hips. 'As if you don't know! I'll ruddy *murder* the young sod, I will!'

By now, Lynn and Duncan were on their feet. Janie gazed to them in utter confusion, as though hoping they could provide the answers – naturally, they couldn't; they looked as stumped as she. She turned back to the woman. 'Right, you. I want to know what's going on here, and I want to know now. Just who the hell d'you think you are, storming into my home spouting your wild demands? *What* "young sod"? Who are you talking about?'

'Joey Hudson, that's who.'

'Eh?' Her mouth fell open. 'My Joey? I don't . . .'

'The one and only, aye. D'you know just what he's gone and done? Shall I tell you?'

Swallowing hard, Janie nodded. 'Tell me.'

What the woman divulged sent a shockwave through the room with the power to strip the strength from Janie's legs; on a cry, she crumbled to the floor. 'You're lying!'

'It's true, all right. Your rotten son is going to be a father.'

Having hurried upstairs on Janie's instruction to fetch the lad in question, Lynn returned grim-faced. She shook her head. 'He's gone.'

'What?'

'Joey must have sneaked from his room and out of the house when he heard the argument. His room's empty, love.'

Though Janie's face crumpled, her tone was like ice. 'I'll skin him alive when I get my hands on him.'

Duncan had made himself scarce with the twins whilst his wife stayed on to offer Janie support. Now, the three women sat in awkward company, unsure what to do next. Joey had scarpered – a sure sign of guilt if ever there was one, Janie was forced to admit. Her devastation was complete.

'He's fifteen years old,' she whispered, hugging herself. 'Fif-bloody-teen. How has this happened?'

'Well, how d'you think? Surely you know by now how babbies are got. Or does your fella take his needs from you in your sleep, you daft—'

'That's enough.' Lynn stared her down coldly. 'Janie's in shock, can't you see? Your nastiness ain't helping matters.'

The woman snorted. 'You reckon this is nasty, do you? By, you've seen nowt yet, let me tell you. So, come on then.' Having turned to Janie, she lifted an eyebrow. 'I want to know where this leaves my daughter. Your son ain't getting off with this one. Oh no, missy. What is it you intend to do?'

'I don't know.' Dear God, she didn't, *couldn't*, think . . . couldn't understand anything right now. 'I must, must speak with Joey and . . . and see what he has to say for himself, I . . .'

'And how are you meant to do that when the bugger's gone? Oh, sod this, I ain't hanging about here going around in circles with you – what would be the point? I've things to be getting on with. You've got my address?'

Janie nodded. 'I'll be in touch soon.'

'Aye, and make sure you do.'

When the front door had banged shut behind the woman, Lynn moved to put her arm across her friend's trembling shoulders. 'Eeh, love . . . I just don't know what to say.'

'No. Me neither.'

'D'you reckon . . . ? I just can't believe . . . your Joey, though? Could it be true?'

'Oh, it's true, all right.'

'Eeh, what will you do?'

Janie closed her eyes. 'I don't know, Lynn. I honestly do not know.'

The hour was approaching four when she saw him.

After seeing to Hilda and Elsie's needs and putting

them to bed, she'd sent Lynn home with the promise she'd call on her should she need her. Then she waited, stare fixed on the door in readiness for her son's knock. It didn't come.

Sleep an impossibility, she'd remained where she was on the sofa, drowning herself in tea and chain-smoking throughout the excruciating night. Midnight passed. One o'clock, two, three – but nothing. Still, she'd waited.

It was mother's instinct which alerted her – had to be, for he made no noise. Rising, she crossed to the window and peered outside. Joey sat hunched on the front step.

Unbolting the door, she opened it and held it wide. 'In.'

He followed her inside without a word.

Voice as low as before, his mother pointed to a chair. 'Sit.'

Again, he obeyed mutely.

Janie sat facing him. The minutes stretched on in thick silence as she waited for Joey to explain. Finally, he lifted his head.

'I'm sorry.'

Just two little words. Yet their meaning said it all.

'It's true.'

'Aye.'

'I never suspected. I never did. Though, looking back now, I see you've been acting shifty forra while. Your reaction to Mrs Reilly telling me she'd spotted you in town . . . and *her* reaction as well, come to think of it. It's like she regretted mentioning it, changed the subject pretty quick, she did, aye. The day of little Bobby and Brian's party . . . You didn't miss it to go off seeing your mates, I bet. Then there was your concern over our Hilda's illness. It was *your* babby you were worried about the measles being passed on to, weren't it? God . . . how have I been so blind?'

'Don't berate yourself, Mam, please.'

Her movements were automatic, void of conscious thought. She crossed to the kitchen and put the kettle on the hob. Fresh pot of tea made, she poured them both a cup and passed her son's across the table. Then she resumed her seat and folded her arms. 'Now. I think you'd better start talking.'

'Her name's Stella. Stella Metcalfe. I'd gone into town to see my mates one Saturday and she were on my tram. We got talking, and well, that's it, really.'

'Except that's not just it, is it? We ain't talking owt as innocent as holding hands or stolen kisses on t' back row of the pictures – she's up the friggin' spout!'

'I wanted so much to tell you. I nearly did a few times, but right at the last minute . . . I couldn't do it. I couldn't. I'm sorry.'

'Not as sorry as you're going to be, my lad. Your fancy piece too. Not by a long chalk.'

Joey lifted his chin. In his eyes, quiet determination sparked. 'I'm not giving her up, Mam. We love each other.'

'Love!' Swinging from her seat, Janie paced the room. 'Bloody love? Youse don't know the meaning of the term, not yet. You're babbies still, don't you see?'

'No, Mam, we ain't. We know what we want.'

'You are fifteen.' Janie threw each syllable at him slowly, concisely. 'More to the point, so is she! It's kiddies having kiddies. You've no idea, have you? Never would I have believed I'd be having this conversation, not with one of mine. Not with you. You stupid, idiotic, brainless young fool!'

'We'll both be sixteen in a few months. Then we'll get wed—'

'Married?' she cut in incredulously. 'Oh, I've heard it all now, I have really. And where will you live, like? *How* will you live? Just listen to yourself, will you? Can you hear this nonsense you're coming out with at all?'

'So what do you suggest then? What, I leave her to face the music alone? The babby, the scandal, everything? Just dump her aside and forget we ever met? That's what you want from a son of yours, is it, aye? That's what you expect of me? Well, is it?'

Janie opened and closed her mouth, but a response wouldn't form; just what could she say to that?

'There's no way out of this, Mam. It's not going to go away. I've responsibilities to face up to, and face them I will. I'm to be a father, and me and Stella will marry, with your blessing or not.'

The last vestige of energy left her, her fight with it. She dropped back into her seat and covered her face with her hands. 'Stupid. *Stu*pid.'

'Aye. I have been, you're right. But, Mam.' Making around the table towards her, he enveloped her sob-wracked body in his arms. 'I'm going to make this right. I swear it. I *have* to.'

For the next few minutes, they rocked each other tightly, the crackles of the small fire the only sound in the dim-lit room.

Janie was the first to break the silence. As the thought occurred, a sigh rose from the depths of her very soul.

'God help the lot of us when your father finds out.'

Chapter 8

THE METCALFE HOUSEHOLD was situated in a grimy nook by Florin Street, no great distance from Velvet Walks. Resenting every second of their journey here and the reason behind it, Janie had barely uttered two words to her son. What would be the point, now, after all? There would be plenty to discuss soon enough.

Stella's mother, who had bulldozed her way into their home and lives the previous day and tipped Janie's world on its head, answered their knock. She threw her stare up and down them both with a curl of her lip. 'You came, then.'

'Looks like it, don't it?' Janie shot back.

'Huh. I'd have wagered on sonny boy here doing a runner for good.'

'Well, that's where you're wrong, Mrs Metcalfe.' Joey spoke for himself. 'Though you're right: I shouldn't have bolted, should have stayed and faced the music. Never will I do that again. I'm here now and I mean to put this right.'

The woman's eyes narrowed. 'And a good thing

128

for you, an' all, you young dog, yer. You'd never have known a minute's peace else – I'd have seen to that.'

'Look.' Janie's patience was clinging on by the briefest thread. 'Are you for inviting us in so's we can talk about this like civilised human beings? Unless, of course, you'd prefer to air your dirty laundry here, on t' step, for the whole lane to hear?' She shrugged. 'It's no skin off my nose, lady.'

Glancing about at the surrounding houses, Mrs Metcalfe attempted a nonchalant sniff, however they could see it was the last thing she wanted. She jerked her head. 'You'd best come in, then.'

Janie's gaze went immediately to the table set against the far wall, where sat the irrefutable Stella. Plump with copper-coloured hair, and hard-faced like her mother, Janie disliked her on sight. She nodded in acknowledgement, but the girl blanked it. The obvious snub rankled, but Janie chose to let it pass. 'I'm Mrs Hudson, Joey's mam.'

Again, Stella looked straight through her as if she wasn't there. Seemingly oblivious, Joey hurried over to her and asked if she was all right. Receiving a clipped affirmative, he stood behind her seat, one hand on her shoulder, as though protector of some high majesty. Janie and Mrs Metcalfe took a chair each facing.

'I'd offer you a brew, only . . . well, I don't want to.'

'Charming,' muttered Janie. Then, taking in the grubby room: 'Mind you, the state of this place, I suppose we must be grateful for small mercies.'

Ignoring her, the woman gave her attention to Joey. 'So.'

'So,' he echoed.

'You're for facing up to your responsibilities, then, I take it?'

He nodded firmly. 'I am, Mrs Metcalfe.'

'Right, well. I've been making some enquiries and I think I've found the perfect wench for t' job. She don't come cheap, mind you, so I hope you've got deep pockets.'

Mother and son peered at her in confusion.

'Deep pockets? What woman?' asked Janie.

'The abortionist, of course. Wait a minute . . .' Noting their horrified faces, she shook her head. 'You surely weren't for thinking that the lass might actually *have* the babby, were youse?'

'That's exactly what she's going to do.' Joey was mauve with outrage. 'For God's sake, we're not killing our flesh and blood! I'm going to marry your Stella and we'll raise the child together. Decent, like.'

'Oh no, I don't think so. She's getting shot of that thing, and that's an end to it. We'd be the talk of the bloody town! I ain't having no one accusing me of raising a slut.'

As her son made to throw back a retort, Janie held up a hand. She addressed the woman calmly, though inside she was feeling anything but. 'Mrs Metcalfe, I'll not deny that all this has come as a shock to me, too. To be perfectly honest in fact, I'm devastated – and absolutely raging to boot. But here's the thing. My lad here is stepping up to his wrongdoing. He means to make an honest lass of your daughter and, from what he's said, that's what Stella wants, an' all. Now, I'm not saying it'll be easy, no. It won't, not for none of us. Yet as their mams, I think it's up to us to see they at least try to make a go of things. For the babby's sake, if nowt else.

'I'll tell you now, I'm not a believer in abortions,' she went on, 'nor will I stand by and watch you force Stella into having one. Whether you like it or no, that's Joey's child she's got there in her belly, too. He has every damn right to his say on what becomes of it. They wanted to act like adults, now they can bloody play at it for real. We must give them half a chance to decide on this on their own.'

'Oh aye? You'd not be spouting all this claptrap were it *your* daughter and not your son what's found theirself in this mess. You're lucky I've not took the poker to the swine!'

'Yes, I would. Lad or lass, it makes no odds to me. If it were really what they wanted—'

'Frig off! She ain't having the brat, and that's that, d'you hear?'

On a cry, Stella jumped to her feet. 'Stop it! Both of you, stop talking like we're not even here!'

'She's right,' added Joey. 'All this arguing ain't doing no good. Please.'

'Aye, you're right – the time for talking's over,' Mrs Metcalfe barked, marching to the door and flinging it wide. 'Sod you Hudsons, and sod your money. We'll find a way of raising the funds without youse. Now get the 'ell out of my house!'

Joey stood his ground. 'I'm going nowhere without Stella.'

'Lad, come away,' Janie told him. 'For now at least.'

'But, Mam—!'

'We're not going to get nowhere today, not like this. Time's needed here, give us all a chance to cool down. Come away.'

His face fell. Shoulders slumping, he nodded. As would a child, he allowed his mother to guide him into the street. 'I love you, Stella!' he called out to the girl over her mother's frame, now blocking the doorway. To her, he added, 'I'll be back, Mrs Metcalfe. You ain't seen the last of me.'

'That's right. And oh, a word to the wise.' Janie pushed her face close to hers. 'You even think of getting Stella seen to whilst our backs are turned, and I warn you, I'll have the police breaking down your door faster than you can say "backstreet butcher".'

'Get gone, you devils, yer!' she yelled back, slamming the door in their faces.

'*She* is the devilish one! Eeh, I don't know. What a to-do.'

'You're right there. D'you know, it's one thing on top of another just now. I'm bone-weary of it, I am.'

Lynn nodded sympathetically. 'Not had it easy of late, love, have you?'

Looking out of the window, Janie watched the sapphire streaks of approaching evening scud the sky. 'Our Hilda getting poorly was the start of it – though, glory be to God, she's mended, now. Our Elsie on t'

132

other hand . . . Well, there's no cure for what she's got, is there?' She'd already filled Lynn in on developments concerning her youngest daughter and, as usual, her friend had proved a mountain of support. 'Mind you, the bed-wetting's stopped, you know, since she told me. I reckon it was the worry what were causing that. She's calmer somehow, now, since getting it all off her chest.'

'And now Joey.' Lynn shook her head.

'Aye – how that's going to pan out is anyone's guess. And to top it all, still there's been norra word from James.'

'What will he do, Janie, when he hears about the babby?'

Again, she released a drawn-out breath. 'He won't be doing cartwheels, lass, put it that way. Oh, it's all such a mess. What next?'

Her friend didn't have the answer. Stretching across, she patted Janie's hand in support; it was all she had.

Joey had taken to his room upon their return – now, as he entered the room and joined them at the table, Janie inwardly winced. Never had she seen him as miserable, so thoroughly beaten down. She reached for her bag on the sideboard and took out her purse. 'Here, lad. Walk to the chippy, will you, please, and get us all chips and pea wet with scraps – take the big blue bowl with you. I haven't the energy tonight for cooking. Go on, the fresh air will clear your head, do you good.'

He accepted the money from her then went to

fetch from the kitchen cupboard the aforementioned bowl, to be filled at the chip shop with golden chips and scraps of fish batter swimming in pea juice which his mother would distribute between the family, as was the working-class custom. When the front door rattled at his back, Janie dropped her head in her hands.

'Oh, Lynn, what's to be done?' she beseeched dully.

'Chin up, love. I'll make you a nice cup of tea, then I'll get in home, let you and the kiddies have your meal and rest up. You never know, things might look better in t' morning.'

Though Janie doubted it very much, she nodded nonetheless. 'Sorry for keeping you away from your own family whilst I bend your ear with my troubles. I do appreciate it, mind, would have likely cracked up good and proper by now if not for you.'

Lynn paused by the door to throw a wink and a smile over her shoulder. 'What are friends for?'

Soon afterwards, having thinly buttered a plate of bread to go with their chips then brewed a fresh pot of tea, Janie called her daughters in from their street games. Busy setting the table, when a knocking came at the door she motioned to Hilda to answer it. 'That'll be your brother back with the grub. Go and let him in, lass.'

'He better not have forgot the scraps, or I'll knock his block off,' said the girl as she got to her feet – Janie couldn't help but smile. Bar a bit of a lingering cough, the lass was back to her usual self, all right; nothing could keep her down for long, thank the Lord.

134

'Mam?' Hilda's voice floated through from the hall.

'Oh, he's not forgot the scraps after all, has he?' Janie wondered aloud to Elsie, who pouted. 'Aye, I know, lass. I were looking forward to them an' all.'

'Mam!'

'All right, Hilda,' she called, tut-tutting and pitying Joey the tongue-lashing he was sure to get from his sister. Leaving the plates, she headed to the hall before a full-scale row broke out. 'It's not the end of the world, lass— Oh.' Coming face to face with the last person she expected – or indeed desired – to see, Janie stopped dead in her tracks. Then, taking in Stella Metcalfe's appearance properly, her mouth drew together in anger. 'What the devil's happened to you? Has that mother of yours done that?'

'I want to see Joey.'

'Come on, come in.'

The girl followed her into her house then turned cold eyes on to her. 'He's not here. Where is he?'

'You two, go upstairs and play forra bit,' Janie instructed her daughters. Then, when she and Stella were alone: 'He's only nipped to the chippy; he'll be back in two shakes of a lamb's tail. Sit down and I'll get you a cup of tea whilst you wait – you look like you could do with one.'

With clear reluctance, Stella did as Janie bid.

Taking stock of the girl's bruised eye and cut lip as she poured out the drink, Janie repeated her earlier question: 'So was it your mother what caused you them injuries?'

'That's right.'

'Eeh, the brute. What possessed her?'

Stella didn't answer. Glancing to her clasped hands in her lap, she shook her head. 'I just want Joey.'

'There, you see. Here he is,' Janie said, abandoning the cups as, just then, knocking came again, heralding his return. 'Hang about whilst I let him in.'

Immediately upon seeing his mother's expression, Joey knew something was amiss. 'Mam?'

'Give us that bowl of grub here and go on through. You've a visitor.'

'Stella?' Entering the room, Joey was horrified. 'Christ, what's happened to you?'

'It were Mam. I set her straight when you'd gone, told her I'll not get rid of the babby. She turned on me, called me all the names under the sun . . . It were horrible. She'll not agree to us marrying, Joey. She won't!'

'Sshhh.' Taking the girl in his arms, he held her close. 'Everything's going to be all right, lass, I promise.'

'But how? With Dad dead, it's her consent I need to get wed until I'm of age. What are we going to *do*?'

Joey looked helplessly to his mother, who sighed. Both were well aware that what the girl spoke was truth.

'That's not all.' Her bottom lip trembling, Stella shook her head again. 'She's thrown me out. She says I'm not to grace her door again until I've seen sense.'

'The rotten . . . !' Janie was incensed. 'She can't do that. You're her daughter.'

'Well, she has.'

'But surely if you were to go back, try to reason with her—'

'No, I daren't! She'll do for me, she will!'

Mother of God, could this day get any worse? Janie flopped wearily into a chair.

'It's the babby I'm most afraid for,' Stella added, turning doe eyes swimming with tears on to Joey. 'She'll do it a mischief next time, given the chance, she will. I'm sure of it.'

'That settles it.' Joey nodded firmly. 'You ain't going back there.'

'But where *will* I go?' cried the girl.

'You can't stop on here.' Janie shook her head. 'It wouldn't be proper.'

'Mam, please! You can't be thinking of booting Stella out on to the street, you can't!'

'Well, of course not. What make of person d'you take me for?'

'But you just said—'

'What I meant was she can't kip the nights beneath *this* roof. That's not to say I haven't somewhere else in mind.'

'Where, Mam?'

Janie went to fetch her coat. 'I'm for asking Mrs Hodgkiss. She's rattling around in that house all by herself, after all, will likely be glad of the company.'

Joey's relief was tangible. 'Eeh, that would be ideal. It's only a few doors down from here,' he explained to Stella. 'We'd not be that far apart.'

'Now don't go counting your chickens,' Janie

warned. 'I refuse to lie to her, will have to be upfront about the circumstances – how she'll take such shocking details, I don't know. She might well say no yet. Let's wait and see what's what when I've spoken to her.'

'And the matter of us marrying?' demanded Stella.

Turning at the door, Janie shot the young madam a frown. 'One thing at a time, eh? I'm norra friggin' miracle worker.'

Sadie listened intently to Janie's explanation. When it was over, she crossed the floor and opened her arms – Janie rushed into them and wept.

'You poor lovey. There now, that's it, you let them tears out.'

'Oh, Mrs Hodgkiss. It's been a terrible time.'

'And no wonder.'

'Then you'll appreciate the predicament I've been put in. I can't just abandon the lass what's carrying my grandchild, can I?'

'No, no.'

'So . . . what d'you say? Me and Joey between us will pay you for her upkeep. I know it's asking a lot from you, it is, but—'

'She's welcome here, can bed down in t' spare room. Aye, I'm happy to take her in.'

'You are?'

''Course, love. To be honest, it'll be nice to have someone around the place.'

Heaving a long breath, Janie smiled. Then, on impulse, she leaned forward and kissed the woman's cheek. 'Ta, Mrs Hodgkiss, ever so. You're a bona fide diamond, what are you?'

Sadie chuckled. 'Well, I've been called some things in my time, but never nowt as nice as that. But ay, I'm not one to argue.'

'I mean every word. Lord knows what we would have done without you.'

'Go on, go and tell the pair what's been decided and fetch Stella round. I'll make her a bite of summat to eat then dig out some spare blankets so's she can get some rest. I bet the lass could do with it.'

After thanking her again, Janie left the house and set off for home. She filled in the young couple on what had transpired then instructed Joey to walk the girl down to Sadie's. She felt suddenly, inexplicably, exhausted.

'Ta for this, Mam.' Joey's words were soft with gratitude. 'I really appreciate it, and Stella does too. Don't you, Stella?' he added smilingly to the po-faced girl, who gave him a brief nod.

I doubt she does, lad, Janie thought. But what would be the point in voicing it? Besides, she was just too tired for anything more this night. 'Go on, Mrs Hodgkiss is expecting you.'

They left, and Janie went to call her daughters down for the belated evening meal. 'I'll just stick the bowl in t' oven; them chips will be stone cold by now,' she told them. 'It shan't be long. Meantimes, Hilda, you can pour us all a well-earned cup of tea.'

'Who were that girl what called, Mam?' asked Elsie.

She hadn't the strength for this, not right now.

139

'Oh . . . Just a friend of our Joey's, lass,' she murmured before escaping from the room.

The food was warmed through and she was dishing it out when footsteps entering the kitchen sounded behind her. 'Almost done. Poor devils, you must be ravenous. Here, give us a hand through with these plates, will you?' she asked, finally turning. Yet who she was met with wasn't one of her children at all, as she'd assumed it would be. Her mouth fell open to form a perfect O.

'Hello, Janie.'

'James?'

'I've come home.'

'James! Oh, my God! But *how* . . . ?'

'One of the lasses let me in.'

'I didn't hear the door go, I . . . Eeh, love!' Dumping the food on to the countertop, she grasped her husband to her in a crushing embrace. 'Thank you, Lord. *Thank* you.'

'Janie . . .' Pulling back, he rubbed a hand across his eyes, and for the first time she noticed the clear strain on his face. 'I'm all in.'

'You're all right—?'

'Aye. Just dog-tired. I think I'll go forra lie-down.'

Still dumbstruck from the shock of his arrival, she could only nod. She watched him leave the room, then she reached for the plates once more and carried them through to her children.

Sitting listening to their chatter, high in excitement that their father was back, Janie could barely process it. Was it true? Had James really just returned?

140

He'd come and gone again so quickly that it didn't feel real at all.

Her mind desperate to be put at ease, she went to fetch an empty cup and filled it with tea from the pot. Doing her best not to spill any in her haste, she hurried upstairs.

'James?'

Soft snores greeted her.

'James, love?'

Again, nothing. Creeping across, she placed the cup on the bedside table and stood staring at him through the gloom. He was still fully dressed in his uniform, she noticed. A slight frown was at his brow – leaning forward, she touched a feathery kiss to it, but it did nothing to smoothe out the creases. He looked dead to the world.

She ran her eyes over him again, in search of injury now, but could see none. Perhaps her night sight *had* been wrong after all? There was a first time for everything. Heart full to bursting, mind free from all other trials, she smiled down at him gently. Then she turned and padded from the room, closing the door quietly behind her.

When she climbed into bed beside him later that night, he didn't stir. Snuggling into his warm body, she soaked up his presence like arid soil in a downpour, and all was well once more.

Chapter 9

JANIE WAS HALFWAY out of bed before she realised the yells were not coming from one of the children's rooms at all, but from the man beside her.

'James? Love, what is it, what's wrong?'

'I'm all out! I'm all out!'

Rushing to light the lamp, she peered at him in horror-filled confusion. His face was putty-grey and slicked with sweat. Eyes squeezed closed, he thrashed his head from side to side on the damp pillow. 'James, it's all right. James—'

'No ammo! I'm all out! No ammo!'

'Love, please.' Emotion choking her throat, she shook him by the shoulders. 'It's a dream, just a dream.'

'Janie?'

'It's me. It's me, I'm here.'

'Janie . . .'

'Oh, lad.' Kneeling beside him on the mattress, she held him tightly, and he clung to her, shaking uncontrollably. 'Oh, my poor sweet love . . . What's happened to you?'

His voice was a whimper. 'Am I home?'

'Aye.'

'Am I really?'

'Yes, love. Sshhh, now, you're here.'

'Oh God. I'm . . . sorry, I . . .'

'It's all right. Everything's going to be all right.'

Encompassed in her arms, James drifted back into a deep sleep. Tears rolling down her cheeks, Janie remained where she was for an age, her hold on him sure and secure.

The following morning, she awoke beside him to find him watching her. His head resting on his arms, looking now calm and relaxed, there was a faint smile at his mouth. She returned it.

'Morning.'

'Morning,' he whispered back.

'How you feeling?'

'Better.'

'Cup of tea?'

'Aye.'

Janie slipped from the bed and donned her dressing gown. A last smile at her husband over her shoulder, then she headed downstairs.

It was early still; the children were all abed. After filling the kettle and placing it on the hob, she sat at the table in the quiet room. Her brain was a mush of thoughts. Last night . . .

Shaking her head, she covered her mouth with her hand. It had been as though James was back on the front line. He'd been screaming for ammunition, his mental being far from his home and bed, locked elsewhere, in unimaginable terror. Certainly, given its evident realism, he couldn't fail to remember that hellish dream. So why hadn't he made mention of it just now? More to the point, why hadn't she?

He'd seemed at peace, that's why; she hadn't wanted to ruin that. And James's own reasoning . . . ? Was he embarrassed? Did he prefer to pretend it hadn't occurred, to save face? Then surely she owed it to him to do likewise? Should he choose to discuss it if and when he felt ready, she'd be here for him. It was all she could do, wasn't it? Dear God, but it had hurt her, though, to see his mind turned so. She just prayed it didn't happen again.

'There you are, love,' she said minutes later, handing him his brew, her tone as natural as she could make it. 'So when did you arrive back in England, then? I've been beside myself with worry, you know. Lynn's husband's returned an' all, but he wrote to let her know, so she was prepared. You didn't half give me a shock last night, lad.'

'A nice shock, I hope?' he shot back.

She was taken aback by his tone. 'Aye, 'course. 'Course it were.'

'Sorry. You're right: I should have got word to you. I just . . . well. I thought I'd surprise you. Our boat reached the port of Dover last week.'

'And it's only yesterday that they issued you with a rail warrant to come home?'

He took a sip of his tea. 'Aye.'

'Eeh. All them wasted days.'

'Aye,' he murmured again.

144

'And how long . . . ?'

'Until I'm called back? Is that what you want to know?'

Biting her lip, she nodded.

'None of us can say. Five days. Mebbe a week. All we were told was to take leave and await further orders.'

'Love?' Covering his hand resting on the bedclothes with hers, Janie spoke carefully, softly. 'Are you sure you're all right? You're different somehow, like you've the worries of the world on your mind. You can talk to me. About owt. You know that, don't you?'

'I'm fine.'

'You're certain? Only you seem—'

'I said I'm fine, woman! Jesus! At least I would be if you'd only give that goddam gob of yours a rest for five minutes.'

'James—!'

'I'm going forra bath.'

Frozen with shock at his outburst, she could but watch as he leapt from the bed and marched from the room, slamming the door behind him. The bathroom door banged shut next, then all was still. In a daze, she rose and made her way downstairs.

'Is Dad all right?' Joey asked her from the table, glancing to the ceiling as she entered.

'Oh. I didn't hear you getting up. Aye, lad. Aye, he's fine.'

'Have you told him yet? Does he know about me and Stella—?'

'No. And keep your voice down,' she hissed, her

145

own gaze now swivelling upwards. Lord above, it was the last thing James needed just now. 'I'll tell him soon, in my own time. So don't you go mentioning it, d'you hear? You say nowt for now.'

The girls were full of questions about their father when they joined their brother for breakfast. Janie offered back brief responses as best she could, however her heart wasn't in it – her mind was elsewhere – and she was glad when they eventually left to collect their cardigans.

'See, Mam.' Pausing on the garden path, Elsie wiggled her arm about, face splitting in a wide smile. 'I told you it would be better when Dad got home.'

'So you did,' said Janie distractedly. 'Well, off you go, now. I'll see youse later.'

With the children packed off to work and school, she cleared the table and washed the dishes, as was her normal routine. But all the while, her thoughts remained stubbornly on her husband; in the end, she abandoned the chores and went to stand by the foot of the stairs.

He hadn't surfaced from the bathroom, and no sound trickled down to her. No faint splashes as he washed, no usual whistling of some cheery tune. The silence was unnaturally heavy. Foreboding, almost.

She was about to climb up to go to him when a rapping came at the front door behind her. Sighing, she turned to answer it.

'He's back, then? I've just passed the girls in t' street – cock-a-hoop they were, the pair. Eeh, you must be that relieved.'

146

Welcoming Lynn and the twins inside, Janie nodded.

'What's up?'

'Nowt,' she began, however there was no fooling her friend.

'No? Then why've you got a face on you like a slapped arse? Out with it, love.'

She shrugged. 'It's just, he's not hisself.'

'How so?'

'I don't rightly know. He's a bit . . . snappy, like.'

'Well, bloody hell, Janie, wouldn't we be? Imagine what the sorry sods have had to deal with these past weeks. It's enough to put the holiest of saints in foul spirits, I'm sure!'

'Your Duncan isn't, is he?'

'Well, no, but—'

'Anyroad, it's not just that,' Janie interjected, crossing to the teapot. 'Last night . . . God, it were terrible. He had this nightmare and . . .' She indicated to the woman to close the living-room door lest the man upstairs overheard, then in a lowered tone: 'The din when I came to . . . I thought one of the kiddies were having a bad dream, or that Hilda had took bad again. But no, it were James. Crying out summat awful, he were. I had to rock him back to sleep, Lynn. Fair broke my heart, it did.'

'Eeh, the poor bloke.'

'I'm just praying it were a one-off. What do you reckon?'

'I don't know, love. It's possible, aye. Have you spoke to him about it?'

147

'No, I didn't like to. He never said nowt about it, so I followed suit. I didn't want him feeling daft, you know?'

'Well, say no more. I know just the thing to put the spring back in his step and fetch a grin to his chops.'

'What's that then?'

'I'm going to organise a bit of a do for our returned heroes. Food, ale, a sing-song . . . It'll be just the ticket, aye, and they deserve nowt less. All the street shall be invited. Say . . . Friday? What d'you say?'

A smile stole across Janie's face. She nodded. 'I say let's do it. Mebbe that's just what James needs.'

'Right then! Leave everything to me. This will be the best bloody party this estate's ever known or I'm not Lynnette Mavis Ball. You'll see.'

Janie could have kissed her. Her thoughtfulness and all-round sunny view in the face of any crisis was like a breath of fresh air. She'd be well and truly lost without this lovely friend of hers. 'Ta, love.'

'I'd best be off to work. Have I to ask Sadie to mind the lads for me this morning, give you and James some peace?'

'Lord, and that's another thing . . . Speaking of her, you've just reminded me.' Janie closed her eyes.

'Oh, what now?'

'Stella Metcalfe turned up yesterday evening. That mam of hers has kicked her out – Mrs Hodgkiss is putting her up.'

'Hell's bells. Does James know?'

'He does not! What with everything else . . . I ain't found the right moment to tell him.'

Lynn's response was firm. 'Then try. It'll be nowt but added hassle for you should he discover the truth from someone else, love.'

'I know. I'll talk to him about it later, God help me. Now, you go on,' she insisted, smiling. 'Bobby and Brian will be just fine here with me. I'll see you in a few hours.'

Janie had settled the boys on the rug and was emptying out the small box of toys when she heard her husband descending the stairs. She hurried into the hall to meet him. 'All right?' she asked tentatively. 'How was your bath?'

'I'm off out.'

'Oh? Where?'

His back to her, he reached for his coat and shrugged it on. 'Thought I'd have a walk to the farm, see Dad.'

'But you've not even had a bite of breakfast yet, James. Let me make summat for you first and—'

'I'm not hungry. See you later.'

'James, please.' Clutching at his sleeve as he made to open the door, Janie gazed up at him imploringly. 'Won't you talk to me, lad? What's wrong?'

He stared at the ground for a moment and she held her breath, convinced he was about to open up to her. Then he lifted his head once more, and her heart sank – his expression was a mask of stone. He seemed to look straight through her.

'See you later,' he repeated, swinging around and leaving the house.

*

149

Refusing to show her upset for fear of worrying the youngsters, Janie put a brave face on things, and by the time Lynn returned from her morning shift to collect her children, she'd almost convinced herself that all was well. Determined to make the rest of the day a better one – and to draw a smile out of her husband, if it killed her – she said goodbye to her neighbour then set off for the shops with grim purpose.

Seymour had a warm greeting waiting for her, as usual. 'Afternoon, Mrs Hudson. You're well, I hope?'

'Afternoon, Mr Briggs. I am, ta, yes.'

'Good, good. The family are well?'

'They are.'

'And your husband? Lynn mentioned he was back from France.'

Busying herself at the tinned-food section so she didn't have to meet his eye, Janie nodded. 'He's gradely, aye.'

'I'm glad to hear it. Now, what can I get you?'

'James's favourite,' she told him with a smile, placing the corned beef on the countertop then pointing to the carrots.

'Corned-beef hash – that's my favourite, an' all.'

'Really, Mr Briggs.'

'Your husband has good taste, Mrs Hudson.'

Guessing what Lynn with her overactive imagination would have had to say had she been privy to the grocer's last statement, innocent as it might be, Janie felt her lips twitch. 'I suppose he has.'

'Here, take these – on me. Go on, I insist,' he pressed, reaching beneath the counter then pushing

150

across a small paper bag of dragees – chocolate- and sugar-coated almonds. 'Two quarters' worth there; them should cheer you up no end.'

'Why would you think I need cheering up?'

Her quiet query brought a cherry flush to his bewhiskered cheeks. He cleared his throat.

'Mr Briggs?'

'Forgive me. I didn't mean to pry. It's just that . . . well, you've a sadness about you in spite of your smile. I thought it would be a welcome gesture.'

'It is. Thank you.'

'You're sure all is well, Mrs Hudson?'

His kindness threatened to undo her resolve. 'It will be, God willing,' she murmured, voice thick. Then, her curiosity getting the better of her: 'Tell me, Mr Briggs. Why are you always so nice to me? The Woodbines for James, the wine, now these dragees . . . And I just know you add a little extra to my rations some days when you think no one is looking. Why?'

Seymour shrugged. 'All shopkeepers have their favourite customers, Mrs Hudson.'

'But why me?' she persisted. Not for one moment, not really deep down, did she hold with Lynn's claims that he had taken a shine to her, however there must be some reason for his attentions and she felt the need to find out.

'If you really must know . . . I'm not blind, Mrs Hudson. I see what the people think of me round here. A bumbling owd fool, and boring to boot.'

'Oh, I'm sure that's not true, Mr Briggs!'

'Not to everyone, mebbe, but the majority. But

151

you . . . you never have done – least, I don't think so. You're always amiable to me. And as the saying goes: one good turn deserves another.'

Janie felt wholly sorry for him. Not to mention ashamed – wasn't she in fact guilty of poking fun at him herself with Lynn, on more than one occasion?

'Mr Briggs . . .' Reaching forward, she patted his hand. 'I, for one, think you're a lovely man, and if others can't see that, then it's them what are the fools. 'Ere,' she added as the thought occurred, and wanting to prove that she meant it, 'there's to be a do in our street for James and Duncan Ball the day after tomorrow – Lynn's organising it. Why don't you come?'

'Aye?'

She nodded. 'I won't take no for an answer.'

'All right, Mrs Hudson. I'd like that very much.'

'Good. I'll see you there, then. Ta-ra for now.'

His face wreathed in a happy smile, he waved her off; returning it, she left the shop lighter of heart than she'd felt in weeks.

'I'm sorry, Janie.'

Busy peeling vegetables by the sink, she turned in surprise at the soft statement and the feel of arms around her waist. 'Eeh, lad. It's me what should be apologising. I ought to have been more mindful of what you'd been through—'

'No. No, love,' James told her, drawing her head towards his chest, upon which she rested her cheek. 'It's me what's in the wrong here. By, I don't deserve you.'

152

It was like a cloak of contentment had wrapped around her – Janie breathed in his scent with a blessed sigh. His walk had been all he'd needed to set him right, blow the troubles from his mind. 'Now that's daft talk. I'm the lucky one, aye.'

He glanced to the pan on the stove. 'Am I right in thinking you're making corned-beef hash?' he asked with a wink.

'That you are, and it shan't be long. Why don't you go and put your feet up with the paper whilst I get on? I'll fetch you through a nice cup of tea.'

James pressed his mouth to hers in a butterfly kiss, smiled, then headed off for his fireside chair. With a fuzzy feeling in her heart and warm smile of her own, Janie returned her attention to preparing the meal.

The evening went without a hitch. It was like the real James was here with them at last, and the whole house felt it. Laughter and high chatter filled their cosy rooms again and all was as it should be once more.

When the children had retired to their beds, Janie made a last pot of tea and went to sit beside her husband on the sofa. She'd turned the gaslight low, and its golden glow, coupled with the flames flickering in the hearth, added a close, romantic feel to the room. Tucking her legs beneath herself, she snuggled into James and closed her eyes. 'This is nice.'

'Aye.'

'It's been so long . . . I'm hungry for you, lad,' she whispered, brushing her lips across his neck, down towards the base of his throat. She felt him swallow

153

hard beneath her kiss, sending fire through her veins. 'Make love to me.'

'Janie . . .'

'Sshhh.' She took his hand and pressed it to her breast. He squeezed gently, his breathing quickening, and she threw back her head and arched her back.

'Please. I can't . . .'

'Don't stop now. Oh, don't stop now,' she begged, carrying his other hand beneath her skirt to the inferno there. 'Lad . . .'

'Do them things stuck either side of your head work at all, or are they just there for decoration?' With a harsh shove, he sent her sprawling against the sofa's arm. 'I said no, damn it!'

Completely stunned, fighting to hold back tears, Janie gazed at him in disbelief. 'What the hell . . . ? What is *wrong* with you?'

'You just . . . you don't *listen*—'

'No. Oh no, James. You're not putting the blame for this one on me. You were enjoying it, I know you were, same as me.' By now, her tears had escaped to cascade down her face. 'How am I meant to understand what's going on in that head of yours if you don't talk to me? I'm worried sick for you – for us.

'It's like a stranger came home from that beach, don't you see?' she went on. 'The last time you were home, compared to this . . . I just can't fathom it. No sweeping me off my feet, now. No tearing one another's clothes off on this very floor or nights out eating chips in the rain like love's young dream. Not even much chatting – and certainly no laughter to speak of. I'm lucky if you decide to toss a smile my way. I can't deal with it, lad. The not knowing . . . Just open up. *Talk.* Don't let's waste what little time we have together arguing, please!'

James had listened to her rant without interruption, his head in his hands. Now, when he lifted his face to look at her, his dark lashes glistened with tears. He opened and closed his mouth then scrunched tight his eyes. 'You deserve better than me. You all do.'

'No, we don't, and nor would we want to! James—'

'Please, Janie. Leave me be.'

'But, lad—!'

'*Please.*'

With a nod of defeat, she rose and crossed to the door. Before departing, she left him with one last thing – a final truth that she couldn't contain and which, no matter how much he tried to push her away, would always be so:

'I love you, James Hudson.'

As she ascended the stairs to bed, her husband's muffled crying was like hot blades in her ears and her heart.

Chapter 10

JANIE AWOKE TO see that James's side of the bed hadn't been slept in.

Tears threatened almost instantly, and loneliness gripped her like a physical thing, making her shiver. She made her way downstairs, expecting him to be curled up on the sofa where she'd left him, but the room was empty. Heaving a sigh, she headed for the kitchen to prepare the children's breakfasts.

He returned in the early evening, drawn-faced and fit to drop. Giving her no explanation as to his absence and with barely a word to anyone else, he disappeared upstairs soon afterwards and spent the next hour and a half holed up in the bathroom before escaping to their bedroom. Janie was nearing her wits' end.

'James, we have to talk,' she announced wearily when he finally joined her in the living room, long after their son and daughters had gone to bed. 'We can't go on like this. Summat's got to give.'

Arms folded, he peered into space in silence.

'Tell me what it was like out there. At Dunkirk. Make me understand.'

'You couldn't,' he murmured.

'Try me.'

He stared at her for a long moment. Then: 'Just drop it.'

'Please, love—'

'I'm warning you, Janie. Drop it, I said.'

'Who is this rude, angry, all-round unpleasant person that I'm looking at, at all? Because it sure as hell ain't my husband. By, but I miss him. Where's he gone, eh? No, please, don't go,' she added quickly when he sprang to his feet, intending to storm from the room. 'There's so much we need to discuss and . . . Joey's to be a father,' she blurted in her desperation.

It worked – James stopped dead in his tracks.

'*What?*'

She nodded to the back of his head. 'I've tried so many times to tell you. Coping with all this on my own . . . it's been torture.'

'The stupid young sod.'

'Aye.'

Lifting his face to the heavens, James shook his head.

'Joey, he . . . he intends to marry the lass when they reach sixteen.'

'There's nowt much else he *can* do, is there?'

'Wait! That's it?' asked Janie incredulously as her husband made to leave.

'What more is there to say?'

'I don't . . . For God's *sake*, James, you can't just walk away after learning summat like this—'

157

'I'm tired, Janie.'

'Aye, and so am I. *Sick* and friggin' tired, if you want to know the truth—!'

'I'm going to bed.'

Stunned, deflated and in utter despair, she watched him disappear without further argument.

She was still in turmoil the following morning when Lynn arrived with the twins. Taking one look at her, the woman shook her head sadly. 'What's troubling you, because I know there's summat – you look ruddy terrible.'

'Oh, love, where to start . . .'

Her neighbour listened with sympathetic tuts and head shakes as Janie spilled out details of recent developments concerning James.

'I just can't believe it, Lynn,' she wept quietly. 'He ain't never during the whole of our marriage laid a finger on me before. Gave me a right shove, he did; my back ain't half sore. He speaks to me like I'm a stranger, looks at me the same way too. He's not eating, barely sleeping . . . And I know he must be going through hell and that I'm being selfish for not doing more to understand, but oh . . . I just want him back.'

'Come here.' Lynn wrapped her in her arms. 'Eeh, you poor love.'

'D'you know the worst thing?' Janie choked against her friend's shoulder. 'It's the fact it's up and down. For short bursts, he's back, he's the man I married, and I'm nearly dying with happiness. Then his mood shifts just like that.' She clicked her fingers. 'And in his

158

place is this other one – nasty, shouting, unreachable – and it's just torture. It is. I'd rather he were horrible all the time than this. Least then I'd know where I stood. I wouldn't be praying for his good side to show itself again, all the while dreading that when it did it wouldn't last, that he could turn on me at any second. The unpredictability . . . it's exhausting.'

'I could ask my husband to have a word with him, talk things through? They went through it together, remember. If there's anyone able to understand, it's Duncan.'

'I don't think it'd do any good, love. Besides, James wouldn't be best pleased that I'd let on to youse – he's embarrassed, I can sense it. D'you know, his mind's that far removed that he barely batted an eyelid last night when I told him about our Joey and the babby.'

'He knows, then, aye?'

'Yes. He said he was a stupid young sod, and that was that. Can you fathom it, Lynn? A revelation like that? Trying to reach him, it's like knitting fog: friggin' impossible. I thought he'd have hit the roof for certain. The change in him . . . it's scary.'

They drew apart, Janie quickly scrubbing at her face as footsteps sounded on the stairs. She threw Lynn a beseeching look, and her friend gave her a 'don't worry, I'll not mention what we've been discussing' smile of reassurance.

'Morning,' James said quietly upon entering, glancing at the women in turn.

'And a lovely one it is, too,' Lynn trilled in her usual sunny fashion, as though nothing was amiss. 'Just look at that sky – the bonniest shade of baby blue you ever saw and not a cloud in sight. So, James. How are you, then?'

'All right, ta. And yourself?'

'Oh, gradely. I were just saying to Janie here, I'm that excited for the do later. We've picked a fine day for it, eh?'

He looked to his wife with a frown, and Janie closed her eyes. She'd forgotten all about that! 'It's just an idea that Lynn had,' she explained. 'She thought it would be nice to arrange a bit of a party in yours and Duncan's honour.'

'Janie ain't half been looking forward to it,' Lynn piped up. 'We all have.'

'Don't fret, though,' his wife hastened to assure him. 'If you're not in favour of it, we can always cancel—'

'No. Don't. It sounds like a good idea.'

'Aye?'

Nodding, James looked deep into her eyes with an expression of such gentle sincerity it took her breath away. She knew he was saying sorry for his previous behaviour, that he was desperate to make it up to her, and hope sparked. Smiling, she reached for his hand and squeezed. To her sheer relief, he returned both.

'Right then, I'll get on. There's much to be done. Eeh, it's going to be a grand day, this, you'll see.' Flashing a discreet wink to Janie, who mouthed a 'thank you' in return, Lynn waved to the twins on the rug and headed off for work. 'Ta-ra for now.'

160

'You're certain you're all right about this?' Janie asked her husband nervously when they were alone, half expecting him to explode into one of his fits of temper, but needing to be sure. ''Cause if you're not . . .'

'I'm so sorry, lass. It's not you, you know, all this . . . the disgusting way I've been treating you . . . None of it is you, none, could never be. I just . . . It's my head, you see. I don't know what . . . I'm sorry, Janie. I'm sorry.'

'Eeh, lad. It's all right. Eeh, come on, now. Come on.'

'I love you so bloody much, lass,' he told her, clinging to her tight, voice gruff with emotion. 'So bloody much.'

Her heart sang. 'And I you, James. Now and for always. We'll get through this together, I promise. We will.'

When eventually he pulled back, he was wearing an easy smile, appeared the most relaxed she'd seen him since his return. 'Any chance of a bite of breakfast, love? I'm ruddy ravenous.'

'Eeh, lad,' she repeated tearfully, drawing him towards her once more, couldn't help it. Could it be possible that she finally had him back?

Listening to him playing with Bobby and Brian as she prepared his food, his laughter like music, she allowed herself to dare to hope.

It seemed the rest of Padbury Way were just as much in need of forgetting their troubles for a few hours – they got into the party spirit with gusto. Wooden chairs were carried outside to line the pavements and

161

each household had contributed a plate of something towards the small buffet, which Lynn had spread out with care on a table outside her home. To wash the food down there were bottles of pale ale for the men, sherry for women who wanted it and tea for those who didn't, and fizzy Tizer pop for the children. All in all, it looked set to be a good knees-up.

James and Duncan, resplendent in full uniform, emerged into the street to a round of rapturous applause. The residents clambered to shake the soldiers' hands and pat them on the back, then Reuben Trent appeared with an ancient-looking violin and they all stamped their feet in time to the lively ditty.

'It's going great, in t' it, love?' Lynn said to Janie a little later as they sat in the warm sunshine. All around them, smiling adults sang and chatted whilst happy children ran about in high spirits. 'Your James looks to be enjoying hisself.'

He really did. Observing him talking animatedly with several other men nearby, Janie sighed in contentment. This was rapidly turning into a grand old day after all.

'Least the Metcalfe girl did the decent thing and stopped indoors.'

'Aye. I think Joey had a word in her ear for his dad's sake, lest it caused a ruckus.'

Lynn nodded. Then, squinting ahead, she rolled her eyes. 'Ey up, here comes owd Briggs. Gawd, which daft bugger invited that stuffy goat?'

'I did,' Janie told her, lifting her arm and giving the grocer a wave. 'Leave him be, he's all right.'

'If you say so. Oh, well, at least he's brought a few bottles with him,' Lynn added, her mood improving rapidly at the prospect of free alcohol. 'You're right, aye – the more the merrier!'

Her friend sauntered off with an overly broad smile to greet the grocer; grinning and shaking her head, Janie went to stand with her husband.

He looked so calm and comfortable – not to mention drop-dead gorgeous, Janie thought – that she found it a struggle not to grab hold of him and plant a great big kiss on his lips, in public or not! 'All right, love?' she murmured, linking her arm in his.

James ran a hand through his hair. 'I am. These people . . . they're a sound lot.'

'You're right there. It was the best thing we ever did, you know, moving to Top o' th' Brow.'

'I'm beginning to think you're right.' He smiled then nodded to where stood the beverages. 'D'you want a top-up, lass?'

'Aye, go on, why not?'

Across the road, Duncan had become the centre of attention. Regaling their neighbours with tales of Dunkirk, he had every man, woman and child hanging on his every word.

'Were you frightened, Mr Ball?' wanted to know an awe-struck youth, as though gazing on some semi-god.

'Pah! Norra bit, lad. Them Jerry kitty-cats can't compete against us lions. Running scared, they were, skriking like babbies for their mams.'

163

Imagining this, the children fell about guffawing.

Glancing around, Janie saw that James had noticed the swelling group, too. Taking slow sips of his drink, his eyes were locked on the storyteller in grim intensity.

'Picture the scene,' Duncan went on, lowering his tone for dramatic effect. 'Sand lifting and swirling around us in the coast winds so we could barely see a hand in front of our faces. Bullets whizzing about our ears without so much as a second's let-up. All the while, the skies burned red from a hundred fires, like a summer's day in hell. Well! "Duncan lad," I says to myself, "this ain't the same as playing football back in owd Blighty, now, is it?"'

The spellbound listeners blinked back at him in disbelief.

'Football?' a child finally asked.

'Aye! A half a French loaf makes for a good enough ball when you're short of the real thing. And bombs did a sound job of marking out the touch lines. Our team won – three–nil.'

'Football?' another youngster echoed, wide-eyed with incredulousness.

Duncan laughed. 'Aye, well. Them Germans weren't up to much – we grew bored. It's God's honest truth,' he insisted, holding up his hands.

Janie made her way over to her husband. She took his hand in hers and pressed it supportively, but he didn't break his gaze. Nor did he acknowledge her when she asked if he wanted to go home. *Blast it. Just as everything was going well, too.* Biting her lip, she lowered her head.

'What happened when the boats came, Mr Ball?' yet someone else wanted to know. 'Did you get seasick?'

'No, no. I've a sturdy stomach, me. It were another adventure in itself. There we were, just thinking how much we could do with a decent cup of English tea, when across the waters came the vessels. Ships of every description there were. Under enemy attack, we queued patiently for our turn to be picked up, but we felt no dejection or fear, not us. Then, in calm order, down the beach we marched and in full kit waded out to sea.' Raising both arms in imitation, he chuckled. 'Holding our cigarettes and rifles high, like this, we were, so not to get them wet. 'Course, they still did! Mind you, our skipper was a good sort and handed out fresh smokes once we were aboard, so no harm done.

'And so, we sets sail. But we hadn't gone very far when this big formation of Nazi bombers came out of nowhere.' At this, a collective gasp went up, and Duncan nodded. 'Oh aye. They were all for sinking our boat, but our RAF boys were ready to protect us – they swooped in and drove the swines off. Anti-aircraft guns from the decks of our warships took their turn next – and boom! They delivered a direct hit. A German plane tumbled from the sky, its shattered pieces flying in all directions, and crashed into the sea.'

Several boys thrust out their small arms and, mimicking aeroplane sounds, ran around in circles, making Duncan smile.

165

'Aye, have no fear, the enemy sustained much heavier losses. Magnificent, we were. The cooperation between us, the army, our RAF, navy and merchant navy was second to none in bringing the operation to a successful conclusion. It will never be forgotten!'

'Good owd Britain!'

'Indeed! Anyroad, where was I . . . ? Oh aye. Our trusty skipper produced a bottle of the finest whisky and us lads enjoyed a reet good jolly-up. Singing "Sailing Home for Dear Old England" loud and clear, we left Dunkirk behind us – but not before shooting the beach a last look. Still fighting mad, we all had the same promise in mind: we'll be back, Jerry. And that we will. The brave men of the BEF – unshaken, unbroken, unbeaten – withstood the full armoured might of Hitler. Next time . . . By! He won't know what's ruddy hit him.'

The crowd whooped and cheered in hearty agreement. Duncan, shoulders back and head high, had the biggest grin. The only people not wearing smiles were Janie and James. She peered up at her husband, and he finally turned to look at her. The haunted expression in his eyes was like nothing she'd seen before; she could have wept for him.

'Come on home, lad, will you?' she pleaded. 'We'll have a cup of tea and . . . rest awhile. What d'you say?'

To her sheer relief, James nodded. Hand in hand, they slipped away to number thirteen.

'All that out there, what Duncan were spouting . . .' said Janie after putting on the kettle then returning to sit beside James on the sofa. 'It were nowt more

166

than bravado for the kiddies' sakes, love, that's all. Don't take it to heart.'

'The way he was going on . . . It were like listening to a movie star discussing a role in his latest film. Like it was all make-believe. Some grand adventure. Filling them children's heads with rubbish. War ain't glamorous. *I* could tell them a few home truths, all right.'

'Tell me instead. Open up. Make me see, understand. Go on, lad.'

'It were all a ploy, this, today,' he murmured, as though he hadn't heard her. 'Her next door organised all this just to get me to stand and listen to that drivel from that husband of hers.'

'What? No, love.'

'They're both in it together.' Rocking back and forth, he spoke in a harsh whisper. 'It's been their plan from the start. They want to humiliate me.'

'No, you're wrong,' Janie insisted gently again, turning him around to face her. 'James . . . you're paranoid, love. They'd never—'

'You don't see them people ever again. Do you hear me?'

'But Lynn's my friend. They both are.'

'Not any more.'

Her rapidly mounting anger erupted. 'Just who d'you think you are, James Hudson, to tell me who I can and can't see?'

'Your husband, that's who! That's an end to it, Janie.'

'No! It bloody well isn't! You're wrong about them good people out there, and shall I tell you for why?

Because you've got a sickness in your head that you won't let out and it's warping your thinking. Dunkirk. What happened? Tell me, for the love of God!'

'That's what you want, is it?' he howled, leaping to his feet like a man possessed – Janie shrank back. 'You really want me to speak it? I tell you what, hows about I show you instead?'

She watched, frozen, as he dragged off his jacket then ripped the shirt from his back, sending buttons spraying across the floor. His vest followed next, then he straightened up and closed his eyes, his breathing ragged.

'Go on. Take a good hard look at what the glorious battle was really like.'

Walking around him slowly, Janie took in every inch of his naked torso through a blur of tears. She tried to speak, but not for the life of her could she get her mouth to form a single word.

'There's the sordid truth of it.'

Oh, my love . . .

His broad back was pitted with shrapnel wounds. Scabs had torn and cracked in places and encrusted blood clung to his skin in livid streaks – it was like something from a nightmare. Yet it was his upper left arm that held her attention and made her cry fresh tears of horror. The puncture here, thick-edged and circular in shape, was undeniable in its truth.

'You were shot.'

'So now you know. Makes for a pretty sight, eh?'

Her night sight . . . She'd been right all along. And so had Elsie, she realised now with terrible clarity.

168

James's injury was in the same position as that at which their daughter had claimed to feel an ache in *her* arm. *Dear Lord.* The child had been experiencing sympathy pains?

'This is why you weren't home sooner. You spent time in hospital, didn't you?'

'Aye.'

'Why in God's name didn't you tell me, James?'

'I didn't want you seeing me like this. *I* didn't want to be reminded . . . Don't you get it? This is just physical – it'll heal with time. The scars inside of my head, on the other hand . . . I worry they're here to stay, Janie, for ever. I just can't . . . I can't *cope* with it, I can't cope!'

'Sshhh. Come here, lad, come here! Eeh, my poor love.'

'I can still hear the shellfire,' he whispered brokenly. 'It's here, all the time; there's no let-up. I often feel I'll go mad.'

'You won't,' she told him fiercely. 'I shan't let you. Now you've let me in, it'll get better, you'll see. I'm going to do my utmost to help you, I promise.'

'Day and night we fought and slept on them gold sands. Each passing hour felt more like a year. Dead and dying lay scattered everywhere. So many . . . Eventually, filthy dirty, dying with thirst and sick with exhaustion, we staggered – a seemingly endless khaki procession – down to the water's edge. Us what could manage it, anyroad. The worst injured, screaming in agony, had to have their shattered bodies carried and dragged there. Anything that would move and float had been sent to fetch us home. We were hauled aboard an old craft and, packed together like sardines, limped off towards the Channel.

'Our boat left by starlight. As we were sailing off, I remember staring out across the beach at this long black mass – like giant seaweed, it looked, in the darkness. But no. It were the men still waiting their turn to be evacuated. And I knew that so many of them wouldn't ever get to leave. Not alive, at any rate. Even us lucky ones weren't out of the woods, mind. The vessels ran a gauntlet of bombs. Those what went up in smoke or sank left men floundering, terrified, in the dark waters. You'd see the lines of machine-gun fire throwing up white foam as they tried to pick the poor souls out, and many were riddled with bullets and past all help by the time they could be rescued.

'One fella on my craft . . .' Here, he paused with a shuddering breath, and Janie, who had listened to his outpouring thus far without interruption encouraged him gently to proceed, aware of how desperately he needed this outlet.

'Go on, love. Tell me.'

'This fella . . . he were real bad, Janie. We'd got to know each other a bit in France – a sound man, he were. One of the best. He were bleeding from his guts summat awful and I fashioned a bandage from his shirt, but it were soaked in no time. I felt so *use*less . . . All the way home, I stopped with him in the little galley whilst he slept, never left his side. And d'you know, he clung on. Right up to the point we were carrying him down the gangway, I thought he might make it. And then he beckoned to me to come closer. Folk had gathered on the quay to welcome us all back, and he had a smile on his face as he listened to their cheers. "I'm home," he whispered. Then he died in my arms.'

Janie had tears pouring down her cheeks. 'Eeh, lad.'

'A wife and seven kiddies he left behind. Where's the justice in that? Such a cruel and senseless waste.'

'I'm so sorry, James.'

'*That's* the reality. Not that fairy tale Duncan Ball told. He were right about one thing, mind: it won't ever be forgotten. No. Not by me, *never.*' He stabbed at his temple. 'It'll be in here 'til my own dying day.'

She held him for what felt like an age. When they drew apart, he appeared calmer, as though getting it off his chest at last had done him some good, just as she'd suspected it would. Despite her devastation for him and all he'd suffered, she couldn't hold back relief. Then he spoke again, and worry swamped her breast once more:

'You were right, you know, Janie. All along, you said I shouldn't join up. Why didn't I listen?' Tight-lipped, slit-eyed, he nodded. 'It's over, now.'

'James . . . what d'you mean?'

'I ain't going back.'

'But, love. It's not up to you, not now—'

'I can't. I won't. That's all there is to it.'

171

Chapter 11

FOR TWO EASE-FILLED days, James made a notable effort, from which the whole family benefitted. He took pains to enquire of his daughters how they were getting along at school and showed interest in their chatter of lessons and classmates. He proved attentive to his wife, was mild-tempered and jocular, and at night made love to her with all the fervour of old. He even sat Joey down and had a calm and thorough talk with him regarding Stella and the child. All in all, things were running smoothly. His mental state appeared vastly improved and relationships were all but healed once more. Janie couldn't have been happier.

Then came the day that each of them had been privately dreading, and which threw everything again into disarray. James received his summons to return to his unit, which was re-forming and re-equipping in readiness to face fresh engagements. He was to catch the early train tomorrow morning.

As he read aloud the words, his face visibly paled. He put down his toast slowly and released a long breath.

Her own breakfast forgotten, Janie groped along the tabletop for his hand. 'Dear God, not yet. We've only just got you back.'

'Aye,' was his only response.

Tuesday seemed to reach them in the blink of an eye. Word had circulated the evening before that Italy had declared war on Britain and France, evoking much anger, but none of that seemed to matter much now as, like some cruel nightmare on a loop, Janie found herself standing in the hall yet again, saying a heartrending goodbye to her husband.

'Don't come to see me off at the train station,' he begged her. 'The last experience of it . . . It was more than I could bear – worse still for you. I won't put you through that a second time.'

Though farewells at home instead would deprive her of some precious minutes in his company, she knew she must respect his wishes. She nodded reluctantly. 'All right, lad, if it's what you want.'

'It ain't what I *want*, Janie. None of it is. I don't want to go,' he finished on a soft whimper.

'Oh, love.'

'I want to stay here with my family.'

'We'd like nowt more than that, an' all. But, well . . .'

'Aye. I know.'

'God speed, James. You make sure to write, d'you hear?'

'Every day,' he vowed, holding her tighter as their bodies shook with the agony of parting.

She watched him walk away down the path and

through the small gate. Every fibre of her being screamed at her to run after him, but she didn't. She mustn't, for what would it achieve bar additional pain for them both?

Her husband paused in the street to blow her a final kiss, which she made a show of catching. Then he turned and continued on his way.

Janie returned inside and closed the door. Sinking on to the sofa, she wrapped her arms around herself and sobbed her broken heart out.

'We must be strong, love. It's all we have.'

Still locked in shock and despair at this latest separation, Janie stared into space without answering.

'Come on, drink your tea,' her neighbour pressed, nudging Janie's cup closer towards her. Duncan had left the previous day and so Lynn knew exactly what the other woman was going through. 'Moping never did anyone any good.'

'But your husband's morale was high, Lynn,' she pointed out miserably. 'James's weren't. I can't believe they've taken him from me again. He's seemed so detached from it all since first receiving the orders . . . I knew, though, that he didn't want to return. He ain't ready. He'll not cope, he'll not, I just know it.'

'He must. There's no other choice, love.'

However, Janie wasn't convinced. And when, days later, a harsh rapping at the door revealed two grim-faced officers of the military police, she knew her concerns hadn't been unfounded.

'Mrs Hudson?'

174

Struggling to scatter the sleep fog from her mind – dawn had barely broken over the grey rooftops – she stood blinking at them for several moments in confused silence. 'Aye?'

'May we speak with you?'

'About what?'

They glanced at one another then back to her. 'Perhaps it would be best if we discussed the matter inside, Mrs Hudson.'

An icy shiver ran down her spine. Nodding, she stepped aside.

'Well?' she forced herself to ask when they were standing in the living room. 'Surely you're not here with bad news about my James? He can't be abroad again so soon, can't have been wounded or . . . worse. Can he? Besides, a telegram would have arrived to inform me of such, were that the case, not youse. Ain't that right?'

'Quite.'

'Then what?'

'I'm afraid your husband has failed to return to his unit, Mrs Hudson. Inasmuch, he has been reported as being AWOL.'

'What?' Dropping unceremoniously into a chair, Janie shook her head. 'But that can't be. I watched him leave with my own two eyes.'

'When was this?'

'Tuesday morning last. I saw him off here, outside this very house.'

The men conversed together in hushed tones then turned their attention back to her. 'It has been

175

assumed that some orders may not have reached their destinations – due to, say, a fault with the postal service – as a small number of soldiers have failed to appear for duty. However, if what you state is correct, that your husband did indeed receive his—'

'Aye,' she cut in quietly as the terrible realisation began to register. 'He did.'

'Then I'm afraid his absence must be construed as wilful desertion.'

'Dear God, no.' She dropped her head in her hands.

'May we conduct a search of the property, Mrs Hudson?'

'But I've just explained, he ain't here.' Then, seeing they wouldn't be dissuaded: 'Oh, look about if you must,' she relented, shrugging in defeat. She felt so incredibly tired of it all. 'I've nowt to hide.'

'Thank you.'

After a thorough search of the downstairs area and back garden, they moved towards the hall. Here, Janie put her foot down:

''Ere, hang on. I've kiddies fast asleep up there,' she told them, moving to block their path. 'You'll scare the poor mites half to death barging into their bedrooms like that. Let me go in front in case they waken, warn them what's occurring.'

To their credit, the men showed understanding and obliged her with a nod. Murmuring her thanks, she led the way upstairs.

'I told you I were telling the truth. He ain't here.'

Having shone their torches into wardrobes, beneath beds and in seemingly every other nook and

176

cranny they could find, including the attic – and, incredibly, without disturbing any of the children – the officers returned with Janie to the living room.

'Can you think where he might be? Anyone else he may have gone to?'

'No, no one.'

'You're certain?'

'Aye. Please, tell me . . . what will become of him?'

'That depends entirely upon Mr Hudson himself. If he has any sense, he'll surrender himself into our custody. The longer he remains missing, the worse it will be for him.'

Christ Almighty, James, what have you done?

'Should he return here or attempt to make contact in any way, you must report it to us immediately. Mrs Hudson, I cannot stress that enough. This is a very serious matter indeed, as I'm sure you'll appreciate.'

'Aye,' she whispered.

When they had gone, Janie paced the floor for several minutes then made herself a pot of tea. She poured herself a cup, lifted it midway to her lips then put it back down. Rising once more, she resumed her senseless treading back and forth. The next thing she became aware of, she was standing outside her neighbour's door. Surprised, she stared at it for a moment. Then she was knocking furiously, her whole body beginning to tremble whilst blind panic crushed her chest: 'Lynn! Lynn!'

'Janie?'

'Oh, love. You'll never believe . . . !'

'Eeh, what's to do?'

Supporting her by the shoulders, Lynn guided her back to her house and lowered her into a chair. Dazed, she offered no protest.

'Tea. Good. Here.'

Janie accepted the cup that her friend placed in her hands and sipped slowly.

'That's it, love. Take your time, it's good for the nerves. All right?' she asked finally when Janie had drained it and was breathing a little easier.

'Yes. No. James has deserted.'

'He never has!'

'What am I going to do?'

For once, Lynn was lost for words. Wide-eyed, she shook her head, stunned.

'The police, they're saying he never arrived. They reckon he's done a runner. He threatened this, you know.' She nodded. 'He told me he couldn't go back. Then he got his orders and he seemed to sort of accept it. He never mentioned again not returning. I dismissed it. I thought it had been just talk, you know? And now he's gone and done it. Where can he be? Just where the hell *is* he?'

'How about that father of his? Happen he's gone there?'

'Albie. Of *course.*'

'Go on, love, go and find out. I'll stop on here and see to the children's breakfasts, get Hilda and Elsie off to school for you.'

'You're sure?'

'Aye, 'course. I'll just fetch in the twins from mine, won't be a tick.'

By the time Janie had hurried up to dress and returned downstairs, Lynn was back and had settled her sleeping sons on the sofa.

'Wish me luck.'

'I've got everything crossed for you, love!'

Heart thudding in desperate anticipation, she donned her coat and hurried from the house.

After knocking and receiving no reply, Janie crossed the farmyard and made towards the stables. Sure enough, she found her father-in-law busy with shovel and straw mucking out one of the stalls.

'Morning, Albie.'

'Janie? What brings you here?'

His reaction told her all she needed to know. There wasn't a trace of answerability or even awareness, thinly veiled or otherwise, in his gaze or voice. Only open surprise. Her spirits plummeted to her toes. 'Oh, *God.*'

'Lass? Summat's wrong, in t' it?'

'Aye.'

'What? James?'

She nodded.

His Adam's apple bobbed in a thick swallow. He breathed deeply. Without another word, he cupped her elbow and led her across the cobbles.

Once inside the house, Janie inclined her head towards the chairs positioned around the large pine-wood table in the centre of the kitchen. 'You're going to need to sit down for this, Albie.'

His creased eyes never leaving hers, he obeyed with no hesitation. He waited until she'd taken a seat too then, finally, he spoke. His voice was like dry leaves. 'Tell me.'

'James . . . I don't know where he is. He's failed to return to his unit.'

The old man's eyes bulged then drew together into thin slits. 'He's AWOL?'

'Aye.'

'My son?'

'Aye, but Albie, things have happened. Things you know nowt about. James, he hasn't been well, you see, and—'

'Hasn't been well? In what way?'

'Shell shock, battle fatigue – call it what you will. He's suffered bad, is still doing. The horror of war was too much for him to handle. He broke under the strain.'

'Are you telling me he's had a mental collapse?' Utter disgust dripped from every word. 'My own flesh and blood's gone yellow?'

Janie was livid. 'Don't you ever call him that, d'you hear? That poor man of mine has been to hell and back! Faced with the threat of death every second of the day and night, is it any wonder his mind is wounded as well as his body? It would surely drive anyone to their limits of sanity.'

'Not me. Nor any other Hudson male what's served his country, for that matter. *I* didn't turn tail and run from the Germans during the last lot, did I? Neither did my father flee from the enemy during the Boer War – nor *his* father in the Crimean War before him, I'll be bound. James is nobbut a ruddy coward!'

'I always knew you were a hard-nosed bugger, Albert Hudson, but this takes the biscuit. This is your own child you're talking of. Ain't you even the slightest bit concerned for his welfare? Where he could be? How he's been sleeping, eating, these days past? Owt could have happened, the way his mind's at. You'd best start praying you don't have cause to regret what you've just said.'

'The only thing I regret is that the law was changed ten years ago outlawing the military death penalty for desertion!' he blasted out, fists clenched.

'You're actually saying that your own son ought to be sentenced to death?' Janie probed in a whisper, completely aghast.

'Sniffed out, tried by court martial and executed for cowardice, aye! Make an example of him!'

'I'm not buying it, Albie. I don't believe you mean that, not truly. Not deep down.'

For the briefest moment, a flicker of self-doubt appeared in the old man's eyes. Then he puffed out his chest and lifted his chin. 'I do, as it goes. King and country expect soldiers to fight to their last. They must face it like men. It's the only way for good to triumph over evil. Shirking one's duty can't ever be condoned nor tolerated. Who's to say that every fella wouldn't try his luck, fake combat exhaustion to get out of it, unless there were clear and dire consequences? Disaster – sheer *anarchy* – would reign. Then where would the British army, the British people, be? For all we know, that's what James could be trying here, because he hasn't the spine for owt else.'

181

'You're wrong. My husband's norra traitor, he's a victim. I've seen with my own two eyes what this war has done to him. Time and understanding are what he needs, for God's sake, not threatening with a firing squad. He was winning, was fighting back against the blackness in his mind. That's courage, not cowardice. You, you're just barbaric. And to top it all, it's you what bullied him into joining up in the first place! He only went along with it to please you, I'm sure. I just . . . I can't believe this you're saying, now. I'd never have expected such downright cruelty – not even from you. I'm appalled, aye. Appalled and ashamed to know you, and I'll not be in your company a second longer. I'm off.'

'You'd best start saying your prayers that he ain't daft enough to turn up here, that's all I can say!' Albie yelled after her as she stormed out of the house and across the yard. 'He'll regret it, Janie, if he does! I'll shop him to the authorities! I will!'

She wouldn't cry, refused to. With a last withering look over her shoulder, she held her head high instead and continued for home. All the while, one thought dominated all the rest: is that what everyone else would believe, too? That James was weak, soft? But it wasn't true! He was the bravest man she knew. He was ill, nothing more. Blast them all! *Oh, love, where are you?*

'Please, Lord, send him home,' she mouthed to the white clouds, her heart physically hurting like nothing before. 'He needs me – and I need him. Eeh, I do.'

'Mam?'

Preoccupied with her crippling ruminations, she didn't see Joey until they were almost abreast with one another. 'Lad. What are you doing here?'

'I'm on my way to the farm, of course, same as I do every morning.'

'Oh. Aye.'

'What are *you* doing here, Mam? Lynn were vague when we asked where you'd got to.'

She had to tell him, couldn't keep back from him something of this magnitude. 'I've been to see Albie. Joey . . .'

'Mam, are you all right? What's happened?'

'Come on.' Taking his arm, she steered him around. 'You'll give work a miss today. I need to talk to you.'

'But Grandad—'

'He'll manage well enough without you for one day, I'm sure,' she shot back, her anger resurfacing at the mention of the man she'd just left. 'This is more important.'

'Lynn left for work as I were setting off for the farm – the twins are with Mrs Hodgkiss,' Joey explained when they were nearing Padbury Way. 'She said she'd leave the door on t' sneck for you in case you didn't have your key.'

Nodding, Janie hurried him along. Once inside, she made straight for the kitchen and put the kettle on for tea – always guaranteed to calm her nerves. By God, did she need that right now.

'The thing is, lad,' she began when they were

183

sitting at the table with their drinks. 'Your dad, he . . . Summat's happened . . . Oh, this is so hard,' she added, running a hand over her tired eyes. After the confrontation with Albie and his devastating reaction, which had shocked her to the core, she couldn't be certain now how her son would react. 'You see, he . . .'

'He's been killed, ain't he?'

'No. No, love. Nowt as bad as that. He's gone AWOL.'

Sitting back in his chair, her son let out air slowly. 'Well, I weren't expecting you to say that. Have you heard from him? Do you know where he is?'

Janie shook her head. 'Not a dicky bird, and I'm worried sick. Your grandad weren't exactly helpful. In fact, he were downright disgusting. Your dad's been ill, lad. Surely you must have noticed he weren't hisself? Albie just can't, or doesn't want to, see it. It's help James needed, and now . . . I just wish I knew where he was!'

'He was different whilst he were home, weren't he?'

'He's suffering with a bit of shell shock, I reckon. I tried to shield you and the girls from the worst of it, didn't want you fretting. When he insisted we should say our goodbyes here at home, I thought it were 'cause he wanted to spare us both a drawn-out and more painful farewell. Now I know it was because he had no intention of catching that train at all. He must have been planning it, yet didn't utter a word. The poor love must have been so scared . . . I just never thought he'd do this.'

Joey reached for his mother's hand. 'Dad will be all right. He'll be lying low forra while, that's all. He'll get in touch with us when he's ready, Mam. The thing is . . .'

'What, lad?'

'Well, what's to be done in t' meantime? How will we manage – with money, I mean? They'll stop his army pay, and your allotment with it, won't they, whilst he's missing? Sorry, I know it sounds heartless mentioning it when Dad's not well – his health matters more, 'course it does – but, Mam, it needs thinking on.'

Gazing at her boy, Janie saw him in this instant for the mature and practical grown-up he was quickly turning into. Pride coursed through her. 'Don't apologise for pointing out the truth. You're right, aye. I hadn't even wondered over that.' She shrugged. 'We just get on with it and manage best we can. It's all we can do. I just need to know he's all right. Right now, that's all what matters.'

'You reckon he's kipping rough someplace?'

'Aye, he must be. I can think of nowhere else bar your grandad's that he could have gone to – and Albie's adamant he's not been near the farm.'

For a few minutes, they were silent with their own ruminations. Then Joey was speaking again and his words sent Janie's blood running cold:

'You don't think Dad would do owt . . . daft . . . Do you, Mam?'

'You mean . . . ? No. No, James would never . . .' she began firmly, and yet doubt had been planted that refused to be shaken. Indescribable terror seized her.

Her husband's mind wasn't his own, was it? Did James have it in him to cause himself harm? Do away with himself? She'd never have given the notion even a second's wondering at any other time; but at present, given his state of mind of late . . . *Please God, no!*

'I'm frightened, Mam.'

Since the day her children were born, she'd endeavoured to do her utmost to buffer them from life's trials and worries – and this she'd always done. Now, however, with this, she found that she couldn't. Her own blinding fear was much too strong to try to attempt it.

Tightening her fingers around his for strength, she nodded. 'Me too, son. Me too.'

When later that day Joey donned his jacket and left the house, Janie assumed he was going to see Stella. He hadn't returned by the time she was ready to dish out the evening meal, and so she sent Hilda to go and knock for him at Mrs Hodgkiss's home – only to discover they hadn't seen him; he hadn't been there at all.

Rain had fallen steadily for hours and the summer sky had long since lost its light when he finally arrived back, tired, cold and soaked to the skin. Needing to feel useful, he'd been out scouring the local forests and fields, he informed Janie. But of his father, there had been no sign.

All options now well and truly exhausted, they sat up throughout the long night in the hope he'd return of his own free will.

He didn't.

It seemed James had vanished like smoke into thin air.

Chapter 12

ANOTHER DAY PASSED, bringing with it the bomb-
shell that Paris had fallen to the Germans – though
Janie barely acknowledged this blow to the Allied
cause with more than a passing sigh, given her private
troubles – then two days, and still there was no word
of James. Then, as she was having a last cigarette at
the back door before bed, Janie spotted a shape flit-
ting across the school field beyond her garden fence.

Her breath caught in her throat. Rushing forward,
she squinted through the wooden slats, but the darkness was too dense. Then a rustle sounded from the
thin undergrowth to her left – gasping, hardly dar-
ing to hope, she whispered out her husband's name.

No response.

She waited a moment then repeated it, this time
adding, 'It's me. Please, love. You can trust me.'

'Janie?'

'Oh, James! It is you!' Scrambling closer, she put
her arm through the fence to him. A familiar hand
wrapped around her searching fingers and she swallowed back a euphoric cry. 'Eeh, my love!'

'Janie. I'm sorry . . .'

'Sshhh. All that can wait. Come on, lad, come indoors. No, not the street way,' she added when he made to turn. 'Scale the fence here, lest someone sees. Quickly now.'

For a long moment, he didn't move, and she thought he'd had a change of heart and would turn tail and run. Then, to her sheer relief, he took hold of the fence.

He pulled himself up, swung his legs over the top and dropped into the garden beside her. Gazing up into his face, Janie allowed herself a tear or two. Then, grasping his arm, she shepherded him across the grass and into the house.

'Lock the door.'

James did as she bid whilst she hurried to put a shovelful of coal on the dying fire. He allowed her to guide him to the hearthside chair, then she was off again: this time to pour him a cup of hot tea and fetch the loaf from the larder.

She knelt in front of him and in silence watched him eat and drink as the heat from the growing flames thawed his shivering body. When, finally, he passed her his empty cup then sank back into the seat's cushions, closing his eyes, she reached for his hand.

'All right?'

'Aye.'

'I'm not angry, James.'

Turning his head from her, he buried his face into his shoulder. 'I'm so sorry, lass.'

'Don't be. None of that matters, now. I'm just glad you're well.'

'I couldn't do it. I can't go back.'

'I know.'

'What am I going to do?'

'We,' she murmured. 'You'll never be alone again, not in this. Not in owt. *We* will find a way, lad. Together, all right? Yes?' she pressed when he didn't respond. 'Say it. You must, I have to hear it.'

'Yes.'

'Promise me.'

'But it's hopeless, though. It is, it—'

'Promise me, James.'

He dragged out a weary sigh. 'I promise.'

'Do you mean it?'

Though his words were flat, he didn't hesitate this time: 'Aye. Aye, Janie.'

'Good. Now, come with me and get yourself out of them filthy clothes. I'll draw you a bath.'

'Why are you being so calm?' he asked her later as she sat on the edge of the tub washing his back with a flannel, every stroke filled with love.

'I told you. I'm just relieved you're all right.'

'You ought to be furious with me after what I've done. I'd not blame you.'

'Well, I'm not.' She meant it wholeheartedly. 'You're home now, and that's all what matters.'

'I saw him, you know. Earlier, the lad. I saw him.'

Janie paused to look at his face. 'You mean Joey?'

'He was looking for me.'

'Aye.'

'I spotted him coming across the woods and I hid in some trees. Calling my name, he were, and I ignored him. I felt terrible about that, still do.'

'Don't fret on that now. What's done is done.'

'I couldn't . . . I didn't want to be found.'

'I understand, and he will too. Put it from your mind.'

They had been conversing in hushed tones so not to disturb the children – now, James's voice rose. 'But I can't, don't you see?'

'Quiet, love, you'll waken the kiddies—'

'No, I must say it. I *must* try to get this through to you. I can't stop here. It's impossible. I shouldn't ever have come tonight; what the hell was I thinking? I can't . . . I'm sorry.'

She watched with increasing concern as he rose abruptly and climbed from the bath. He secured a towel around his waist and left the bathroom – frowning, she followed him back downstairs.

When she entered the living room, she found him perched on the edge of the sofa with his head in his hands and went to sit beside him. 'James, what are you saying?'

'I'll not fetch trouble to this door, Janie. They'll not rest, the police. You can bet your life on it. They shan't 'til they've got me, and I can't drag you and the kiddies through that. I won't. This is my mess. I ran. *I've* created it, and I must deal with it on my own. I have to go.'

'Sit the frig down.'

She delivered the order with such force that James, having half risen, paused to glance at her in surprise.

'I said sit, damn it!'

Wordlessly, he did. Nodding, Janie continued.

'Now you listen to me, and listen good. You are going nowhere. No ifs or buts, no more excuses, you're stopping put and that's that. This is where you belong, with us at home. We'd not have it any other way.'

'Janie, I'm a wanted man. I've deserted my unit in the middle of a war. They ain't going to let this drop, for God's sake.'

'We'll make it work somehow.'

'What? And how the devil do you suppose we do that? No, lass, I'm done for.'

'Only if they find you,' she murmured with grim focus. Her eyes were like steel. 'And that they shan't do, not if I've owt to do with it.'

Now, it was his turn to ask: 'What are you saying?'

'I'm saying that we work together on this, all of us. That you're not going back to no bloody battle. Nothing and no one's taking you away again.' She took a determined breath. 'I'm saying we're for hiding you, lad. Here, at home.'

'But—'

'But what?' shot back his wife, hands on hips.

'This is madness.'

'Aye, but desperate times call for desperate measures.'

'I won't put you through this! I won't!'

192

'I'm afraid you ain't gorra say in it, love. We're a family, and families stick together.'

'We, we can't . . . Janie, it'd never work.'

'Happen it will, happen it won't. By, but we're going to give it a damn good try.'

The fight seemed to drain from him in a rapid gush. He dropped back into the sofa, head bowed.

She drew him against her in a swift hug then folded her arms with renewed purpose. 'Right, come on, lad, shake yourself! I'm going to need your help.'

'What d'you want me to do?'

'First things first: nip upstairs and fetch your tools,' she instructed. 'I've got an idea.'

When the children arrived downstairs for breakfast a little later and saw their father sitting drinking a cup of tea at the table, their faces were a picture. Squealing in delight, the girls ran to throw their arms around him, and he hugged them back with just as much fervour.

'Eeh, I've missed you, my lasses.'

'Are you home for ever, now, Dad?' asked Elsie, hopping excitedly from foot to foot.

Sharing a look with her husband, Janie answered for him. 'Well, you see, love, the army has decided to let your dad have a bit of a holiday at home as a special treat. Ain't that nice? The thing is, all t' other soldiers might get jealous if they find out, so we have to try and keep it hush-hush. All right?'

Their youngest daughter nodded readily. Though Hilda's expression was one of mild bemusement, she did the same. Only Joey, who had juddered to a halt in the doorway upon setting eyes on James and remained there still, didn't respond. He was staring at the floor in silence.

'Remember, not a word,' Janie reiterated as lightly as she could manage, as though it was all some fun and harmless game, when the girls were about to leave for school. To attempt to conceal James's return would have been impossible, and to reveal to them at such tender ages that this was in fact a dangerous secret would have been unwise. The pressure on them would have been immense. To her mind, this was surely the safer option all round. 'Not to your teachers – not even your friends. You promise?'

'Can't I tell even my bestest friend, Mam?' begged Elsie. 'She'd not say nowt, honest she wouldn't—'

'No, lass. You mustn't let on to no one. No one at all,' Janie insisted, trying her best to smile, despite the worry coiling her guts, and was relieved when the child gave a reluctant nod. 'That's a good girl. Go on, now, off to school. I'll see youse both later.'

Alone now with Joey, the adults sat facing him in uneasy silence and waited for him to speak. He'd uttered not a word throughout the meal, and each was somewhat dreading learning his reaction. There was no pulling the wool over his eyes, no fobbing him off with some cock-and-bull tale as they had his sisters, after all. He knew exactly what was playing out here.

Joey continued slowly stirring his porridge as though in a world of his own; finally, Janie could bear it no longer. 'Well, lad? Ain't you going to say owt?'

194

'What do you *want* me to say?'

'You know what we're about, don't you? What we plan to do?'

He pushed away his bowl and nodded.

'So . . . ? Do we have your cooperation?'

'You mean will I help with keeping Dad hidden?'

Her husband lowered his chin, his shame painfully clear, and Janie reached for his hand. 'That's right,' she told her son. 'We'll not lose him. He ain't ever going back.'

'But should the police come back . . . ? What then?'

'I've thought of all that. Here, come here.' She rose and crossed towards the sideboard. Frowning, her son followed, and she motioned to him to grab hold of one end of the dark wood furniture whilst she gripped the other. 'Right, pull,' she said. 'Gently now, that's it.'

Joey's surprise when the item glided across the floor effortlessly was plain to see. He dropped to his knees to inspect its underside. 'You've added castor wheels to the bottom.'

'They're from that little table in my bedroom. They make shifting this a lot easier – not to mention quicker – don't they?'

'But why . . . ?'

'Look.' She pointed to the space where the sideboard had recently been standing. 'See the bare boards?'

'The oilcloth's been cut away.'

'And I'll show you for why.'

Her son watched with increasing interest as, with the aid of a screwdriver, she prised up the corners of

195

several pre-loosened floorboards and lifted them out, exposing the roomy void beneath. When eventually he raised his head to look at her, there was a definite glimmer of belief in his stare. 'Dad's to hunker down under the floorboards?'

'Aye. Should the authorities come knocking, he can be down there and everything put back in less than half a minute. We tested it out last night. Nowt looks out of place if done right, so there's no reason why anyone would suspect or ever think to search there.'

'I hate this.'

At the tortured statement, Janie and Joey swivelled around to look at the man in question.

'This isn't right. I shouldn't *be* here.'

'Yes, you should. This is your home,' Janie insisted fiercely. Then, turning to her son with pleading in her gaze, knowing James needed his reassurance too: 'That's right, in t' it, lad?'

Joey glanced from the makeshift bunker and back to his father. Then he crossed the room to stand before him. 'Aye,' he said quietly, placing a hand on James's shoulder. 'Ain't no one taking you away, Dad.'

'Eeh, lad,' he choked back.

With tears in her eyes, Janie gave Joey a nod of gratitude, which he acknowledged with a small smile. However, their demeanours soon changed when, moments later, the slamming of the front door rattled through the house.

Frozen in shared horror, they hadn't time to either

196

move or speak, could only watch as their visitor breezed into the room.

'Morning, all— Oh!' Their neighbour stopped dead in her tracks.

'How did you get in?' Janie demanded.

'The door was open. The girls mustn't have shut it proper when they left.' Turning her attention to James, Lynn smiled. 'Eeh, hello, lad. You're a sight for sore eyes.'

'Hello, Lynn,' he murmured, visibly cringing.

'Come on, time you left for work,' Janie intervened as an awkward silence took hold, shooing Joey to the hall. 'And norra word to the owd 'un,' she warned as he took his leave. The prospect of Albie getting wind of James's return didn't bear thinking about, blast him. 'He's not to know nowt, all right?'

'Aye, Mam.'

Satisfied, she returned to the living room to find that James had taken himself off to the kitchen – and that Lynn was eagerly waiting to put to her some pressing questions:

'He's back? What's going on? How did it happen, and when?'

'Not here,' she told her quietly. 'Hang on whilst I ask James if he'll keep an eye to the twins. I'll walk to the shops with you and we can talk on the way. Don't worry, I'll warn him not to open the door to no one whilst I'm out.'

'Well?' Lynn asked minutes later when she and her friend emerged into the street. 'Spit it out, love, the suspense is killing me.'

'As you can see, he's back. Glory be to God. I spotted him on t' school field last night and persuaded him to come home.'

'You mean . . . ?'

Biting her lip, Janie nodded. 'They ain't having him again, he's stopping put. We're . . . we're for hiding him at ours.'

'By 'eck, Janie.' Lynn released a shaky breath. 'Where? Just how will you manage it?'

'I don't know.' Now, for the first time, she didn't feel quite so strong. Saying it out loud to her friend had brought about a definite nag of doubt – her confidence in her plan began to wane. She halted to take some deep breaths. 'I've promised him. I didn't know what else to do, I . . . I'll not let him go, Lynn, I'll not!'

'Eeh, what a mess.'

'Aye.'

Linking her arm through Janie's and leading them on once more, Lynn sighed. 'I understand, I do.'

'You mean you're not angry? I thought mebbe . . . I were worried you might disapprove, fall out with us even. I didn't want you or anyone else knowing.'

'Ay, come on, love.' Drawing her to a standstill, she stared her straight in the eye. 'Did you really believe that of me? I thought you knew me better by now. You're my friend for life, aye, through thick and thin. I'd support you in owt. Anyroad, I don't blame you at all. Were it my Duncan, I'd be of the same mind as you.'

'You really mean it?'

Lynn nodded. 'I'd do anything to have him home – legal or otherwise. More so if he were unwell like James is, poor sod. Don't fret, girl. I reckon you're doing the right thing.'

'It ain't going to be easy, though, Lynn, is it?'

'No. Then again, nowt worth doing ever is.'

Feeling slightly brighter, Janie gave her a thankful smile. 'I suppose not, love, no. What would I do without you, eh?'

Lynn held a hand to her brow theatrically, announcing in mock horror, 'Ooh, perish the thought! Now, come on, let's get a wriggle on before I'm late, or owd Seymour will be having ruddy kittens.'

They arrived at the grocer's just in time to spot Mr Briggs affixing a small card in the shop window. He disappeared to return to his duties and the women made their way over to inspect it.

'It can't be an advertisement for a new assistant, can it, love? I'm not for losing my job, am I?' a worried Lynn asked, biting her lip.

'Hang on, let me look. No, see, it's not that,' Janie reassured her, pointing at the writing. 'It says "Cleaner wanted", that's all.'

'Oh, thank God for that.' Lynn placed a hand on her chest. 'I thought happen I'd pushed him too far at last and he'd decided to give me the shove!'

But Janie had stopped listening, was too preoccupied with the notice still to offer a response. Her own heart beginning to drum in excitement, she hurried on ahead into the shop.

'Morning, Mrs Hudson.'

'Morning, Mr Briggs.' Janie gave him her most winning smile. 'The sign you've just stuck up on the pane, there . . . "Cleaner wanted", it says.'

'That's right.'

'For here in the grocer's, is it?'

'My home, actually. I normally have a woman what comes in regular to see to its upkeep, but she's away to Preston at the week's end to live with her daughter.'

'Oh, I see. Well . . . d'you think I could be considered for the position?'

The man raised his eyebrows in surprise. 'You?'

'Aye, why not?'

'But don't you have your hands full of a daytime, minding Lynn's lads?'

She smiled again in relief, thought for a moment he was about to dismiss her idea outright. 'Oh yes, but that'll be no hardship. I could fetch Bobby and Brian along with me. They'd be no trouble.'

'Well, I suppose . . .'

'I'd do a good job, Mr Briggs. I won't let you down.'

'I don't doubt that forra minute.' His own face stretched in a pleased expression. 'All right, Mrs Hudson, aye. I'd be only too happy to offer you the job.'

'Eeh, Mr Briggs.' Janie could have punched the air in satisfaction. With James now minus his army pay, she'd fretted how they would manage. This extra income could well be the answer to her prayers. 'When would you like me to start?'

'Say . . . tomorrow morning? Pop into the shop here and I'll have the keys ready and waiting for you.

We'll go over your duties and rate of pay then, all right?'

'Aye. Ta very much. And don't fret: as I said, the twins will cause no bother, I'll see to that.'

Seymour smiled, nodded. Then, glancing from her to Lynn, a slight frown touched his brow. 'Where are the little 'uns today?'

The women gazed back at him mutely. They couldn't very well reveal the truth, could they? To Janie's horror, she felt her cheeks begin to fill with guilty colour and was about to attempt an explanation when her friend intervened:

'They're with Sadie Hodgkiss,' she blurted. 'Aye, that's right. She offered to watch them whilst Janie did her shopping—'

'Morning, all!' a familiar voice rang out, cutting Lynn off.

Glancing around at the new arrival – and coming face to face with the very person they had been discussing – Janie closed her eyes in despair. *God above, no . . .*

'Oh. Hello, Sadie,' said Lynn meekly.

The grocer was looking from one to the other in mild curiosity. Janie tried to laugh off the incident as being merely a slip of the tongue:

'No, Lynn,' she told her lightly, though inside her anxiety was mounting, 'Mrs Hodgkiss ain't got the twins. Our Hilda's watching them, remember?'

'Oh? Ohh!' Understanding, Lynn nodded. 'Aye, that's right. I were getting mixed up.'

'The lass unwell again, is she?' asked Seymour.

'Aye, but . . . but it's nowt serious,' Janie stuttered. 'A touch of the bellyache, that's all. I thought it best to keep her off school, though, just to be on the safe side . . . Oh, for frig's sake!' she added on a hiss in the next breath, closing her eyes once again as, to her disbelief, another customer entered the shop in that moment to unveil this second explanation as another pack of lies – Hilda's class teacher!

'Aspirin, please,' the young woman begged of Seymour, squinting across the counter at him in obvious discomfort – whilst Janie did her best to blend into the background, praying she wouldn't notice her.

No such luck.

Turning to leave, the teacher glanced in her direction and paused to smile. 'Hello, Mrs Hudson.'

'Hm? Oh. I didn't see you there, Miss Swain. Good morning,' she mumbled back.

'Splitting headache.' She brandished her purchase with a wince. 'The headmistress offered to sit with my class whilst I slipped out to the shop. Mind you, your Hilda did offer her services first.'

Damn! All eyes were on her now. Just how would she talk her way out of this one? *Could this day possibly get much worse?*

'She assured me she'd keep the others in check in my absence,' the teacher went on, chuckling. 'Knowing your daughter, I don't doubt for a second that she'd have made a jolly fine job of it, capable girl that she is.'

'Bossy, more like,' Janie said, forcing a weak smile and wishing the ground would open up and swallow her whole.

202

Miss Swain laughed. 'However, I thought it best to decline all the same, just to be on the safe side!'

'Very wise, I'm sure.'

'Well, I'd better get back. Goodbye.'

Janie waved her on her way then forced her eyes around to meet those of Seymour and Sadie. They were frowning and staring straight back at her, clearly awaiting an explanation, and she felt tears clog her throat. How she loathed all this deceit. *Think,* her mind yelled. *Say something – anything!*

'Elsie!' Lynn exclaimed suddenly. Eyes flashing warning, she nodded to Janie. 'It's Elsie what's poorly and off school, love, not your Hilda. Ain't that right?'

'Aye.' Too choked to offer anything further – and too bone-weary of it all to even much care any more – Janie made her excuses and beat a hasty retreat.

Throughout the short journey home, one thought dominated all others: this was day one. The very first morning of what had become their new existence, and already she was making mistakes? How would she uphold this treachery, maintain this double life, for the foreseeable future? And yet so much depended on its success. Why had they found themselves in this terrible, terrifying mess? It was all so unfair!

They had no choice.

Lord help them, she'd just have to try twice as hard from here on in.

Lynn was of the same mind when she called into number thirteen that evening.

Drawing Janie to one side, she shook her head. 'Jesus, Janie, that scene in the shop earlier . . .'

'I know, I know. I've never been so mortified nor frightened in all my life. I were sure the truth would come spilling out at any moment.'

'Well, that's summat we can't risk again.' Lynn glanced around. 'Where are the kiddies, playing out?'

'Aye, and our Joey's gone to see Stella.'

'Right, that means we've time to have a talk. I think it's best that me, you and James sit down and sort through what's to be done.'

Husband and wife followed their neighbour's instruction without protest, crossing to the table and taking a seat in readiness for whatever it was she had to say.

'I've had my thinking cap on, and I've come up with a few ideas,' Lynn continued, folding her arms with a purposeful nod. 'I reckon it goes without mentioning that it's norra good idea to leave the twins with James again, should you need to go out, Janie.'

'Oh, fear not. I've learned my lesson there, that's for sure!'

'And I also don't think it's wise that you, James, are left at home alone, neither. You can't manage with putting back the floorboards and sideboard on your own. If the police catch wind of you being here, they'll likely not stop at knocking – it'll be no good sitting tight and waiting for them to go away. Should they take it into their heads to bash the door in, you're buggered, lad.'

He sighed. 'Aye.'

'So, this is what we're going to do. Each day when Janie must leave the house, you'll creep round to mine, all right? Go the rear way and over the fence – I'll leave the back door unlocked. I doubt the authorities will think to check at mine. Well, it's worth a shot, at any rate, eh?'

'Lynn, you're certain about this?' Janie asked her, overcome with gratitude.

''Course I am. I told you I'm here to help, in any way I can, and I meant it. Now, the next bit of advice I have is that, from now on, you should think about kipping in the living room. It'll be far easier to get James in that hole in the ground if you're woken from your slumbers in here than it would be in bed. Once you've roused, dived up and staggered half asleep downstairs, precious seconds would have been lost – summat you can ill afford to squander when time is of the essence.'

'I never even thought of that,' admitted Janie, nodding. 'We must stay one step ahead, aye. It's a sound idea, love.'

'Well, there's one or two more where that came from, so you just sit back and lend me your lugholes . . .'

'Why are you doing this, Lynn?' James asked some time later when their planning had exhausted itself and they were sat with a well-earned cup of tea. Like his eyes, his tone was soft. 'Don't get me wrong, I'm more grateful than I can put into words, I am. But well . . . You've no reason whatever to get yourself involved, barely know us really, yet you're choosing to put your neck on the line. Why?'

205

'Because Janie's my friend – you both are,' she answered simply. 'I love the bones of youse all. You've cared for your family since day one, and you've made a fine job of it, I can see that. Now, in your hour of need, they want to do the same for you – and I'm here to help them. Will that do you?'

A benign smile lit his face. 'Aye, I'd say so. Ta, love. I won't ever forget it.'

'Eeh, you two, give over,' Janie sniffed, but her heart was fit to burst. 'You'll have me bawling into my brew in a minute.'

'Don't go doing that, it'll finish up all salty. And 'ere, you don't want to go wasting a good sup, not now . . .'

Frowning at her friend, Janie cocked her head. 'Not now? And why's that, then?'

'Ain't you heard, love?' Lynn was struggling to keep a straight face. 'They reckon tea is soon heading for the ration.'

'What?'

'Aye. And you a right brew belly as well. How will you cope at all?'

'Oh God, no, don't let it be true. Owt but that. *Blast* that friggin' Hitler to hell.'

And to think she'd dared to question earlier whether this day could get any worse!

Chapter 13

THE FOLLOWING DAYS trotted along without hiccup. There were no more slips of the tongue to
outsiders, no mistakes, no suspicion. Moreover, there
had been no further visits from the police, much to
their relief. It seemed that wherever the authorities
reckoned James could be hiding out, it wasn't at
home. Nonetheless, the family remained vigilant,
would have been foolish not to. To let their guard
down would have been inviting trouble, they knew.
All the same, it was a relief to finally allow their frayed
nerves a bit of a holiday. They just prayed that things
would continue to flow as smoothly as they were
doing up to now.

The only bug in the ointment was the increasingly
fragile subject of money. James despised the fact that
his wife had had to take on a second job to supple-
ment their household income, and it had begun to
affect his mood. Now, it wasn't so much memories of
war that plagued his mind, he admitted, but instead
crippling emasculation. However, there was no question of altering things for now; life was how it was,

and Janie told him so. Yet it did little to stem his pain of inadequacy or stop her feeling rotten for his predicament.

This morning, however, she'd determinedly put their problems to one side. This nineteenth day of June was a significant one – her son's sixteenth birthday. She was adamant that they would mark the occasion, if not with a party and fancy gifts, then at the very least with peace and love, as it deserved to be.

By, but it didn't seem two minutes since she was bouncing her firstborn on her knee, she reflected as she made the short journey to Seymour's home on Bridson Lane. It fair brought a tear to her eye to think on it. It seemed she'd blinked, and poof – the years were gone, melted away like smoke. How strange to think he was almost fully grown now, with a child of his own on the way. Just where did time go at all?

She still wore a nostalgic smile as she parked the twins' pram beneath the front window and lifted the chubby bundles into her arms. And her gladness grew, a feeling of tranquillity coming over her again along with it, when she entered the house.

The grocer's home wasn't what you would call grand, yet it possessed a quiet charm that pleased her senses in ways she hadn't the words to describe. Stuffed with dark Victorian furniture and odds and ends that had seen better days, it was nevertheless welcoming in a sentimental sort of way. It evoked within her fond memories of weekend visits to her grandparents' dwelling as a child – though, here, there was one marked difference that set it apart: reading matter.

There were bookshelves squeezed into every available corner; some tall, some short – all filled to overflowing with row upon row of publications in a varying array of styles and subjects. Ancient-looking tomes bound in black and ox-blood leather, well-read volumes with frayed cloth spines, newer softback novels and hardback classics, handbooks, manuals and guides – the personal library was an impressive one. Not that Janie did much reading; she had neither the time nor the inclination, and besides, her basic education left a lot to be desired. Still, they were nice to look at, and she made a point of taking care to replace everything exactly as it had been when dusting.

His books clearly meant a great deal to Seymour – a means of filling the empty evenings? she'd pondered more than once, always with a tug of sadness. She'd learned from him that his wife had died from Spanish flu twenty years before. The pandemic that had taken hold towards the end of the last war and swiftly spread across the globe had claimed tens of millions of lives – an unfathomably devastating number.

How lonely he must be without even the comfort of children to ease somewhat his companionlessness. And how much the odd kind word must indeed mean to a body in his situation – a fact he'd hinted to her not so long ago in the shop, but which only now was she able to fully appreciate. In light of this, she'd found herself warming towards him further. If only more folk would make the effort to look beyond his somewhat curmudgeonly manner and get to know him a little better, they would see he wasn't so bad after all.

Janie had her chores completed in no time and, with her thoughts now on the birthday tea she had planned, she headed for home to begin preparations. After settling Bobby and Brian on the rug with some toys, she hung up her coat in the hall. Then, as had become the new habit, she went upstairs and knocked three times on the adjoining bedroom wall to alert her husband, who was next door, that she was back, and that it was safe to return. He entered through the back door moments later and she lifted her face to him for a kiss.

'Cup of tea, love?'

'I'll do it,' he said quickly, making for the kitchen before she could stop him, and she let her protests die on her lips.

It was James's way of feeling useful, she knew. Upon her return, he'd insist on brewing a pot and making up a plate of something for her and the twins' lunch. He'd then order her to sit down and put her feet up for a while, tell her that her own household duties could wait until she was rested up.

Though she'd assured him that her new cleaning job was hardly taxing – truth be told, she could have done it standing on her head – he wouldn't hear of it, and she'd learned to just let him have his way in this, for it made him feel better. Still, she wished he'd relax more and realise that it mattered not one iota to her that circumstances were changed. God willing,

210

they would manage on her and Joey's wages, there was no need for him to fret; he couldn't help it, could he? Simply having him here safe and well was contribution enough.

'I'm thinking of doing us a nice tea today for our Joey's birthday,' she told James when she was sipping her drink. 'A salt-beef stew and dumplings, aye. I know how much he enjoys that. And mebbe a bread pudding for afters; I reckon the sugar will stretch to that. Mind you, I'm all out of cinnamon . . . I'll have to see if I can cadge a bit off Lynn. So what d'you reckon? The lad'll like that, won't he?'

Pausing in his task of cutting the twins' fish paste and tomato sandwiches into small squares, he smiled. ''Course he will, aye. I do wish we could have got him a better gift, mind. A couple of shirts and a next-to-new cap don't seem enough really for a special milestone such as this one.'

'No, don't be daft, Joey loved them. Besides, he understands how things are right now, what with money being tight—' She cut herself off quickly and chewed her lip. Curse her tongue! 'I'm sorry. I didn't mean . . .'

'Yes, you did – and you're right. We're struggling to make ends meet, lass, and it's my fault. If only there were summat I could *do*.'

Janie went to stand behind him, put her arms around his neck and rested her cheek against his. 'You did all you needed to by coming home,' she murmured. 'You're free from danger, love, and that means more to us than a king's ransom. Nowt else matters.'

211

'I love youse all so much, Janie. I'll make it up to you someday . . . somehow.'

'I know. Now,' she added brightly a little later, crossing the room to collect her coat. 'It looks like the twins are finished with their grub, so I'll just give their hands and faces a wipe, then we'll nip to the shops. I have to get some suet so's I can make a start on t' pudding.'

Rising with a nod, James headed once more for the back door to wait out her return at their neighbour's. 'Give us a knock when you're back.'

'Will do. Oh, and whilst you're there, have a look in the kitchen, please, and see if you can find that cinnamon I need. Lynn won't mind.'

'I am useful for summat after all,' he mumbled beneath his breath as he left the house – but not quietly enough that his wife didn't catch the bitter-sounding remark.

Alone, she glanced to the heavens with a weary sigh. Then she straightened her shoulders and, dragging in place an all-is-well smile, set off to make her purchases.

'Eeh, summat smells good.'

Janie welcomed her son home from work with a big hug. 'It's your birthday treat. I hope you're hungry!'

Grinning, he rubbed his hands. 'Starving, Mam.'

'Good, well, the lasses are across the way playing at their friend's house, so you relax and enjoy the quiet awhile. Go on, sit yourself down and pour yourself a sup of tea whilst I finish the meal off. It won't be long.'

'Erm . . . Mam?'

Having reached the door, she turned back to smile. 'Aye, lad?'

'Would it be all right if I asked Stella to join us?'

'Oh. But—'

'Please, as it's a celebration. I'd really like her to be here.'

Janie flicked her eyes towards her husband. 'You *can't*, lad, remember . . . ?'

'She knows.'

'What?'

Breaking his stare from her horrified expression, Joey gave a guilty shrug. 'She's soon to be family, Mam. She had a right to know—'

'You've told that girl that your dad's deserted from the army, that we're hiding him at home under the floorboards? She knows *every*thing?'

'She'll not breathe a word about it, not to no one. She promised.'

'Are you bloody mad?' Janie was livid. 'You had no right! Who's to say she won't blab? For Christ's sake, the girl's little more than a stranger—!'

'Not to *me* she ain't.'

'Aye, don't we know it! Look where that's got you! You had no right telling that girl owt, d'you hear me? No right at all.'

'Stella's carrying my child and she's soon to be my wife. We shouldn't have secrets. What's more, I'd be grateful if you'd stop referring to her as "that girl". She's gorra name, you know.'

'Oh aye, I could think of a few all right!'

'And what's that meant to mean?' Eyes narrowing,

he lifted his chin. 'Well, come on, Mam, let's have it. What names would they be, then? Slut? Tart?'

'That's enough,' James interceded quietly. 'Don't use language like that to your mother.'

'No, I want to know what these names are.'

Getting to his feet, he pointed a finger at his son. 'I said hold your tongue. Your mam's worked up is all. She meant no harm. So just calm down, boy, and—'

'Boy?' The word seemed to ignite his flame of anger into a raging inferno. 'Bleedin' *boy*? Don't you call me that, not ever again! It's me what's fetching in a wage around here, me what's the breadwinner. It's me what's keeping your wife and children in food and clothing and putting a roof over our heads. *Me* what's working all the hours God sends whilst you sit here waiting to bolt into that bloody hole in the ground like a lily-livered coward. Boy? I'm more of a man than you'll ever be!'

A stunned silence held the room and its occupants frozen for some seconds – Janie recovered first. Rushing forward, she delivered an ear-ringing slap to Joey's face. He staggered back in shock and she thrust a hand out again, this time grasping his collar to pull his face close to hers. Her tear-heavy words were like ice:

'You vicious, cruel-mouthed little sod, how *dare* you! One more remark like that and, God help me, you'll feel more than the back of my hand. I'll give you the thrashing of your friggin' *life*, my lad, d'you understand?'

214

'Janie.' James's voice was low with pain. 'Leave it, it doesn't matter—'

''Course it matters! I ain't having him speak about you like that.'

'But it's true. Every word.'

'No, it *isn't*,' she shot back through gritted teeth. Then, turning once more to her son: 'You, apologise. Now.'

Face stiff, Joey looked past her at nothing. As the seconds grew and he remained tight-lipped, she shook him harder.

'You deaf? I said apologise.'

'No.'

'Why, you hard-faced young—!'

'I'm getting out of here,' Joey spat. He turned on his heel and stormed from the house before his parents even had time to blink.

Janie ran after him into the street: 'Lad, wait! Where you going?'

'Grandad's,' he yelled back without turning. 'Now leave me alone!'

She returned indoors in a daze and slumped on to the sofa. James came to sit beside her and she dropped her head on to his shoulder. 'I wanted everything to be special today, and now it's all ruined. Everything's falling apart lately. Just what's the friggin' point in anything at all?'

'Janie, lass ... I'm for handing myself in to the police in t' morning.'

'What?'

'I'd sooner die than have my son ashamed of me. I'm going, I must.'

'D'you know what, James?' Dragging herself to her feet, she held her arms wide. 'Do what the hell you like, because I'm past caring. I'm sick to the back teeth of the lot of it. I've nowt left to give.'

'Wait, please, we have to talk about this – where you going?'

'Bed.'

'But—'

'Leave me be, James. Just leave me bloody be.'

He did, and blindly she made her way upstairs, shutting the bedroom door behind her. She kicked off her shoes and climbed beneath the covers, mind and body numb, to stare unseeing at the ceiling.

'Janie! Janie, get up!'

'Hmm? What time is it?'

'Gone half three.'

'What the devil . . . ? Are the police here?'

'No, no. Quick, come *on!*'

Opening one eye, she peered up at James through the darkness. A headache throbbed at her temples and a terrible whining filled her ears – groaning, she swatted him away. 'Let me sleep, will you? I feel rotten.'

'Janie—'

'Please. I just need to sleep.'

'Christ sake, woman!'

''Ere, what . . . ?' she cried groggily as she felt herself being hauled from the bed and into her husband's arms. He set off at a run, through the door and down the stairs, before depositing her in the hall, where, to her confusion, her daughters stood waiting with coats draped over their nightclothes, their small white faces wreathed in fright. Janie knuckled at her eyes. 'What . . . ?'

'Can't you hear it?' James shook her in desperate panic. 'The siren's going off. We're having an air raid.'

His statement acted like a slap to the face – she sprang to her senses in an instant. 'My God . . .'

'I peeked around the blind. Folk are out there just standing in the road in shock, gazing up at the sky, bloody fools – well, not us. Into the shelter. And here, don't forget your masks.'

'You reckon there'll be a gas-bomb attack?'

'Who knows. Now, come on, hurry!' he ordered, bundling them all towards the back door and into the star-pricked night.

Out here, the warbling wail from the siren located on the roof of the shops was much louder. They raced across the dewy grass and ducked inside the metal contraption in the corner of the garden. Feeling around in the darkness, Janie located the thin wooden bench running along one side and guided her daughters down on to it. By now, the terrified youngsters were crying and, as she sat between them and put her arms around them, holding them against her tightly, she murmured words of comfort. Yet, inside, she too was quailing.

Bolton's first air-raid warning.

She'd forgotten how terrible a noise the signal

was. The town's authorities had sounded them once or twice during controlled tests at the outset of war last year, but this time was different. Tonight was no practice run. The enemy was upon them. Mother of God, were they about to die? *This couldn't be happening. It couldn't!*

In her fear-dumb state, one thought had thus far failed to reach her. When it did, she went icy all over and a scream of pure horror ripped from her, reverberating off the steel walls: 'Joey! Dear Lord, my lad!'

'No!' James yelled, pushing his wife back as she made to dash from the shelter – and it was only then that Janie realised he'd made no attempt to join them inside, was still standing in the garden. 'I just wanted to get youse settled before I left . . . *I'm* going to find the lad.'

'But, James, you can't—!'

'I must. I have to know he's safe.'

Before she could stop him, her husband turned and was gone, swallowed up in the inky night. Gasping in breaths and struggling not to hyperventilate, she flopped back down on to the seat. Immediately, the girls clung to her, and she prayed for all she was worth.

Minutes slipped by as they awaited their fate, and nothing happened. No drone of plane engines above, no explosions. Bar the distant shrill of Ralph Robertson's whistle, which carried on the breeze as the warden performed his ARP duties, all was still as the grave. Nevertheless, they remained poised with dread, prepared for the worst.

After what felt like days, another blare from the

siren finally sounded over the rooftops. The flat, continuous note was as loud as the first, only this heralded something else entirely – the all-clear. Danger had passed.

Weak with shock and with tears of relief pouring down their cheeks, the trio climbed hesitantly from the damp-smelling confines and emerged into the sharp air.

They stood for a moment, gazing up at the clear sky. Then, without a word, they headed across the garden and into the house.

Janie made a beeline for the mantel to scan the clock atop. To her surprise, she discovered that a mere half an hour had passed. Heading next to the window, she moved aside the blackout blind and scanned the street, but of her menfolk there was no sign.

Her blind terror for her son had lessened in the knowledge that the alarm had clearly been a false one. Now, her worries focused on James's fate instead. Not for anything had she meant what she'd snapped to him last night – of course she wasn't past caring or wanting him to go back. What was playing out at the farm this very moment? Had James come face to face with his father yet? Would Albie really decide to inform on him when he did?

A small group of neighbours stood huddled by old Reuben's house across the road, talking quietly; spotting Lynn and the twins amongst them, she slapped a hand to her mouth. Her poor friend! In all the chaos, she hadn't given her a thought. The Balls didn't even have a shelter! After putting an exhausted

Hilda and Elsie back to bed, she returned downstairs and hurried outside.

'Love?' Janie beckoned her across. 'Are youse all right?'

Giving her a quick hug, Lynn nodded. 'I'm still bloody shaking, mind. Eeh, I thought we were goners, then. I did.'

'Aye, and me. I am sorry for not coming to find you, only what with one thing and another . . .'

'James?' her friend whispered.

'You don't know the half of it. But never mind my problems; what about you, where did you go?'

'Mr Trent brought us into his Anderson, God bless him. Apparently, enemy planes were spotted in the vicinity – why, though? I don't understand it. What would Jerry want with us? They won't be back, won't waste their bombs on our town, surely? Bolton ain't got nowt worth their while blowing up: no docks or shipyards or airfields, nowt much of military importance.'

'God knows how their warped minds work, love. All's we can do, I suppose, is pray they stop away. It makes me sick, you know, to think they were so nearby, horrible gits.'

Lynn gave a shudder. 'Aye. I'll tell you one thing, mind, I ain't taking no chances next time. I'm having that shelter what's piled up in bits in our garden built. Duncan never got round to it when it got delivered last year, didn't see the point. Truth be told, neither did I until tonight. One of the fellas on t' street will oblige if I ask, I'm sure.'

Nodding in agreement, Janie glanced back to her house. 'I'd best get in, love, I've left the kiddies on their own. Will you come in for a brew?'

'No, I'll get the babbies home and in bed, ta all the same.'

'Oh, has anyone checked in on Mrs Hodgkiss and Stella?' Janie asked suddenly as the thought occurred.

'I'm sure someone would have done; Ralph Robertson, perhaps.'

'Aye, you're probably right. I reckon I should start making more of an effort with the girl, you know,' she added quietly. 'For our Joey's sake, like.'

'Has summat occurred?'

'Nowt what won't keep – I'll fill you in next time I see you. Well, ta-ra, lass. You take care.'

'And youse. Ta-ra, love.'

Before departing to their respective homes, the women shot an involuntary look upwards, sharing the same hope: that those Germans wouldn't be back to sully their skies a second time. Then, flashing one another a smile, they hurried indoors.

The hour was approaching six when James finally returned home. Springing from the sofa, where she'd been dozing lightly, Janie ran to greet him in the hall. When she saw who was in his company, her chest constricted; she let out a small gasp. 'Son . . .'

'Hello, Mam.' Shuffling awkwardly on the spot, head lowered, he glanced up at her from beneath his lashes. 'Mam . . . so sorry . . .'

'Sshhh. It's forgotten, lad. All in the past. I thought . . . I thought I were going to lose you

221

tonight . . . Come here.' She held out her arms and he rushed into them, wrapping her in a crushing embrace. Catching her husband's eye over Joey, she saw that he was smiling. He inclined his head to her in a silent message that he and his son had straightened things out between themselves already and that all was well, and she breathed in relief.

'I don't think them things I said, really I don't,' Joey murmured into her shoulder. 'I behaved terribly, and I'm sorry. It won't ever happen again. I don't know what came over me, I . . .'

'All right, come and sit down,' she soothed, guiding the lad into the living room. 'I know what set you off,' she continued when they were seated at the table. 'It were me and the things I said about Stella.'

'All the same, I had no right—'

'Hang on, hear me out,' she interjected, taking his hand. 'We both said things we didn't mean, it's true. Thing is, I'm the adult here and I should have acted better. What's more, I started it. You got het up because I were being rotten about the lass you love. There's no crime in that, lad. In fact, I admire you for it. Your dad would have reacted exactly the same, had someone been bad-mouthing me like that, because he loves me. It's shown me how much Stella means to you. So, from here on in, I'm going to make more of an effort with her. I should have tried from the start, I know, but well . . . I couldn't take to her somehow. Maybe that's on me and, if that's the case, I apologise for it. I'll try from today. I promise.'

'You really mean it, Mam?'

'I do.'

A weight seemed to rise from him. He closed his eyes. 'I know Stella can seem a bit standoffish at times, but she means no harm by it – it's just her way. And though she'll not admit it, she's frightened, Mam. What's more, I just know she's upset over how things have panned out with Mrs Metcalfe, and that she misses her. No matter what the woman's done, it's still her mam, after all.'

Janie lowered her eyes with not a little shame. How hadn't she realised all this herself? That poor lass must be scared witless, young as she was. Abandoned by her own mother, forced to flee to a strange area in the midst of a war and lodge amongst people she knew not a thing about – unmarried and pregnant into the bargain. All the while well aware that her future in-laws were less than pleased with her and the situation . . . No wonder she was the way she was. Janie felt wholly sorry.

'Tonight's made me see things different. Staring death in the face like that for all we knew . . .' She took her husband's and son's hands in hers and kissed them in turn. 'We've to make each day count from now on. Family first, always. That includes Stella. Yes?'

'Aye,' they agreed in unison.

'It'll be her birthday soon, won't it?'

'August, Mam.'

'Right, well, I think I ought to pay that mother of hers another visit, make her see sense this time. She'll give her consent to youse wedding, if it's the last thing I do.'

'Eeh. Ta, Mam!'

Janie smiled. 'As for you,' she continued, training her soft gaze on to James, 'we'll have no more talk of you doing owt foolish. You're going nowhere. All right?'

'Aye,' he confirmed – though Janie saw he was struggling to meet her eye. She nodded knowingly.

'I take it Albie wasn't jumping for joy when he saw you tonight?'

'You could say that.'

'He threatened to shop you?'

There was raw hurt in her husband's response. 'Aye.'

'Well, I guess a visit to the farm's in order first then. Don't fret,' she assured them in a voice steady with purpose. 'I'll make everything all right. You just see if I don't.'

And she meant it. Nothing – *no* one – would stand in the way of her family's happiness from now on.

Heaven help anyone who even thought to try.

Chapter 14

'CAN I COME IN?'

It was evident by his expression that she was the last person he expected to see. He stood his ground in the doorway and folded his arms.

'Please, Albie,' she pressed gently.

A deep frown knitted his brow. Then, with obvious reluctance, he stepped aside. 'Make it quick, mind. I've work to be getting along with.'

Janie traced his steps down the passageway and into the kitchen. He flicked his chin, indicating that she could sit, but she shook her head. 'I'll not, thank you all the same. What I have to say shan't take long.'

'Well?'

She bunched her hands, concealed from view inside the sleeves of her coat, into fists. Tighter still, until her nails bit painfully into her palms, making her eyes water. Next, she set her bottom lip wobbling. Then, covering her face, she burst into what she hoped were convincing sobs.

After a few moments, an uncomfortable Albie

shuffled towards her. He patted her back awkwardly. 'Now then. No need for all this.'

'I'm sorry,' she blubbered, forcing a hiccup. 'I can't help it. James, he . . . I've lost him!'

'The police?'

'Aye. They came for him not an hour since and took him away. Just what am I going to do?' she wailed, throwing her arms about the old man's neck.

'There now, come on.' He led her to a chair and lowered her into it. 'For what it's worth, it weren't me, you know, what dobbed him in.'

'I believe you.'

'Not that I wouldn't have done, mind, given the chance, but well . . . It's been taken out of my hands, now, so that's that. You must try to understand, it's for the best.'

Blowing her nose on her hankie, Janie nodded. 'I suppose you're right. It *is* his duty, after all. I see it now.'

'That's right. And you're not to fret none. I'll see that you and the kiddies are looked after whilst he's gone.'

'You mean it?' she asked, gazing up at him with wide, shiny eyes – and was gratified to see his face soften. 'We can really rely on you, Albie?'

''Course, aye. For owt.'

This was it, where she went in for the kill.

All morning, she'd thought this through thoroughly, perfecting her scheme. She'd taken a risk but was now confident that she'd pulled it off, that this route had been the best one to take with him. He needed to think himself the big man, the person in charge, always had. In the face of her apparent meekness and submission, he was finding her impossible to resist. Had she gone in all guns blazing, he'd have fought back stubbornly, and all would have been lost. She'd had to play this – him – differently, and it was working. It was stroking his ego to have her pleading for his assistance.

'There is one thing,' she murmured. 'I don't hardly know how to utter it . . .'

'Aye?'

'I reckon there's only you in all the world what can make this right, Albie.'

Expanding his chest in self-importance, he nodded as though in clear agreement. 'You're likely right, there. So come on, lass. Let's hear it. What d'you need me to do for you?'

'It's more our Joey what's in need, if truth be told. Oh, Albie, say you'll help us. Please!'

Twenty minutes later, Janie made off for the tram stop in quiet triumph, her father-in-law's allegiance secured.

All that remained now was to put the final part of her plan into action. Of successfully bringing around to her way of thinking the next person on her list, she was much more confident.

'What the bleedin' hell do *you* want?'

This time, Janie attempted no false civility. She matched Mrs Metcalfe's hostility completely. 'I have summat to say to you.'

'I don't want to listen, so just get gone and don't come—'

'Oh, you'll want to hear this,' she butted in, stepping forward. 'I have a proposition for you – one you'd be daft not to take up, believe me.'

The woman's eyes narrowed to slits, her curiosity piqued. 'Well, in that case . . .' She held the door wide.

Nodding grimly, Janie followed her inside.

Hilda and Elsie, a little tired but none the worse for their experience, had gone to school as usual, and on Janie's instruction Lynn had asked Mrs Hodgkiss to watch the twins today, so it was just James and Joey at home. They looked up expectantly as Janie entered the house and, after removing her coat and hanging it up, she went to join them at the table.

Glancing at them in turn, she allowed herself the shadow of a smile. 'It's sorted.'

'What is?' asked James.

'Everything. Albie shan't be alerting the authorities about you being here, and Mrs Metcalfe will give her consent for Stella and Joey to wed.'

Her husband and son were gobsmacked. It was the latter who eventually managed to rasp, 'How on earth did you manage it, Mam?'

Janie gave them a rundown of events. 'So you see,' she finished, 'Albie has agreed to . . . reward, shall we say, Stella's mam in exchange for her cooperation.'

'Pay her off, you mean,' Joey muttered.

'Bribery?' threw in James. 'Good God, love. Is that really the path we ought to tread?'

'And what would you have had me do instead, eh?

228

That woman wouldn't have budged. Our first grand-child would have been branded with the stigma of bastard for life – and the innocent mite's parents wouldn't have fared much better neither. Our son and Stella will be the talk of the town if they're unable to do things proper. Knowing her the little I do, I reckoned Mrs Metcalfe would cave if there were summat in it for her, and I were right. I think it's best not to tell Stella, mind. The truth would crush her. Let her believe her mam did the decent thing through the goodness of her heart and nowt more.'

Joey nodded agreement. Then: 'Does Grandad really believe that Dad's been arrested?'

'He does, and it's got him off our backs. He can't inform on someone what's already been apprehended – at least so he thinks. We've heard the last from that quarter, fret not on that score.'

'How did he react when you told him?'

Sympathy sparked for her husband. Hope flickered in his eyes and she knew what he wanted her to say, but she couldn't – wouldn't – lie to him. Her tone was gentle. 'He's glad to think the police have caught up with you. Sorry, love, but it's true.'

James shrugged. 'I suspected as much. Mind you . . .'

'What?'

'Well, I can't help feeling bad that we've conned him out of his money. I get your reasoning with regards to that Metcalfe piece, but still . . . It's not right, Janie.'

'I could see no other way. Besides, he were only too willing. Honest, he was. To take charge of the

229

situation, feel as if he were saving us bunch of inadequates from ourselves ... He'll not miss it anyroad, ain't short of a bob or two.'

'All the same . . .'

'Look, James. What's done is done. At the end of the day, that wicked owd sod was prepared to sign your death warrant – his own son! I don't enjoy being manipulative; by, I don't, no. But desperate times, and all that . . . I did what had to be done for my family, as would anyone. What's more, I regret nowt. So there you have it. God willing, and keeping everything crossed, our luck is at long last on the turn.'

There was no more to say on the matter and the subject was dropped. Janie made a pot of tea and, when she'd poured each of them a cup, she brought up her other idea, which she'd had shortly before on the journey back to Breightmet.

'I want you to invite Stella to join us for some grub,' she told Joey. 'That birthday tea I made you didn't exactly go to plan, did it? So, we'll make up for it tonight.'

He smiled. 'Aye, all right. I'd like that, Mam. I know Stella will appreciate it too.'

'Good, that's settled then. Why not go and see her now, see what she says? I'll walk with you on my way to Mr Briggs's; I haven't even been there yet today, what with everything else ... I'll call in at the shops on t' way back and pick up summat for our meal.'

An hour and a half later, Janie let herself out of the grocer's house with a yawn. What with the interrupted sleep last night and her trekking about Bolton visiting Albie and Mrs Metcalfe this morning, her cleaning work now had sucked the last of her energy from her – and there was still the rest of the day to get through yet, she reminded herself with a groan. She'd sleep well tonight, all right! Pray to God they had no more raids, that's all she could say. Another early-hours Nazi ambushing like the last would be the final straw.

Throughout her preparation of the evening meal, Elsie shadowed her movements in the kitchen, which was out of character for her. Like Hilda, she'd normally be out in the street with friends at this time of day, but earlier, when her sister had asked her to join them in a game of hopscotch, Elsie had declined. Finally, after tripping over the youngster for a second time, Janie turned to her, hands on hips: 'Lass, you're under my feet again – what is the matter with you? And don't bother trying to tell me nowt's wrong like you did the last time I asked, because I know there's summat on your mind. Come on, you can talk to me.'

'I do want to, Mam, but . . .'

'But what?'

'I don't understand what it means.'

'What *what* means?' she pressed. Then her brow cleared and she enquired quietly: 'Have you heard summat, lass?'

Frowning, Elsie nodded.

'Another one of them special voices, was it?'

'Aye.'

'And what was it you were shown?'

'It were about a babby. A little girl. And our Joey . . . our Joey were her dad.'

Janie released air slowly. 'I see.'

'But he's not having a babby, is he? He can't be; he ain't even gorra wife! So this voice, it can't be true this time, can it? So why did I hear it, Mam? Why?'

Biting her lip, Janie drew her towards her in a hug. They had deemed it best that Hilda and Elsie were not told about the pregnancy, yet now . . . Was it time to try to explain to her daughters how matters stood?

How on earth would she and James find the right words for them to understand without confusing them? More important still, could they be trusted not to speak of it outside of this house? The last thing they all needed was Joey and Stella's business becoming common knowledge. Folk could and would arrive at their own conclusions once the marriage was announced, but by then everything would be all proper and above board – gossip was sure to abate soon enough. Was there any point in ruffling feathers just yet, when it could be avoided?

'Try and put it from your mind, lass,' she said at last, her decision made. 'Mebbe all will become clear shortly. Now then, why don't you go on outside 'til tea's done, eh?'

Lighter in mood now she'd unburdened her mind, Elsie skipped off to play. Alone, Janie went over and over the revelation as she resumed her duties – and despite herself, she couldn't contain a smile. *A*

232

granddaughter. Eeh, imagine that. The new life shortly to join the fold had suddenly become a lot more real – she could hardly wait, now, to meet her.

Stella arrived as the food was being dished out – endeavouring to start off on the right footing, as she'd vowed, Janie welcomed her warmly.

'Ta for coming. We're glad to have you, lass. Won't you sit down?'

Wearing a look of mild surprise, the girl nodded and took the chair closest to Joey's. Glancing around at the Hudsons in turn, there was about her an air of guardedness.

'So. You've settled in down the street all right, then?' Janie asked her as they ate.

'That's right.'

She nodded. Sadie had revealed as much, had had no problems with her new lodger so far. In fact, she seemed to have taken a definite shine to Stella. 'And you're keeping well, aye?'

'Well enough,' came back the strained reply.

'That's good. It's just you never seem to be around whenever I pay my usual tea visit to Mrs Hodgkiss, so I ain't had the chance to ask before now—'

'That's 'cause I purposely avoid you. I take myself off to my room when I know you're due with the twins.'

'Oh.' Thrown by the bluntness, Janie didn't know what else to say. 'I see.'

'Well, let's face it: it's saved a lot of trouble all round, me keeping out of your way, ain't it?'

She couldn't help but admire the girl's honesty. 'I

233

suppose it has. The thing is, Stella, I reckon we ought to try a bit harder, now. Well, *I* should, aye. When all's said and done, you'll be one of the family soon, and . . .' Spotting her daughters' bemused expressions, she cursed herself beneath her breath. So, it seemed the time *had* come to be honest with them after all. Well, partially at least. 'That's right, lasses, you may as well know: Stella ain't just our Joey's friend, as we've had you believe. She's his betrothed.'

'You're getting wed?' Hilda asked her brother.

Taking Stella's hand with a smile, he nodded. 'That's right. Just as soon as she turns sixteen, in a few weeks.'

'But . . . you're too young. Only older folk do that.'

'Age don't matter, our Hilda, when you're in love,' Joey told her, then laughed when she made vomiting noises at what she clearly deemed his soppiness. 'One day, you'll meet a lad and fall in love, and then you'll understand—'

'Ew, I shan't! Lads are 'orrible!'

He ruffled her hair affectionately. 'Aye, well, we'll see about that.'

Janie had been watching her youngest daughter in readiness – now, as Elsie's eyes widened and she opened her mouth to blurt out her vision, Janie was quick to get in first:

'Just think, you might both be aunties by this time next year. That'll be nice, eh?'

However, Elsie wouldn't be quietened: 'A girl! That's what the babby will be!'

'Well, we'll have to see, won't we?' her mother said

lightly, playing the prediction down – though, secretly, it pained her to do it.

All her life, she'd tried to hide from people this 'gift' she herself had been given. Not even in the comfort of her family home as a child had she been able to discuss or try to make sense of it – her mother wouldn't tolerate it. She'd resented her for that for years, still did to some extent. An explanation as to what they saw in their dreams would have eased her troubled mind so very much – instead, she'd had to go through the pain and confusion of figuring it all out herself. And now, here she was, doing the same thing with Elsie: brushing her ability beneath the carpet in front of others, pretending it didn't exist. Making her suppress it at home, same as she'd had to do. It wasn't right.

'Talking of the wedding . . . Mrs Hudson?'

Lost in her tumultuous thoughts, Janie only realised Stella was addressing her when she touched her arm. 'Sorry, lass, I were in a world of my own there. What were you saying?'

'I just . . . I just wanted to let you know . . . Thank you.' Her demeanour was uncharacteristically soft. 'Joey told me what you did, that you went to see Mam again and managed to bring her round to the idea.'

Not quite able to meet her gaze, she shook her head. 'You've no need to thank me, Stella.'

'All the same, I appreciate it. Truly.'

So many secrets and lies . . . Swallowing a sigh, Janie returned her attention to her food.

Moments later, a heavy thump sounded on the door.

The room froze. Then Joey was on his feet. Fast as a flash, he had the sideboard pulled out and the floorboards lifted before the rest of them had time to blink.

'Quick, Dad!'

Dropping his fork and sending it clattering to the table, James bolted into the makeshift bunker. Janie rushed to assist her son and, within seconds, they had everything back in its usual place. After taking a deep breath, Joey went to answer the knock, and Janie, taking in her daughters' baffled expressions, held a warning finger to her lips.

'Not a word,' she whispered. 'You've seen norra thing of your dad if anyone asks.'

Before they had chance to respond, the living-room door opened and Joey re-entered. Following close behind was the local warden and a uniformed policeman.

Doing her level best to ignore her banging heart and retain her composure, Janie acknowledged them with an incline of her head.

'Evening, Mrs Hudson—'

She cut Ralph off quietly: 'I know why you're both here. And I'm here to tell youse the same thing I told them last officers: my husband ain't here.'

'James hasn't been in touch at all?' the policeman put to her.

'That's right. We ain't none of us seen hide nor hair of him.'

He frowned deeply. Then, crossing the room, he nodded to the children. 'And how about you lot, then? Have either of *you* seen your father of late?'

Janie held her breath. To her horror, she saw her daughters inadvertently swivel their eyes towards the sideboard – she stepped forward quickly. 'Don't you pester my kiddies with questions. Can't you see you're upsetting them? I've told you how matters lie, so just you leave them be!'

His brow furrowed further. 'Mrs Hudson, the army won't rest until your husband is found, and neither will we. Now, if there is anything you can tell us, anything at all—'

'There ain't.'

'Then I assume you have no objections to my looking around?'

The tension was palpable. Though, inside, Janie was a bag of nerves, she shook her head. 'None at all,' she insisted. 'Look where you like.'

When the officer had disappeared upstairs, Ralph shook his head. 'I happened to be passing when I saw him approaching your house. Learning what his business was, I decided to accompany him to offer my support. Support to you, that is, Mrs Hudson,' he added, much to her surprise.

'Oh? Oh. Right.'

'From what I've seen of your family since you moved here to Top o' th' Brow, you seem a decent lot, with honest souls to boot. I knew you'd not be harbouring James, that there had to be some other explanation for his disappearance, and I told him so. All the same, the officer has a job to do, I'm afraid . . . But don't worry, we'll be out of your hair soon enough.'

Rooting around inside her mind for something to say, guilt stabbed. *Yet more deceit.* Would it ever end? 'Eeh, Mr Robertson . . .' she finally managed. 'Thank you.'

'Are we all done here?' he asked soon afterwards when the policeman rejoined them, his search having yielded nothing.

'For now.' Then, turning to Janie: 'If Mr Hudson *does* turn up, however . . .'

'I'll be sure to inform you of such,' she assured him.

'Very well. Then I'll bid you good evening and let you all get back to your meal.'

Seeing his eyes move beyond her to linger on the table, Janie felt the colour abandon her face and she almost staggered. *The plates* . . . Surely he'd realise there was one place set too many! Oh, good God. There could be no possibility of talking her way out of this one. *How could she have been so stupid?* Heart shattering, she closed her eyes and waited – but to her astonishment, his accusation never came.

'Goodbye, Mrs Hudson, everyone,' said Ralph instead, and she was just in time to witness him lead the policeman out. The front door clicked shut and they were gone.

Stumbling to a chair, she dropped into it, shaking from head to toe. 'Friggin' hell!'

Joey was as white as tripe. He nodded agreement. 'By, that were a close call.'

'But I don't understand . . . Your dad's plate. Where is it?'

It was Stella who provided the answer. She rose and crossed to the dresser, and, in growing surprise, Janie watched her open a drawer and bring the half-eaten meal out, cutlery and all.

'You?'

The girl shrugged her shoulders. 'I slipped it out of sight when Joey went to open the door.'

She'd been too distracted in securing her daughters' silence to notice. Oh, the dear, clever lass! 'Ta, Stella, ever so,' she murmured earnestly, reaching for her hand and squeezing. 'I'll not forget this.'

'It's all right,' came back her easy reply. 'What are family for?'

That you most definitely are – more than ever after today, she told her with her eyes, smiling. Stella had come to the rescue, had proven her loyalty to them without a doubt. She was a fully-fledged member of the Hudson clan, now. Furthermore, Janie couldn't have been happier of the fact.

It seemed she really had got this girl all wrong after all.

Later, as the world lay sleeping, Janie found her rest interrupted once again. Only it wasn't the wail of the air-raid siren now that dragged her from her slumbers, but a night sight. And it was one which left her lying awake in the darkness, restless with confusion, for a long time afterwards.

In her vision, she'd been holding an infant.

She was certain it was her future granddaughter – only, when she looked down, she'd seen that the baby was in fact a boy. And yet as she looked into his perfect little face, she'd known, *known* without a shadow of doubt, that Elsie's prediction was truth. So just what did it mean?

Was there more than one child on the way?

Could Stella Metcalfe in fact be having twins?

If that were the case – and Janie could think of no other explanation – then Lord help them. One newborn, even for seasoned parents, was difficult enough!

Chapter 15

THE FOLLOWING MORNING, when Elsie had left the breakfast table to go and get washed and dressed for school, Hilda put down her spoon and folded her arms. 'Right, now she's out of the way, I want to know what's going on.'

Sharing a look with James, Janie tried to make light of it: 'Nowt's going on, lass. Now hurry up and finish your porridge and go and get ready yourself, else you'll be late for school—'

'I'm not daft, you know. It's eleven I am, not two. You all think I'm a babby still what can't be trusted, but I can. Dad ain't meant to be here at all, is he? That's why he hid from the police and Mr Robertson. As for him,' she went on, prodding her thumb in Joey's direction, 'he's got that Stella in t' family way and that's why they're getting wed! I know it happens 'cause I've heard Maud Dyke in my class talking about it. Her sister got caught with a babby and had to marry her chap—'

'Hilda!' James cut in, mortified.

'Well, it's true, Dad! Maud said—'

Janie silenced them both with a flap of her hand. Then, sighing in defeat, she nodded. The time for honesty had come. 'You're correct, aye. Your dad isn't here on some holiday that the army's granted him, he's deserted. War's a terrible thing, lass, and he witnessed some things at Dunkirk that . . . made his mind poorly. He ain't strong enough no more to be a soldier, so he's stopping put here. As for our Joey . . . aye. Him and Stella are to have a child. It's not ideal, no, but what's done is done and they're trying to make the best of it. All right?'

Face solemn, Hilda bobbed her head. 'Ta, Mam, for telling me,' she announced with an air of maturity. 'And don't fret none; I'll not tell a soul.'

A smile lifted the corners of Janie's mouth and she reached over to stroke Hilda's hair. What with everything else lately eating up her attention, she seemed to have missed sight of the fact that her elder daughter was indeed growing up. 'I know you won't. You're a good girl.'

'So, is that the lot or is there owt else I should know?'

James and Joey couldn't hold back a chuckle at this fresh demand from the youngster, but Janie found herself biting her lip. She *did* have something extra to get off her chest, didn't she? And utter it she must – it wasn't going away, after all. Now was as good a time as any:

'Speak the truth and shame the devil, that's what they say, in t' it?' she said in a rush. 'Well, there's summat else I think you should all know, summat important I've been putting off telling youse. You see, I've got . . . powers, like.'

'Eh?' Joey and Hilda exclaimed in unison.

'Janie . . .' Frowning questioningly, James reached for his wife's hand. 'You decided years ago that you'd never tell them about the night sights . . . are you sure about this?'

'Aye, love, I am.'

'But why? Why now?'

'Because . . .' She took a deep breath. 'Because our Elsie's the same way.'

He released a low whistle. 'I see.'

'You knew there were a chance, didn't you, as did I? It's the females of my family what have this . . . thing,' she continued now to her children. 'Well, some of us, anyroad. My mam and my granny before her. Me. And now our Elsie. Things come to us in our dreams. Clues about the future, about what's to happen. Only the lass upstairs . . . she's got summat a bit different, I reckon. Summat stronger than any of us have had. She gets these flashes, these clues, when she's awake – feels stuff as well. Your arm,' Janie added to her husband. 'She knew, I reckon, you'd be shot. It were like sympathy pains she had. I ain't never had owt like that; nor did my mam or granny neither. Elsie, she's . . . she's got summat even more special, aye.'

'Why didn't you tell us about this gift of yours years ago?' asked Joey after a long moment, breaking through the stunned silence.

'I didn't want to scare and confuse you, I suppose . . . I don't know. You have to understand

243

what it's like having this: it's norra gift to most of us. We see the bad as well as the good, and sometimes . . . sometimes, it feels more like a curse. But now our Elsie . . . She's going to need our support. *All* our support, d'you see what I'm saying? She didn't ask for this – none of us do – and her so young . . . I'll not have it being some grubby secret no more, and that's why youse had to know. She's not to feel ashamed for summat she can't control.'

'Do I have it, Mam?'

Seeing the spark of excitement in Hilda's eyes, Janie was struck with conflicting emotions. On the one hand, she was relieved that the girl wasn't horri-fied or scathing of the confession she'd just heard, yet how to explain without upsetting her that only certain ones were chosen? She shook her head, say-ing gently, 'No, lass, I don't think so. We'd have noticed by now.'

'But that's not fair. Why Elsie and not me?'

'I don't know.'

'But I'm the eldest.'

'Eeh, lass. It doesn't work like that. It just . . . happens. Some get it, some don't. It can't be explained. Take it from me, though: in my opinion, you're the lucky one. If I could choose, I'd want to be just like you.'

This seemed to placate Hilda. She nodded thoughtfully. 'I'll look after our Elsie from now on, Mam. I will, honest. And just let anyone at school say owt to her – I'll thump their bleedin' heads in.'

Janie laughed out loud, though there were tears in

her eyes. 'I should tell you off for swearing, my girl, but . . . I'll let it ride just this once, seeing as you meant well by what you said. Elsie's lucky to have you.'

When soon afterwards Hilda disappeared upstairs to get ready for school and Joey took the dirty breakfast dishes out to the kitchen, James pulled his wife into his arms and held her close.

'What's this in aid of?' she asked softly, snuggling into him.

'I wanted to wait until we were alone to tell you . . . Eeh, I'm that proud of you, love. You're not to worry, you know. Whatever life throws our way, we'll get through it as a family. We'll manage, aye.'

'We always do,' she murmured with a smile, dropping a light kiss on to the tip of his nose.

'I'll have more than that, if you please,' James said on a low growl, nuzzling her neck and making her laugh. 'My lips ain't half jealous of my damn nose—'

'Cooee!' a voice from outside trilled suddenly, breaking the moment. 'Only me, Janie love.'

James released his wife with a groan; grinning, Janie went to let Lynn and the twins in, saying over her shoulder, 'Sorry, stud, but duty calls!'

'I'll get you later, my girl.'

'Ooh. Promises, promises!'

Janie was still smiling as she opened the door; her friend cocked her head quizzically. 'Oh aye? You look happy this morning.'

'Do I?'

'Like the cat what got the cream,' she insisted with a wicked wink.

245

'Go on with you!' Janie shooed her inside. 'You and your one-track mind – I despair, I do.'

''Ere, have you heard?' Lynn asked after greeting James, and like the flicking of a switch her face held now not a trace of amusement. 'That siren warning the other night? Word has it that it weren't a false alarm, as folk thought. Some German bombers carrying high explosives had come making scattered raids, and one plane managed to make it into Lancashire. A district in Accrington copped for it – that's only about twelve miles from us, can you believe it? – and a few houses were flattened. Whether they were going for a specific target – a colliery, mebbe, some reckon – or whether it were just a random attack, we'll likely never know for sure.'

Janie held a hand to her throat. 'Oh God. Was anyone . . . ?'

'Aye, three killed, poor souls. An owdish couple and their daughter. Twenty-one, she was, with her whole life in front of her. Mind you, the aircraft was shot down, so that's summat to be glad about at least.'

'Them Jerry swines!' Janie was raging. The northwest's first air attack – where would it end? 'None of the bigger cities in England have even been bombed proper yet, have they – why us? I mean, it would have been tragic wherever it happened but, good God, it's so unexpected. And too close for comfort, to boot. Bolton might have been spared, aye, but next time . . .' The notion was too terrible to contemplate. 'Did you get around to having your shelter built?' she added suddenly, turning to Lynn with wild eyes.

246

And when her friend shook her head: 'Right, well, that's getting seen to today. Who knows if we'll have another raid – we'll not take the risk.'

'Leave the Anderson to me,' James began, but Janie cut him off with a click of her tongue:

'Don't talk daft; you can't do it, can you? What if you're spotted?'

'I'll erect it, Mam,' offered Joey, catching the tail end of the conversation as he joined them in the living room. 'As you said, it's better to be safe than sorry.'

'You're sure? Ain't you at the farm today?' asked Lynn.

'No. I figured it's best I give the place a wide berth forra few days.'

Having been filled in on developments yesterday by Janie, Lynn nodded, understanding. 'Your grandad will grow used to the news of the babby, given time. Well, I'll be off to work. You'll find all the materials at the bottom of my garden, lad, and the instruction guide on how to put the shelter together is in the dresser drawer in my living room – just let yourself in, the back door's open. Ta for this, I'm grateful.'

Once she'd seen her daughters off to school, Janie took a blanket into her back garden and, after spreading it out on the grass, sat Bobby and Brian down with a few toys. The summer sky was of the brightest blue and not a cloud marred its glass-like expanse. Tilting her face to the high-sitting sun, she welcomed its warming beams on her skin and breathed in the fresh air. Feeling calmer now, she returned to the kitchen to put on the kettle.

247

As she brewed the tea, she smiled to herself. Joey's grumbles from next door drifted through to her as he banged and thumped about, constructing Lynn's shelter. It seemed the task was already getting the better of him. However, she knew he wouldn't give in; hell would ice over before he admitted defeat, stubborn bugger that he was. She went to switch on the wireless, glad to discover Home Service Friday were playing 'film music: popular tunes from the musical screen' – her favourite. Turning up the volume so that the velvety strains would carry outside, she took her son a well-deserved brew.

'Here, lad.' Janie passed the cup over the garden fence. 'Get that down you.'

He wiped the perspiration from his brow and smiled wryly. 'Ta – I need this!'

'It's a pity you and your dad couldn't have done it together after all.'

'Is he all right?'

'Aye. He's enjoying a cup of tea with the paper.'

'He didn't half look downcast, Mam, when I volunteered with the Anderson in his place.'

Swallowing down a mouthful of tea, she shrugged sadly. 'It's a case of him having to get used to it, in t' it? Things can't be helped; it is what it is.'

James was still on her mind a short while later. Calling out to her son, who had returned to his work next door, to keep an eye to the twins, she headed inside.

'All right, love?'

Sat slouched in his fireside chair, her husband nodded without looking up. 'Aye.'

248

'You're sure? Only—'

'Ssh. What was that?'

Frowning, Janie turned towards the window, which she'd opened earlier to allow a little breeze into the humid room, and now she heard it too: footsteps coming up the front path.

Muttering a curse, she bolted for the sideboard and had it and the few loose boards beneath lifted in seconds. However, no knock was forthcoming and, when she listened harder, she realised with confusion that whoever was out there had passed right by her front door and was making their way through the ginnel between the houses. *Who on earth . . . ?*

'Stay out of sight,' she warned James. 'I'll find out what's going on.'

Janie hurried back outside to investigate. She heard Seymour's voice before she saw him. He'd passed through the ginnel by now and was standing with Joey in Lynn's garden – halting, she called across to him in surprise: 'Morning, Mr Briggs.'

'Mrs Hudson. Hello.'

'Is everything all right?'

He nodded towards the six corrugated panels lying in a heap on the grass. 'Lynn mentioned what your son here was about – a reet kind deed it is too. As I have nowt on this morning, I thought he might appreciate a helping hand.'

'Oh.' She'd intended to go to her cleaning job shortly – it would have to be this afternoon, now, instead. James couldn't very well sneak across to hunker down in Lynn's house in her absence, could he, not with Seymour here? And she couldn't risk leaving her husband home alone. Nonetheless, the gesture was a nice one and Janie was touched. 'That were thoughtful of you.'

'I'll say,' agreed Joey with a grin. 'This lark is harder than I thought it would be.'

His own face breaking into a smile, the grocer loosened his tie and rolled up his shirtsleeves. 'Right, lad, let's get started. I reckon we'll make short work of this between us.'

'I'll get you a cup of tea, Mr Briggs,' Janie told him, casting him through the fence a soft look, which he returned.

'Lovely.'

'I shan't be a minute.'

'Well?' James wanted to know the moment she re-entered the room. 'Who was it?'

'Oh, just Mr Briggs from the shop. He's offered to aid our Joey with the shelter.'

'Why?'

She blinked back in bewilderment. His tone had been abrupt, harsh even. 'Just to be nice, I suppose. It doesn't bother you, does it?'

''Course it soddin' does! Don't you think I'd give anything to be the one out there with the lad right now? Sorry,' he added, running a hand through his hair. 'I didn't mean to snap, only . . . I feel fit for nowt, lass, and I hate it.'

She stroked his cheek. 'I know. I'm sorry.'

'Don't be, it's not your fault. Just ignore me. I'll be all right.'

'You're sure?' she asked, though she was already inching back towards the kitchen. These morose episodes could be exhausting and, right now, though not apathetic to his situation, she hadn't the strength to face it. To her relief, he nodded and she hastened from the room.

Her son and employer worked hard, and in no time the Anderson began to take shape. The metre-deep hole was dug primarily by Joey, him having the energy of youth on his side, then Seymour's skills of organisation and patient planning came to the fore and the first steel sheets were soon bolted into place. The rest followed steadily, man and boy communicating calmly all the while, and finally they had reached the last task: piling earth on to the curved roof to hold the shelter's position securely.

Throughout, Janie had watched their progress through one eye, squinting in the sun on the blanket between the twins with a cup of tea in her hand, the wireless playing softly in the background, and knew a sense of contentment. Birds chirruped pleasantly above, mingling with the soothing hum of a solitary bee nearby drifting lazily from flower to flower, and for just a short while at least her tribulations seemed as though belonging to another lifetime. A stranger looking in would never believe there was a conflict raging – in her own household as well as abroad. In this moment, all was peaceful, and she savoured it.

'Ey up, here comes trouble,' announced Joey, who was taking a rest on his shovel, flicking his head towards Top o' th' Brow School in the distance.

251

Following his gaze, Janie saw that pupils were spilling from its doors for their quarter-hour breaktime and that her daughters, having spotted their presence, were making a beeline for them across the playing field. She went to greet them at the fence.

'Hello, my lasses. Having a good day, are youse?' she asked when they had skidded to a halt on the opposite side, pink-cheeked and panting for breath.

The next few minutes were taken up with them regaling her with the morning's lessons and general classroom antics – during which Janie noticed Seymour listening in keenly. And as the girls continued chattering ten to the dozen, as children do, a light smile broke through to hover at his mouth. Not for the first time, she was reminded about his life and missed opportunities – parenthood, for one – and how he must regret not having experienced before moments such as this.

When the conversation finally exhausted itself, the grocer spoke. Motioning to his and Joey's handiwork, he asked, 'What d'you reckon, then, lasses? Will it pass muster with Mrs Ball?'

Meeting his eye shyly, Elsie nodded. Hilda however, never one to withhold her opinion, chewed at her bottom lip in consideration before declaring: 'It looks a bit wonky to me.'

Joey scrunched up his face in indignation. 'Wonky, my foot! We've toiled hard on that; there's nowt up with it, cheeky article.'

Seymour was chuckling, clearly enjoying the exchange. 'You think, do you, lass?'

Tilting her chin, face serious in deliberation, Hilda scrutinised the shelter again. Then: 'Aye – it's definitely askew. Lynn will not be pleased,' she added to her brother. 'Ah well, our Joey, you'll just have to knock it down and start again, won't you?'

'What! You must be joking! There's no way I'm . . .' His words petered out, his temper with them, as the girl threw back her blonde head and laughed. 'Oh, I see . . . you little swine, yer!'

'I had you going, though, didn't I?' she chortled, hopping from foot to foot in glee, clearly delighted with herself. 'Now come on, admit it.'

'Aye, all right. Only forra second or two, mind. I were just playing along with you the rest of the time.'

'Huh – yeah right! You great fat liar—!'

'Now now, that's enough of that,' Janie intervened with a roll of her eyes before a full-scale squabble broke out. Seymour, on the other hand, looked to be enjoying every minute. Pulling out his hanky, he wiped the tears of mirth from his eyes, and she couldn't help smiling. 'Terrible, they are, Mr Briggs, honest. Any excuse forra ruddy argument!'

'All harmless fun, all harmless fun,' he replied with a definite hint of fondness in his tone, and again he and Janie shared a smile.

'Oh God, we'd better go. Best not keep owd fish-face waiting,' said Hilda as a sudden clanging rang out. Teacher Mr Fisher had appeared on the school steps and was swinging a bell back and forth, signalling the end of play. 'Come on, our Elsie,' she added, taking the youngster's hand, which heartened their mother to see – it seemed Hilda had indeed been serious in her recent vow to look after her sibling from now on.

'Hang about,' Seymour called as they made to bolt. He rummaged around in his waistcoat pocket and produced two black-and-white-striped humbugs, which he passed to the girls through the wooden slats. 'Go on, you can eat them on the way.'

Delighted, they accepted with a polite thank-you and popped the hard-boiled peppermint sweets into their mouths. Then, waving, they skittered off to join their classmates lining up in neat rows on the yard.

'That was kind of you,' said Janie when they had gone. 'You'll be a friend to them for life, now!'

The grocer seemed pleased at this. 'They're good kiddies. They're a credit to you, Mrs Hudson.'

A feeling of quiet pride ran through her. 'Aye, they are, and ta.'

Shooting a glance to the shelter, Seymour sniffed. 'Well, that's that.' He sounded almost regretful. 'I'll be on my way, then.'

'Thanks again, Mr Briggs,' Joey said. 'I'll see you out.'

He nodded. Then, turning to look at Janie, he smiled. 'Ta-ra, Mrs Hudson.'

'Ta-ra.'

He continued staring at her as though he would say more. However, he didn't; instead, he touched his hat in farewell and walked away.

Still wearing a quiet smile, Janie returned to the

blanket with a sense of happiness for a morning well spent.

'You just had to rub my nose in it, didn't you?' muttered James later, when they were retiring for the night.

'What?'

'You heard me. Did you think I didn't know? I saw you from the window.'

Janie was flummoxed. 'Saw what, love?'

'You. Giggling and carrying on with that boss of yours, when it should have been me out there with my wife and kids. Youse looked like a proper cosy little unit, aye. Well, you're my family, are you listening? *Mine!*'

'For God's sake.' She turned her back on him and his anger with a jaded sigh. 'It wasn't like that, and you know it. Mr Briggs was being neighbourly, that's all.'

'Aye, and the rest.'

'There's no "rest" to it. We'd have rather had you with us, 'course we would, but that weren't possible, was it? Now just drop it, will you?'

James stomped across the room to push the two armchairs together – his makeshift bed – and lay down, turning his back to her without saying goodnight.

Instinct had her moving forward to go to him, to apologise, make everything better. Then sudden weariness overtook her and, with a shake of her head, she crossed to the sofa instead.

Peering at her husband's shape in the darkness,

hot tears stung. Then her thoughts switched to the hazy hours earlier that day, the sun and peace and laughter – the way Seymour had spoken to her with only kindness in his tone. He'd complimented her on her children, he'd smiled and he'd made her feel calm. *Calm.* The emotion felt like a stranger to her these days. There had been no pressure or backbiting, no accusations, no guilt. Only ease of mind; what she wouldn't give to know that now – always.

Closing her eyes, she pictured him at this moment, two streets away in his own home surrounded by his books, feet up with a cup of tea, ruminating gladly on his morning having been as enjoyable as hers. And as she settled down to sleep, a smile went with her.

Chapter 16

'OH GOD, NOT AGAIN.'

'Is that . . . ?'

'Aye,' Janie confirmed, springing from the sofa and rushing for the hall. 'I'll get the kiddies downstairs, you grab the things from the kitchen. Come on, James, quick!'

A handful of minutes later, the family found themselves hunched on the benches of the damp shelter for a second night – all except Joey. He'd insisted he must be with Stella to look after her and, before his mother could argue the point, had pelted down the road to sit this next raid out in Mrs Hodgkiss's shelter.

The Hudsons had at least the comfort of warmth and light this time. In anticipation of further raids, Janie had prepared what she called their 'shelter pack' – a wicker basket that she'd filled with blankets and candles and which she kept by the back door in readiness. Alongside these essential items were the family's identity cards and ration books, as well as birth and marriage certificates. Should the house suffer a hit, their important documents would be saved – and a whole load of hassle that came with the reissuing of such things into the bargain.

'I'm cold,' Hilda stated.

'I'm tired,' added Elsie.

'Here, lasses, lie down.' By the light of a guttering candle, Janie settled them at each end of the wooden seat and covered them with a blanket. She folded two others and slipped one each beneath the girls' heads to act as pillows. 'Fingers crossed, you'll be back in your beds again shortly. For now, try to get some sleep here.'

'Aye, Mam,' Elsie said, stifling a yawn.

'I'm *sick* of that Hitler, me,' huffed her sister before she too closed her eyes.

Squatting on the floor between them, Janie stroked their hair until their breathing had steadied in sleep then went to sit beside James on the bench opposite. She glanced his way, but he made no effort to acknowledge her in return. Instead, he continued staring ahead at nothing, mouth set, arms folded, and she looked away again with a small sigh.

His moods were worse than ever. She was lucky if she managed to get more than two words from him, let alone anything even remotely resembling a smile. He'd retreated into himself too deeply for her to reach and it seared more than she could have imagined it would. He was hurting, she knew that, but what could she do? The more she tried to understand him, to sympathise, the more he turned from her. He seemed hell-bent on pushing her away and she was at a loss, now, how to make things right.

'At least Jerry gave us the weekend off, eh?' she murmured after a while, attempting a stab at conversation, desperate to lighten the atmosphere. 'Mind you, I might have to keep the girls off school. If this goes on for much longer, they'll be fit for nowt come the morning. It ain't right sending them in exhausted, poor loves.'

James brought his gaze to his daughters. 'It's not right, is it?'

Surprised that he'd responded – she'd fully expected the usual stony silence – she shook her head. 'No. No, it ain't.'

'Them bastards need defeating, and soon.'

'And they will be, you mark my words—'

'Aye?' he barked, cutting her off. He finally turned to look at her, and there was such a level of burning fury in his gaze that Janie gasped. 'You reckon so, do you?' he went on in a growl. 'And how are we meant to see them Germans beat when filthy cowards like me sit idly at home doing nowt to stop it? Go on, you tell me that!'

Not this again. 'Love . . .'

'I'm a disgrace, Janie. I sicken myself.'

'James, please—'

'I'm not fit to call myself a man. I'd sooner be dead than live another day, another *hour*, with this crippling shame. I just can't do it any more!'

She reached out to comfort him, but he shrugged her off savagely and she let her hands fall back to her sides. Nothing she did would have the slightest impact, nor would he listen to anything she had to say, so what

259

was the point? Dropping her head, she allowed the tense silence to envelop them once again.

All remained still beyond the shelter. No sound of a rattle or handbell, which the ARP warden would use to alert the people of a gas attack. The searchlights would have difficulty locating enemy aircraft this night owing to low-lying cloud, but still there was no roar of engines overhead. No bomb blasts.

Eventually, the all-clear wailed its 'raiders passed' signal. Without a word, Janie and James rose. They lifted into their arms a slumbering daughter each and carried them across the garden and into the house. Joey arrived home as his parents were returning downstairs from putting the girls to bed, and Janie encouraged him to go on up too and get some rest. This he did, and she went to join her husband in the living room, closing the door softly behind her.

'I love you.'

Having already returned to his armchair bed, James kept his eyes closed and didn't respond. Fighting back her anguish, Janie climbed beneath the covers on the sofa and closed her eyes.

'Open up!'

In the same moment that the thunderous demand reached them from outside there came an ear-splitting crack as the front door crashed inwards. Janie and James barely had time to raise their heads from their pillows before half a dozen men in uniform stormed the room yelling instructions, rifles pointed:

'Up! Up!'

'My God . . .' Janie choked on a gasp as she was forcibly wrenched to her feet. A torch was shone into her face, its lurid glare momentarily blinding her. Yet she didn't require the power of sight to know that, across the room, her husband was encountering the same treatment.

'James Hudson?' a voice boomed.

His quiet response was unpanicked. 'Aye, that's me.'

'You are under arrest. Come with us.'

'Please!' Janie cried, rushing forward and attempting to yank aside the large hands that had seized James, but it was no use – the officer's grip held firm. 'You can't take him, you *can't*!'

'It's all right, lass. Everything's going to be all right.'

'No!'

'Janie, you must accept it.' Her husband's tone was calm, measured. 'It's time. Just know that I love you, more than owt else in this world, and always will.'

'James!' she screamed over and over, her feet tripping over themselves in hot pursuit of him as he was bundled past her, down the path and into the vehicle waiting ready by the roadside. Then he was gone. The strength left her legs and she crumbled into a heap on the hard ground, sobbing loudly. 'Oh, my love! My love!'

'Janie?' It was Lynn, barefooted in her nightgown, disturbed by the ruckus. 'Come on, love, come on.'

Janie felt her friend's hands go under her and help her to her feet. She allowed her to lead her back inside the house, but not for anything could she quell the agonised whimpers that tore from her or the tears cascading like a burst riverbank, doubted they would ever stop.

'He's gone.'

'I know, Janie. Eeh, you poor love.'

'What will I do?'

'For a start, you can answer some questions,' a grim-faced officer interjected. 'Knowingly harbouring a deserter – particularly in wartime – is a serious offence, Mrs Hudson. It would be in your own best interests to tell us exactly what we need to know.'

'I'll sit with them,' Lynn offered soothingly as movement sounded above, alerting them that the children were awake. 'You'll be all right?' she asked Janie, shooting the man standing over her a dark look.

'Aye. See to the kiddies.'

When her friend had gone, Janie waited with dread for the expected grilling but, to her consternation, it never came. Instead, the officer nodded to a colleague standing nearby. Then the pair crossed the room, making straight for the sideboard.

She could only watch in numbing astonishment as they pulled the furniture out and stooped to examine the floorboards beneath. How could they possibly . . . ? 'Lord, no,' she croaked as realisation slammed home, bringing with it a wave of such horror, swiftly followed by rage, that she could barely snatch in a breath. 'This ain't a random visit like before at all. You knew for certain James was here because you were informed. I'm right, ain't I?'

'Such details matter not—'

'They do to me!' Trembling uncontrollably, she dived to her feet. 'Who was it, eh? Who told youse?'

'Mrs Hudson, hold your calm. You are doing yourself no favours.'

Void now of rational thinking, she sank back into her seat with a feeling of drowning. Questions were put to her, but she was incapable of answering any of them, and in the end the frustrated officers took their leave with the promise that they would be calling on her again.

Alone, Janie could focus still on nothing – and wouldn't for a long time afterwards – but that one, all-consuming thought: just who could hate them so much to want to rip their entire lives to shreds, and why?

'My heart is broken.'

Pouring out tea, Lynn clicked her tongue sympathetically.

'I don't understand it. It makes no sense, none of it.'

'And you say they made a beeline straight for the sideboard? They searched nowhere else?'

'Not this time, no. It was like that officer knew exactly what to go for. Someone tipped them off, Lynn.'

The women sat in tense silence for a few minutes with their own thoughts – predominantly that it seemed Janie was indeed right, and just who could it have been who informed?

'Well, I know it weren't me,' her friend said finally. Eyes thoughtful, she rubbed her chin. 'Who else knew about the floorboards hideout?'

'Me and the kids.'

'There's no chance one of the lasses might have let it slip to one of their friends . . . ?'

Janie shook her head. 'They're adamant, Lynn, and I believe them.'

'Right, so, if it ain't Hilda or Elsie, and you certainly didn't say nowt, then that just leaves . . . No, he *wouldn't*.'

'My Joey?' Janie gave a huff of derision. 'No, not him, never.'

'But then who else—?'

She cut Lynn off suddenly with a shuddering gasp. 'Oh, my God.'

'What?'

'Stella!'

'Eeh, no . . . !'

'How could I have forgot?' Janie choked, nodding wildly. '*Stella* knew.'

'Now, love, listen to me,' said Lynn as Janie leapt to her feet to pace the room. 'You must be absolutely certain before you go rushing in accusing her. If you're wrong—'

'How can I be wrong? There's no one else!'

'But if by some chance you are . . . It would cause a merry ruddy storm of trouble. Joey might never forgive you.'

The ticking of the clock filled the room for several moments as Janie stood dithering. Then the Metcalfe girl's face – her expression one of disdain with a smirk hovering nearby, which Janie recognised so well – slammed into her mind and her trickling anger grew to a raging torrent, obscuring all other thought. She began to tremble, her breathing ragged.

'Stella's been aloof with us all since day one, does nowt but stare down her nose at us, has *never* liked us,' she seethed, her hands bunching into fists. 'Oh, she put on a fine enough show when she came here for her tea, the night she learned about the hidey-hole over there, aye, I grant you. But I see her game, now, all right. It were nobbut play-acting for our Joey's sake. That vindictive little bitch *has* done this, she has. I'll rip her friggin' head off!'

'Janie. Janie love, wait,' Lynn entreated, but her friend was beyond all listening and she had no choice but to hurry after Janie as she charged purposefully from the house.

'Hello, love—'

'Where is she?' Janie hissed, cutting through Sadie's greeting like a hot knife through butter. Before the bewildered woman could respond, Janie shoved her aside and stalked inside.

She found Stella dozing by the fire as though she hadn't a care in the world – and this stoked her fury further still. Marching forward, she gripped the girl by the front of her blouse and hauled her to her feet.

''Ere, Janie love!' Sadie attempted to intervene but backed off when Janie pointed a quivering finger in her face.

'This evil young cow has some questions to answer, so just you keep out of it, Mrs Hodgkiss,' she growled. Then, turning back to a baffled-looking Stella: 'Why? Why did you do it, eh?'

265

'Do what?'

'Don't even *think* to deny it to me. Don't you dare. I've been wracking my brains – could it be Albie? Your mam, even? Both have axes to grind, and I wouldn't put it past either to want to hurt us. But it can't be, no, because they knew nowt about the sideboard. It was you. *You* went squealing to the police about my James. Go on, admit it!'

Stella shrugged herself free from Janie's hold then folded her arms. 'You believe that, do you?' she put to her mildly – her calmness threw Janie.

'Well, of course I bloody do! The law knew exactly where to look. There's . . . there's no one else—'

'No?' Raising an eyebrow, the girl swivelled her gaze to a point beyond Janie's shoulder. 'You're sure about that?'

Frowning, Janie turned slowly. The person staring back at her – the *truth* – brought a wave of nausea to her guts – she gasped. 'You?'

'I told Sadie all about it,' Stella went on. 'Happen I shouldn't have . . . but well, I never dreamed she'd do this. I reckon it's her you should be haranguing, not me.'

The words were barely registering. Janie side-stepped to the mantel to cling to its edge for support. She was going to faint, she was . . . 'You?' she murmured again to the older woman.

'Janie . . . Janie, I can explain—!'

'After everything I've done for you? You were my *friend*.'

'I am still!' Her wet face wreathed in horror, Sadie

266

made to reach out to Janie, but she leapt back from her with a cry. 'Love, I never meant . . . The girl's got it all wrong, she has—'

'Did you blab?'

'Love, please—'

'Did you: yes or no?'

'Well aye, but—'

'I need to get out of here.' Choking out devastated sobs, Janie looked to Lynn in desperation. 'I need to get out of here!'

'Aye, come on,' her friend told her, leading her to the front door. 'Come on away, now.'

'Wait!'

At Stella's cry, Janie paused to glance around. The girl rushed forward and grasped her hands, and Janie blinked back through a blur of tears. 'Lass . . . I'm sorry, I am—'

'Don't leave me here. Please, Mrs Hudson. I can't stop on any more, now, after what she's done. I can't.'

Flicking her eyes towards Sadie, Janie's lip curled. She nodded. 'Aye. Collect your things, lass, and come on back with me.'

'But . . . ! But . . . !'

'But nowt,' Janie told Mrs Hodgkiss as Stella raced upstairs to pack. 'You, you've finished with me, finished with *all* of my family, from this day. You're lucky I'm not tearing you limb from limb, you wicked owd bitch! How could you do it, eh? To me, what's been nowt but kindness to you when no bugger else wanted to give you the time of day . . . and aye, I can see why, now! I tell you summat,' she added, thrusting her face

267

into Sadie's, and her words had taken on a chilling tone. 'Should harm come to my husband because of this – because of *you* – I swear to God I'll do for you. Make no mistake about that. Do you understand?'

'Janie . . . Love . . .'

'Do you understand?' she repeated, swatting aside the older woman's arm with a grunt of disgust as she attempted to take her hand.

'I'm sorry. I'm *sorry.*'

'Get out of my way.' Pushing past her, Janie strode from the room, a silent Lynn trailing close behind. Meeting Stella, clutching her bundle of belongings, in the hall, Janie motioned for her to follow, and the trio stepped outside.

'Please, love. Please!'

Janie didn't look back. Chin high, heart shattered, she continued for home, Sadie's cries ringing in her ears all the way.

'I can't believe you could have thought it was Stella.'

Despite the good fire, Janie sat shivering beneath the shawl wrapped around her shoulders. 'I'm sorry.'

'I mean, she'd never do such a thing,' Joey went on with a shake of his head, taking the girl's hands in his own. 'What possessed you?'

'Lad, I'm *sorry.*'

'Leave her be, Joey.' Extracting herself from him, Stella rose and went to crouch in front of Janie. She reached out and patted her shoulder. 'Can't you see your mam's upset?'

'No, lass, he's right.' Covering her face with her

hands, Janie sighed. 'I shouldn't have thought it of you. It were wrong. It's just . . . there was no one else – or so I reckoned.'

'I never should have mentioned it to Mrs Hodgkiss, and I'm sorry for it. I believed her trustworthy but see now I were mistaken.'

'Aye, and me.' The pain of betrayal seared deeper still. Dipping her head, Janie wiped the fresh tears that had formed with the back of her hand. 'I've been nowt but good to that woman, and she goes and does this. I'm fair broken-hearted, I am.'

'Never mind, Mrs Hudson. James will come back in one piece, you'll see.' Stella nodded with conviction. 'In t' meantime, you've got us. We'll not let you down.'

'Aye, Mam, Stella's right.' Voice soft now with contrition, Joey came to kneel beside his future wife. 'We're here.'

'And us,' piped Hilda, pulling Elsie along to perch with her on the arm of Janie's chair.

'Eeh, youse lot.' Janie was overcome. 'What would I do without you, eh?'

'Go up to bed, Mrs Hudson, and have a lie-down,' Stella said. 'I'll see to the kiddies and the evening meal.'

'Oh, I don't know, love . . .'

Rising, Stella stared down at her, hands on hips. 'I insist.'

She *could* do with resting her banging head for a while . . . 'All right, then, if you're sure?'

'I am. Go on.'

Nodding, Janie left the room and headed upstairs. Crawling gratefully into bed, she heaved a long breath and closed her eyes.

Sleep wouldn't come, of course not; she doubted whether she'd ever know its release again. However, just being alone to gather her tumultuous thoughts was enough right now – and much needed. She'd genuinely feared earlier that she might be in danger of suffering a complete mental collapse, so intense had the terrible emotions been. Naturally, answers were what she craved still, more than anything else. But she knew that, for now at least, they would remain out of her reach, and so she must be content with darkness and peace going some way to soothing her torture.

James.

Where was he? Was he frightened? Was he missing home, missing her as much as she yearned for him? Just how would he bear this? He couldn't go back to battle, wouldn't cope with it again. Why – *why* – had this happened?

Sadie Hodgkiss's image slithered into her mind and she gripped the bedclothes with both hands. The stab of hurt and loss was indescribable. Never would she forgive the woman this.

The tear it had ripped through their friendship was irreparable – and still Janie was no nearer to understanding *why*. Yet did it even matter? What was done was done, and nothing would change that. However, Janie was as steadfast on one thing as she'd been when first delivering it: her threat to Sadie should her cruel talk cost him his life.

Nothing on this green earth would protect her from Janie's murderous revenge should that come about.

Chapter 17

WEEKS DRIFTED BY in a haze. A prisoner of her unshakeable grief, Janie allowed herself to be swept along without resistance.

Stella had proved her weight in gold throughout the living nightmare that was now her soon-to-be mother-in-law's world. At the girl's own insistence, she'd taken on the most taxing of the household chores to enable Janie to rest whilst she got over her shock, and had shown herself to be as diligent and capable as someone twice her age. Janie didn't know what she'd have done without her.

Lynn, on the other hand, was a different matter. Though it pained Janie to face up to it, her best friend had been a bit of a let-down. If there was one person she could be confident to have her back in her hour of need, it was Lynn. Or so Janie had assumed. The reality had turned out to be massively disappointing.

Lynn didn't admit she believed Sadie a victim of injustice – not in so many words, at any rate. And dreading hearing the truth, Janie had thus far resisted asking the woman's opinion outright. However, she sensed Lynn's feelings keenly at how matters had panned out and, inevitably, as time went on, it had begun to drive a wedge between the pair.

Now, as a quiet July slowly gave way to August and the dreaded late-night air-raid warnings started up again, adding further worry to those already clogging her mind, Janie longed for her friend's companionship and support more than ever before. But she was at a loss how to put things right and hadn't the strength of spirit just now to attempt it. In return, and much to her bewilderment, Lynn showed no signs of wanting to rectify things either.

Today, as had become usual of late, Lynn dropped off Bobby and Brian and left again for work with barely a word in between. Janie watched her go with a sigh and, after settling the boys, headed to the kitchen. She'd filled the kettle and put it on the hob and was swilling out the teapot before she remembered – 'Damn it!' she muttered beneath her breath. Slamming down the teapot and turning off the heat, she retraced her steps back to the living room.

As predicted, tea had indeed found its way on to the ration list. For citizens of one of the greatest tea-drinking nations in the world, the cutbacks had come as a heavy blow. None more so than to Janie. The beverage, which she'd come to rely on over the years to calm her frayed nerves if and when required, was more necessity than luxury so far as she was concerned, and her disgust at having to eke out her precious two-ounce weekly allowance – which stretched, if you were lucky, to two weakish cups per day – only grew with time. Now, more than ever, she'd have killed for an endless supply of strong sweet brews.

With a shrug, she donned her knitted turban and pinny and got started on the housework, whilst Stella kept an eye to the twins. She'd washed and scrubbed the front step and cleaned the windows and was on her way to pour out the bowl of dirty water she was carrying down the sink when a dull ache struck beneath her ribs. Pausing, she sucked in some air and rubbed the offending spot. Within moments, the pain had subsided and, thinking no more of it, she continued with her duties.

Being Monday and what was widely acknowledged as wash day, her last task was to fill the dolly tub with hot water. The dirty clothes went in next, and she was pounding the muck from them with the posser when, once more, the throb returned to her stomach. This time, she ignored it and again, soon afterwards, it disappeared. When it hit for a third time as she was dragging out the large wooden mangle, she barely paid it heed. It went as quickly as before and, without further thought, she continued with her chore of wringing out the excess water from the garments then carried them across the garden to hang them out.

Today and every other wash day, her old street – and each road and lane surrounding it – would be festooned from end to end with lines of clothing billowing in the breeze. Top o' th' Brow was different. Here, housewives didn't have to suffer the embarrassment of their family's underwear and other items

274

which had seen better days flapping away in public for all to see. Nor did they run the risk of having their snowy laundry ruined by dust should the coalman pass through on his round, or by children with devilment in mind. Instead, residents of these new estates, with their closed-off back gardens, were afforded the luxuries of privacy and protection – something Janie marvelled at still.

Fixing in place the last peg, she glanced to the sky and nodded in satisfaction. It was a fine day with not a hint of rain – this lot should be dry by the time she returned from her cleaning job.

'You'll be all right with the babbies whilst I'm gone?' she asked Stella on her way to the hall to collect her coat.

'Aye, Mrs Hudson.'

'Ta, lass, I shan't be long. If they get hungry in t' meantime, there's some butties made up for them in t' kitchen. All right?'

'Aye. Go on, you get off. Don't fret, they're in safe hands.'

Janie didn't doubt this. The girl had shown herself more than capable over the weeks in helping her care for Brian and Bobby. Besides, the practice would come in useful. Janie was confident that Stella, in spite of her limited years, would make a good mother in the none-too-distant future.

Passing down Padbury Way and on along New Lane, she shot the shops several glances in the hope of spotting Lynn outside snatching a break, but her friend didn't appear. Figuring that the grocer's must be keeping her particularly busy at present, Janie swallowed a sigh and continued on her way.

She let herself into Seymour's house and after hanging up her coat crossed to the kitchen to collect the polish and dusters from the low cupboard. As she was rising, the ache from earlier attacked – only this time, it was much more intense. Gasping, she pressed the area, but the pain refused to ease and, in the next moment, dizziness swooped. She felt her eyelids grow heavy and was dimly aware of the cleaning utensils slipping from her hands to clatter across the floor, then all went black.

'Where am I?'

'Don't try to talk, save your strength.'

The voice was familiar, but Janie couldn't prise her eyelids open to confirm the speaker's identity. 'Mr Briggs? Is that you?'

'Aye, lass.'

'What happened?'

The grocer helped her into a sitting position and leaned her back against the kitchen cupboard for support. Her eyes finally flickered open and she squinted around in groggy confusion.

'What happened?' she asked again. 'My head feels woolly . . .' Nothing made sense.

'Try to stay calm, lass. The doctor's on his way.'

'Doctor? I don't understand . . .'

'Ssh. Rest. All will be well.'

She must have dozed off again, for the next thing she was aware of was first one eyelid then the other being lifted, and the face of the young medical man who had treated Hilda's German measles swam into focus.

'Mrs Hudson? Can you hear me?'

'Aye,' she murmured.

'Mr Briggs informs me that he left his shop to collect something from home and found you unresponsive on the floor here. A stroke of fortune his timely arrival was, too. Are you able to tell me what happened?'

She shook her head. Then remembrance tapped through the brain fog and she nodded. 'I do recall I had a pain. Sharp, it were, beneath my ribs. It wouldn't go away like the other times.'

'Other times. You've experienced this before?'

'Aye, but that last pain were a bad 'un, worse than any before. I don't remember nowt after that.'

Frowning, the doctor examined her stomach for several moments, pressing here and there with the instruction she was to tell him if it hurt. Finally, he rose. His expression was grave.

'Doctor?' Her hands stilling in her task of repositioning her clothing, Janie felt fingers of dread snake her spine. 'What is it, what's wrong with me?'

'Nothing that plenty of rest won't cure. You've been working far too hard for someone in your condition. This episode today is your body's way of telling you to slow down—'

'Sorry, what?' she cut in, but one word replaying itself inside her head. 'Condition? What condition?'

'You mean you don't know?'

'Know what, Doctor?'

277

The man lifted his eyebrows. 'You're expecting, Mrs Hudson.'

Janie peered back at him in numb silence. Then: 'A child?'

'Well, unless you're a medical wonder and have a baby elephant growing in there, then yes: I'd put my money on it definitely being a child!'

'My God . . . Oh, my *God*.'

At her wail of distress, all trace of amusement left the doctor's countenance. He cleared his throat. 'Forgive me, that was crass of me. It wasn't my intention to upset you—'

'It's not that. I just . . . Oh, what am I going to do?' Great, shuddering sobs tore from her. 'I want my husband! I want James!'

Looking decidedly uncomfortable, the doctor mumbled something to Seymour and the grocer hurried out. Moments later, he was back. Only now, he wasn't alone – catching sight of the figure who had followed him inside, Janie let out a cry:

'Lynn!'

'Eeh. What's to do?'

'Oh, Lynn, I'm glad you're here.' Janie clung to her. 'I . . . I flaked out and . . . Please, love, take me home.'

''Course I will. There you go, that's it, you lean on me,' her friend soothed, helping her to her feet and supporting her to the door. 'We'll have you by your hearth with a nice cup of tea in two shakes of a lamb's tail. Easy now, take your time. I've got you, love, I've got you.'

Arriving at her house, Janie gave Stella a quick, watered-down explanation as to what had occurred. Then, taking a deep breath, she motioned to the twins. The time had come. 'Would you take the little 'uns next door for a bit?' she asked the girl. 'I need to talk with Lynn in private.'

Alone, the women sat facing each other across the table.

'I'm in the family way, Lynn.'

'You never are. Ay, Janie . . . How d'you feel about it?'

'Terrified, if I'm honest. I don't think I can do this without James. Just how will I manage?'

'You'll cope just fine, love, because you must. Besides, you're not on your own. You've always got me.'

'Have I, though?' she asked quietly, then bit her lip when her friend glanced away. 'You see, I'm not so sure any more.'

Silence descended. Lynn's gaze was firmly rooted to the tablecloth and, soon, Janie could stand it no longer. After scrambling around inside her head for the right words, she swallowed down her anxiousness and began:

'What's happened, love, at all? It ain't been the same between us since all the trouble with that one a few doors away, and I hate it. I've . . . well, I've missed you.'

Lynn's voice was barely audible. 'I've missed you, an' all.'

'Then why? Is it that you don't believe Mrs Hodgkiss is guilty?' There, she'd said it. Janie held her breath.

279

'At first I didn't, no. I admit it.'

Swallowing down the pain this brought, Janie nodded. 'Go on.'

'Well. I thought you'd been too quick to take Stella's word for it; she's just a slip of a lass after all, could have blurted all that to save her own neck. I thought Sadie were treated unfairly, that she weren't given a chance to fully explain.'

'And now?'

'Now, I see you were in the right all along. Thing is, by the time I realised it, we'd drifted too far apart and I didn't feel able to speak of it to you.'

'So what changed your mind?'

'I went to see her.'

'Mrs Hodgkiss?'

'Aye. I needed to hear it myself from her own two lips.'

'And?' Janie whispered.

'Sadie confessed.'

'She admitted she'd spoken to the police about James? She said those very words?'

'Aye.'

'I *knew* it.' Her hands beginning to shake with pent-up anger, Janie released air slowly. She mustn't allow herself to get too worked up, she knew. Not now, with the baby to think about. 'Why, Lynn? Why did she do it?'

Her friend shrugged her shoulders. 'She said she didn't know and clammed up pretty soon afterwards, refused to discuss it with me further. She regretted it right away, apparently, but couldn't take the words back once they were out – what was done was done.'

This unequivocal proof that she'd been right all along brought Janie not a shred of relief. Vindication wouldn't ever make her feel the slightest bit better – how could it? Someone she'd deemed a close friend had betrayed her in the worst way possible and there was no getting away from that. There was no forgetting the agonising fact. Nor could she ever forgive it.

'I can't get over what a rotten bitch I've been,' Lynn was saying now, and her tone was thick with tears. 'It must have been awful for you these weeks, and where was I? Not by your side, as I should have been, that's for sure. I just didn't know how to put things right, Janie, didn't think you'd listen to my apology even if I tried – nor would I have blamed you for it.' Reaching for her friend's hand, she squeezed it tenderly. 'Tell me,' she beseeched. 'What's it been like? Please, I want to know. Perhaps then I can start to make it right.'

Wiping away her own tears, Janie laughed mirthlessly. 'It's been bloody hellish, love, if you must know. News spread like wildfire around here, as you can imagine. I've seen folk staring whenever I go out, have heard them whispering behind my back. I just ignore it, but that don't mean it hurts any the less. Ralph the warden especially weren't best pleased. He stuck up for us, after all, and to discover he'd been hoodwinked along with the authorities . . . well.

281

I ain't his favourite person at the minute, put it that way.'

'Swines! Just you let me witness any nastiness thrown in your direction and watch what happens. I'll rip the gossiping buggers to shreds!'

Despite herself, Janie smiled. This was her friend, all right. The real Lynn Ball she knew and loved. Bolshy, brave and loyal to a fault. *This* was what she'd so sorely missed. 'Ta, lass.'

'And what of James?' Lynn's voice, now, was soft. 'Have you had word?'

'He's doing a spell in military prison.'

'Eeh, love.'

'The case ain't made it into the papers, mind, nor shall it: such stories are bad for public morale, apparently. That's one small mercy, I suppose. He doesn't reckon they'll keep him where he is for long, though. They're for giving him a second chance, he says, to prove himself worthy of the British army.'

'So he's to be shoved back into circulation, so to speak?'

Janie nodded. 'Top and bottom of it is they need all the men they can get.'

'Poor sod.'

'He don't seem to think so. Not no more. D'you know, Lynn, it's almost like he's at peace. I can't explain it . . . It's like, now he's been caught and knows he's going back to battle, he feels better somehow. He does, I could hear it in his letter. It's right – or at least he thinks so. It's his duty, where he should be, you know? When I think back to the night them officers

282

come breaking down our door, and I picture James's face before they dragged him out to the van, d'you know what I remember? He didn't seem scared, not a bit. He looked relieved. Aye. Like a great ton weight had been lifted from his shoulders. He were glad.'

Lynn shook her head sympathetically. 'You said yourself, though, didn't you, he'd been getting worse. That his feelings of inadequacy were growing and he was becoming more morose with each day what passed. Happen . . . well. Happen the time was right.'

'It doesn't make it any easier to bear, though, love. I don't half fear for him – and God, how I miss him. Who knows when he'll next be granted leave home – how will they trust him not to go AWOL again if they do? I might never see him again, not for years and years . . . And to think I used to get impatient with him. His moods, you know? Hate myself for that, I do. He was going through torture, and all I could think about was myself and how he was getting on my nerves . . .' She paused to clear the lump from her throat. 'That sounds wicked, don't it?'

'No, love. You were an angel to that man, did all you could, and James would say the same. Don't you doubt that. 'Ere, did you ever hear owt back from the police about your part in it?' added Lynn. 'You know, you hiding James here?'

'No. The dear love claimed in the written confession the police had him sign that it were all his idea, that he forced me to do it. They took his word for it. I'm in the clear.'

'Thank the Lord for that. More so, now, in light of your news,' her friend finished, a smile spreading over her face. Leaning forward, she laid a hand on Janie's stomach. 'Didn't you have a clue, love?'

'I had missed one or two of my monthlies, but well – what with all the stress I'd been under, I didn't think nowt of it. Eeh, just fancy it . . . me and my own child having new babbies at the same time! Friggin' hell.'

The other woman chuckled. Then, seeing the look that had passed over Janie's face, she frowned. 'Love?'

'Oh, Lynn.' It suddenly all made perfect sense. 'The babby . . . Our Elsie said our Joey was going to have a daughter . . . but then I had a night sight of me holding a little lad, and I thought that were Stella's, too, that she was going to have twins . . . But no, no. It was mine. I'm having a son.'

'Aw, Janie love, that's gradely!'

As a slow grin spread across her face, she finally allowed herself to agree.

'Here we go again – everybody up!' Janie called, hauling herself from her bed and out on to the small landing, dragging on her dressing gown as she went.

She threw open her daughters' door: 'Hilda, Elsie, up. You too, Stella,' she added, thumping on her son's door – Joey had given up his bed for the girl upon her arrival here from Sadie's, and was himself sleeping down on the sofa. 'Shake a leg, come on!'

Her daughters appeared with tousled hair and,

knuckling their tired eyes, hurried downstairs. Hearing Joey's door finally creak open, Janie nodded and was about to follow the girls to the kitchen when something made her turn back. To her horror, she saw not only Stella emerging from the bedroom but her son, too.

'You spent the night together?' she hissed.

Flushing at having been caught out, Joey pulled an apologetic face. 'Sorry, Mam . . .'

'What did you do, sneak up to Stella's bed like a thief in the night the minute the house was akip? You young dog, yer! Roll on when the two of you are wed, that's all I can say! In the meantime, the damage might have been done already, but I'll have no carryings-on beneath my roof, d'you hear . . . ? Oh, go on, shift yourselves, the pair of you, and get down to the shelter,' she snapped, jostling them towards the stairs. 'We'll talk about this later.'

'You ought to be resting, Mrs Hudson, the doctor said,' Stella stated on a yawn.

'Aye, as if Jerry's going to concern himself with a little detail like that! Now go on, straight to the garden – and, Joey, don't you forget to grab the basket on your way out.'

They settled themselves on the narrow benches and, after lighting a candle, Janie passed the basket around. 'Grab yourselves a blanket and get wrapped up. There's a newspaper and a comic or two, an' all, if anyone fancies them to help pass the time.'

Hilda and Elsie grabbed the comics whilst Joey opted for the paper. Stella had brought along her sewing box. She'd been occupied for days in making a peg rug to go in front of her own hearth when she and Joey eventually secured a home of their own. Extracting a handful of old rags, she set to cutting them into strips to be hooked on to the canvas web in her lap.

As usual, all was quiet outside. An owl hooted and the faint bark of a dog sounded in the distance. Folding her arms, Janie closed her eyes, hoping they wouldn't be kept out this night for too long.

'Janie?'

Opening her eyes again, she frowned. 'Did you hear that?' she asked.

'Can you hear me?' the voice called again before the others could answer Janie – tentatively, she popped her head outside:

'Hello?'

'It's me,' the speaker responded.

'Lynn?'

'Aye! Fancy some company, love?'

Grinning and shaking her head, Janie answered that she would. 'Come on around here to our Anderson, lass!' she told her. 'Be quick, mind. The Germans could be nearby, for all we know – you don't want a ruddy bomb landing on your head, do you!'

Lynn, a twin in each arm, was through their adjoining back gate and across the garden in seconds. 'Budge up, cocks!' she laughed, shuffling inside the Hudsons' shelter and plonking herself down on a bench. 'Eeh, that's better. It ain't half lonely out in that one of mine with just the babbies here for conversation.'

'Here,' said Janie, handing a blanket across. 'Cover the mites up.'

'Ta, love. Ay, I came prepared, an' all – look what I've got.' Reaching inside her coat, Lynn pulled out a beige stone bottle. 'Sup of tea, anyone?'

Janie laughed out loud. 'Would you look at us? It's like a ruddy party we're for having!'

'Aye well. If Hitler reckons he's for breaking our spirits, he's got another think coming! Now then, who's forra sing-song?'

By the time the all-clear rang out some twenty minutes later, the group was having so much fun that they were actually sorry to leave. With a collective 'Aw!' they rose reluctantly, and after gathering up their things stepped out into the black night.

'Ta-ra, then,' Lynn trilled as she headed for home. 'Same time tomorrow night, eh, lovies?'

Janie was still smiling as she bundled her family indoors and up to bed. For the dozenth time that day, she reminded herself how fortunate she was to have her wonderful friend back. She'd have moved heaven and earth to have James here, too, of course she would, but in the meantime, Lynn made a grand substitute. And Janie knew deep down in her heart that everything was going to be all right.

Chapter 18

JOEY AND STELLA were married in a swift but pleasant registry office ceremony on the last Saturday of September. True to her word, Mrs Metcalfe had given her consent and, though she failed to show up to watch her daughter exchange her vows, everyone was simply relieved that the wedding had managed to go ahead at all.

James's absence was the cause of a few long faces and several tears on Janie's part. However, just as James would have wanted, the family had been determined to put their hurt aside for a few short hours and had in the main succeeded, though he wasn't far from all of their minds throughout the day.

Albie, on the other hand, *had* been in attendance, in his stiff dark suit, as had Lynn and Seymour Briggs – he'd generously offered to supply a few foodstuffs from his shop for the wedding tea afterwards, and so Janie had felt it only right to extend to him an invite, which he'd readily accepted.

Owing to money being tight, a new frock for the bride had been out of the question, and so Janie had dug out the one she had worn on the day she herself became Mrs Hudson.

With some clever alterations, and paying close attention to the midriff area in particular – her swollen stomach was these days becoming impossible to conceal – Stella had managed to transform the dress and had looked quite beautiful, everyone agreed. That her mother would never get to see her like this, she'd accepted with a sad shrug of her shoulders. Not even the sudden wailing of the siren as Janie and Lynn had been helping her to get ready on the morning had thrown the girl off her stride – luckily, the all-clear was given within a handful of minutes. She'd refused to let anything spoil her special day and the occasion had gone without further hitch.

Then, weeks later, the grocer had come through for them again. He'd made mention to Janie that he had a few contacts, and would she like him to put in a word about a house for the newly-weds to rent? What strings he managed to pull, she didn't know, but it had worked. Joey and Stella had secured shortly afterwards a two-bedroomed house on neighbouring Aldercroft Avenue. Albie had helped them to furnish it with the basics from a second-hand shop, and had even raised his grandson's wage to enable him to adequately support his new family.

Janie was delighted to have the couple so close by and had showed her gratitude to Seymour by asking him to join her and her family one evening in a celebratory meal, which he'd seemed to enjoy immensely. As with Lynn, he'd become a firm friend of late, and Janie didn't know now what she'd do without him.

Now, as she and Lynn crossed through town in the December afternoon, all thoughts of weddings and jollity in general were far from their minds. The weather was harsh, the winds biting. Frost had settled on the sandbags stacked against buildings' frontages, placed to protect against bomb blasts, and folks' breaths fanned their hat-covered heads in great white clouds. With the prospect of warming their icy toes by the fire with a nice cup of tea dominating their thoughts, the women hurried on to make their final yuletide purchases.

The sight of Woolworths on the corner of Bridge Street and Deansgate, the 'owd lady' – a large statue of Britannia – standing gracefully atop its roof keeping a watchful eye over the good people of Bolton, was a welcome one. Arms linked, Janie and Lynn made a beeline for its doors.

Inside it was warm and bright and teeming with shoppers; they paused to look around. Then, smiling, they made their way across to the toys department. They took their time perusing the counter and the selection of sixpenny games and playthings on offer in search of the perfect stocking fillers. War or no, they were determined to try to make this the best Christmas they could.

Janie chose playing cards, a jigsaw and picture book each for Hilda and Elsie, as well as woollen socks and gloves for Joey and Stella, whilst Lynn opted for two small clockwork trains and wooden boats which floated in water for Bobby and Brian. Not only would the items prove great fun for the youngsters, they would provide much-needed distraction when in the shelters, they knew. After all, the Anderson was feeling more like a second home these days.

Following Dunkirk, Germany had devised a strategy to take Britain by sea. In order to stop the RAF mounting a defence against their advancing troopships, they had first to establish air superiority. And so had begun in the hot summer the Battle of Britain – a major aerial attack on the United Kingdom. However, the Germans hadn't anticipated the RAF's might and determination – by the date of the planned invasion, the Luftwaffe was defeated. And so commenced in the autumn Germany's next tactic: fierce bombing raids on the capital and other major cities – a period known as the Blitz.

Now, places of war weapons production weren't all that faced destruction – innocent civilians also became the target. A great many people were dead already, plenty more injured, and countless homes had been blown to rubble. Evacuees who had returned home during the Phoney War had been hastily sent back to the safety of their billets in the countryside. Men and women alike, driven by anger to 'get back at Jerry', joined up in their droves. Families were essentially torn asunder. And yet, if the enemy thought to cow them, they were sorely mistaken. Such wanton death and devastation had had the opposite effect on morale: it had served only to strengthen the people's resolve. Nothing would break their spirits. They would *never* surrender.

'Right, I think we're done,' Janie was relieved to announce some time later as she and Lynn emerged into the bland afternoon.

Her friend was quick to agree. 'Thank God! Come on, love, let's get home. I could murder a brew.'

Hooking baskets bulging with packages over their arms, they set off to catch the tram.

They had gone no more than a few yards when the all-too-familiar wavering wail pierced the skies – the women froze. Within seconds, the rest of town had followed suit; traffic and shoppers alike ground to a standstill. Then people were hurrying for the public shelters – Janie and Lynn took to their heels with the rest of them.

An assistant was standing outside the door of a nearby store, directing people into the building's cellar, and the women rushed for cover. They found a space and, praying they wouldn't be here too long, settled down in grim resignation to wait for the raid to pass.

Warnings had become increasingly regular. Throughout September and October, the sirens had been in almost daily operation. Nor did the enemy limit their unwanted visitations to the hours of darkness – these days, the mad sprint to safety could occur at any time of the day or night. People also saw much lengthier waits for the 'raiders passed' signal to sound. A three- or four-hour bout sat shivering in the shelter was not uncommon – and neither was but a single alert on any given date. In some instances, they would no sooner be released by the all-clear and climb back gratefully into bed when the siren would yell yet again, and up they would drag themselves, to return like rabbits to their burrows.

Things were indeed livening up. They heard planes overhead on occasion, now, and saw anti-aircraft guns in use, the storm of shells flashing silver-gold through the black heavens. Along with everyone else, Janie would cross her fingers and hope that enemy aircraft would be brought down – which sometimes they were. Such instances had become almost normal. However, there was one thing she doubted they would ever grow used to, and that was the bombs.

Raiders appeared to operate in a huge circle – so far, Bolton had miraculously escaped relatively unscathed. Attacks on neighbouring towns and cities, however, had become devastatingly predictable.

Manchester, Salford and Liverpool, in particular, were shown little mercy and some nights received terrific bombardment for hours and hours on end. Listening to the heavy thuds in the distance, imagining the onslaught those residents were suffering, brought tears of anguish and fury to every eye. All too often, Janie and the others would finally emerge from the Anderson to be met with a sky glowing red from the enormous fires raging miles away. Subdued with pity for the poor souls whose districts had taken a battering, and praying fervently theirs wouldn't be next, they would slink away indoors to await the next call to action.

Janie was just glad to have her friend by her side

during such episodes. Lynn's dash with her boys to the Hudsons' shelter the moment the siren sent out its dismal message had become routine, and the woman's cheery presence helped alleviate the fear tremendously.

Now, as she huddled with strangers in the dank underground space, Janie wished more than anything that she was in her own back garden; she'd never been in a raid away from home before. Fancy getting caught out whilst doing a spot of Christmas shopping – did Jerry have no sense of occasion or compassion at all? Her daughters at school, her son with his grandfather on the farm, and Stella babysitting Bobby and Brian, she refused to dwell upon. The feeling of helplessness was unbearable. They would be hunkering down as she and Lynn were, Janie assured herself over and over. They were safe. They were. *Please God.*

'I pray the kiddies are all right,' Lynn murmured, as though reading her thoughts; swallowing hard, Janie nodded agreement.

'They'll be fine, love. Hopefully, we'll be on our way soon,' she added, though her words held little conviction, even to her own ears. They had known more semblance of respite from the sirens in November and early December than in previous months, it was true, but the warnings seemed to be picking up once more. Last week, they had spent just short of twenty hours overall in their Anderson – Janie had counted – and secretly she worried they were in for a long spell now. 'Aye,' she lied in reiteration nonetheless, for her friend's sake. 'I'm sure of it.'

'Janie? Janie Hudson?'

The sudden call close to her ear had Janie turning with a frown to squint through the gloom. The speaker's face was in shadow, but she was sure she recognised the voice: 'Sorry, who is it?' she asked.

'It's me, Jean Giggs. You remember; I lived a few doors up from you at Velvet Walks.'

'Jean ... Jean! 'Course I remember you.' Janie pressed her arm in greeting. 'How are you?'

'Not too bad, love, and you? The children are well?'

'Aye, love, aye.'

Jean's teeth flashed in a smile. 'That's good.'

'And how's everyone doing at Velvet Walks?' Janie asked eventually, guilt stabbing at not having been back to visit in so long. 'Mrs Reilly's good, aye?'

'Eeh, ain't you heard?' Jean shook her head. 'The owd girl kicked the bucket a few months back. Summat to do with her heart, they reckoned. Sorry, Janie; I know how fond you were of her.'

She was speechless with grief. Imagining that dear woman dying alone in that festering hovel she'd called a home with only the rats for company was more than she could bear. And to think she'd never even got to say goodbye ... 'May God bless her!' she choked.

'Janie love?' It was Lynn. She shook her friend by the shoulder. 'That's the siren sounding, love. Let's get going, eh?'

The all-clear. So lost was she in her emotions, she hadn't noticed. She nodded. 'Aye, love, get me out of here.'

Throughout the journey back to Breightmet, Lynn

attempted several times to engage Janie in conversation. However, she was too consumed with her own thoughts to manage replies of more than one syllable, and Lynn eventually left her to her brooding.

It was later that night as the pair were sitting in number thirteen's shelter with their children – the sirens had sounded once again not long after the evening meal – that Janie finally felt able to open up to her friend.

'Let's hope this one is over as quick as the one earlier, eh?' Lynn was saying, stroking her sons' heads as they lay snuggled together sleeping peacefully on the bench beside her. 'I thought we were going to be in that cellar a lot longer than the quarter of an hour or so that it was – didn't you? Ay, guess what, though? Good news. Reuben Trent across the way were telling me earlier that this afternoon's raider was brought down. Apparently, one of our aircrafts was seen doing a victory roll in t' sky – that's what they do when they score a hit. Bloody well done, that man, I say. If only we could catch them all, then this rotten war would be over and done with. In't that right, love? *Love?* Janie, are you even listening?'

'Sorry.' Readjusting the blankets covering her daughters, Janie sighed. 'I don't know where my head's at today at all . . . Actually, I do,' she admitted quietly. 'Oh, Lynn, I just don't know what to do . . .'

'About what? Love, what's troubling you? Is it your friend, the one what you found out passed away?'

'Aye. Well, partly. You see . . .' She paused to shake her head. How could she put into words what had been dominating her mind since hearing of Mrs Reilly's demise? She didn't even understand the thoughts herself. 'It's just that since getting that news from Jean Giggs, I can't stop picturing another owd woman sat all alone in her house, day after day . . .'

'Another . . . ? What owd woman, love?'

'Mrs Hodgkiss,' Janie whispered. 'I know, I know, I shouldn't be giving her even a second of consideration after what she's done, yet . . . I feel sorry for her, Lynn. I can't help it. She only had us in the whole of the world and now . . .'

'Will you go and see her?' asked her friend softly.

'I don't know. I don't know if I could do it after what she's done, all what's passed . . . 'Course, we've crossed paths a few times – it's impossible not to, given how close we dwell to each other – but I look the other way and walk right by. Norra word has gone between us since I confronted her that day, and I'm not sure whether I could change that – nor if I want to. And yet . . . It's just . . . Oh God, I'm not making much sense, am I?'

Lynn leaned across to pat her hand. 'Aye, you are. I understand what you're getting at. You feel bad for a soul what's on their own and no doubt miserable. No matter who that soul is, whether it's Sadie or no, makes no odds. And d'you know why?'

'Because I'm a ruddy fool?'

'No. It's because you're kind, Janie. You've gorra solid golden heart, and that's the truth. Question is, can you find it *in* that heart to forgive and forget? Happen if you could finally draw the truth from her

297

as to why she informed on James, you could start to put it all behind youse for good. No harm can come from trying, surely?'

Lapsing into silence, Janie returned to her own musings.

By the time the siren released the strain of the all-clear an hour later, her mind was made up.

'Lad? Eeh, what's to do?'

Panting for breath on the doorstep, a terrified-looking Joey pointed through the moonlit winter morning in the direction of Aldercroft Avenue. 'Stella . . . The babby . . . !'

'Have her pains started?' Janie asked, at the same time reaching towards the hook on the wall beside her where hung her coat, which she threw on over her dressing gown.

'Help her, Mam, please. She's asking for you.'

Instructing her son to stay put to keep an eye to his sisters – the birthing room was, after all, no place for the father – she hastened into the silent street in her slippered feet and turned right for New Lane.

Here, she rapped smartly on the door of number twenty-four, where lived the local midwife, and when the tousled grey head appeared at the upstairs window, beckoned her down. Less than a minute later, the two of them were making their hurried way to Stella and Joey's house.

The front door was ajar, and Janie led the way inside. 'Stella, lass?' she called.

'Oh, thank God! I'm in here, Mrs Hudson!'

'All right, I'm here, lass. Nice deep breaths,' she soothed, dropping to her knees on the floor before the sofa, upon which lay the puffing and grunting girl. 'How long ago did the pains start?'

'I don't know, they woke me up . . . about half an hour or so, I think.'

'Right, well, we're in for a long wait yet.'

'I'm not due 'til the new year, it's too early.'

'Well, I don't reckon it's for waiting. Anyroad, a few weeks either way don't matter much.'

Scrambling for Janie's hand, Stella began to whimper. 'I can't do it! I can't!'

''Course you can. There's no need for fretting 'cause I'm going to help you every step of the way, all right? I know it's your own mam you'd likely rather have by your side, and I'm sorry for you there, lass, but I'm afraid I'll have to do.'

'No, I don't want her. I'm glad it's you. Mrs Hudson, the way I've behaved towards you in t' past . . . I'm sorry. Honest I am. I just . . . I knew you didn't like me, so I went on t' defensive, yet I wanted you to like me more than owt, but I didn't know how to go about making it happen, and—'

'Sshh, now,' Janie murmured thickly, cutting short her tearful rambling. 'All that's been and gone, and everything's different these days. You just keep calm and concentrate on the babby, lass. Just listen to what your body's telling you and you'll not go far wrong.'

'Oh Lord. Oh, the pain's coming back.' Gripping the sofa's cushions, Stella gritted her teeth. 'I'm so scared! It hurts so . . . *much*!' On the last word, she let out a beast-like cry and the midwife ducked beneath her nightdress to examine her.

'The head's crowning.'

'Already?' Janie was stunned. She cast the girl a grin. 'By 'eck, lass, it's nearly over!'

'When I say, I want you to give a big, firm push,' the midwife instructed. Then, in the next breath: 'And it's here!' she announced, catching the slithery life form in her firm grip.

Janie could hardly believe it; it had all happened so quickly. 'Eeh, lass. You clever, clever girl! You did it.'

'You've gorra fine and healthy daughter,' smiled the midwife.

Laughing and crying, Stella held out her arms for the squawking bundle that the woman had finished wrapping in a towel. Holding her close, she gazed into the child's face in wonder. 'Hello, little 'un.'

Janie was overcome with emotion. Chuckling and wiping her wet cheeks, she pressed a feather-like kiss to her granddaughter's dark hair. 'You're an angel, that's what you are.'

'Me and Joey agreed that if we had a girl, we'd name her Josephine. Josie for short.'

'Josie.' Janie smiled through fresh tears. 'Ay, that's bonny.'

'Right, we're all done,' said the midwife shortly afterwards with a relieved nod. 'You didn't lose much blood and the afterbirth came away no problem – you didn't even tear. Talk about swift and simple. I've never known owt like it, lass, you're a natural.'

After she'd gone, Janie made Stella comfortable

and brewed her a well-earned cup of tea. Then she kissed the new mother's cheek, gave Josie a last gentle cuddle and slipped from the house to collect Joey.

Her head and her heart overflowing with joy and love, she felt she could have floated the short journey home. And with the brand-new babe dominating her thoughts now and for days to come, her decision to visit Sadie Hodgkiss was completely forgotten.

Chapter 19

'MORNING, MRS HUDSON. And how's the new arrival to the family fettling?'

Giving Seymour a big smile, Janie sighed happily. 'Josie's doing just gradely, Mr Briggs. She's already got her parents wrapped around her little finger; ruddy besotted, they are. That goes for Hilda and Elsie, an' all – round at Aldercroft now, they are; it's a task trying to prise the pair away.'

'And you? You're all right?'

Following her fainting episode in his house, he put this question to her each morning, now, without fail; Janie couldn't help but feel touched by his concern for her well-being. As was usual, she answered with a reassuring nod.

It was the morning of Christmas Eve and there was a festive feeling in the small shop. Sprigs of holly dotted the shelves, and one or two simple decorations adorned the walls. In the streets, and despite the dreaded smell of snow in the air, Top o' th' Brow's residents seemed particularly cheery this day and greeted one another even more warmly than usual. It was as though, by some unspoken agreement, they too had decided to make the most of the yuletide period for all they were worth – distraction from the realities of war for a few short days was sorely needed. *If only everyone could be at home, contented and secure in the bosom of their family, where they belonged, everything would have been perfect . . .*

'There was no getting any work out of Lynn, giddy as she was, so I let her leave. She's gone to the train station early to while away the time from there,' said the grocer, as though he'd plucked the theme of Janie's ruminations from her mind – swallowing down her pain, she forced another smile.

'She's fair daft with excitement to have Duncan here for the holidays; aye, and who can blame her? I'd give owt to have—' Janie paused to bite her lip. 'But well, it is what it is, eh? No point in moping over what can't be changed.'

Duncan's battalion had been retained in Britain on home defence duties protecting vulnerable points, and as such he was afforded short sporadic leaves. James, on the other hand, wasn't so lucky. Though he'd completed his time in the army jail, he was now away training Lord knew where for offensive operations. And that meant only one thing: they were planning to send him overseas to fight again.

If his shell shock hadn't reared its cruel head again yet, then it soon would. How would he cope – and without her by his side? Would he even survive his next battle stint? Oh, if only she could speak with him in the flesh, see for herself how he fared – *hold tight to him and never let go.* But she couldn't. She couldn't, and now the twenty-fourth was upon them already and this made everything harder still. She was sick with heartache at the prospect of him not being home for Christmas.

They corresponded regularly, but the written word was no substitute for face-to-face communication – how could it be? In particular, having been forced to inform him he was to be a father again via letter had upset her immensely. That was no way in which to relay such monumental news, was it? No meeting of lips or avid embrace, no spoken endearments. No sitting to discuss the matter at length or opportunity to plan. No celebration.

Though his clear pleasure had shone from the pages of his return note, it just wasn't the same, and she knew it was something she'd for ever bitterly regret. It was true again when informing him of Josie's arrival. And when he'd eventually get to see his first grandchild was anyone's guess. He should be *here*. Damn Germany, damn Hitler and damn this bloody war!

'Is that the lot, Mrs Hudson? Can I get you anything else?'

Placing the last of her purchases on the counter, Janie shook her head, saying quietly now, her earlier chirpiness gone, 'Just them for now, Mr Briggs.'

'Are you all right?'

After trying but failing to clear with several blinks eyes now swimming with tears, she lowered her chin. 'I will be. It's just . . . It's a difficult time of year to be without the ones you love, you know?'

Seymour nodded with clear understanding. 'I do.'

''Course, aye, sorry.' So consumed was she in her own disconsolation, she hadn't given a thought to his even deeper experience of such loss – she inwardly cursed her tactlessness. 'You must miss your wife.'

'Oh aye. But well, as you say . . . if summat can't be changed, then where's the point in dwelling on it?'

Sensing his inward pain and deeming it kinder to put a halt on this particular line of discussion, Janie was about to agree with him and change the subject when the door opening behind her snared her attention. She gave a cursory glance around – and stopped dead in her tracks. *No, not her. Not now.*

Sadie herself had, upon spotting Janie, juddered to a standstill in the doorway. Mouth slack with unexpectedness, eyes wide, she looked like a rabbit caught in headlights. 'Janie . . .'

'Don't.' Despite herself, despite the expectation of the season and her determination to follow its code of goodwill to all, despite her recent – and only now remembered – decision to seek the woman out to attempt to build bridges, the bubbling resentment of old had resurfaced at the sight of her, and Janie was powerless to stem it. 'Just don't, Mrs Hodgkiss . . .'

'Eeh . . . love—'

'I said, *don't* speak to me,' Janie warned again in a low tone. 'Because, right now, the way I'm feeling, I'm liable to say summat I'll regret.'

In the ensuing silence, a customer perusing the shelves nearby gave a sniff. She followed this up with a mumble of something that Janie didn't quite catch – Janie turned on her, eyes like slits:

'What did you just say?'

'Well, if you must know . . .' The woman slammed the tin she'd been holding back on to the shelf. 'I reckon you're a ruddy hypocrite, Janie Hudson, that's what! Standing there lording it over this poor wench here like you're summat special – and for what, I ask you? Speaking up about your low-bellied husband? So she should, too – and ay, I'll tell you this for nowt: I'd have done the same in a heartbeat, aye. Making out you're the blameless one when all the while you were helping to conceal your man – huh, and that description's a debatable one! – whilst *our* brave fellas are out there doing their duty, risking life and limb? You ought to be ashamed.'

For several moments longer following the outburst, shock held Janie frozen. Then a torrent of rage – and crippling hurt – burst from her in a howl. She pointed a quivering finger in the customer's face. 'You viper-tongued owd *bitch*, yer! You know nowt, d'you hear me? Nowt, about me or my James. Keep your nose out of my affairs or, so help me, I'll break the bleedin' thing!' Leaving the woman standing agape with astonishment, Janie directed her attention to Sadie. 'As for you . . . You've ruined our lives, d'you know that? And for why? Why did you have to go and poke your great fat hooter into summat what didn't concern you? I'll never forgive you, you wicked bloody witch – never!'

Seymour attempted to touch Janie's arm in sympathy, but she shook her head wildly, sending her tears cascading down her face. 'You stop away from

306

me, too!' she cried. 'I wish to God we'd never moved here . . . Just leave me alone, the lot of you!'

'Lass . . .'

But Janie was past listening. Shoving past a silently weeping Sadie, she took to her heels and ran from the shop.

She reached home in seconds and slammed the door firmly behind her. Then, as the last vestige of her resolve dissipated, she fell to her knees on the hall floor and sobbed herself hoarse.

When the sound of knocking pierced through her malady, bringing reality crashing back, she lifted her head towards the door with a frown of dread, hadn't the strength for further battle now. Hiccuping back her emotion, she dragged herself to her feet. 'Who is it?'

'It's me, Seymour. Open up, there's a good lass.'

Chewing her thumbnail, she stared at the door warily. 'What d'you want, Mr Briggs?'

'Just to talk, that's all.'

She shuffled forward and reached out a hand. Shaking her head, she let it fall back to her side. Then she heaved a sigh and repeated the action, turning the latch this time and pulling back the door a little to peer through puffy eyes around the crack.

'Just to talk,' he repeated gently, inching forward; then, when she opened the door fully, he stepped inside with a disarming smile. 'Oh, and to give you this.'

'What is it?' she asked, eyeing the string bag he was holding up.

'Your shopping. You left it behind.'

A blush crept up her neck. 'Ta,' she murmured.

'You've no need to feel embarrassed, you know. Not with me.'

His words, spoken with such understanding and kindness, were the undoing of her; her face crumbled. 'Oh, Mr Briggs . . .'

'Ay. Come here, come here.'

Janie felt his arms go about her and clung to him. 'Fancy making a public exhibition of myself like that in the middle of the shop. I'll never live it down, I won't!'

'Don't take on so,' he hushed, and his tone and hold were secure and comforting, fatherly almost. 'It'll all be forgotten about come the new year. Besides, you were upset; no one will blame you for it.'

'Oh, they will! She did, that customer, whoever she was. My name's mud round here, now, since . . . well, *you* know. James deserting.' She felt him nod. 'He's no coward, Mr Briggs. It's the shell shock, it sent his mind daft after Dunkirk. He'd never have done it, else.'

'I figured as much.'

'And yet you've never made mention of it, not once. Not to sympathise or criticise nor owt else in between.'

The grocer's response was simple: 'Don't think I weren't sorry for you and what you must have been going through. No – I kept my tongue because it were none of my business. If you'd have wanted my opinion on t' matter, you'd have asked for it. You didn't, so I left it at that. The last thing I wanted to do was upset you in any way.'

Pulling back to look at him, Janie flashed a wobbly smile. 'You're a sound friend, you, Mr Briggs, and I mean that. Aye, the best.'

'It's nice to hear you say that. Very nice.'

'Aye well. I don't seem to have many pals left lately, and that's the truth. Mrs Hodgkiss . . . Eeh, I didn't mean for any of that to happen just now, really. I'd told myself I were ready to hear her out, proper like. I wanted to try and put all the bad feeling behind me. And now look how things stand: it's worse than ever. And I regret that, I do. It was dwelling on James, you see, what did it. I just miss him so much. I want him *home*.'

'Aye, I know.'

She wept a little more then extracted herself from him with a determined nod. 'I'm all right, now.'

'You're sure?'

'Aye, I feel better.' And she meant it. 'Sorry,' she added. 'Skriking all over your shirt front like that; I don't know what came over me.'

Seymour tut-tutted aside her apologies. 'You were upset – and for good reason. There's no shame in it, lass.'

'Mr Briggs?' she said suddenly as a thought occurred. 'Aye?'

'What are your plans for tomorrow? Only I thought . . . would you like to have your dinner here?'

His face was a picture of shocked delight. 'Spend Christmas with you and the kiddies?'

'Aye. Well, me and the lasses, at any rate. Joey and Stella have decided on a quiet day with Josie at their

309

house, what with it being their first Christmas. And Lynn and the twins shan't be coming here now, as we'd arranged, not with Duncan coming home; they'll want to spend the day together as a family. So, if you've nowt else on . . . ?'

'No, nowt.'

'Then you'll come?'

'I'd be over the moon to accept, aye. Thank you.'

'Thank *you*,' she insisted. Then, on impulse, she leaned forward and kissed his cheek. 'For everything. We'll see you tomorrow, then.'

Smiling from ear to ear, the man took his leave and Janie went to put her groceries away with a small smile of her own. Yet, all too soon, Sadie's face slammed back into her thoughts, leaving her instantly despondent once more.

The feeling refused to leave her throughout the day. Even bedtime brought no respite; every time she closed her eyes, the older woman's distraught expression in the shop doorway would assault her mind and she'd wince anew with guilt and regret.

By late morning on Christmas Day, Janie was close to breaking point. Finally, having just finished peeling the last of the veg for dinner, she could hold out no longer – she wiped her hands on her pinny and headed for the living room. Her daughters were sat cross-legged before the fire, immersed in their new gifts, and she addressed Hilda apologetically: 'Sorry, lass, to drag you from your games, but I need you to run an errand for me.'

310

'Aw, Mam, do I have to?'

'Aye, you do. Go on, there's a good girl; you can be there and back in half a minute if you're quick.'

Sighing, her daughter got to her feet. 'All right. Where is it you want me to go?'

Janie nodded to fortify her resolution. 'Mrs Hodgkiss's. Tell her . . . Tell her I want to speak with her, will you? Ask her if she can nip round.'

The girl went off to fulfil her request and, after some seconds, Janie sloped across to the window to keep a look-out on the frosty street. Then, moments later, there they were: the youngest striding in front, eager to return to her place by her hearth, the elder yet smaller-looking of the two, swamped as she was in her too-large coat, trailing behind with definite fore-boding and trepidation. Taking a deep breath, Janie moved to the door to admit them.

'Go on inside, lass,' she told Hilda. And when she'd gone: 'Mrs Hodgkiss. Will you come in?' she asked quietly.

Though Sadie's eyes screamed confusion, she accepted nonetheless, and they made in silence for the kitchen.

Janie closed the door and turned to face her. She cleared her throat; once, twice. Then she licked her lips and said in a rush, 'Mrs Hodgkiss, would you join us for dinner?'

To say the other woman was surprised was putting it mildly; her jaw slackened in sheer disbelief. She shook her head. 'But why?'

'Because you're alone, and no one deserves to be on their own on Christmas Day. And because . . . because I'd like you to.'

'But, love, after everything . . . ?'

'We do have to sit down and talk about that, aye. I need to understand why, Mrs Hodgkiss – *why* would you do what you did? – before there's any chance of us trying to put the whole horrible mess to bed. That's if you want to, of course?'

'Oh, I do! Eeh, love, I'd like nowt better than to have my friend back, I would, I . . .' She paused to press her fingers to her quivering lips. 'I ain't half missed you, you know. All of youse – especially them bonny twins. Mornings ain't the same these days without your lovely visits for a natter over a sup of tea and a biscuit.'

Janie felt a lump rising to her throat. 'I've missed that, too,' she whispered. 'You must have been very lonely these past months.'

'Oh, summat awful! And what with not even Stella to keep me company . . .' She dropped her gaze. 'How is she?'

'Gradely.'

'And the new babby?'

'Aye, the same.'

Sadie smiled wistfully. 'By, but you are lucky, Janie. You've really got it all, you know.'

'Not everything,' she murmured. 'I don't have my husband home no more, remember?'

'Oh, love. Love . . .'

'Tell me why. Why did you go to the authorities?'

Sadie's reply had Janie jerking back in shock.

'Mrs Hodgkiss . . . what did you say?'

'I said I never,' the older woman repeated.

'But I don't understand . . . You *said*—'

'Aye, and it were a lie. I spoke to no policeman about your James or anything else.'

Janie was utterly baffled. 'Why would you admit to such a terrible thing if it weren't true?'

'You'll not believe me.'

'Try me.'

'You'll like it even less . . .'

Dread was rolling through her guts, now. 'Mrs Hodgkiss. Please. Just tell me.'

'I did open my big gob about James, that much is correct, but it weren't to no member of the law – it were to Reuben Trent, across the way. It just sort of came out, honest; I could have chewed my tongue off at my carelessness. When you confronted Stella and she pointed the finger of suspicion my way, I were horrified, love. Not because I were guilty of what I were accused of but because I believed then that it must have been Reuben, that he'd gone to the police with the information I'd let slip. It was only after, when I was going through what you'd said in my mind, that I remembered summat: the sideboard.

'You'd said that the officers had known exactly where to look – only I never made mention of the hiding place to Reuben. As God is my witness, I didn't, and so he couldn't have been the one to squeal, could he? I wanted to come and tell you, I did, but your anger that day had fair frightened me

313

and I didn't think forra minute you'd take my word for it besides. I were still plucking up courage to come and see you when, the next thing I knew, Stella turns up. She said she were sorry, that she'd had to make you believe I'd blown the whistle so as you didn't think to blame her.

'She were adamant she hadn't informed on James but reckoned you'd not trust that, reckoned you hated her and would use this to split her and Joey up. She begged me to keep quiet and let you go on thinking it were me. I didn't want to, 'course I never, but she were crying and pleading and it pained me to see her distressed; I'd grown to love her as my own, you see. So, in t' end, I gave in. I told her I'd not seek you out, and I never.

'Lynn knew summat were fishy, mind. She tried to get the truth from me, but I couldn't let Stella down – a promise were a promise. But now . . .' Here, Sadie paused for breath and closed her eyes. 'Eeh, I can't lie to you, love. Not no more. I'll tell you summat else, an' all – it's a relief to finally get it all off my chest.'

Janie's head was swimming. For a full minute, she said nothing; she couldn't have strung a sentence together for neither love nor money, so intense was her dumbfoundedness. 'This . . . It was Stella's doing?' she eventually rasped. 'All of it? For all this time? And I didn't have the slightest inkling?'

'Why would you? Nay, it's my fault for keeping quiet so long. I should have said summat—'

'You're friggin' right you should!' Janie was livid. 'That wicked young bitch has been laughing up her sleeve at me for months and I had no idea. *None.* Fancy her doing all this, causing all this misery and heartache just to save her own skin—!'

'But, love, would you have believed her?' Sadie cut in gently. 'Had she sworn to you and gone on swearing that she weren't the culprit, would you have let it drop? That's what she were fearful of. I don't blame her for what she did; she's just a slip of a lass and acted out of desperation. Nay, and nor should you, neither. It's the real offender what deserves your anger, not no one else.'

Sagging with the plain truth of it, Janie nodded. 'But who? Who could it be? There's nobody other than us what knows. It doesn't make any sense.'

'Janie love.' Sadie's voice was now little above a whisper, and she was wringing her hands. 'I do have one person in mind, but . . .'

'But what? Who is it, Mrs Hodgkiss?'

'Eeh, I can't . . .'

'Tell me. Who do you suspect?'

'Stella, I . . . I could be mistaken, but I don't think she were telling the whole story, don't think it were simply fear of you believing her guilty. Mebbe . . . well, mebbe she . . .'

'No,' Janie croaked, her hand straying to her throat. 'You're not saying you reckon she were protecting someone . . . protecting Joey? No, he wouldn't. He *wouldn't!*'

And yet . . .

Like clips from some monstrous movie, snippets of memory played through her mind against her will.

315

She saw her son standing up to his father when he'd taken umbrage at being addressed as 'boy'. She saw afresh the murderous rage and undeniable contempt in his gaze. And she heard again the vitriol he'd spat about James being less than a man, of him being a coward. Now, a worm of doubt was burrowing inside her brain, and not for the life of her could she evict it. The more she tried, the deeper it slithered and settled there, and she gripped the hair at her temples with a whimper.

'It can't be true. It can't!'

And yet her proclamation of denial sounded hollow to her own ears.

Just what was she going to do?

The bare reality was simple, at least to her – she did nothing.

What would it achieve?

This she'd asked herself a hundred times as, as though in a trance, she'd cut short the discussion with Sadie and got on with the Christmas dinner.

The revelation would shatter her family to dust. Never would they be the same again, were the truth to get out. If indeed it was the truth ... *But of course it is – who else?* her mind would yell, crushing her heart to pulp. It all fitted. Her son would have regretted it afterwards – of this she was certain – but the fact remained: the deed was done, it was too late, and always would be, to turn back the clock.

Seymour arrived at some point and, though he surely must have been surprised to see Sadie present,

he didn't voice it. Janie greeted him with what enthusiasm she could muster, but it felt as though she was
in some nightmarish fog from which she couldn't
shake free, like she wasn't here at all. And she wasn't;
not mentally, at any rate. Her head was somewhere
else entirely and would remain there perhaps for
ever, she was sure of it. How could she ever get over
this? Her own flesh and blood. *James's* own flesh and
blood. To turn on him in such a truly wicked way as
this. This was torture – the agony was killing her
inside . . .

'Merry Christmas, everyone,' the grocer announced
with high-spiritedness, raising his glass – in automatic
action, Janie followed suit with a half-smile.

'This looks gradely, love,' said Sadie, gazing with
appreciation at the meal – again, Janie responded as
was expected of her:

'Well, tuck in,' she said, and the small smile
reached her lips once more. 'There's chicken left,
an' all, for anyone what fancies extras. Albie, my
father-in-law, fetched two good-sized 'uns around for
today, killed from his own farm, so there's plenty. I'd
have asked him to join us, but he don't do gather-
ings, prefers his own company even on Christmas.'

'Well, I for one wouldn't have missed it for the
world,' stated Seymour, casting her a soft glance.

'Nor me,' Sadie agreed with the self-same expression of warm thankfulness.

Doing her level best to suppress a moan of
distress – her chest felt tight and she had a feeling
upon her as though she was being smothered – Janie

317

murmured something along the lines of them being more than welcome then turned her attention to her food, desperate for distraction.

It was towards the early evening, not long after Sadie had left, when Joey and Stella popped by. The young couple breezed in on a gust of wintry air and greeted everyone with enthusiasm. They were glowing with happiness and festive cheer, and Janie had to turn away for fear of breaking down completely. Then her daughter-in-law placed Josie, who was wrapped up snugly against the elements, into her arms, and Janie's pain eased just a little. She drank in the delicate features, pressed a feathery kiss to each creamy, plump cheek and the rosebud mouth, and smiled.

'Merry Christmas, Mam.'

Turning to her son, she searched his face for a moment as though expecting a trace of . . . what? she asked herself. Concealed guilt? But there was nothing. Only affection for her shone from his eyes, and maternal love banged through her breast in response; it was impossible to contain. She gave her cheek to him to kiss, which he did soundly, then she followed the action with Stella.

'Merry Christmas, Mrs Hudson.'

Once more, she looked for some clue, but as with Joey, the girl's expression was one of open friendliness; Janie didn't know whether to be hopeful or upset. Had she and Sadie got their assumption completely wrong? Or were these two standing before her now the best damned actors in the history of mankind? And how would she ever get to know? For one thing was certain: she wouldn't confront him.

The top and bottom of it was she was terrified of the answer. To hear him admit it from his own two lips . . . she'd wither from the heartache of it all. Besides, the repercussions were too devastating to contemplate. As for James ever finding out . . . She shuddered to imagine what it would do to him. Her family, her life, would be broken. She couldn't risk it, couldn't lose her son and her grandchild, would sooner die.

'Mam?' It was Joey. His voice sliced through her agonising and she blinked across at him in overwhelming indecision. 'Are you all right?'

'Aye,' she croaked past the lump threatening to choke her. 'Tired, is all.'

'You're sure?'

Again, that niggle of doubt as to whether she was doing the right thing made itself known. Then her eyes strayed to her granddaughter and she nodded.

Banking down her emotions, she kept her mouth firmly shut.

Chapter 20

September 1941

'EEH, IT'S WARM.'

Fanning herself with a newspaper, Lynn nodded across to Stella. 'Aye, lass. I like it warm, but this is too warm.'

Janie, seated between them, bouncing baby Robinson on her lap, couldn't help but chuckle. 'It's not that ruddy warm.'

'Oh, it is, it's warm!' the women responded in unison – then burst out laughing.

It was a beautiful mid-month morning and the three of them were enjoying a relaxing cup of tea in Janie's back garden. Bobby and Brian were toddling around the grass chasing a butterfly whilst Josie, having not yet mastered walking, stood clinging to her mother's skirt, looking on their game enviously.

Lynn and Stella had fallen pregnant again around the same time, shortly after Janie had given birth in March. Now, the glorious weather was proving burdensome in their encumbered state – both were in agreement that the year's end, which was when their children were due, couldn't come soon enough.

'He's a placid little thing, ain't he?' Lynn remarked with a smile as she watched Robinson snuggle against his mother's chest, put his thumb into his mouth and drop off to sleep. She smoothed a hand over the clear rise of her stomach. 'Let's hope this one is as well behaved when it gets here. Mind you . . .' She guffawed ruefully. 'Knowing my luck, it'll take after the twins and have me run ragged from dawn 'til dusk instead.'

'Mebbe it's twins again, Lynn,' said Stella, giving Janie a wink.

'Oh, my good God, lass, don't say that! Eeh, no, not again. I'd not cope, I wouldn't!'

Laughing, the younger woman swatted a fly away lazily. ''Ere, I'd best not tease, else it might be me what finds myself having two as my comeuppance.'

'I hope you ruddy do! Then you'd know what hard work is, lass, let me tell you.'

'Have youse thought on names yet?' Janie asked them, then rolled her eyes when the pair glanced towards Robinson with a grin. 'Don't fret, I shan't be giving you any suggestions. I know you're both too uncultured to appreciate them, anyroad, even if I did!'

Lynn and Stella shared a laugh, and Janie shook her head at them both in mock offence with a click of her tongue. 'Well, you can say what you want, because I like the mite's name. It's different, aye.'

'You've got that right,' the others tittered behind

their hands – aware it was all in good humour, Janie poked her tongue out at them.

She'd got the idea from a story that Seymour had lent to her: *Robinson Crusoe*. She'd taken to borrowing books from him towards the end of her pregnancy as a means of relaxation, and the name of the lead character in that particular tale had caught her attention right away. It was unusual, and she liked it – more to the point, so did James. Seymour had also reacted positively to her choice, and so the matter had been settled. It suited the baby perfectly, she reckoned.

Now, as her eye caught the Anderson shelter, slouched forlornly in the corner of the garden, she released an easy sigh. Air-raid warnings had eased off considerably during this new year. They received only a smattering of wails these days, and the siren had lain silent, now, since early July – the only alert of that month – and, even then, it had been but a twenty-minute wait before the all-clear followed.

Residents were slowly beginning to relax; it felt great to think they might finally be getting back to some mode of normality. In fact, if not for the rationing and endless queueing, it was again sometimes difficult to believe there was a war on at all – in their town, at least. If you counted out the absence of their menfolk, of course. That was indeed a hardship they continued to share with the rest of the country.

Feeling a hand stroking her nape, Janie turned her head to smile up at her husband. 'All right?'

James nodded. Then, motioning to the other

women, who were by now dozing in the sunshine, he smiled. 'They look all in.'

'I know, poor loves. Being in t' family way does that to you.'

'Aye, I'll bet. I'll keep an eye to the little 'uns whilst their mams rest.' He took a seat on the back door-step beside her chair then held out his arms for his son. 'Come on, pass the bruiser over to me, lass.'

As he gazed adoringly at Robinson, Janie hugged herself with a feeling of contentment. Spotting her grandfather, Josie made a beeline for him and crawled across, and James lifted her on to his knee and planted a kiss on her brow. Watching on, the warm-ness inside Janie's breast intensified. She draped an arm around her man's shoulders, lifted her face to the sky and closed her eyes in bliss.

This was how it was meant to be, how it should *always* be, and she was loath to fritter even a single millisecond of it. All too soon, James would be gone again – off to face God alone knew what – but right now, he was here, they were all together, and she wouldn't dwell on what the near future might bring. One day at a time was how she was taking it, for it was simpler and more enjoyable that way. Nothing would spoil this precious time.

That he wasn't having to hide away on this occa-sion made it all the more special.

His battalion had recently converted to a recon-naissance corps and, having been on fresh training throughout the summer, he was home with the army's full approval on a fortnight's leave.

323

No diving for the space beneath the floorboards whenever a knock came at the door, no fear. Not that they made much mention these days of what had passed, preferring instead to leave all of that behind them, where it belonged. Even the odd resident hereabouts who had been critical of his actions appeared inclined now that he'd paid his dues and was doing the right thing, so to speak, to let things lie.

That whole stress-filled episode was, mercifully, behind them. Well, to some extent, at any rate, Janie reminded herself, her eyes swivelling to Stella.

Simply accepting that it was how it was, James hadn't made mention once as to who could have been responsible for his recapture – and Janie was glad of it. Whether she'd have been able to conceal from him her suspicions had he asked her outright, she honestly couldn't say. All she could do was pray she wouldn't be put to the test. As for her own feelings on the betrayal . . . she'd tried her damnedest to put it from her mind.

Still only she and Sadie were in possession of the knowledge; Janie had sworn the other woman to secrecy, and she'd promised not to breathe a word. Nor had anyone else learned of Stella's role in it all – and the girl was unaware that Janie knew. As a means of explaining her renewed friendship with Sadie, Janie had remarked casually to her daughter-in-law that she hadn't asked the older woman the ins and outs but had merely decided to let bygones be bygones. And with a look of unequivocal relief, Stella had accepted this unquestioningly.

324

The women roused a short while later. Soon afterwards, they bade Janie and James goodbye and returned to their respective dwellings and duties, and Janie did likewise: leaving Robinson in his father's care, she headed off to Seymour's house to do her cleaning. Eager to be back with her family, she had the place finished in record time; gratefully, she set off home again to give her husband and son a cuddle and begin preparing the evening meal. She was peeling the last of the potatoes when her daughters arrived home from school. She'd put down the knife and turned to greet them, yet one look at Elsie and her smile froze on her lips. She wore an expression Janie recognised only too well, now.

'Lass? The voices . . . ?' Then, at her nod: 'D'you want to tell me what they said?'

The girl shrugged. 'It were daft.'

'Was it?'

'Aye. And disgusting, an' all. Mam, it made me want to be sick!'

Frowning, Janie crouched down to her level. 'What did the words show you, lass?'

'Maggots.'

'Eh?'

'Maggots, Mam. In a cup. And Dad was eating them.'

'That was all? Nowt else?'

'No.'

Straightening back up again, Janie scratched her head. 'A cup full of maggots . . . ? What the devil does that mean?'

She was still pondering on it later as she and her husband climbed into bed:

'James?'

Her looked to her with a yawn. 'Aye, love?'

'James . . . have you ever had maggots?' she asked, feeling mightily foolish the moment the question was out.

'What do you mean, "had"?'

'Eaten.'

'What?' Laughing, he pulled a face. 'Why would you ask that?'

'Have you?' she pressed him.

'Well, I have put them under my tongue once or twice when fishing as a lad. It helps keep them warm on a cold day, you see. But as for having eaten them . . . God no. 'Course not.'

She told him what Elsie had revealed. 'It's flummoxed me, it has really. What could it mean at all?'

Yawning again, he let his shoulders rise and fall then snuggled down beneath the blankets. 'Christ knows, lass. That is one prediction our Elsie's got wrong, aye. This I know, because I'd sooner waste away than feast on bloody maggots.' Smiling, he pulled her into his arms. 'Now, what says you put that nonsense from your mind, eh, and give me a kiss instead?'

Just as Janie feared, the days seemed to speed by in half a heartbeat. Before they knew it, it was time for James to leave them.

She harboured no concerns about him not returning to duty. These days, he seemed more himself, focused of mind. Not upbeat exactly, no. But then again, not the quailing wreck of old who had come back from the beaches of France. He'd found a middle ground that worked for him. He wouldn't desert again. Whether this stability would remain with him once he was thrust back into the thick of it, however, she didn't know. All she could do was pray that it would; it was all she had.

'Eeh, but I'll miss you,' she whispered, holding him close to her on the station platform. 'Promise me you'll be all right, love.'

'I promise. I love you.'

'And I you, with all my heart.'

She watched the train shunt and chuff its way out of sight before turning sadly and making her way home – back to the house that she just knew wouldn't feel the same again, now.

Weeks later, she received from James a letter stating he and his comrades had 'met' the King – His Majesty had been conducting his preliminary inspection of the troops – and that they were likely to be leaving for an as yet unknown destination very soon. This was followed up with a note a month later to say he was fit and well and was now overseas – though where, owing to security reasons, he was unable to specify. And then . . . nothing.

Initially, Janie tried not to worry. Yet, as the days and weeks passed without further contact, her resolve began to wane and anxiety slowly crept in. Another Christmas came and went and still there was no news. By the new year, having convinced herself he'd been killed, she was half mad with terror. Then, one morning, she arrived back from her cleaning job to discover not one but two postcards awaiting her on the hall floor.

With a cry, she scooped them up and pressed them tightly against her heart in blessed relief, eyes closed. Then, laughing, she brought them back up and devoured every glorious word.

Both were dated early December and must have got delayed in the post – clicking her tongue, she read on. The messages were brief, but that mattered not to her; he was alive, that was the most important thing. He told her he loved her and to give the children a hug and kiss from him, and that he'd try to write again when he could. Walking on air, she went to put the kettle on to read them all over again with a cup of tea.

Little did she know in that moment – and it was probably for the best – that two incidents were hovering just around the corner which were set to tip her world into immeasurable turmoil.

The first occurred shortly into February. Janie awoke from a terrible night sight that had her bolting up in tears, coughing and gasping for breath.

She'd dreamed she was looking out at a vast expanse of sea. The sky was cloudless and not a ripple marred the waters; the morning was a beautiful one. Then a low roar had drawn her attention and, to her horror, she turned to find herself looking at a large liner engulfed in flames.

She knew without question that aboard, it was

packed full of soldiers – and that James was amongst them, below decks in the troop transport quarters. The noise was terrific and thick black smoke was filling her lungs, but for the life of her she couldn't tear her eyes from the devastating scene. A bellowed order went up to abandon ship, and men, a number wounded or badly burned, began diving what had to be over fifty feet into the water. Some were sucked into the huge propellers and extinguished instantly. Others floated off to slowly drown.

Seconds later, the inferno faded to nothing and she'd opened her eyes to find herself back in her own bedroom.

The vision refused to leave her, and her emotions were shot to pieces. She would burst into uncontrollable sobbing at random points throughout the days, and neither her friends' nor loved ones' attempts at comfort could penetrate her misery. Worse still, there were no more letters from James. Her husband was dead. In her darkest moments, Janie wished she was with him.

'There's been no telegram, though, neither,' Lynn would remind her as the weeks rolled on, desperate to bolster her friend's spirits. 'So long as there's no official word of him having been killed, there's hope. Cling to that, love, for all you're worth. You *must*.'

Janie tried. Oh, did she.

It did little good.

A message was received in early April from the War Office confirming her worst fears: James had been reported as missing. The sea had indeed claimed her most precious victim.

'Singapore, it said. Why? What business had he there? He said to me when he was last home on leave that his regiment was destined for the desert. Some of the men had told him so, reckoned they were soon to be kitted out with tropical gear: topees, beige shirts and shorts, that sort of thing. Singapore ain't desert, is it? It's jungle. So why were they there? It's not what they were trained for. It makes no sense to me, none. And why did Japan decide to stick their oar in on this war, anyroad? Ain't we got enough to contend with with the Germans? As for that lot at them big offices . . . what do they mean by "missing", like? Why not just come out and say it: he's dead. Gone. Never to return. James . . . James is dead, he's dead, he—!'

'Ssh, love, come on now,' said Lynn, stroking Janie's head, which was resting on her lap. There were tears in her voice. 'Please, try and rest. All this talk . . . you're making yourself ill.'

'I want my husband.'

'Eeh, I know, love, I know. Oh,' she added, glancing in the direction of the door as a knock sounded. Gently, she drew Janie up and rose from the sofa. Easing her friend back down into the space she'd just vacated, she tucked the blanket covering her more securely around her shoulders. 'You just lie there, love, whilst I see who's calling. Don't worry, I'll get rid of them.'

Janie heard the front door opening, and muffled

voices. Then Lynn's head appeared around the living-room door: 'It's Seymour. Have I to tell him you're not up to visitors?'

'No,' she murmured. 'It's all right, let him in.'

The grocer waited whilst she pulled herself up into a sitting position then sat down beside her. His face was grave. 'I figured summat was wrong when Lynn didn't show for work so thought I'd best come and check.'

'That were my fault,' Janie told him. 'I gorra message this morning, you see, and Lynn came straight round . . . She didn't want to leave me.'

'Mrs Hudson, what on earth's happened?'

Reaching for the sheet of paper emblazoned with its official-looking stamps and mind-shattering words, she handed it to him blindly. 'Read it for yourself.'

He scanned it in silence and sighed deeply. Then, turning to Lynn, he said, 'Could you give us a few minutes alone? Perhaps you could take the children to Mrs Hodgkiss's . . . ?'

'Aye, 'course. I got Hilda and Elsie off to school earlier on, reckoned they'd be better off there. So it's just these four.' She motioned to Bobby, Brian and Robinson playing quietly in front of the fire then flicked her chin towards the window, beyond which lay sleeping her new daughter in the pram outside.

'Mrs Hodgkiss will be in her element when you turn up with these lot,' said Janie with a brief smile.

'You'll be all right, won't you, whilst I'm gone?'

'Aye, Lynn. And ta, love.'

Seymour saw the woman and children out and

331

returned to his seat. Again, he read through the letter then lifted his eyes to Janie.

'So?' she asked quietly.

'Mr Hudson was posted as missing on the fifteenth of February at Singapore. You mentioned a bit back that he thought he were facing desert warfare . . . ?'

'Aye! Exactly! So what the devil was he doing going to the jungles? Unless . . . Eeh, Mr Briggs, you don't reckon they could have got it wrong, do you?' She knew she was clutching at straws, knew it was pointless even contemplating this, but desperation had her doing it anyway. 'It could be possible, couldn't it? Surely mistakes happen . . . sometimes. They've *got* to.'

His voice was soft. 'No. I'm sorry, but I don't believe this has been sent in error. I do think you're right about one thing, mind: your husband likely was on his way to someplace else initially.'

'Then what could have happened? Why did his regiment change route?'

'Well, when Japan invaded Malaya at the beginning of December, it looked likely that they would strike Singapore next. As both places were under British rule, we had to act. If my memory serves me right, I read in the papers that the government gave orders for troops that could be spared to be withdrawn or diverted from other theatres to act as reinforcements in defending said island. Not that it made much difference, like. Singapore capitulated to the Japanese anyway.'

'Aye,' she replied thoughtfully. 'So you're saying that James was amongst these troops you mentioned?

That him and his comrades were redirected from where they should have been going to help with Singapore island instead?'

'In my opinion, aye, it seems so. Remember, though, them Japs were busy last year, weren't they: Malaya weren't all they targeted, no. They attacked the US naval base at Pearl Harbor around the same time as well, which has prompted America to join the war. They took their time about it, though, eh, them Yanks? But well, better late than never, I suppose. Their support will aid us to victory, aye. With any luck, it'll all be over soon.'

As it was wont to, suddenly, the acrid taste of smoke assaulted the back of her throat just as it had in her dream, and she shook her head. 'It won't make no difference to my James. It can't. It's already too late for him.'

Frowning, the grocer pointed to the letter he still held. 'But it says here that him being classed as missing don't necessarily mean he's been killed. He could have just been separated from his regiment and can't be traced; that would account for it, right enough. Or, worst-case scenario, he were taken prisoner by the Japanese when Singapore fell. After all, reports that men have been captured by the enemy take time to reach the country—'

'No.' Janie was adamant. 'It's not none of them things. He . . . He lost his life on a vessel.'

'What vessel?'

'I don't know, a big one on fire at sea.'

'Mrs Hudson, what makes you think that?'

'I just do.' She glanced at him then away again quickly. She couldn't tell him; it just didn't feel right to. Eyes widening, she turned to him expectantly. 'You ain't heard owt about a ship being burned out in the waters, have you, Mr Briggs? There's been no talk, nowt in the papers?'

He shook his head. 'As you know, them lot in authority tend to be tight-lipped about stuff like that until well after the event. But, Mrs Hudson,' he added, patting her hand, 'I'm sure you're mistaken, in any case. It's likely just your imagination thinking up the worst.'

Not wanting now to discuss the subject with him further, she nodded. 'Aye, you're probably right. Take no notice of me, Mr Briggs. I'm physically and mentally wrung out, that's all.'

As she was tucking her daughters into bed that night, Janie put something to Elsie that she'd resisted saying up to now: she asked her whether she'd had any more 'voices' about her dad.

Thumb planted firmly in her mouth, the girl shook her head.

'You're sure, lass? I don't like to pressure you on matters like this – promised myself, if I'm honest, that I never would – but it's important.' She eased Elsie's hand away from her face in an attempt to encourage her to talk. 'Just try to remember. Is there owt at all you can think of that you might have forgot to mention?'

'Only the maggots, Mam.'

'Try now, lass. Go on, close your eyes and see what happens.'

'I don't want to.'

'*Please*, lass, for me.'

With a less-than-pleased pout, she did as her mother instructed. Watching on, seeing the lids flickering in concentration, Janie held her breath.

'Well?' she finally whispered.

Elsie's eyes sprang open. 'Nope. Nowt. Just a cup of dirty maggots, like before.' With that, she popped the digit back where it had been, signalling an end to further discussion.

Lying in her own bed minutes later, Janie let her tears roll unchecked. Why, oh why, couldn't they pick and choose what vision they received and when? Just a snippet of a clue, anything at all to let them know with complete certainty her husband's fate, was all she asked. But then life was never that simple, was it? *Damn it all.*

There was but one thing left to do. It remained the only option left open to her. She must play the waiting game.

If her night sight was wrong, she'd receive a letter stating James was a prisoner of war, and there would be hope. If her night sight was right, it would be a telegram instead, announcing 'supposed drowned', and she too would cease to ever exist again.

It was in God's hands now.

Chapter 21

THE BOLTON EVENING NEWS
Wednesday, 20 May 1942

Empress of Asia Bombed and Sunk

It was announced officially in Ottawa yesterday that the Canadian Pacific liner Empress of Asia *was sunk on 5 February.*

The 16,000-ton vessel was transporting troops to Singapore when, six miles outside the island, it was attacked by Japanese dive-bombers. They hurled some eighty bombs, five of which were direct hits.

Fires quickly broke out and flames roared through the liner. The lifeboats were destroyed, and some soldiers and crew trapped by the blaze were forced to leap into the waters.

The Australian sloop Yarra *soon sprang to the rescue and worked tirelessly to pick up as many men as they could. By and by, the* Empress of Asia *drifted through a minefield before beaching, where she burned out.*

About 100 seamen and the majority of the 2,500 Imperial troops on-board escaped.

Janie heard the voice calling her name as though through a wall of thick glass. It hadn't the power to touch her. Gaze fused to the newspaper in her hands, she opened her mouth in a silent scream.

Seymour reached her side just as welcomed darkness swooped. On a merciful sigh, she tumbled into a dead faint in his arms.

Chapter 22

'I DON'T WANT to see him, Lynn.'

'But, love—'

'I said no! Get them out of here, now, the pair of them!'

Having ground to a halt on the threshold at her venomous greeting, Joey and Stella stared at Janie as though she were mad.

'Out,' she repeated to them on a growl. 'Get gone and never come back.'

'Mam, what in Christ's name—!'

'Proud of yourself, are you? Well? You low-down young devil, yer! Oh, what's up?' she added, springing to her feet. 'Did you think I wouldn't find out? Well, I did. I know all about your wicked friggin' act, so don't you come the innocent here. Your poor father's dead because of you and I never want to see you again!'

Utterly stunned, Joey seemed incapable of anything but shaking his head. Stella didn't appear much better.

'Well, what are youse still doing here? Get gone!'

'We don't actually know whether James . . . not yet,

338

at any rate,' Lynn reassured the couple quietly. 'All the same, I think you'd better go. It's for the best, just 'til she's had chance to gather her senses, like.'

Janie snorted. 'Oh, I've done that already. I'm seeing clearly for the first time in a long time, don't you worry about that!'

'Go on, take yourselves off home,' pressed Lynn, shepherding Joey and Stella back into the hall. And, too shocked to argue, they went without further protest.

'Good riddance,' Janie announced when her friend returned to the living room after seeing them out. 'If they've any brains, they'll stop away, an' all.'

'What the bloody *hell* has got into you?' The woman's voice was hollow with horror. 'I'd never have believed you capable had I not witnessed that with my own eyes . . . Why turn on your own son, of all people?'

'You know nowt.'

'Then tell me. What could the lad possibly have done to make you treat him as cruelly as that?'

Pressure was filling Janie's chest. She couldn't breathe. Up it rose – up, further, until it burst from her in a strangled howl. Collapsing on to the sofa, she dropped her head in her hands.

'Love, what is going on? Speak to me.'

'He . . . He . . .'

'He what?'

'Joey were the one what informed on James.'

Lynn slapped a hand to her mouth, smothering a gasp. 'No . . . You're certain?'

339

'Oh, am I. There can be no doubt. But I can't pretend otherwise, not now. I can't forgive him, neither. God, what am I going to do?'

'I just . . . I have no words. Eeh, love.'

'I've lost him just as surely as I've lost my husband. Josie and baby Bert along with them, too. Even that still sticks in my craw, you know, them naming the new child after Albie and not James,' she muttered as an aside. 'Mind you, the hypocrisy would have likely choked me if Joey had named him after his father, knowing what he'd done . . . Oh, Lynn. Why is all this happening? Will this living nightmare never know an end?'

'But, Janie, like Seymour pointed out when he helped you home earlier from the shop, you've still not had a telegram yet, remember? Aye, you saw that article, and aye, it must have been a horrible thing to read, but, love . . . All those survivors . . . James could very well have been one of them. Can't you just try and wait to see what the outcome will be?'

'Lynn, I know already. My night sights have never been wrong yet. I saw that ship ablaze with him stuck on-board deep below decks as clear as I'm seeing you now. There's no way he could have got out. He's gone, I know it. It's only a matter of time until the office bigwigs confirm it.'

Joey remained cemented in Janie's mind for the remainder of the evening. Although, as she'd stated to her friend earlier, she couldn't forgive him, still she was haunted by shame at what had transpired, and how. She'd said some terrible things. His hurt

340

had been absolute; she'd seen it plainly. But her rage had numbed her emotions towards him completely. Now, she regretted that most of all. She could have handled things so much better than she had.

Her daughters had already gone to bed and Janie had just settled a fractious Robinson in his cot in the room that was once Joey's when light knocking at the front door reached her ears. Her heart drummed a painful beat. *Joey*. He'd come to talk things out. She hesitated for the briefest moment. Then her feet jerked forward of their own accord and she was running down the stairs.

'Evening.'

'Mr Briggs.' Her face drooped in disappointment. 'Hello.'

'Sorry, I know it's late . . . Please can I come in? There's summat I'd like to speak to you about.'

'It's nothing bad, is it? Nowt's happened?'

'No, no.'

Frowning, Janie nodded. 'All right then, aye. Come on through.'

Seymour halted in front of the fire and removed his hat. He fidgeted with it as though in nervousness, but he made no attempt at talk. Finally, Janie lifted an eyebrow questioningly.

'Mr Briggs? There was summat you wanted to say . . . ?'

'Aye. Aye, sorry.' He cleared his throat. 'Well, Mrs Hudson, the thing is . . . I wanted to ask . . . I mean, what I wanted to say was . . .'

'Go on,' she encouraged, sensing his discomfiture

341

and curious to know what all this was about. 'What is it?'

'The position you find yourself in ain't ideal. Now that your husband's officially reported as missing, you're likely set to face financial hardship shortly. Until concrete proof comes through of Mr Hudson having been made a prisoner of war, the authorities must class him as presumed killed – it's just the way they do things, I'm afraid. When that happens, his allotment pay to you from his army wages plus the dependants' allowance you receive from the government will be replaced with a much smaller widow's pension. 'Course, once it's proven he is in enemy hands, your usual allowance should be restored – minus the allotment pay, mind you, as his wages will be suspended and held on account until his release—'

'You still think I'm wrong about him being a casualty on that ship, don't you?' she cut in quietly.

'Well . . . I admit I was surprised when you spotted that article about the sunken liner today. It did seem to fit, after hearing your suspicions . . .'

'Yet you still believe it just a coincidence,' she finished for him.

'Mebbe, aye. I don't know. And what's more, it makes no difference really to what I've been trying to say. Whether Mr Hudson went down on that vessel or is indeed a prisoner of war, it'll still amount to the same thing: for the remainder of this war and perhaps beyond, you're going to find things a struggle.' Here, the grocer paused to clear his throat again. Then he added: 'And I want to help.'

342

'You do? But why?'

'Because I have the means. And because I want to; I really, *really* do.'

She had to admit the worry of money had crossed her own mind. The family were coping all right when James's pay was resumed following his apprehension by the military police – until Joey wed and moved out, at any rate. She'd definitely felt the pinch with the loss of his pay packet. Expenditures for food, housing, clothing and medical care, to name but a few, all added up. However, with well-practised frugality, she'd just about been managing. Seymour was right: mere survival would be a battle in itself soon. Nevertheless, she couldn't have him thinking of her as a charity case, wouldn't take his handouts – for herself as well as him.

'Forget your pride, Mrs Hudson. And don't harbour worries that you'd be taking advantage of my good nature, neither, because you'd not be – I want to do this,' the grocer said now, as though he'd seen inside her mind. 'This is my choice, my decision—'

'Mr Briggs, look. I know you mean well, but it's not possible. I can't let you do it. We'll cope, God willing, somehow.'

'And what if you don't?' he insisted quietly. 'All the best intentions in the world won't put grub on t' table, or keep the rain off your head should the rent run into arrears—'

'Even so.'

'Move in with me,' he blurted.

Janie gazed at him. 'What?'

343

'There's plenty of room for us and the kiddies. Please. You'd be making an owd man very happy.'

'Oh, Mr Briggs.' *Had Lynn actually been right about his feelings for her all along?* 'I don't think of you in that way. I'm sorry.'

'Don't be. It don't matter, not really. I just want to look after you, that's all.' He dropped his stare. 'I'm so lonely, lass. What's more, I know you are, too.'

She was; oh, more than she could ever put into words.

'How long since you last saw your husband?'

'Eight months.' Her tone was heavy with emotion.

'That's a long time.'

'Aye. It is.'

Seymour came to stand in front of her. Tentatively, he put out his hand and caressed her cheek, and Janie closed her eyes.

'Mr Briggs . . .'

'In your heart of hearts, you don't believe Mr Hudson is ever coming back, do you?'

Tears squeezed themselves free to roll down her cheeks. 'No.'

'And can you say with all honesty that you'll bear the rest of your life alone?'

'No,' she choked again.

'Then allow me in. Let me be a part of it and, I swear to you, you'll never know a moment's unhappiness again.'

His hand was still stroking her face and, despite herself, she pressed into it further, welcoming the comfort of warm skin against her own. *It had been so very long*. 'The grief and pain, the fear and never-ending worry . . . It's like, lately, I've turned mad in the head with it all.'

'It's too much to cope with, ain't it?'

'It is.'

'I'm here now. You're not by yourself any more.'

The words were like gentle music, the prospect of their meaning a healing balm to her battered soul.

'I'd never let you down,' he murmured.

'No. No, I don't believe you would.'

'I know we could make a good team, Janie.'

Finally, she opened her eyes. The corners of her lips peaked in a smile. 'That's the first time you've ever called me by my name.'

'Do you mind?'

She shook her head. 'No, Seymour.'

They stared at each other for a long moment. Seymour was the first to break their gaze. With evident reluctance, he let his arm fall back to his side and put on his hat.

'I'd better go.'

'Aye,' she whispered.

'Think over what I've said. Will you, Janie?'

To her own surprise, she found herself nodding.

'Mam?'

Busy on her hands and knees donkey-stoning the front step, Janie froze at the hesitant call. Slowly, she turned her head. Her son was standing by the closed garden gate, as though unsure whether to enter.

'Mam . . .'

'Come in,' she said quietly.

They sat facing one another across the table. The air between them was so thick you could have hung your jacket on it.

'You're not needed at the farm today?' she asked at last, the flat question slicing through the silence like a hot blade through wax.

'I'm for going in a bit later today, wanted to come and see you first.' Dragging out a sigh, Joey shook his head. 'Yesterday . . . Mam, what the hell did it mean?'

Her tone was weary. 'Don't pretend you don't know.'

'But I don't! I know you've been upset over that night sight—'

'Huh. That's the understatement of the year. Out of my mind would be nearer to the point.'

'And you're fearful of Dad having been . . .' He paused to swallow hard. 'But, Mam, the things you said . . . it ain't fair you taking your pain out on me.'

'That's what you reckon I was doing, is it? All right, aye, mebbe I was,' she conceded, softer now, after a moment. 'I went about it the wrong way and it were cruel, some of the things I spat. Cruel, but nonetheless true, mind.'

'You said it were my fault that Dad's . . . that he's . . .'

'Dead?'

'Aye.'

'Ain't it?'

His eyes deepened in devastation. 'No, Mam. Why would you think that?'

'Joey—'

'If Dad is . . . if he has been killed, it's not through no fault of mine. How can it be? What is it *I'm* meant to have done?'

Her anger at this blatant hard-facedness was rising, but she forced it back down. A scene like the one before would solve nothing. She folded her arms. 'You informed on him, didn't you?' It was more statement than question. 'For the love of God, don't try to deny it.'

Anguish screamed from his gaze. A single tear made a slow track down his cheek and splashed on to the tablecloth.

'You sealed your own father's fate – why? How will you ever live with yourself?'

'It weren't me.'

'You're a liar.'

'It's your head; you're poorly. Please, Mam—'

'Just go.' She motioned to the door. 'I need time to . . . to *try* to . . . Whether I will ever be able to forgive you, I don't at this moment know. Go. Leave me be, lad.'

His chin touching his chest, Joey scraped back his chair. He'd made it midway across the room when, suddenly, he rushed back towards her to throw his arms around her neck. On a cry, her own heart torn to tatters, Janie clung to him.

'I love you, Mam.'

In the next instant, he'd turned and was gone.

'And I love you, my lad,' she mouthed to the closed

347

door, and she thought she would die with the pain of it all.

Throughout the years to come, Janie was to wonder often how she hadn't.

The following day, a letter arrived confirming what she'd known all along.

Trooper J. Hudson, no. 3646201 of 18th Reconnaissance Corps, lately The Loyal Regiment, had perished aboard the *Empress of Asia*.

Chapter 23

November 1944

'YOU'LL FINISH UP without a hair left in your skull, lass, if you don't leave it be. Honestly, it looks fine.'

Driving another pin into the voluminous 'victory roll' curl at the front of her head, Hilda stepped back from the mirror to assess her reflection. She twisted her neck left to right then pulled a face. 'Are you sure?'

'Aye. Mind you,' Janie went on innocently, sharing a smile with Lynn, who was seated beside her, 'I don't know why you're titivating yourself up just to sit in your mate's house. Makes no sense to me, that. After all, it's not like anyone's going to see you . . . is it?'

Her daughter attempted a nonchalant shrug, but her face had turned blood red. 'No, 'course not,' she responded, a touch too defensively. 'But well . . . I just thought I'd make the effort forra change, that's all.'

''Course you did,' said her mother. Then, to herself, with an amused roll of her eyes, she added, *You must think I were born bloody yesterday, my lass!*

Hilda had turned fifteen in the spring just passed and was developing into a beautiful young woman. Her delicate appearance contrasted wildly with her feisty personality and made her all the more intriguing – particularly of late to the opposite sex, Janie had begun to notice. The soft features and honey-coloured hair coupled with an outspoken nature, wicked sense of humour and deep protectiveness towards those she loved was a winning combination. She was on the road to becoming a force to be reckoned with, and Janie was inordinately proud of her.

'Anyroad, I must concentrate all my efforts on my hairstyle to look half decent, don't I? There's not much chance of looking nice any other way, is there, thanks to the bloody clothing ration?'

'Language, missy,' Janie scolded; however, Hilda did have a point. With many factories having been taken over for essential war work, clothing restrictions had inevitably come into force; though at the start of it, several years ago, the girl hadn't much noticed. Now, at the age she was, it had become a major bugbear and one which her daughter bitterly complained about on a daily basis. It was understandable. All teenagers wanted to be seen as fashionable, after all, but in the current climate of course it just wasn't possible.

'Eeh, the outfit I saw in a magazine the other week . . .' Hilda went on dreamily. 'You should have seen it – *gorgeous*, it were. A forest-green suit, the skirt and bolero appliquéd with black along the hemlines.

Silk stockings, silk scarf and matching gloves, finished off with kitten-heeled court shoes and a doll hat worn at a jaunty angle with a feather in the front.'

'I've been saving my own clothing coupons up for you, lass,' Janie reminded her. 'With what you've already collected, you should have enough for a new rig-out by Christmas.'

'Aye, summat ugly, I'm betting. I understand we have to save fabric but, by God, them utility designs are *so* drab!'

'Well, it's like it or lump it. The latest Paris fashions it shan't be, but it'll be better than nowt, won't it?'

Catching the edge in her mother's tone, Hilda pulled an apologetic face. 'I know. Ta, Mam, I am grateful, really. I can't wait, neither. Just look at the state of this ancient thing, my best skirt,' she said, prodding at the navy woollen garment in disgust. 'It's older than you are.'

'Oh, ta very much!'

Hilda grinned. 'You know what I mean.'

'Oh, I do. And look now, today: another ruddy year older. I feel every one of them as well – and more besides.'

'Well, you don't look it.' Stooping, Hilda kissed her mother's cheek. 'Ta-ra, then, I'm off now. Ta-ra, Lynn.'

'I want you back by nine o'clock, lass, and no arguments,' her mother called to her as she disappeared into the hall to don her coat.

'Aw, Mam! Barbara only lives in the next street.'

'I don't care whether she lives in Greenroyd Avenue or Timbuktu. I'm not having you wandering

351

about alone now these dark evenings have set in. Besides, you've got work in the morning,' she reminded her. Hilda had begun as an assistant at the confectioner's nearby since leaving school, a position she really enjoyed. 'You don't want to be turning up tomorrow boss-eyed through lack of a good night's kip, do you? Nine o'clock on the dot, or else.'

The women shared a wince as the front door banged shut at the disgruntled girl's back.

'Eeh, she's a card, your Hilda,' chuckled Lynn.

'A moody piece when she can't get her own way, more like! Slamming about like that – she'll think so if she's woken Robinson.' Janie cocked her head towards the stairs, then, when only silence greeted her, nodded in relief. 'Thank God for that.'

'The lass spends most of her time round at this friend's house, now, don't she?' Lynn observed as she sipped her tea.

'Aye. She's gone tonight to read the latest *Vogue* magazine Barbara's just bought and listen to the eight o'clock music-hall programme with her on t' wireless – aye, and pigs might fly if that's all the young minx has got in mind! It's Barbara's brother what's the real attraction; I'd put money on it, in fact.'

'She's growing up. It's only natural.'

'I know that, Lynn, only . . .'

'You're worried she might go down the same path Joey did at her age?'

'Well, wouldn't you? I couldn't bear that a second time.'

Lynn clicked her tongue reassuringly. 'No, you've

352

nowt to fret about there, I don't reckon. Hilda's the sensible sort, has her head screwed on.'

'Aye well, let's just hope you're right, love.'

'Mind you, it'll only get worse with time,' her friend continued with a wink. 'The lass will be off to the dance halls soon enough, won't she? God help you then with her blossoming good looks – she's sure to have the lads flocking, you wait and see.'

'Give over, you, winding me up,' Janie said with a lopsided smile when her friend began to laugh impishly. 'You're terrible, that's what.'

'Aye, and that's why you love me, in t' it!'

Janie's eyes softened. It warmed her heart to see the woman looking happy – it had been in short supply for the Ball couple of late.

Duncan's battalion had fought in North Africa the previous year and he'd been fortunate to survive the episode unscathed. His next posting to Italy, however, had proved a different story. He'd been knocked unconscious on the battlefront during a heavy enemy assault, and when he woke days later it was to discover he was minus a leg.

Invalided out of the army, he'd returned to civvy street six months ago, his war over. However, he'd struggled since to accept his condition, and his explosive outbursts of devastation and frustration had put a strain on his marriage.

Lynn being Lynn, she did her best to play their problems down and appear optimistic, but she couldn't fool Janie. Janie understood only too well the ravages of war on men and their families. Oh, she did. And just as Lynn had done her utmost to support her when going through the nightmare with James, so Janie was steadfast in her quest to do the same in her friend's hour of need.

Now, as they drank in companionable silence the rest of their tea, Janie stole another glance at her neighbour over the rim of her cup. And as she always did whenever thoughts of Duncan struck, she knew a rush of merciful relief that he'd survived. Had he been killed . . . She shuddered to dwell on the prospect. Her apparent night-sight prediction that their husbands would return to them could very well have destroyed everything. Well meaning as the untruth had been, she just thanked the Almighty it hadn't come back to haunt her.

Did Lynn ever wonder over it, too? she asked herself suddenly. After all, it hadn't fully come to pass, really, had it? James wasn't coming back. Yet her friend had never made mention of the vision having been wrong in this sense. Then again, why would she? What could it have gained? She wouldn't have wanted to remind Janie of the fact, no, would have seen it as rubbing salt into her wounds. Not that anything *could* have made Janie's pain worse, mind you. Mother of God, the hell she'd suffered . . .

'That must be Joey and Stella come to mind the kiddies for you – blimey, is it that time already?' exclaimed Lynn now, bringing Janie back to the present with a bump. 'I'll show them in, love, then I'll get off home and let you be on your way.'

'Aye. Ta, love.'

'Well, you don't want to keep Seymour waiting, do you?'

'No. I suppose not.'

'Have a nice evening, you two, and I'll see you tomorrow.'

She bade her friend goodbye then, thankful for the few moments alone in which to compose herself – thoughts of James had brought tears to her eyes that she'd rather not shed – she rose and crossed to the mirror. She'd just finished making herself presentable when her son and daughter-in-law entered the room, Josie and Bert in tow. She smiled at them in turn. 'All right?'

'Happy Birthday, Mam.' Joey enveloped her in a hug then pulled back to extract a paper-wrapped package from the inside pocket of his jacket. 'Sorry, it ain't much . . .'

'No, I love it! Ay, but you shouldn't go wasting your money on me, though.'

'Aye, well, you're worth it.'

Removing the stopper from the small bottle, she took a long sniff then dabbed a little of the scent behind her ears. 'Eeh, smells nice, that does, thanks, lad. Thanks, Stella,' she added as the woman kissed her cheek. 'Now then, I put Robinson down early; the little love was worn out. And Elsie's playing up in her room. Are youse certain you don't mind sitting in with them? I'm not putting you out? I'm sure Seymour will understand if I cancel—'

'Don't you dare,' said her son. 'You enjoy yourself, you deserve it. 'Course we don't mind – it's not like you ain't watched ours for us enough times, is it? Go on then, don't leave the fella waiting, get your coat on.'

'All right, all right, I'm going. By, your daddy's a bossy-boots, in't he?' Janie asked her grandchildren teasingly, and chuckled when they nodded agreement. 'Right, I'll see youse later. I shan't be gone more than an hour or two, but if the little 'uns here get tired in t' meantime, just settle them down in my bed. Ta-ra, then.'

Outside, she paused to glance back at the door and her precious family beyond, and a grateful smile stroked her lips. Then, fastening her coat against the cutting weather, she set off through the darkened streets for Bridson Lane.

Seymour greeted her warmly. 'Come in, lass, come in.'

'I'm not late, am I?'

'No, no. You're right on time. Go on through.'

Janie led the way into the living room – and stopped dead in her tracks. 'Oh, Seymour . . .'

'Will it pass muster?' he asked hopefully.

Taking in the beautifully laid table complete with matching dinner service and ornate candelabra from which burned already several candles, illuminating the space in cosy golden light, she nodded. 'Eeh, aye. You must have gone to a lot of trouble.'

'I promised you a lovely birthday meal, didn't I? And I always mean what I say. Besides, you deserve nowt but the best.'

Turning to face him, she pressed her lips gently to his cheek. 'Thanks, Seymour.'

356

'Can I take your coat?'

Janie passed it to him, saying, 'What's on the menu, then? Summat smells good, whatever it is.'

'My speciality: devilled fish and green vegetables.'

She raised an eyebrow. 'You've cooked it before, then?'

'Well . . .' Pulling a face, he shook his head. 'To be honest, no. I cut the recipe out of the paper.'

'Then why lie?' she laughed.

'I wanted to impress you.'

Her eyes softened and her voice was earnest. 'You already do, so no more pretending.'

'No more pretending,' he murmured in agreement. He pulled out a chair for her with a theatrical flourish. 'Madam.'

'Why thank you, kind sir,' she said, sitting down with a smile.

'Wine?'

She held up her glass. 'I don't mind if I do. Just a small measure, mind.'

They chatted for a while then Seymour rose to check on the food; alone, Janie swayed her head in time to the orchestral strains flowing quietly from the wireless set with a sense of contentment. There was something about this house that never failed to put her at her ease and, right now, she could think of nowhere else she'd rather be.

'Janie? Janie, I'm sorry . . . you couldn't lend me a hand in here, could you?'

Rolling her eyes and grinning, she made her way to the kitchen, calling as she went, 'Eeh, I hope you've not ruined the grub, I'm famished— Oh.' Slapping a hand to her mouth, she juddered to a halt. The grocer was down on one knee and was holding a ring aloft. She took in the scene in stunned horror. 'Seymour . . .'

'Sshhh. Let me explain—'

'What the hell are you doing?'

'Janie . . . I . . .'

'No.' She took a step back. 'Don't do this.'

'I must. I've waited so long . . . I love you.'

'Oh God.' This couldn't be happening. 'Oh *God.*'

Seymour came to stand in front of her. His expression was one of sheer fear. 'Don't turn me down. Say you'll marry me, lass. Please.'

A mammoth sigh escaped her. Taking his hand, she led him back to the table. 'Come on. Sit down.'

He perched on the edge of his chair and, peering at her through eyes wide with dread, waited in silence for her to speak.

She took another deep breath. 'I can't marry you, Seymour.'

'But why?'

'Well, the main reason being because it wouldn't be right. I don't love you.'

He let his shoulders sag. 'Still? I thought . . . I thought you'd grow to feel the same for me in time.'

'I *am* fond of you, honest I am—'

'But not enough to wed me.' He dropped his head in his hands and his tone was hoarse. 'If you only knew how long I've been planning this, how much I've dreamed about it . . . Won't you at least think about it? Please, Janie?'

Tears were welling; she blinked them back furiously. 'There would be no point. Seymour ... I'm still in love with my husband and always will be.'

'James? But, lass, he ain't coming back.'

'Don't you think I know that?' she snapped. 'Jesus Christ, I think of nowt else! My every waking hour is spent going over that one truth in my mind – I just wish to God I could make it not be so. But I can't, can I? He's gone from me for ever. And yet it changes nowt and never can: I love James Hudson now and always. There can never be room in my heart for anyone else. Never.'

'I see.'

Seeing Seymour's face crumple, her anger receded. She closed her eyes.

'I've tried my damnedest not to give you false hope. It's the reason why I turned down your offer all that time ago of me and the kiddies moving in here with you: I didn't want to risk you getting the wrong impression. When you realised I'd not be swayed, you suggested instead helping me out with my rent – I didn't want to accept, if I'm honest. But I could see how much it meant to you to have me do so; and aye, it has been a big help, it has – I shudder to think how we'd have managed without you. Yet I always saw it as a token of your generosity and friendship, nowt more. If I was wrong in that ... if you've been doing it in the belief I'd one day get together with you, then I'm sorry, but—'

'It's not. 'Course it's not. I help you because I want to.'

359

'I can't be bought, Seymour.'

'I know. I know. That's not how I'd have wanted to win you round, anyroad. You'd have had to come to me through love, nowt less.'

'And that I can't do.'

'No.'

'I'm so sorry, Seymour.'

He nodded miserably. 'We've had some good times, though, eh?'

'Oh, the best,' she was quick to reassure him. 'You're one of my closest mates; I don't ever want that to change.'

'D'you mean that?'

''Course I do! Seymour, you've become very special to me over the years, really you have. I don't want to lose you over this, couldn't bear it. Can't we just put tonight from our minds and carry on as before?'

'I don't know, Janie, whether I can . . .'

'Please?' she pressed. 'Please just try?'

After what felt like an age, and much to her relief, he nodded. 'Let's pretend this never happened, lass, all right?'

'Aye.'

Smiling ruefully, he patted her hand. 'Sorry if I embarrassed you.'

'You didn't,' she lied to save his feelings. 'We'll say no more about it.'

'I suppose you'll be going, now, won't you?'

She feigned surprise. 'Going? And why would I do that?'

'Well, I just thought mebbe you'd not want to stick around . . . ?'

'And miss out on that devilled fish? Not on your nelly!'

Janie waited until she'd turned the corner into New Lane before leaning against a garden fence and sucking in great gulps of air.

How she'd remained strong in there, she'd never know. Now, in the seclusion of the deserted street, she allowed the pretence to fall away and gave her emotions free rein.

Guilt at Seymour's devastation when she'd turned him down, coupled with anger that he should have placed her in such a mortifying position in the first place, predominated. Overriding all else, however, was the fresh sear of loss for the man she truly loved and could never have again.

She'd toiled so very hard in clawing back some semblance of a life during the past few years. There had been times during those early dark days when she'd been convinced she'd never get over the agony of losing him. And yet, by some miracle, she had. She'd had to keep going, *had* to force herself from bed each morning, force sustenance down her throat, force herself to wash, to clean the house and see to the children's needs – always forced. But she'd nonetheless done it, hadn't had a choice.

Though still unaware that Janie had fooled him and that James had been hiding out for all those weeks at home, there had been no question of keeping from her father-in-law his fate – he'd had to be told of his son's death. The old man had clasped her to him and wept like an infant, proving to Janie that his pomp and bluster were just that all along. Unity in grief saw that they got along better these days than they had ever done in the past. Yet, Albie's devastation had been nothing compared to that of her children . . . And it was for them alone that everything since had been for.

For the little ones' sakes, if certainly not her own, she'd pushed on just a little further each day, and somehow, *somehow*, she'd come through the other side into a world not as it was before – it could never be that – but something resembling manageable. A new normal, if you will. And that, she knew, had been achieved in no small part by the help of her friends, both Lynn and Seymour equally.

She learned to shut down thoughts of James as soon as they began to rise – she had to, if not to send herself stark-staring mad. As time passed, she'd got better at it until, now, she barely dwelled upon the memory of him at all. It was how she coped, was all she had, and she clung to this crutch for all she was worth.

People relied on her. She couldn't drown in her misery, couldn't afford to risk herself going under. She *couldn't*. That didn't mean, though, that her husband was forgotten. Never. She'd have sold her soul to the devil himself and done so with a smile on her face to have him back for even just a minute.

'You promised me, James,' she whispered to the

blanket of stars above her as she dragged herself on towards home. 'You held me in your arms on that station platform, you looked me straight in the eye, and you vowed you'd come back. But you didn't. You didn't, and now I'll for ever be alone. How could you go and leave me like this? My own sweet love . . .'

'I didn't expect you back so soon,' Joey said when his mother entered the house. 'Is everything all right?'

Her heartache tucked neatly away once more and the much-rehearsed smile fixed firmly back in place, Janie nodded. 'Aye, 'course it is. I had a gradely time and the birthday meal was lovely.'

'That's good. The kiddies have been no bother.'

Glancing about and seeing that Josie and Bert weren't there, she inclined her head to the ceiling. 'The little 'uns asleep, are they? You may as well leave them where they are; they can stop here tonight, save them being disturbed.'

'You're sure, Mrs Hudson?' asked Stella.

'Aye, lass. I'll fetch them across to yours in t' morning.'

The couple had donned their outdoor gear in readiness to leave for home, but when they reached the hall Joey suddenly looked back. He stared at Janie for a moment and a small frown tugged at his eyebrows. He turned to his wife. 'You go on ahead, love. I'll follow in a minute.'

'Why, what's up?'

'Nowt,' he assured her with a smile. 'I just want a quick word with Mam about summat.'

Though puzzled, the woman nodded nonetheless

and, after bidding her mother-in-law goodbye, left the house.

Alone with her son, Janie tilted her chin questioningly. 'Well, lad? What was it you wanted to talk to me about?'

'Summat's happened.'

'What? No, it's not.'

'Mam, I know you. Tell me what's afoot.'

She opened her mouth to continue to protest then closed it again. 'I thought I'd done a good enough job of hiding it . . . It's Seymour.' Her words were barely above a whisper and she struggled to meet Joey's eye. 'He's asked me to marry him.'

'Oh.'

She waited and, when no further response was forthcoming, said, 'Oh? That's all you've got to say on t' matter? Ain't you even shocked?'

'No, 'course not. I've seen it coming forra while. If I'm honest, I thought it would have come long before now.'

'Really?'

He chuckled at her expression. 'It's as plain as the nose on your face that he loves you, Mam. You didn't guess at all?'

'Well . . . I suppose I've sort of always known he felt summat for me that went a bit deeper than friendship,' she admitted to her son – and to herself, she realised, for the first time. 'I just couldn't be completely sure, and Seymour never came straight out with it.'

'Until tonight.'

'Aye,' she murmured. 'Until tonight.'

Joey's tone now was just as quiet. 'Did you accept?'

''Course I didn't.'

'Why?'

His quick-fire reply threw her. She glanced away. 'Because I don't love him.'

'Does it matter?'

'What?'

'I mean ... well.' Shrugging, Joey ran a hand through his dark hair. 'You're fond of him, ain't you?'

'Well, yes, but—'

'Can't that be enough – for now at least? You never know, it could grow into summat deeper with time.'

Her brow furrowed. 'Why are you saying all this?'

His answer came without hesitation: 'I want to see you happy.'

'And what makes you think I'm not?'

'Because I see it in your eyes, Mam. It never goes away, however much you try to mask it. You're lonely, and it hurts me to know it. Don't you think you deserve to start enjoying life again?'

Silence descended. Janie breathed deeply. 'Whether I deserve to is neither here nor there. I can't ... can't ever.'

'But why?'

'Why d'you think?' she cried, thumping the table-top and sending the teapot rattling.

His Adam's apple bobbed in a deep swallow. 'I don't know.'

'Really? Come off it, lad, don't play dim. It's because of your dad, all right? Pleased now, are you? I love James, damn it, and I won't ever stop!'

Joey closed his eyes as though a great weight had been removed from his shoulders. 'I'm sorry. I knew what you meant all along; I just had to make you say it.'

'Say it . . . ? Say what?'

'Dad's name. D'you know that's the first time you've uttered it in front of me for nigh on three years?'

Janie blinked back mutely. *Surely not . . .*

'I know why. It's because you worry that if you mention him whilst I'm there, then all your old resentment for me will come rushing back. I'm right, ain't I?'

'I don't know,' she whispered. 'I hadn't even realised . . .'

'That you were doing it?'

'Aye.'

'I have, Mam. I've always known. And it hurts, so *bad.*' Tears dripped openly down his face. 'D'you know the worst part?'

She shook her head.

'I'm not guilty of what you accuse me of.'

'Lad—'

'I'm not.'

'No? Then who is?'

'I don't know.'

'Don't do this . . .' She turned from him and folded her arms. 'I've warned you before – just don't. It's taken so much to get to where we are today. Don't dredge it up again, not now. It'll solve nowt.'

Joey released air slowly. 'Mam?'

'Aye?'

'Will we ever move on from this? Truly?'

'I'm trying. It's all I've done since day one ...'
Then: 'I don't know, lad,' she admitted finally. 'I
honestly do not know.'

'Mam?' he repeated quietly.

'Aye?'

'Can I hug you, Mam?'

'Eeh, lad.'

Holding her son close, Janie cried for all that had
passed and all that should have been. And she cursed
Adolf Hitler to hell's damnation, for starting this
whole hideous nightmare in the first place, and
wished he'd never been born.

Chapter 24

May 1945

'IT'LL BE SAUSAGES, I reckon.'

'I don't care what it is so long as it's summat normal,' piped up another housewife, and the rest of the line muttered agreement.

Janie and Lynn were amongst them. Lynn was enjoying a rare Saturday afternoon off and the two women had been chatting by their front doors when they noticed a group forming outside the butcher's – hurrying inside their houses to grab their purses and ration books, they had hastened down to the shops to join the queue. They hadn't a clue what they were waiting for, but whatever delivery the butcher had had in, it was worth finding out. They just prayed that, whatever it was, it hadn't all gone by the time it was their turn to be served. Shortages had grown worse of late, and meat was one of them.

'Even that tinned American meat, that Spam stuff, is becoming hard to get your hands on nowadays,' stated another customer with a shake of her head.

'Mind you, I'd take that any day of the week over the other rubbish they've been trying to force on to us lately. Horse and whale meat, I ask you! It's bloomin' disgusting.'

Her companion nodded. 'I'm sick of offal and tripe, an' all ... Oh, see 'ere, the line's moving, Freda – come on, budge up, lass.'

Everyone shuffled forward a step or two before stalling once more. To add to their disgruntlement, a slight drizzle started up; with a collective sigh, the women pulled their scarves around their heads more securely. They seemed to spend half of their lives queueing these days.

The minutes wore on and, inevitably, talk soon turned to war. Whispers had begun circulating just recently that things might very well be reaching a conclusion, and the country had become gripped with tense and hopeful expectancy.

'They reckon it'll be over any time now. As quick as next week, apparently. I don't know why they can't just get on with it and put us out of our misery.'

'Well, I for one won't hold my breath,' responded a stout woman with a decisive sniff. 'I'm paying no heed to rumours; it's the Prime Minister I want to hear say it, or nowt at all, and that's that.'

'Aye,' said another. 'Until owd Winnie confirms it from his own two lips, I'm not building my hopes up.'

'Mind you,' reasoned Lynn, joining in, 'surely the end *can't* be far off, given that Berlin fell the other day. And if rumours are to be believed, and Hitler really is dead . . .'

'I hope the swine's not done away with himself,' growled Janie. 'He'd be out of it, then, and that's not right. He should be made accountable for what he's done. He deserves to suffer.'

'They ought to hang the devil up by his heels and beat him to death – slowly and publicly!'

'Aye, shooting is too good for him,' threw in someone else. 'My son ain't ever coming home because of him. Worst day of my life, it was, when that telegram boy knocked. The lad's poor face as well, bless him; he looked scared to death when I answered the door to him. 'Course, he knew what news he'd brought me and wanted to be away quick sharp, but he had to make sure it reached me, didn't he, so had to wait around until I'd read it.'

Janie had only been half listening; at this now, her ears pricked up. She frowned. She hadn't received a telegram, had she? Her being informed of James's death had come in the form of a standard letter. Neither had it been hand delivered but sent instead through the usual channels by post. Then again, this woman's son, she knew, had been killed in France at the start of hostilities – perhaps protocol was changed later on, or maybe things were done differently depending on the theatre of war, she reasoned. Aye, that must be it.

'Mind you,' the woman who had been speaking went on, 'my husband were more upset when the letter of condolence from the King and Queen arrived. Well, I say upset ... bleedin' livid would be nearer the truth. Had a right dicky fit, he did. He reckoned a few generic lines from them toffs down in that London in exchange for our lad's life just wouldn't cut it; ripped the message to shreds, he did.'

Janie's frown had returned. She shook her head. 'I never got one of them.'

The woman turned to give her a sympathetic smile. 'What, love, you got nowt from the monarch?'

'No, I didn't.'

'Eeh, that's not on. The least they could have done was send you some words of thanks as well. I thought it was the done thing, that. Mind you, the post can be all to cock at times, can't it? Happen yours just went astray.'

'Aye, you're no doubt right,' Janie concurred, adding with definite bitterness, 'anyroad, it wouldn't have made a difference, would it? As your husband said, that's no substitute for what we lost.'

Just then, the inclement weather intensified and a blast of rain fell from the heavens, drenching the shoppers in seconds – with cries of protest, they huddled as near to the building as they could manage.

'M' lady,' said a voice close to Janie's ear.

Turning, a smile crept over her face to see Seymour had appeared from the grocer's next door – and it stretched into a grin when from behind his back he brought out an umbrella. He opened it up and, standing to attention like a trusty butler, held it above her head.

'Briggs to the rescue, at your service,' he announced.

She sensed the customers watching on in interest and even heard the odd one titter, but she didn't care.

371

Let them assume what they liked; she knew the truth, that she and Seymour were just friends, and that was all that mattered. 'What are you like?' she said to him with warm fondness. 'You daft ha'porth, yer.'

He winked, but before he had chance to utter anything there came a flurry of activity at the head of the queue and a shout went up:

'Well, that were a waste of time – bloody whale meat again.'

Used to disappointment by now, the line of people took the news with good humour: 'Whale meat again, don't know where, don't know when . . . !' they belted out together before dissolving into laughter.

Chuckling along, Janie, Lynn and Seymour held back whilst the crowd dispersed, then the grocer nodded to his shop.

'I've left the place unattended; I'd best get back inside before I'm robbed blind. I'll see you later?' he added to Janie alone.

'You will. Ta-ra for now.'

She and Lynn had crossed the road and were almost home when the latter said quietly, 'And to think you were daft enough to turn him down.'

Janie gave her friend a sidelong look. 'What's that meant to mean?'

'It means I think you need your bumps feeling. That bloke would tread barefoot over hot coals if he thought it would please you. Treats you like a queen, he does.'

'You've changed your tune. You laughed your socks off six months ago when I told you he'd proposed.'

'Aye well, that were then.' She shrugged. 'Happen war's changed me, I don't know. What I can say is this: I've had time to get used to the idea and I reckon now that you passed up on a good thing. He ain't so bad, really. A woman could do a lot worse for herself.'

'For what it's worth, I believe you're right,' Janie murmured. 'And that's the problem, Lynn: it's only now that I've started to see it.'

Having reached their gates, her friend drew her to a halt. Her voice was soft. 'Eeh, love. You never said.'

'What would have been the point in telling you? My chance with Seymour has been and gone. I need to leave it in t' past, where it belongs.'

Janie's shifting feelings over time had surprised even herself. Uncertainty was her partner now and she was at a loss what to make of it. Just as she'd always sworn, her level of love for James was the same; it hadn't diminished in the slightest and never would. Yet neither had her loneliness. This only grew deeper with each day that passed, and she dreaded dwelling on the future and what the rest of her life with no one by her side might be like.

She still didn't love Seymour and doubted she ever would. However, she was steadfast in her certainty on one thing: he would have made a good companion. The best. Solid and dependable, he would have never let her down. And wasn't that better than nothing at all? Even following her rejection of him he'd remained exactly the same towards her. He'd done his utmost to ensure there was no awkwardness between them and seemed not the slightest bit resentful, was as kind and attentive as ever, in fact. So why was she only lately able to appreciate this – him? Moreover, why had she been so hasty in turning his offer down?

'This passage of time means nowt – Seymour would take you in a heartbeat still and you know it,' Lynn was saying now. 'I can't begin to imagine how you've suffered, how hard it must be for you, but, love . . . James has been dead over three years. The time must come eventually when you have to move on.'

Though it pained her to do it, Janie nodded agreement. 'Our Joey said much the same thing when I told him what Seymour had asked. Maybe . . . maybe you're both right.'

'It's not that you'll be letting go of James completely, love. More tucking his memory safely to the back of your mind instead.'

'Aye.'

'He'll always be with you. No matter what happens or whoever you're with. You know?'

'Aye,' she whispered thickly again.

'Mull it over, eh?'

She knew she didn't need to reassure her friend of that. She was going to find it impossible to think of anything else.

As fate would have it, events two days later were to prove Janie's assumption wrong. For, along with the rest of Britain, but one thing was soon dominating her mind: it seemed the rumours had been correct after all. The end of the war was indeed nigh.

'You're sure, love?' Janie asked the woman who had just burst into her house with the incredible news.

'Aye! Hostilities have ceased – they've just said so on t' wireless. Weren't you listening?'

'Ruddy valve has gone in my set, and you know how hard it is these days to find a replacement . . . You definitely heard right?'

Taking her hands, Lynn giggled. '*Yes*. An official announcement will be broadcast by Mr Churchill at three o'clock tomorrow afternoon. So there you have it. Tomorrow, the glorious eighth day of May, is to be Victory in Europe Day. We've won, love. Eeh, can you believe it?'

Overcome with amazement but also bewilderment, Janie shook her head. It had been so long in the coming she couldn't bring herself to hope it could be true.

'Well, you'd best start, girl, 'cause I ain't telling no lies. Oh, and another thing: there's to be street parties up and down the land in the coming days to celebrate, and we're certainly not going to miss out! So, you make sure you get a good night's sleep tonight, because we've a hard day's work ahead of us tomorrow.'

Tears had filled Janie's eyes and she was grinning so wide she thought her face might break. 'Oh, Lynn. It's really over!'

Her friend laughed on a sob. Then, pulling Janie to her feet, she took her face in her hands and planted a great smacking kiss on her lips. 'Rule friggin' Britannia!'

*

375

Whilst thousands of Boltonians on this monumental day looked forward to flocking to Victoria Square in the centre of town, most residents of Top o' th' Brow were preparing for a more intimate celebration.

Everyone had a task to do, and adults and children alike had been up since the break of dawn. In every street and household, the air itself seemed to crackle with feverish anticipation – not even the intermittent showers could dampen the carnival spirit.

As well as hanging shop-bought Union Jacks, women and girls had spent the best part of the morning making bunting by sewing together triangles cut from donated material, and soon the wet road was splashed in welcome colours of red, white and blue adorning picket fences and strewn across the houses. With a bonfire also planned later, lads, meanwhile, had made themselves useful, collecting whatever wood they could lay their hands on, which they stored from the rain in the now redundant Anderson shelters. Rubbish that people had been unable to burn owing to the blackout restrictions, and which had been amassing in back gardens for almost six years, would also help to feed the flames.

Soon, tables had been placed end to end in the centre of the street in readiness for the modest feast. Neighbours had pooled their rations and, though it would mean going short on food over the following days, all agreed it was worth it.

Then at 3 p.m., Winston Churchill reached them on the breeze – someone had placed their wireless set on the sill and thrown the window wide so every-one could listen together – and a hush fell on the gathering. His stirring voice, which they all knew so well and which had got them through so many dark days, was comforting, and more than one person had a tear in their eye. They hung on his every syl-lable as he spoke of developments, and when he reminded them that, although the German war was at an end, Japan had still to be defeated, each gave a sombre nod.

News of the terrible conditions endured by their men taken prisoner in the Far East had begun to fil-ter through at the beginning of last year and had shocked the nation. The blistering heat, harsh ter-rain and all manner of tropical diseases, not to mention the snakes and elephants and tigers that were rumoured to abound in what seemed a strange corner of the world, would have been enough on their own for them to contend with. Yet, as the pub-lic learned, the true horror they faced lay not with nature but with man.

Stories of ill treatment at the hands of their barbaric captors were to any right-minded person incompre-hensible. Starved, overworked, beaten and tortured, their suffering was impossible to imagine – and soul-destroying for their family members on the home front in knowledge of the fact. However, with Europe now at peace, the first flickers of hope were ignited. Surely Japan too would surrender soon? It had to.

The Prime Minister went on to say that, neverthe-less, Great Britain may allow itself a brief period of rejoicing, and the atmosphere slowly lifted once more. Then those golden words – 'Advance Britannia! Long live the cause of freedom! God save the King!' – and rapturous cheering burst from every man, woman and child.

An impromptu chorus of 'For He's a Jolly Good Fellow' went up, then a line was formed and, amidst much laughter, they all danced the conga.

'All right?' a smiling Lynn asked Janie a little later when they broke off to lean panting against their gates.

'Aye. I were just thinking, you know, love, that I'm glad—' She paused to shake her head. 'Not glad, no, that would be wicked. What I mean is, I'm beginning to think it was kinder in the long run for my James to go when he did rather than him ending up captured by them Nips. Least he was spared all that. Dwelling over the years on what he might have been going through . . . It would have sent me barmy, that, I reckon.'

'Oh, you're right there.'

'Tens of thousands of our boys, just languishing out there . . . It's hard to fathom, in t' it?'

The other woman sighed agreement. 'Poor souls.'

'Peace will come for them and their loved ones, too, won't it, Lynn?'

'Aye, it will. D'you know, I'm proud of you,' she added, squeezing Janie's arm. 'I know how hard today must be for you, but you're doing bloody brilliantly.'

Her response was simple: 'I ain't got much of a choice, have I? Oh, I had a bit of a weep early on this morning, 'course I did. But wearing a long face won't bring my husband back, will it? And besides, I owe it to the kiddies to stay strong. They deserve this party after all they've had to cope with – by God, they do. I'll not spoil that for them, not for nowt.'

The friends hugged, then, motioning to where Seymour Briggs stood nearby watching Janie, Lynn asked, 'Did you manage to make your mind up about him, then?'

Janie's cheeks reddened at the sudden question, and she stopped herself from uttering the words just in time. *She had made her decision, yes.* However, just for a little while longer at least, she wanted to keep it to herself. The time would come soon enough . . . 'Not yet,' she told her. And before Lynn could press her further, and much to Janie's relief, Reuben Trent started up his trusty violin, and she dragged Lynn back into the road. 'Come on, you, time for a dance!'

A short time afterwards, whilst everyone was getting on with their enjoyment, Janie slipped unseen from the jollifications.

Sitting snug in the pocket of her pinny was her key for letting herself into Seymour's for work, and as she turned on to New Lane she fingered it nervously. Then a smile slowly crept across her face and, picking up speed, she hurried on to Bridson Lane.

Inside the house, she made straight for the dresser and pulled open the middle drawer. There it was, just as she'd known it would be: the ring with which he'd proposed to her. She'd spotted it here months ago when tidying some papers whilst doing her cleaning.

Her hand hovered above the small square box for a few seconds, then she plucked it out and eased open the lid.

The diamond set atop the gold band winked at her as though in greeting. Her smile returning, she lifted it from its velvet bed and dropped it into her pocket.

She'd locked up and was nearing the garden gate when a voice high in good spirits called hello – glancing to her left, she raised a surprised eyebrow at the figure approaching. Though she didn't recognise him – men came and went in his line of work all the time – there was no mistaking who he was, given his uniform.

'Oh, hello. I didn't expect we'd see any of your lot today. Ain't it meant to be a holiday, given the occasion?'

The postman chuckled. 'Aye well, that's our postmaster for you – work must come first. Not to worry, I'm almost done on my round, then it's off home to begin the celebrations.'

Taking in his somewhat glazed stare and slack-jawed grin, she could see that, despite what he'd said, he'd clearly already started these 'celebrations' some time ago. 'Are you sozzled?' she asked, laughing.

'Mebbe a bit, aye. It's not my fault, mind. Nearly every street I've called at insisted I partake in a wee nip to drink to the grand news – they'd not take no for an answer!'

'I'll bet! Oh, are them for this house here?' she added, pointing to the letters he held.

380

'Aye.'

'Well, give them to me and I'll pass them on to the owner. I'm just on my way to see him now; he's a friend of mine.'

The postman handed them over then touched his hat to her in farewell. 'Ta-ra, missis!'

Bidding him goodbye, she watched him for a moment weaving along on his way, then, shaking her head with a smile, she popped the post alongside the ring and key and turned back in the direction of home.

She arrived in her street to discover that no one seemed to have noticed her absence; breathing in relief, she merged inconspicuously into the crowd.

After locating her youngest offspring, who were engrossed with a group of other happy children by the gas lamp, around which a pair of skipping ropes had been thrown to make a swing, she headed across to Joey and Stella. 'All right, lad, lass? Them two look to be enjoying themselves,' she said warmly, motioning to where sat her grandchildren with Mrs Hodgkiss at the long table, waving small flags and with paper hats on their heads. Included in Sadie's contribution to the buffet were tinned plums, which had been sitting at the back of her pantry since the outbreak of war and which she'd been saving for a celebration such as this, and the children were tucking into the sticky sweet treat with relish.

'Aye. It's a good turn-out, in t' it?'

'It is. 'Ere, have you seen owt of our Hilda?'

Smiling, Joey jerked his chin up ahead. Following his direction, Janie clicked her tongue to find her daughter standing with her friend Barbara and her brother.

'She's a bold piece, that one. I knew she had her sights set on that lad; look how she's making cow eyes at him.'

'I wonder what Dad would have made of it?' Though Joey attempted a laugh, the sadness within the words was plain.

She touched his arm. 'I reckon he'd have booted that lad's backside back to his own street before he had time to blink,' she murmured, and they shared a soft smile.

When her son and daughter-in-law had moved off to attend to their children, Janie let her gaze travel over the heads in search of Seymour. She spotted him across the road, chatting with Duncan Ball. As if sensing he was being watched, the grocer glanced her way, and his eyes filled with what she could only describe as deep and heavy loss – the sight of it brought a throb of pain to her chest. Slipping her hand inside her pocket, she stroked the ring. Then she took a deep breath and made her way towards him.

'All right?'

'Aye. You?'

He nodded.

'Seymour, I wanted to . . . to tell you . . .'

'What is it, lass?'

Under the cover of her pinny, she twisted the marriage band that had joined her with James and whispered in her mind that she would always love him. Then, for the first time in over twenty-two years, she eased it from her finger and replaced it with Seymour's engagement ring. When finally she brought out her hand to show him, her eyes were swimming with tears.

'Janie . . .'

'Come on,' she told him, and linking him, she led him to her house, where they could talk in private.

When they were in the living room, she stood facing him for a moment in silence. Then she held out her arms and the grocer grasped her to him in a crushing embrace.

'My love.'

'I wanted to surprise you.'

'Eeh, you did that, all right!' he cried brokenly. 'But why? Why now? What changed your mind?'

She shrugged. 'Happen I think that today is a day for fresh beginnings. I do want to make a good go of this with you, Seymour, but perhaps . . . well, let's keep the news to ourselves forra while, eh? And we don't have to dwell on marriage just yet, do we? We could try a long engagement instead, see how things go?'

He didn't hesitate: 'Aye, lass, aye, whatever you say. I'll give you all the time you need if it means I get to call you my wife at some point. It's more than I ever dared dream . . . Eeh, love.' Drawing her closer, he covered her mouth with his in a smothering kiss – on impulse, she pulled back.

'Sorry, Seymour . . .'

'What's the matter? Surely I can kiss you, can't I, now you're promised to me?'

She searched for an excuse but could think of

nothing plausible. Truth was, the touch of his lips upon hers had felt so very wrong – wrong and slightly nauseating, she was both ashamed and alarmed to admit to herself. 'Well . . .' she floundered. 'I just . . .'

'Go on, let me have one little kiss,' he breathed, his arms snaking back around her. And, feeling unable to resist, she nodded.

This time, she closed her eyes in the hope it would make it better.

It didn't.

Instantly, her body made to jerk from his, but she forced herself to remain still. Not that she could have distanced herself even if she'd tried; he'd pressed himself up against her so tightly she was powerless to move a muscle. Then, horror of horrors: *Oh Lord, no,* she cringed inwardly as she felt his hardness throb against her stomach. His mouth sought hers again, his tongue wrapping around her own as though he meant to devour her, and it took all of her strength not to gag. Finally, it was over. He pulled back and she grabbed the opportunity with both hands; in a heartbeat, she'd disentangled herself and moved back towards the hall.

'Can't we spend just a bit more time on our own?' he wheedled, his face flushed and his breathing heavy.

She forced herself to smile. 'We'd best not. Folk will be wondering where we've got to.'

As she followed Seymour down the path, her racing mind was in turmoil.

Christ, what had she done?

*

384

'Duncan's been great today.' Lynn's tone was gentle with hope. 'I reckon he's finally turned a corner, you know?'

Following her gaze to where the man in question sat, enjoying black peas and potato pie with his children at the table, Janie's eyes creased in thankfulness for her friend. And yet, much to her shame, at the same time she couldn't stem the bite of envy.

Duncan was much changed since the last party this street had known. The hero returned had dazzled with vitality and confidence – now, he seemed to prefer to quietly blend into the background. He'd found it hard adjusting to life at home after spending so long in the army, and more difficult still his altered appearance and all that went with it. And yet, in the long run, it hadn't left too deep a scar on his marriage.

Of course, the Balls still had some way to go, but he and his wife would get through it because they had on their side an ally much stronger than any trials the future might see fit to place in their path: love. Seeing how Lynn looked at him with such pure adoration was almost too much for Janie. For she'd had that once, and more. An intenseness and all-consuming connection such as that was hard to explain to someone who had never been fortunate enough to experience it. That was gone for her now, and she'd never know it again. The pain at the truth of it was unparalleled.

And what was she left with? Her stare swivelled in the direction of her new fiancé and her guts tightened in disenchantment. It just didn't feel *right*. Or perhaps she was being unfair? she asked of herself, desperation having her scramble in search of anything that might by some miracle make this better. Maybe she hadn't given him a chance . . . ? But no – her mind refused to even consider analysing it. She'd made a terrible mistake. Worse still, it was an irreversible one, surely? How could she break things off with him now? After making him wait so long for her, then to finally change her mind . . . she couldn't reject him again. She didn't have it in her for such cruelty. *God lend me the strength to get through this.*

The first fingers of dusk had begun stroking the sky. On the open grassland at the top of the street, people were getting the bonfire ready for lighting. An effigy of the dead Führer which the children had made lay nearby in readiness to burn on top in a final show of defiance – the atmosphere buzzed with expectancy.

Soon, orange flames were roaring to the sky, adding their glow to other fires dotting the hills in the distance – it was a surreal sight after so many years of enforced darkness. Younger children, who had never known peacetime and in whom it was instilled that red skies meant the Blitz and bombs and danger, began to whimper, but they soon brightened up again when Hitler's scarecrow was sent whizzing on to the bonfire amidst deafening cheers.

Watching with Elsie and Robinson the hypnotic flames dancing in the cool breeze, Janie jumped when a hand touched her shoulder. It was Seymour, and she forced herself to return his smile.

'What are you thinking?' he asked her quietly.

'I'm thinking what a farce the war was. The whole bloody lot of it.'

'D'you reckon we might all be celebrating prematurely?'

'That fighting might flare up again, you mean?' She nodded. 'Aye, I suppose I do a bit.'

She knew she wasn't the only one. Now the initial gladness and excitement were wearing off, an air of foreboding had settled and the crowd was somewhat subdued. Those who had had one drink too many were becoming maudlin about their lost men – feeling her own emotions rising, Janie knew it was time to call it a day.

'I think I'll get the kids home, now, Seymour, they're worn out. I'll see you tomorrow,' she hastened to add when he made to follow. 'Goodnight, God bless.'

'Janie?' he called when she was abreast with the gate, and she was forced to swallow a sigh of irritation.

'Aye?'

'Thank you.'

'For what?'

'Making me the happiest man alive. Ta-ra, lass.'

For a long moment she remained where she was and watched until he'd disappeared down the street. Then, frowning, she turned and headed inside.

'Some of the kiddies at the party were crying earlier,' said Elsie as her mother was tucking her into bed.

'Oh? And why's that?'

'They thought their dads would be back today, now the war's ended. They'd been keeping a look-out at the corner and got upset when they never showed. Their mams gave them a hug, and I heard one telling them that it will take a good few weeks to get all the men home.' She paused for a second and a smile lit her face. 'Eeh, I can't wait for mine to get here.'

Janie was horrified. She shook her head. 'No, lass. Your dad . . . he died, remember? He can't ever come home. Eeh, lass . . .'

Elsie was frowning. She nodded. 'Aye. I forgot.'

'You're all right, love?'

'Aye, just tired, I think.'

'Well, you close your eyes and get some sleep, eh? You'll feel better in t' morning.'

Downstairs, Janie lowered herself down on to the sofa, closed her own eyes and released a long breath. She had an ache in her heart and her throat felt thick, but before she could give way to it the opening of the front door sounded; wiping her eyes, she plastered in place a smile.

'By, it's been a gradely day.' Hilda flopped down beside her mother. 'It's like a graveyard in here; is there nowt on t' wireless, Mam?'

'The King's doing a speech at nine, I think.'

The girl pulled a face and got to her feet. 'I might just get off to bed.'

'Goodnight, God bless, lass,' she said, lifting her

388

cheek for a kiss. 'Don't make too much noise, will you? The little 'uns are already down.'

'I'll not. Night, Mam.'

Alone, the silence seemed to seep into every nook and crevice of the room, and Janie shivered. Looking down, she studied the ring on her left hand for an age. She slipped it off and laid it on the arm of her seat.

Her hand went next to the pocket of her pinny in search of James's band. However, it wasn't cold metal that met her touch but paper – frowning, she brought it out. *Seymour's post.* She'd forgotten all about it. She placed it beside the grocer's engagement ring and once again reached inside her pocket. Her beloved wedding ring was soon back on her finger where it belonged; she admired it for a moment and pressed her lips to it gently. Then she rose and lifted the other things from the sofa.

Seymour's ring she placed on the mantel shelf until she'd next be forced to wear it tomorrow. His post, which she would give to him in the morning, she propped against an ornament close by.

She was about to turn away when a word on the forefront item of post caught her eye: *Mrs.* Frowning, she plucked it from the pile. It was a postcard addressed to her.

In a dream-like state, she took in the red blocky shapes in the top-right corner and knew instinctively it was Japanese writing. Slowly, she turned the card over.

In bold black type, *Imperial Japanese Army* screamed back at her. She read the four short lines beneath it:

I am interned in Thailand.
My health is excellent.
I am working for pay.
Please see that you and the children are taken care of.

Janie's gaze dropped further. The final scrawl had the power to cease her breathing.

My love to you all,
James

Chapter 25

'MAM? MAM, WHAT in hell—?'

'Get up. I need you to mind your sister and brother.'

'Why, where you going? Wait, you can't just shake me awake like this and not tell me what—'

'Just do as you're told, Hilda,' Janie ordered on a bark. She stalked from the bedroom and sprinted down the stairs.

The next thing she was aware of was standing on Seymour's step. Lifting her bunched fists, she drew back her arms and pummelled on the door.

'What the . . . ? What the . . . ?'

Janie shoved the astonished grocer aside and barged into the house. Numb to every other feeling bar an engulfing fury, the degree of which frightened her, she turned to face him.

'Lass, what—'

'You dirty, evil *bastard*.'

Opening and closing his mouth, Seymour gazed at her as though she were mad.

'How could you do it?'

'For God's sake, do what?'

On a cry, she launched the postcard she was still gripping into his face then watched the range of emotions pass over it as he scanned the contents. 'How?' she repeated on a rasp.

He staggered to his chair and dropped into it. His colour was corpse grey. 'Mr Hudson's survived . . . I dreaded this happening.'

'You dreaded . . . ? I thought at first it was all innocent, that it had been delivered here instead of Padbury Way in error. It stood to reason, given the state the postman was in . . . But then I saw the address.' Retrieving the card from him, she thrust it towards his face again and stabbed at the proof printed there. 'Bridson Lane, it says. There is no mistake, is there?'

'No,' he whispered.

'James is alive.'

'Lass . . .'

'Why? *How?*'

'I had the army authorities redirect your post here. I told them you were my daughter and that you'd moved in with me for support whilst your husband was away. They didn't question it.'

'The message. The one saying he'd gone down on the *Empress of Asia*—'

'I forged it. I remembered I had a typewriter stored away in t' attic and . . . Well, you seemed so convinced anyway, I thought I was doing you a favour. I thought it would help put your pain to bed, like, help you move on.'

392

Her brain was spinning. The lack of a telegram boy, the fact the notification had been via letter . . . How had she dismissed those things so out of hand? As for her night sight . . . she'd simply assumed . . . *Lord, she'd been so blind.*

'All this time . . .'

'Janie, please, I—'

'You had me believe my husband was dead for all this time? Three *years*, when all along . . . You knew he wasn't, knew he'd survived that liner, that he was a prisoner of war, and yet . . . You've been receiving my post – my every word from him – for *all this time*?' Her whole being trembled with fearsome rage. 'What were you hoping: that he wouldn't survive? Is that it? That he'd perish out there in that godforsaken camp and I'd never have to find out?'

'It was all I could do. Dwelling on if he should return . . . It caused me endless turmoil.'

'Oh, my heart bleeds for you! You poor thing!' Her lip curled in hatred. 'What the hell do you suppose *I've* gone through in that time? That you can sit there and think only of yourself . . . ? Why, eh? Why did you do it?'

'Because I love you! I thought . . . with him out of the way—'

'What? That I'd fall into your arms instead?' She laughed harshly. 'My God, you're pathetic!'

'Well, didn't you?'

'Didn't I what?'

'Come to me eventually. I guess my plan weren't so ridiculous after all.'

'My accepting your proposal? Is that what you mean? It's the biggest mistake I've ever made in my life – I realised it within seconds.'

'Aye? It didn't look like that to me. When we kissed . . . You wanted me, I could feel it.'

'What?' Her stomach lurched at the memory. 'I wanted only companionship from you. Loneliness had turned my thinking; I was desperate not to spend the rest of my days on my own. But *you* . . . How did I misjudge you so badly? Talk about naïve. *You* had much more than just company in mind, didn't you? God, the feel of your hands on me . . . pawing and grabbing at me like that – it made me sick. Did you really think I could ever want you in that way after someone like James? He makes every last inch of me ache for his touch and always has. The things he can do to me . . . what I do to him . . .'

'Please. Don't.'

'My body begs for him inside me. It *screams* for him—'

'Stop it!' Seymour cried, covering his ears with his hands. 'It's not true. You want me.'

'You?' she pressed on, desperate to inflict upon him just a fraction of the agony she was feeling. 'You mean naught to me. You're nothing, nothing at all.'

'You're killing me, Janie!'

'Good! I hope to Christ you do drop down and die after this, you cruel swine, yer. You deserve nowt less. Now,' she added, holding out her hand, 'I want my post. Every last letter and card you stole . . . Give them to me.'

394

'I can't. I fed them to the fire.'

'I could wring your bloody neck for you, you devil, yer!'

'Janie, lass . . .' The grocer rose and closed the space between them. 'Lass, come on, now. You don't mean all this you're saying—'

'What?'

'I know you. You love me, now, not him. I bided my time, didn't I? I gave you ample opportunity to get over him. And it worked, it did; you came to want me instead. It ain't too late. It doesn't have to be over. James . . . James would want you to be happy. He'll understand—'

'I can't believe I'm hearing this,' she cut in incredulously.

'Lass, you can't stay chained to a ghost for ever.'

'Except he's not a bloody ghost, is he? He's alive!'

'That makes no odds, not really.'

'What are you *talk*ing about . . . ?'

'No odds at all,' he continued feverishly, as though he hadn't heard. 'Aye. Not if you don't want it to—'

'You're norra full bob, you,' she told him in a whisper, tapping her temple. 'I was alone, heartbroken and vulnerable, and you took advantage of me. That's all. There's no love between us, there never was.'

He chuckled and rolled his eyes as though she was an imbecile for even considering it. 'How can you say that? Shall I tell you when I first felt it, that spark? Properly felt it, I mean? That day I helped your lad put up the shelter for Lynn. Summat changed between us that afternoon. It did. And well, when I spotted that sideboard, it seemed to confirm it. It was like a sign from God—'

'What?'

Thrown off his stride, Seymour blinked. 'I said, love, it was like a sign from God—'

'Sideboard?' Her every nerve had turned to ice. 'You . . . It was *you*? You informed on James?'

His face dropped. Then, sighing, he held up his hands. 'You might as well know. It won't make no difference to an unshakeable love like ours. I know you'll come to understand eventually that it was for the best—'

'Tell me!'

'It was as I was leaving after the Anderson had been built. I nipped into the kitchen on my way to put my cup in t' sink, and that's when I saw it. Your sideboard – it had been pulled out from the wall.'

She'd heard footsteps outside and, believing it to be the police, had hurried to hide her husband. They soon realised their mistake but had forgotten to put the furniture back. And all this time she'd thought . . . *Joey. My God, this can't be happening* . . .

'That weren't all, mind,' Seymour was saying now, though Janie could barely hear him past the blood thundering through her ears. 'You see, I just happened to glance to the empty space where the sideboard should have been, and what did I spy? Torn oilcloth. Disturbed floorboards. And I knew then – there was no other explanation for such a thing: you had been hiding Mr Hudson all along.

'Course, we'd all heard the rumours flying around, but I never thought they might be true. And yet it was. The proof was there.'

'So you got my sick husband taken away to have me to yourself? You pretended to be my friend, lied to my face . . . My relationship with my son is all but ruined because of you!' she screeched, making a grab for him, intent on clawing the flesh from his face. Even when the grocer caught her wrists she continued to fight him like a woman possessed. 'Wicked, wicked bastard!'

'Sorry.'

That one word, so utterly and completely meaningless in its inadequacy, seemed to carry a strange sort of power – Janie fell still. She stepped back from the man and peered at him in calmness, and suddenly none of it mattered now. He had nothing, whilst she had everything. He was destined for a lifetime of misery and loneliness, whilst she would know only joy and togetherness with her family – all of them. *James.* He was alive. Her husband was coming home.

Rising euphoria bubbled and fizzed before bursting from her in hysterical laughter. She turned and walked away.

'Janie, lass, wait, where—?'

'I'm going.'

'But . . . what about us?'

Looking at him over her shoulder, her tone was cool and collected. 'Goodbye, Mr Briggs.'

The keen breeze felt glorious on her flushed skin and she sniffed it hungrily; it seemed all the sweeter this night somehow. Then she was running, from what very nearly could have been, and on, on, instead towards hopeful redemption and new beginnings.

'Rice.' The word fell from Janie's lips suddenly as she reached Aldercroft Avenue. 'Friggin' maggots, I ask yer . . .'

Shaking her head with a smile, she knocked on Joey's door.

Epilogue

November 1945

'WHY DON'T WE nip forra drink? I'm sure our Hilda won't mind keeping an eye to the lass and lad.'

'Aye?' Janie's face spread in a smile. Then, realising he'd probably forgotten, him only just becoming reacquainted with the place: 'It's a different kettle of fish here, mind, remember? We'd have to catch some transport into town.'

'We might as well make a proper night of it, then? How's about I treat you to the pictures afterwards?'

'Eeh. I'd like that, love, aye.'

'Fingers crossed we'll manage to get some seats on the back row, eh?'

'James!' Janie scolded, her cheeks pinkening as the children grinned at his quip. 'What are you like!'

With a wink and a smile, he took himself off to fetch their coats.

After a glass of sherry and pint of mild in the Balmoral Hotel, they cut through town, busy with dance halls, cafés and pubs, towards the junction of

399

Bradshawgate and Trinity Street, where the Queen's Cinema was situated. Tonight, there was no threat of air attacks or risks the blackout posed. Holding tight to her husband's hand anyway, Janie allowed him to lead the way.

When they emerged from the picture house two hours later – relaxed and fuzzy inside with the sheer completion of being together – it was drizzling with rain. Not that they were going to allow that to dampen their spirits. Laughing, they headed out into the star-pricked dark, hastening inside a fish-and-chip shop at the first opportunity. Feeling sixteen again, they ate their supper straight from the salt-and-vinegar-soaked paper, under the shelter of a nearby doorway. Finally, tired but happy with their evening, they set off once more to catch the last bus back.

'All right?' asked Janie softly as they journeyed home, snuggled side by side.

Though James nodded, she caught that now-familiar flash of uncertainty in his eyes, and she moved in just that little bit closer.

There was no denying that, like millions of other men who had gone to war, he was changed by what he had seen and suffered. Adjusting to normal life hadn't been easy and he still had a way to go – they all did. But by God, they were trying. And so long as they had each other, they couldn't go far wrong.

'We will be, love,' she vowed. 'We will be.'

ABOUT THE AUTHOR

Emma Hornby lives on a tight-knit working-class estate in Bolton and has read sagas all her life. Before pursuing her career as a novelist, she had a variety of jobs, from care assistant for the elderly to working in a Blackpool rock factory. She was inspired to write after researching her family history; like the characters in her books, many generations of her family eked out life amidst the squalor and poverty of Lancashire's slums.

You can follow her on
Twitter @EmmaHornbyBooks and on
Facebook at www.facebook.com/
emmahornbyauthor